Tasche shook himself loose from the trance that had gripped him. His heart was pounding. His head was pounding. His hands were shaking. His eyes burned—but he had done it!

The creature materializing before him towered above him, as tall as six men, broad as a building, glowing like coals in the heart of a fire: smoldering black lace over molten crimson that flared even brighter in dozens of spots as the winds swirled around the beast. Its limbs were massive, like ancient trees, and all four of them ended in reptilian claws. Each talon had a dry, dull sheen like freshly fired iron.

He turned to Haggel and found exactly what he was looking for: a face filled with awe, astonishment, and terror. This was the expression that would fill the faces of any fools who sought to oppose him. The last expression. . . .

certainly be difficult to sustain. But three-to-one odds

FROST

MARK A. GARLAND
&
CHARLES G. MCGRAW

472-7569
Tania

FROST

Copyright © 2000 by Mark A. Garland & Charles G. McGraw

A Baen Books Original

Baen Publishing Enterprises
P.O. Box 1403
Riverdale, NY 10471
www.baen.com

ISBN: 0-671-31943-4

Cover art by David Mattingly

First printing, October 2000

Distributed by Simon & Schuster
1230 Avenue of the Americas
New York, NY 10020

Typeset by Brilliant Press
Printed in the United States of America

For John, Chris, Janine and
Laurie

                              M. G.

For Ed — may your journey
through life be full of grand
adventures.

                         Love, Dad

Greg
940-9421

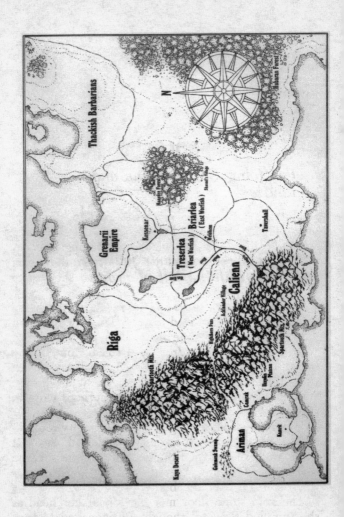

PROLOGUE

Madia awoke with a start. She sat up, a fateful dream fading slowly, and held her breath as she stared into the blackness of her chambers, listening. She saw nothing, heard nothing, yet one image from the dream remained in her thoughts, and she knew she had to find Frost.

Her dress these days was usually that befitting royalty, whether she liked it or not, but for now that didn't matter—only time mattered now. She pulled a robe over her nightdress and rushed out of the room, still barefoot, into the darkened hallway. Which was odd since lamps were kept lit at all hours. Whatever hour it was, she thought, perhaps close to sunrise.

She hurried on, feeling her way through the darkness until she found the stairs and started down. It wasn't until she reached the bottom that she realized something untoward was indeed going on: *That* was when she fell over the body.

The cold stone floor met the top of her head as she tumbled forward, though she managed to turn

the fall into a roll that spared her skull the full force
of the impact. She expected the worst after that—
an attack by someone, or several someones. She
tensed, ready. Nothing happened. Nothing stirred.

She gathered herself up and went on her hands
and knees back to the still figure at the foot of the
stairwell. A man, she determined, not very large and
certainly not very strong, and absolutely dead, though
she couldn't feel any wounds, or any blood. His hands
held no weapons, but she found a rather substantial
sword soon enough, lying near the body.

Light glowed behind her in the hallway, drawing
near; not a lamp or candles, this light had a cold
paleness and a rose hue, and did not flicker at all.

"Frost?" she whispered.

"Good morning," Frost answered, his voice low and
steady, unaffected.

Madia could see his very large form now, a robust
silhouette dressed in robes and floppy hat. The light
followed as if tethered to him. She had never seen
this particular shade of sorcery before, but Frost
seemed to have a nearly endless supply, and to delight
in them all.

Madia let down her guard. No one else would still
be about now that Frost had shown himself, of that
she could be sure.

"What in the name of the Greater Gods are you
up to?" Madia asked, rising from the floor.

She saw the others then, Sharryl and Rosivok,
Frost's two remaining Subartan warriors. They emerged
from the darkness just behind the great wizard, following him precisely in step. Madia had been the
other, the third corner of Frost's defensive triangle,
but an entire kingdom needed her now. She had
resigned herself to that, and to the idea that she might
never again fight at their sides. Soon enough Frost
would choose another, though she knew of no one
in all Ariman who could fill a Subartan's boots. At

least these three had decided to stay in Kamrit for a time, Madia thought, so they could talk about all they had been through together, all the changes to be made, and the possibilities to come. And give her time to talk them all into staying even longer.

"He's one of yours," Frost said. He raised his left hand and waved it slowly. One by one the lamps on the walls came to life, illuminating the great hall as it should have been and the body at Madia's cold feet. She looked down, examining the man. She didn't know his name, but he was a personal servant in the castle. *A cook*, she thought, *or a meal server*. She'd seen him about his duties. Frost's handiwork was evident now. The man's hair was utterly white, his face and hands shriveled as if by very great age, his clothes far too bulky. A lifetime burned up in a matter of minutes. A victim of the spell that had given the large sorcerer his name, unknown decades ago.

"He hoped to find the Blade unattended while I slept," Frost went on. "He ran."

"He took the false sword," Madia added, glancing at the weapon that lay nearby. The last man to do so had ended the same way. She looked up then. *Frost is capable of kindness*, she thought, and Madia was anything but quick to judge these days, but they'd agreed that anyone caught trying to steal the Demon Blade should be dealt with swiftly, and permanently. Such action would set an example, but it also eliminated the chance of a repeat offense.

"I'll have him removed," Madia said quietly.

"That makes three in all," Sharryl said. She was looking about the room as if some unnoticed hazard might still be about.

"Three too many," Rosivok said.

"At this rate, you will be running low on staff by midsummer," Frost sighed, a bit dramatically, while the magic glow faded behind him.

Madia chuckled at this. "Agreed," she said, "but

we of course have many more servants, most of them more sensible. At least I hope so, and summer is still three months off."

"Some things," Frost said, "cannot be put off."

"What things?" Madia asked, noting only now that Frost was fully dressed in his traveling tunics, that both the Subartans were wearing their cloth and leather armor under heavy tunics, and had satchels on their backs. Madia felt a lump form in her throat.

"Simple servants are already throwing away their lives, men who do not have even the smallest knowledge of what the Demon Blade is. They imagine its value, and feel its pull, perhaps. But they are only the beginning, the first chill breezes of a coming storm."

"You and the Blade are safest here within these walls, protected by my army—and my sword as well, if it comes to that," Madia said. "We have had this conversation."

Frost shrugged. "There were fewer dead men at the time." He turned to his two Subartans, a silent exchange, then they all stepped nearer. Frost held out one thick, steady hand. Madia put her hand in his. Even in the dim glimmer of lamplight she could see the truth in his eyes.

The good-bye.

"Where will you go?"

"Where I must go, especially now. And all as well; this journey is something I have put off for far too long." Frost took a breath, and let his eyes close for just an instant.

"I will require a mule with pack," he said.

"When?" Madia asked.

"I leave with the dawn."

CHAPTER ONE

Frost snatched up his walking stick and kicked dirt over the little fire, snuffing it out. He moved back until he felt a tree at the clearing's edge press against his spine. Ahead, just beyond the clearing's other edge, he could hear faint sounds of movement, a rustle of branches, the crack of a twig underfoot—though whose feet he could not be sure. Not his Subartans, they would make no sound, until . . .

A curious stillness spread through the forest. Frost held his breath, closed his eyes, and reached out to the darkness beyond. He could sense the others, and he decided they were the same ones that had been following him since he and his Subartans had left Kamrit on their journey northward. Until now this group had been well back, nothing more than a hinted presence, persistent but small and unremarkable.

He heard a man call out over a sudden jumble of clanking, scuffling and more snarled voices. Then a shriek that briefly combined fear and astonishment before it was snuffed out. Shouts came after that. "No!" Frost heard; then another man uttered a brief, defiant cry. A moment later, on the clearing's far side, three figures emerged: His Subartans, Sharryl and Rosivok, and another man the likes of which Frost had not expected. He stood straight and unmoving, waiting with Sharryl and Rosivok to either side. A man in his thirties, well fed but not quite fat, and gloriously dressed. Even in the pale light of moon and stars, Frost could see that his pants and tunic were finely tailored and sewn with a layered pattern. The jerkin he wore was made of fur, probably ermine. His head was topped by a wide, flat cap of a stiffer material than Frost's, probably leather.

Frost moved slowly to the center of the little clearing.

"Your friends here have killed both of my men," the man said, tipping his cap toward the trees behind him.

Frost looked to Sharryl, then Rosivok, who nodded somewhat heavily and said, "They drew their swords."

"Your men asked to die," Frost said. "Why are you here, and why do you bring fools?"

"Business," the man said. "I am known as Cantor, a merchant, the richest in all Calienn. As for my men I cannot be responsible for every action of a few hired troops, but I will tell you we had no intention of attacking your camp. I am here to make a purchase."

"You have been a merchant for a while?"

"It has been my life."

Frost leaned on his walking stick, studying the other man. "Odd," he said, "that with so much experience, you could make so many errors all at once."

"I myself have made no errors, sir, as you will see."

"You hire fools, you invite your own death by your lack of manners, you seek to buy from those with nothing for sale. I can only assume that your past successes have been due to accident and luck."

"Luck?" the merchant said. "Hardly. Though I am not surprised that one known to rely often on magic, tricks and gimmickry might put stock in such things. You do have something to sell, and I am willing to pay any price you might ask."

Frost could not see Cantor's eyes clearly, but almost as much could be known about a man by observing his manner, listening to his tone and words. Frost thought this fellow rather confident considering the circumstances, even arrogant—almost to the point of being patronizing—and a bit flamboyant as well. No sorcerer, though, that was certain, but otherwise he reminded Frost of no one so much as himself.

"You have been misinformed," Frost said. "You have no useful knowledge of me, and I have no patience to enlighten you. I will let you leave, alive, but you will gain nothing else here tonight."

Cantor came forward two steps, and Rosivok met him. Frost waved the Subartan off, then let the other approach. When they were no more than four paces apart Frost raised his hand again, and Cantor stopped.

"The Demon Blade," Cantor said, firmly, but still civil. "All of Ariman knows you have it. I will not pretend to bargain with you, we both know how much the piece is worth. I will pay whatever you want, but you must sell it to me.

"Who else is competent or rich enough? In any case, it may be your only chance to survive."

Now Frost stepped closer, and leaned toward the merchant. "Is there a reason I should fear you?"

"No, no, of course not. I bring no threats, only a warning. There are many who would as soon take the Blade from your dead body. It is wise to expect that most of them know you intend to cross the Spartooth Mountains, or they will, soon enough. The story of the battle you fought in Ariman has become a legend that grows daily—a battle won by a single sorcerer who used the Demon Blade to slay thousands, to kill a demon, to restore the throne in Kamrit—most remarkable."

"I had help," Frost noted, "but go on."

"I must confess, I was terribly undecided whether to buy the Blade itself, or also to buy the man who has apparently unlocked its ancient secrets. As I see it, both are of equal value, but neither is of very great value alone."

Frost tipped his head, considering Cantor from a fresh angle. "I may have to amend my judgment of you," he said. "Such truths are usually too obvious for most men to see."

"Agreed," Cantor said with a slight bow of his head, "but I am not most men. In the end I decided the Blade alone was the wisest choice. While it is of limited value without you, I believe that—most men being what they are—very few of those interested in buying the Blade will allow that to matter. There are other considerations as well. People are often unreliable, difficult, sometimes impossible to deal with, and a sorcerer known to be eccentric in the past, and wielding an all but unimaginable power in the present, could easily prove the most troublesome sort of all.

"No, I do not welcome that misery. Just the Blade will do. Once we get to Calienn we can part company, and it will be my concern alone, not yours."

Frost pondered his response for a moment, then decided he'd had enough of the shadows that veiled the other's features. He bent and collected two thick pieces of a broken branch from the small pile his Subartans had gathered, then tossed them into the fire. He spoke to the embers under the dirt, then used his walking stick to stir the darkened coals. The fire flared up and caught on the fresh branches, illuminating faces.

Cantor's eyes were very much what Frost had expected, cool and steady, focussed, but moving with perhaps a bit too much nervous energy.

"What you suggest holds a certain appeal," he told the merchant. "To be rid of the responsibility, the worry, the temptation, and perhaps most of all the need constantly to look over my shoulder. You are proof that when I look, I find someone there all too often. But the responsibility is the catch." He moved back to his spot and sat down again on the trunk of a fallen tree, then indicated that Cantor should do the same. He did and sat cross-legged, something Frost had not imagined him limber enough to accomplish.

"I have given endless thought to what might happen if the Blade fell into the wrong hands," Frost continued, "and then there is the reality that, no matter what else, it ought to be in the hands of the Keeper appointed to hold it by the ancients. If it were up to you, would you do less?"

Frost watched the other's eyes meet his. Cantor was ignoring everything and everyone else and concentrating instead on Frost, trying to read him just as Frost was trying to read Cantor.

"It is hard to say," Cantor answered after a moment.

"I am sure it is," Frost said. "I already have my own answers to those questions, which is why I cannot sell you the Blade. While your price might be most generous, the final cost of selling it to you would surely be greater, and I would have to live with that. The Blade has already burdened me more than any man can know, but there is only one way I can ever be rid of it."

"I sympathize, truly," Cantor said, beginning to sound like a man trying to sell a used wagon and team, "but I can all but promise you the Blade will bring your deaths if you do not give it up. Powerful lords and those that serve them will spend lives and kingdoms to hold the Blade, as well as countless lesser men."

"Lesser men and merchants," Frost replied.

Cantor took the barb in stride. He folded his arms and tipped his head back slightly, reflective. "How can you be sure that the one who buys the Blade from me will not be the very one who was meant to have it, the very one you seek? This is sometimes the way the world works."

"Seldom," Frost said.

Cantor nodded. "That's true."

"Who do you know that wants the Blade?" Frost asked. "I would know my enemies."

Cantor smiled too broadly at this. He took a deep breath, let it out and took another. "No one. Anyone. All who think they have the slightest chance of taking it, or corrupting you, which I admit to my dismay seems somewhat unlikely."

"Is there anyone in particular?"

Cantor shrugged. "Perhaps. Keep the Blade, and I am sure you will find out more than you care to know."

Frost stabbed the end of his walking stick into the earth and stood up. "As I said, Cantor, you may go with your life and whatever else you brought along. But go, now, and do not cross my notice again."

"But—" Cantor held his words as Rosivok grabbed him under his right arm and began to lift him by it.

"But you have killed my guards!" he managed.

"They insisted," Sharryl reminded him as she moved to flank Cantor on the left.

"You will think of me as your life ends, Frost, of the chance I offered you. An offer that remains open."

"You have made no offer," Frost called after him. "Name your price."

"The truth," Frost said.

"Once you have the truth, I may have to start over again, bargaining with someone new."

"It is a perilous life," Frost replied.

"As well you know, but it is a risk I may take," Cantor said. Rosivok began to escort the merchant away. "Wait!" Cantor shouted, struggling. "You would set me out on the road alone at night?"

Frost shrugged. "I would."

"Then I make you another offer. I will pay for your protection, that of you and your able warriors. Let me pay you your best fee. I have three horses as well, somewhere in these woods."

"They have run off," Rosivok said without cheer.

"You may have helped?" Frost asked his retainer. The warrior nodded.

"No matter." Cantor said. "With or without the horses, I am traveling home to Calienn, therefore we must share the same road, and I can think of no one I would trust more. You have the means and reputation of a survivor. Besides, it will give me so many more chances to attempt to sway you to reconsider."

"You possess a sober honesty that continues to surprise me," Frost admitted.

"Something we share, I trust?"

Frost glanced at his Subartans. Neither of them seemed amused at the prospect. On the other hand, Frost had long enjoyed a free-lance lifestyle, one that allowed him to go where he pleased, be as he pleased, and earn the wages of royalty when the need, or the notion, arose. All that had changed for now, and for the foreseeable future, with the notable exception of Cantor's offer . . .

"How will I sleep with the likes of you in my camp?" Frost asked.

"Half as soundly as I with you," Cantor replied.

"Agreed," Frost said. "I will take my payment in gold when we reach your manor in Calienn and I will take your life without notice if you attempt to cross me."

"That is not my way."

"An honest merchant?" Frost prodded.

"Not always," Cantor replied. "But it is a luxury I can afford these days."

The right answer, Frost thought, satisfied. "It will not be an easy journey," he said. "We climb the plateau tomorrow and the mountains lie only two days beyond. We have escaped the notice of most in these lowlands, but that will be more difficult from this point on. For tonight, I suggest you get some rest."

"Have you ever been to Calienn?" Cantor asked.

"I have," Frost said, though he had the impression that Cantor already knew.

"Good, it will give us something to talk about."

The look on Cantor's face was too smug. There were indeed more secrets that might be uncovered through lengthy verbal sparring, if Frost's assessment of the merchant was at all correct. For tonight, it would keep. The journey ahead would provide occasions enough.

"Much to talk about," Frost agreed. Before they parted ways, he would know what Cantor knew. The camp's small fire was dying again, letting the darkness back into the clearing, letting it surround them. "Good night," Frost added, though that was something he expected none of them could truly count on for a long time to come.

Frost stood still and silent, eyes closed, hands wrapped around the walking stick planted firmly in front of him, his forehead pressed gently against its smooth wood. The warmth of the rising sun, the fresh breezes, the chatter of birds and the steady rhythms of blood and breath within him he had eased out of his consciousness, until only the whispers of the spell spoke to him, gathering to him the faint breath of others.

It was a simple bit of sorcery he'd learned as a boy and mastered ages ago, so far as one could master such things. The key had been to learn to recognize the auras of human beings as separate from those of other life, and then to adapt a spell to find them. Like picking one voice out at a crowded inn. Difficult, but not impossible, and the spell worked much better in a place like this, where few human beings were likely to be.

He opened his eyes and looked up at the rough rock walls that sloped away on either side toward the sky, then he breathed a heavy sigh. The trip was not getting any shorter. They'd been nearly a month on the road all told—two weeks to the Ikaydin Plateau, nearly two weeks more walking since then—but the journey had been made harder by the necessity of staying away from villagers and towns, and sleeping in spurts so that crossing the dry, open Ikaydin Plateau could be done mostly by night.

A stop in Lencia had been the only night indoors, a short respite before spending the last two days climbing to reach Highthorn Pass, which itself only marked the beginning of further hardship from difficult terrain, colder nights, and the greatest prospects yet of being ambushed—none of it the least bit appealing to Frost. Sharryl and Rosivok said almost nothing by way of complaints, they seldom did, but he knew they felt the same. Cantor kept to himself as well, curiously so in fact, though Frost was less certain of his reasons.

Frost had no special desire to talk to Cantor, but it would have made the days pass easier. For now, though, there was a new, more immediate concern. Only three days into their trek over the Spartooth Mountains, and trouble had already found them. Worse, Frost sensed a subtle, disturbing difference in one of the unknowns that trailed them so slowly and diligently, keeping themselves hidden among the more challenging rocks and banks above the pass—*magic*.

"A difficult place to defend," Rosivok said, taking his turn at leading the mule as the three set out walking again.

"Agreed," Sharryl said. She flanked Frost on the left, Rosivok to the right, their shining, two-edged subartas slung at the ready on their right arms. Frost carried only his walking stick. Beneath his cloak, sheathed, wrapped and strapped securely to his very broad back, he carried the Demon Blade as well. But there it would stay, at least until they reached their destination. *Though perhaps*, he thought wearily, *long after that as well*.

"I am considering our options," Frost replied. He had some ideas, and had already begun rehearsing the appropriate spells in his mind. For now he could do nothing more, yet more, certainly, would be required, and probably before the day was done.

"That fellow in Camrak, the one with the scarred ear, I still think he would have made a fair replacement," Sharryl said.

"He was too young," Rosivok said, after they'd walked in silence for several paces.

"For you, perhaps," Sharryl said.

Frost glanced at her, saw her nearly about to smile. She had taken an instant liking to the lad, and he to her.

"He may have been old enough to fight by day," Frost said, "but I am not so sure he could have survived many nights with Sharryl."

"Though he did show promise," Sharryl said. "One night together is hardly enough."

"Enough for him," Rosivok said, and added a grunt. "He never did turn up at all next day."

"True," Sharryl said, "but I would have found him."

Now a smile, Frost saw, and allowed one of his own. He too had spent such a night with her, as had Rosivok, though all three of them had had very different reasons. The Subartans of the Kaya Desert were supreme warriors, born and bred, each one a match for any three men, and they were remarkably capable in other physical activities as well, though only when the mood came upon them, which was as curious and unpredictable an event as the weather.

"Strength and stamina are often required for more practical activities as well," Cantor said, apparently in support of Rosivok's views on the matter.

"True," Frost said. "If he failed to manage with Sharryl he may well have failed us all."

"Hmph," Sharryl grunted this time, but then she looked at the others. "It is still unfortunate," she added, trudging a bit heavily.

"We will find another third," Frost said, taking her meaning. "Let me show you." With that he stopped and untied the little pouch he carried since the desert, since before he'd known of Subartans, containing a handful of stones reputed to be most useful in learning what lay ahead, or which way to go on more difficult matters. Frost reached in the pouch and gathered the stones, just half a handful these days, then he bent and scattered them on the hard packed trail. "There, you see?" he said, examining the pattern. "This grouping here, and that small group there, then this clear line connecting the two."

"I never knew a crack in the ground could be counted in the reading," Sharryl said.

"Nor I," said Rosivok.

Cantor covered a smirk. Frost shook his head, then sighed. "By my eyes, I wish I knew." He scooped up the stones once more and blew the dirt off them, then returned them to the pouch. "Still, the signs are all around, I think. We must be patient, and wait for the right one. A third who can be trusted as one of you. A weak link serves no one."

"Unless the odds become too unfavorable," Sharryl said.

"You need another warrior?" Cantor asked.

Rosivok managed a nod.

"Subartans prefer it," Frost explained, "but in a fight there is never time to baby-sit. The third member of a defensive triangle must be as strong as the other two, or missing altogether, at least in theory. Though it was possible to imagine that while being overrun, such standards might seem a bit harsh."

Cantor shrugged. "For the right price, a suitable candidate should be easy enough to hire."

"With Sharryl and Rosivok, equality is beyond the reach of most," Frost said.

There had been talk among them of returning to the desert lands for a time, to renew old acquaintances, but more importantly to find a true Subartan to take the place of the one that had been lost, so many years ago—and those that had taken his place since then. The idea was more than tempting, but in the end, for several reasons more important, Frost had decided on another direction. He had made himself a promise, and he was not about to change his mind.

Frost slowed his pace. Here the pass wound around a particularly tall spire of barren rocks that rose like a great hand poised to slap down on passers-by. The left side was lower, with only small bits of shrubbery and a few dwarfed trees. Not wide enough for Frost's liking, but there was nothing to be done about it. At least the terrain offered little in the way of accommodation to highwaymen or opportunists. Which was why the group still following them was not close at hand. For now.

Frost tried once again to concentrate on their subtle glimmers of consciousness out among the rocks. It would be easier now that he knew what he was looking for. He sensed nothing different; they must still be some distance away.

"Do you know where they are?" Rosivok asked.

"Behind, I think, but they will catch up," Frost answered.

"They have taken another way, above the trail," Rosivok said, following Frost's gaze to the cliffs overhead. "They are resourceful."

"No doubt," Frost said, speculating on the confrontation that lay ahead and feeling quite weary of it all, of the many and sundry who had come and would come seeking the Demon Blade, so long as he held it. Which was the other half of the reason he was headed this way, headed . . . home. "All of this," he grumbled, "I never intended."

The Subartans quietly nodded.

"You still have my offer," Cantor said calmly.

"And you still have my answer," Frost replied without pause, but he let the mood drag him down as they continued walking. He watched the pack mule plodding evenly, dully, and almost envied the beast its oblivion. He hadn't asked to be the one, hadn't wanted the responsibility, the attention, the troubles or the pain. The Demon Blade held in his hands alone had saved the world, just as it had so many centuries ago in the hands of many others. But his wondrous feat remained a puzzle he had yet to fully resolve, while the Blade had become a personal hardship, Frost's curse.

"Tomorrow, I say, we will have company," Sharryl said, as if making a wager.

"Why do the Greater Gods insist that every time I traverse a mountain pass I must be set upon by hostiles?" Frost muttered. The last time they had passed this way it had been wolves and banshees that descended on them, and the Demon Blade had been a hundred leagues away at the time.

Rosivok grumbled quietly while Sharryl rolled her eyes. Frost caught it. "Your thoughts?" he asked.

"That is what mountain passes are good for, after all," Sharryl replied, making an even less exuberant face.

"After all," Frost repeated.

"It is not your fault, of course," she added.

"Perhaps, in a way, it is. Have I read the omens wrong? Do I test my luck too often and thereby wear it out? Do I lack the necessary charms required?"

"What charms?"

"I have no idea, but there are many, I'm sure."

"Perhaps I have done myself a disservice, throwing in with you," Cantor said.

"Of course you have," Frost said.

"No doubt you've done it all wrong, as have we," Rosivok told Frost, "but that does not change anything, not usually,"

Frost had no reply to that. He let out a sour sigh, then went back to walking, back to his spells, to planning, to alternatives, and to seeking auras—to his surprise he found one, and instantly stopped.

Someone else, casting about as he was. The spell was similar to his and therefore likely as effective. *At least I must assume it is,* Frost thought. He was still unable to determine for certain whether this other came behind them on the trail, or waited somewhere up ahead.

"What?" Sharryl asked, turning from him and eyeing the shadows along with Rosivok.

"The same ones I sensed before," Frost said.

"Can you tell yet how many?" Rosivok asked.

"Perhaps a dozen, perhaps more," Frost replied, "but one is unique, an adept of some resource, and cautious, a capable adversary I would wager."

"You said they would come from all directions, and use every means," Rosivok reminded. "An adept is not so unexpected."

"No," Frost said.

"None of it is," Cantor said. "Since the battle in Ariman, rumors of the Blade have spread like autumn fires."

Frost felt the other's words rest heavily upon him. There had always been rumors, of course, and men had sought the Demon Blade for centuries, though until now the rumors and seekers had managed without him being at the center. Frost let a frown find his face.

"All true," he said, "but I had hoped those inclined to look for the Blade would continue to look in

Kamrit for a time. So formidable a challenge so soon is troubling."

"A challenge short-lived," Rosivok stated, caressing the twin blades of his subarta. Sharryl nodded in solidarity.

"Well, that's reassuring," Cantor said, apparently sincere.

"We will need to deal with them properly," Frost said. "There are many questions I would ask of them, if I can. Which way they have come, for one, and which way they are going."

"If they come from behind, then traveling on means leaving many such dangers behind," Cantor wondered aloud, "but if they come from those lands that lie ahead . . ."

"Yes," Frost said.

"We will invite them to join our camp tonight," Sharryl said, waving as if to someone in the rocks above. "And ask them!"

"They will come to us without invitation, I am sure," Frost replied.

"Not that I'm worried, mind you," Cantor said, examining the high rocks himself now. "But what do you plan to do?"

"We must become the hunters, not the hunted," Rosivok said.

"What—" Cantor started, but Frost held his hand up, cutting the merchant off, and stood considering Rosivok's last words for a time.

Something more than a simple hide-and-pounce strategy would be required and nothing could be taken for granted. Old, reliable spells would be best. Frost looked at the sun and the day was growing old. The others would not come near this night, which gave them time to make camp for the night, and make their plans. He looked to his Subartans and smiled. "Indeed," he said at last, "we shall."

❖   ❖   ❖

"If I seek him out he will sense it. Even now he is seeking me," Frost said, "but in so doing he gives his own position away, more or less."

"How much less?" Sharryl asked, crouched with Frost and Rosivok behind a scattered pile of fallen rocks and boulders along the trail.

"It is almost certain they did not sleep last night," Frost replied, "and they are ahead of us now. Precisely where will not matter for long."

"A good night's sleep will be our advantage," Rosivok offered, confident.

"I hardly slept a bit," Cantor said. He was crouched just behind the others, and was apparently not terribly interested in sharing the view. "So many days and nights on the road are bad enough, but all this stalking . . ."

"Yet that is something anyone who wishes to hold the Demon Blade should expect," Frost said.

"I would hold it only after I am home, where my own guards can protect me, and only until I can sell it to a suitable buyer," Cantor said. "If I had purchased the Blade from you in Kamrit, how would I get it safely home? No, you are welcome to it until then. A bit of sleep is better than none at all."

Frost glanced back at the merchant with fresh regard. He hated to admit it, even to himself, but there was something about Cantor he was actually starting to like. He simply nodded, then turned away and tugged at the reins of the mule, testing to be sure they were snug beneath the rock that held them. Now Sharryl and Rosivok stood guard, their backs to Frost as he closed his eyes, focussed his mind and set about casting his spells.

A winter at Kamrit had restored him to his full and celebrated weight, enough stored mass to fuel even the most vigorous sessions of spell-casting, yet he had managed to keep enough muscle underneath it all to remain an asset to himself, not a burden; a necessity in those instances when strength or a bit of unexpected agility might be required.

Keeping the extra padding was a more difficult task when walking across an entire realm, but good hospitality had been found all along the way; a cottage here, a tiny village there, where people were eager to trade a meal and provisions for a bit of helpful sorcery to ease some affliction or pestilence, or a few copper coins. Game had been plentiful as well, and Rosivok and Sharryl were capable hunters of most any sort of creature, not just men.

"Now, join hands," Frost said, standing exactly between the others. He reached out and took Sharryl's hand in his left, Rosivok's in his right, then he instructed the Subartans to touch the mule with their free hands. Next he recited the long sequence of phrases he had assembled, enabling the spell. As he spoke the spell's final phrase, he felt strength and energy begin to seep out of his body, calories being burned, magic being done. He had overcome the dizziness decades ago, along with the unsettling waves of fatigue that came after it, usually in direct proportion to the size of the task. This time, the sensation lasted only an instant.

"Step back," he said, keeping the hands held tight. The three of them retreated one step, yet remained with the mule as well. Three perfectly created simulacrums, three illusions hand-in-hand standing exactly where the real trio had been, still touching the mule. Frost had guessed that those who were following them would not know about Cantor, and each image added to the spell made the task many times more difficult, so he had left the merchant out.

Frost let go, then went around and took the reins of the mule again, and pulled them free. "Come, mule," he said, leading the creature out from behind the rocks. The three newly created images followed, all walking realistically enough, though they stayed quite close to the mule.

"Go down the trail, mule," Frost told the animal. It seemed to understand completely. After picking its way to the level ground it set off trotting up the path as if being led. The three false glamours walked along. "I have tethered the spell to the beast," Frost said, as he came back. "It will draw energy from the animal."

"Will it survive?" Cantor asked, stretching his neck to watch the mule go.

"The spell will only last a short time, and the drain is not enough to do real harm; a good mule is not easily replaced."

Cantor nodded. "What happens next?" he asked.

"The others will reveal themselves when they attempt to strike," Rosivok said, clearly savoring the idea.

"We must be in position to take advantage of that," Frost said. "Else all my hard work will go wasted, and perhaps the mule."

"Will you require survivors?" Sharryl asked, wearing the same satisfied smirk as Rosivok.

Frost shrugged. "One or two."

"This way, up and over those boulders," Rosivok said. He wasted no time in setting off up the smooth rock slope beside them, then scrambling over a series of massive rocks and debris left over from a slide, long ago. Not steep, but treacherous. Sharryl went next. She tossed a rope back down to Frost, and he and Cantor used it to pull themselves up and after the others.

The midday sun was hidden behind a soupy layer of light gray clouds, and the breezes of the day before had stilled, leaving the air damp and warm and smelling of distant rains.

All of which Frost considered nearly ideal. Wind direction and the scents it might carry were of little concern, and without the harsh rays of the sun intruding on them and degrading them, his simulacrums looked all the more real and would remain that way longer. With luck—which he wasn't at all sure the omens foretold—the waiting troops and their ignoble sorcerer friend would never know what hit them.

"Not much further," Frost said, as the group forded a crevasse and began working their way along a narrow bit of ledge. Rock faces far below obscured the trail from here, and so them as well. Frost considered his second option, if the first did not prove satisfactory. Whoever his opponent was, Frost had no choice but to assume he would know enough to plan a proper assault, one that would be swift and leave little room for a capable response. A direct attack by sorcery was problematic, since there were very few spells that could quickly disable even a mediocre practitioner of the arts. In order to be effective, any such spell would require skill and control, and a generous, sustained expenditure of energy, leaving one in a state of temporary but intense fatigue, and quite vulnerable, if the attempt was to fail.

No, it was more likely that the other would take a defensive tack and build his most effective warding spells around each of his soldiers and himself. After all, they outnumbered Frost and his Subartans at least three to one. Sufficiently protected, a troop of able soldiers might have enough time to defeat the two Subartans, and keep Frost himself busy while secondary measures were taken.

Even trained and enhanced, a human body was capable of only so much effort, could turn stored fat into usable energy only so quickly. A sustained, combined physical and magical assault could ultimately succeed even against Frost.

So the first option, simply to stand and fight on equal terms, held little appeal. Frost's second option involved far less effort.

The ledge emptied onto a small, rounded plateau

that offered poor footing, but a clear view of the trail below. A long, straight stretch was visible, with slopes and rock falls on either side. A perfect place for a surprise.

The mule walked dutifully along accompanied by its three conjured companions. Frost looked to the rocks and cliffs ahead, checking both sides of the pass, top to bottom, checking even the skies lest some airborne threat take them unawares. His best efforts turned up nothing out of the ordinary.

"We will hold here for now," Frost said, "and observe." But the instant he looked down again he saw something he did not expect. The carefully constructed images that strode beside the mule were fading, then were suddenly gone.

"Not you?" Sharryl asked, eyeing the event suspiciously along with Rosivok.

"No," Frost confirmed.

"What then?" Rosivok asked, a question simply put, in the event that plans had changed.

Frost allowed himself a hard frown while he considered his reply. To be able so easily to counter such an illusion his opponent had somehow anticipated both the spell's specific nature and Frost's means of accomplishing it. "I must assume he knows something of me and my ways."

"Many do," Rosivok said.

"I am known and acclaimed by bards and emulated by all manner of adepts in many lands," Frost said honestly. "Perhaps my fame has finally caught up with me."

"You are quite famous," Cantor said. "I had no trouble learning all I wanted to know. Though just now I would like to know how worried I should be?"

"Stay back and behind cover, and your worries will be small," Sharryl said.

Frost rubbed his chin bemusedly with the top of his walking stick and watched the mule walk further on, all alone. He could sense the other sorcerer's presence with the proper effort now, and more faintly, the fading aura of the finely crafted spell he had used to so effortlessly dismantle Frost's careful work.

"There, on the crest," Rosivok said. Frost looked up. Ahead of them on the far escarpment, a little more than a good arrow's throw away, the others had shown themselves.

Frost recognized his opponent, even though the distance was too great to see the details of his features. Imadis had always worn black, one of the few sorcerers to do so because of the color's associative nature, the stigma of darkness. But Imadis had reveled in the fear his fashions inspired in common folk and lords alike. He was not a disciple of the darkness, and mortal through and through, but he was nonetheless quite capable. Some years older than Frost, he hailed from a land due north of the Kaya deserts where much of the year the snow and ice made the living unbearable for most—Frost included. Cold lands did not necessarily breed cold people, but Imadis, for all that Frost had seen, could never be held as evidence of that.

"You know him?" Cantor asked.

Frost glanced at him over his right shoulder, and found the merchant's eyes fixed on the figures ahead. It was not panic that he saw there, Cantor wasn't one for that, not yet at least, but Frost decided without another thought that this was a man who had known combat only in the telling.

"I sense something familiar about him," Sharryl said, her voice charged, her body bobbing a bit in place.

"As well you may," Frost said. "We met before in Tavershall, years ago."

"An opportunist, if I recall," Sharryl said.

"A scoundrel," Rosivok corrected.

Frost nodded.

"Not exactly old friends, then?" Cantor asked, his voice shaky but holding up, as he was.

"Imadis likes to play many ends against the middle, and likes to use anyone available to realize his goals, no matter the cost," Frost answered him. "We have met twice before."

He and Imadis had spent several days together in another town the year before, simply sharing bread, ale and conversation. Frost had found Imadis agreeable enough, though he seemed more mercenary that most.

More recently they'd crossed paths in Tavershall where Frost had been commissioned to lend his resources to a local lord with a poisoned well, a problem that many in the city thought had something to do with a curse of some kind. An old woman known to be something of a hedge witch and, to her misfortune, a truly clumsy thief, had drowned in the well one night. Her body floated there for days before being hauled up and buried. Frost had arrived only to find Imadis already working on the problem, and claiming the fee.

"The well will be pure again in a few days," Imadis promised. Frost had no doubt this would come to pass as promised, but he suspected it would have no matter what Imadis did. Then he discovered the truth.

Frost had followed the poison to its source and found it to be a small spring at the edge of the city. Empty urns lay in the woods nearby, though the smell inside them told the tale. The well had indeed been poisoned—by Imadis himself. "Do you deny it?" Frost had demanded, after confronting the sorcerer privately and laying out his accusations.

"It is true," Imadis had replied. "And what of it? I have been here, bored and wasting in this town for weeks. I could not help but notice the opportunity recent events seemed to present. You don't strike me as the kind of fellow who would have done differently, had you but thought of it first."

"Think what you will," Frost had said, then he'd walked straight into the town square and exposed the scheme. Imadis publicly denied everything, then left town under cover of darkness. Frost had seen or heard nothing of him since.

"I recall there being no more than three or four men with him in Tavershall," Rosivok said.

"That number has more than tripled," Sharryl said.

"Yet nothing else has changed," Frost muttered.

"There is no hope of negotiation?" Cantor asked, stolid, turning to Frost.

"No," Frost said.

Cantor swallowed hard. "What then?"

"I am well prepared, but surprise will not be the advantage I had hoped for, and there is no time to reconsider. I will do what I can. My Subartans must meet those that survive."

Frost turned to Sharryl and Rosivok. "I will stay here, you two go there," he pointed toward the low land between the two rises, "but be assured Imadis knows what he is about, and will have predicaments planned for us."

Again, silent nods.

"What of me?" Cantor asked.

"Get back, and stay out of sight."

Cantor nodded, and seemed to have no trouble at all finding a suitable spot to vanish into.

Frost closed his eyes and tried to concentrate while his warriors left his side—itself a rare event—and set off down the rocks to meet their enemies.

His first task was to diminish the soldiers' warding spells. Though this would require a bit of guesswork, since countermeasures relied most heavily on knowing precisely the type of spell one was to counter, and a great deal of effort, in this situation, would certainly be difficult to sustain. But three-to-one odds meant these soldiers had more to fear from magic than battle, and were likely protected in matched proportion, so Frost had prepared a spell designed to remove nothing at all.

Instead, the spell he worked to finish now would use the energy of the soldiers' own warding spells to make them heavy—a burden of great, relentless weight, and one the attacking soldiers would be forced to drag with them into battle. Sluggish and struggling, they would be vulnerable. Rosivok and Sharryl would have to do the rest.

As for the sorcerer himself, Frost had decided to rely on a variation of his oldest and most effective—if somewhat opprobrious—spells, one of the few he knew that might work against another adept. Though how well, or how quickly, he could not be sure. . . .

Much depended on Imadis himself. Already Frost could feel the presence of the other's spell workings, a rarefied glimmer of sorcery in the air. Though strangely, nothing yet seemed directed at anyone or anything in particular. Frost waited, working his first spell near to completion while the soldiers all stood there on the next ridge, perhaps waiting for Frost to make a move. Perhaps, one Imadis could then counter.

You will fail, he told Imadis, attempting to send his thoughts directly to the other, guessing Imadis would be listening.

No . . .

The answer came weak, but Frost took this as a sign of nothing. Imadis might not be as practiced as Frost at speaking in thoughts, or he might be trying to influence Frost's preparedness, encouraging overconfidence; which was something Frost had to admit he was occasionally prone to. Today, however, he would not succumb.

Sharryl and Rosivok had crossed the low point between the two hills and were headed up the adjacent rocky slope now, approaching Imadis. The waiting troops enjoyed the double advantage of numbers and possession of the high ground even without Imadis' help. Frost could wait no longer. He finished the spell, and discovered at once that he had guessed entirely wrong.

He found nothing to latch onto, to work with, to reshape or pervert. No warding spells were present at all. He had wasted precious time and energies and accomplished nothing.

There . . . It was Imadis again, his thoughts somewhat clearer now, and most disquieting. Frost quelled his impulse for anger—no time for that, either.

If they had no wardings they would pay the price, including Imadis. Bringing all his will and concentration to the effort, Frost abandoned his earlier work and quickly recited the phrases that would empower his single most effective spell. Next he added those few last words that would extend the spell's focus to all those who stood on the other ridge, then he added his binding phrase. A nearly impossible task, but Frost could attempt nothing less if—

He felt the drain on his body immediately, the rapidly growing fatigue that made him feel as if he'd suddenly gone two days without sleep. But it felt good at first, the way all gainful exercise could make one feel, especially when the results could be easily measured. That would change.

Frost kept focussing, continuing the effort, and waited for the inevitable graying of his targets, the withering, the dying that came from extreme and sudden age. A complex spell, so widely implemented, but he had used this one many times before and perfected its every nuance, making it versatile, yet entirely under his control.

No, he heard Imadis say again in thought.

He looked more closely from within and concentrated on the feel of the spell, the push of absorption combined with the gentle rebound that let him know his targets were being affected. He felt nothing, as though the spell was being deflected or altered somehow. *Or redirected,* he suddenly realized.

Frost felt a cold foreboding grip his gut. If Imadis knew anything about Frost, he would know of the aging spell. *Of course!* He had devised some means of sidestepping it, was even now acting like a lightning rod, drawing Frost's efforts away from his men and around himself, then sending the energy off into earth or air. Frost wasn't sure how, but it was working. His best efforts were failing. Sharryl and Rosivok were rushing to their deaths.

That, Frost vowed in silence, would not come to pass.

He began to withdraw from the spell and gathered his wits about him. For all that was happening, Imadis seemed quite preoccupied. Frost held him hard in his gaze and waited for the visceral rejoinder that would mark the moment of contact, but the wait went on, his stare went unanswered. Which meant Imadis was lending his full concentration to that irksome tangle of sorcery he was using to protect his soldiers from Frost's assault. Or he was working on other magics as well, and combined, they had taxed him to his limits.

Warding spells were the simplest of all and Frost had perfected a number of them over the years; the one he wore at this very moment, for instance. Properly enhanced, a warding spell could reflect an assault from any direction. Which offered a possibility.

Frost let the aging spell go completely. He took a breath, then spat out the single phrase that would transfer his own warding spell to Imadis. A gift of sorts. He owed Imadis that much at least.

The effect was immediate. Imadis howled loudly enough to carry across the ravine between them, then he spun halfway around, shaking his head, flailing his arms about as if insects were swarming after him.

Whatever he'd been using to reroute Frost's spells, it had flashed back and bitten him like a rabid dog.

"Now!" Frost said, clearly and loudly, "I continue." He returned to the aging spell, though this time he aimed it only at Imadis' soldiers, concentrating on the nearest of them first. Cut off from their master's protections, the desired effects began to appear.

The soldiers had stood fast, waiting for their two hapless adversaries to reach them at the top of the ridge so they could cut them down at their leisure. Frost concentrated on his spell, feeding it with measured precision from his considerable body stores. The soldiers' postures began to arch forward. The hair that poked out from underneath their short, wide-rimmed helmets was clearly turning white, especially on the nearest of them. Frost did not allow himself even a smile as he glanced up, but he felt a certain satisfaction well up inside him.

The feeling vanished as his displaced warding spell dissolved. Frost fought to hold the spell's energy intact, working two spells at once, but it was already too late for that. No form or function remained, only his own great exertion, and all of that being wasted.

With a shudder, Frost let the effort die. The soldiers had already grown older and diminished, some more than others, but none had been vanquished.

Rosivok and Sharryl, each with their subartas lashed to their right arms and a short sword in the other hand, reached the ridge an instant later and struck the first blows. Frost watched Rosivok slice a man nearly in half, then Sharryl felled a second and a third, then Rosivok another. But as Frost watched he found reason for fresh concern. The soldiers that fell kept moving, rolling about in pain, long after they should have lain still. Then one of them gathered himself and rose again, first to one knee, then one foot, until he stood up once more, ready to take up the fight again. Frost could see blood on the soldier's armor, evidence of his wound, but not nearly enough.

Another spell! Frost felt exasperation clawing at his throat, his wits. Imadis wasn't so talented when they'd last met. He had been practicing and apparently studying Frost with devotion. Flattering on the one hand, though quite inconvenient at the moment. Imadis had anticipated Frost's every move, or nearly so.

The two Subartans were heavily engaged, fighting with all their skills and strengths, yet each blow proved only temporary. Imadis' men could be wounded, but they would not die. The ones least affected by Frost's aging spell were at the fore now, forcing Sharryl and Rosivok back down the steep rock face while the others began to form a semicircle around the warriors. Frost saw Sharryl flinch as she took a sharp blow to the leather-shielded calf of her left leg. She rallied with a fierce, rapid combination—first the subarta, then the sword—and Frost saw her nearest opponent's left leg come off cleanly just above the knee. The man fell in a heap, screaming at the sky and rolling, hands gripping at the stump. The bleeding seemed to stop quickly enough, but the soldier stayed down, the fight gone out of him.

One down, Frost thought. But even his Subartans were only human, and could only keep this effort up another few moments before they began to falter or were overwhelmed. Imadis and his men would then come for him once Sharryl and Rosivok had fallen, intent on taking the prize that had driven them to risk their lives in the first place.

No! Frost vowed. He was not about to lose those two, they had been through too many years and battles together, and had become too well suited for each other—to Frost. *Think of something . . .* He still heard Imadis' thoughts faintly, more emotion than words, but the sorcerer was clearly growing excited in response to Frost's own desperate thoughts. Frost needed a completely new plan, one Imadis hadn't already thought of.

Both Subartans turned abruptly and lunged down the rock toward the hollow between the two rises. Four soldiers remained with Imadis, leaving eight of them still able to make pursuit. Frost watched the larger group. They were being so careful as they edged down the steep rocks, minding each step so as not to fall, looking almost comical, but when they reached the bottom any trace of humor was lost. The battle raged again, this time head to head, shoulder to shoulder. Despite their feebleness, though, the attackers' numbers and their damnable habit of healing after every good blow kept the outcome grim.

Frost . . .

Imadis was calling to him, but why?

The reason came fiercely clear as the sickness struck at Frost from within and began to overwhelm him. His body broke into a cold, soaking sweat as his insides churned, as his body began to ache. He felt the urge to heave up what little bread and cheese he had eaten for breakfast; then he swayed, dizzy as the fever continued to rise rapidly, high enough to cook what few wits he had left. Imadis had prepared this spell carefully and at length, had fashioned it to follow the name directly into Frost's mind and body once Imadis had spoken it properly, and Frost had taken it to heart.

Frost's own warding spells were useless against it, since he had given his best preparation to Imadis only moments ago. That was certainly the most admirable part of Imadis' considerable plan, or the luckiest. He had used his familiarity with Frost's ways and methods to good result.

Frost felt himself swaying as if blown by a wind, though the air was quite still. A fresh surge of nausea churned his belly. He had nearly been destroyed in the encounter with the demon prince, Tyrr, a disaster that had left him beaten and empty, unwilling and unable to attempt even the smallest sorceries, and lacking the smallest hope of ever finding confidence again. But this was only a man, a sorcerer such as himself. Until the battle with Tyrr at Kamrit, Frost had never lost before, and he intended never to lose again.

With that thought his right knee buckled, and he found himself kneeling on the rocks trying to catch his breath, so dizzy and weak that he could barely move.

The Blade, Imadis was saying, thinking, dreaming— as a starving man dreams of feasts—*The Demon Blade*.

Frost heard Sharryl and Rosivok shout out from below, the howls of warriors about to be overwhelmed yet roaring back at the imminence of that fate, raging at their own ends with a courage they would never abandon.

There were no spells, nothing Frost could think of now, nothing he could do that would turn the battle. There were other warding spells, some different enough, perhaps, to break Imadis' hold on him for a time. *Long enough to save myself*, Frost guessed, though even those seemed too difficult just now— and then what? Sharryl and Rosivok would not be helped and his demise would still be inevitable.

Frost's mind reeled from fever and frustration, from the certain knowledge that whatever he did, he had only the time and stamina and presence of mind to make perhaps one effort. Only one. Then, either way . . .

Frost let his cloak drop from his shoulders. The world spun around as he moved his head. Sweat from his forehead ran and burned his eyes. He gasped at the heaviness of the breath in his lungs and the sweat-soaked clothing that clung to him. He wanted to slump back onto his haunches but he fought that urge.

He needed to kneel at least, to do what he knew he should not do, what he had promised himself on the battlefield in Ariman he would never do again.

If it is the Demon Blade you want, then you shall have it! Frost thought. He reached up to his shoulder and pulled the strap down, around, then groped at the linens that kept the Blade itself hidden from the world. Next he took the hilt, first in one hand, then the other, and pulled the sword from its sheath.

Now what? he thought, reeling still. His successes with the Blade involved the most complicated, unlikely and unpalatable confluence of sorceries ever imagined. Spells that drew energy, but turned inside out, spells like those he was using to sense Imadis' thoughts, but turned on their side, deflection and warding spells turned completely around, a chant that aided in focussing, another that helped repel. The knowledge of a lifetime scavenged, bastardized, adapted to a purpose even Frost could barely understand. It had worked once—worked too well—and he had nearly died in the attempt. It would take half a lifetime of working with the Blade to learn how to control it without destroying himself, or others. But for now, he had only a moment, and hardly any wits at all.

Frost focussed on the far hill where Imadis stood feeding the spells that kept his soldiers alive, and kept him in such agony. As he had done before he raised the Blade and braced himself, remembering as best he could, whispering the words, the sounds barely leaving his lips. The first time he had tried this feat the Blade had used nearly all the energy he could give; it had drained much of the life out of those who stood near at the time. Sharryl, Rosivok and Madia had nearly died. Then he had tried again—reduced to a bag of bones, he'd tried again—gambling with the only thing he had left, his life, he'd tried. *As I must do now.*

"Sharryl, Rosivok, to me!"

They heard and without hesitation they turned and headed up the hill, Imadis' aged but determined troops trailing after them. The moment the two Subartans reached the top Frost had them get well behind him, then he concentrated on both Imadis and the soldiers just below, now no more than fifty paces away. Darkness took him briefly as he finished the last phrases of the spell, and added his binding phrase. He blinked, and saw a brilliant flash of blue-white fire explode from the Blade and cross across the distance between the two sorcerers. It turned slightly green, then red, strengthening, blindingly radiant now—so great a concentration of unearthly power that Frost could not truly comprehend it, even though he knew something of what to expect. A second blaze ignited, arching off, down and left, to the climbing soldiers just below.

Frost paid desperate attention, first to the accuracy of his aim, something he could only get a sense of, and then to his mind's ear as Imadis screamed out in horror as Frost's aim proved true. He watched even more closely for the moment when the blaze would turn suddenly white once more—the instant when it ceased to draw energy from Imadis and the soldiers below, and went after a new source of energy. The nearest source.

Beneath him the earth began to shake. He hadn't noticed that before, in the valley that had been the battlefield in Ariman. Hadn't noticed it here until just now. He wasn't even sure whether it was the earth or his own body that shook, or whether the brutal coldness he felt seeping into his knees and back was real or an imagined part of the panic and confusion his body was being subjected to.

The heat was real. The flesh of his hands and face burned from the fierce radiance of the Blade's energy streams; and the inevitable pain within was real as well, like countless thousands of tiny hot embers touching every fiber of nerve, muscle, bone. Unbearable, but if he was not careful, it would get worse as quickly as . . .

Imadis screamed out as if his very soul was being torn from him. Then Frost felt the sword grow heavier, felt that the strain of his efforts to force the fusion of so many makeshift spells had suddenly become unbearable.

He felt the hunger next, terrifying, bottomless, a cold beyond thought or touch. The torrent of flame was turning white once more and he understood in that instant what would happen, what he must do, and that it might already be too late.

His gut turned hard as the pain exploded inside him—even as he tried to let go of everything, the spells, the world, the Demon Blade itself—but as he did the pain found its center in his chest and the weight of twenty horses came to rest on his ribs. Reality seemed to slow nearly to a stop, as if the pain had weighted it down. He couldn't get away, couldn't put two thoughts in a row, couldn't stop.

His ears were ringing, but the sound seemed to come from beyond himself, from beyond the air around him and the earth on which he stood, a sound like the tearing of a fabric never seen or touched by mortal minds. The notion was abstract, yet intensely terrifying, and sent him groping back through twisting layers of pain, magic and substance in search of the release that should have come—should have come ages ago.

Let go. . . .

The darkness gripped him, then blinding light that touched off a final explosion of pain inside him, and severed his last ties with self, with flesh . . . with the world. He collapsed on the rocks, but the rocks ran away from underneath him, and he felt himself begin to tumble over the edge. He couldn't see, couldn't breathe, couldn't move any part of his body as it fell.

His mind seemed suddenly taken with observing everything from a detached point of view. Nothing seemed real but the pain. Then reality found him, and touched him with a hammer as big as the mountain itself.

He felt hands clutching at his clothing, pulling him backward. Or perhaps he only imagined he did. He tried to open his eyes, he thought he had, but only darkness filled his mind. Then even his most errant thoughts began to fade again, until he lost them in the growing void—a place where, he was certain, he would never find them again.

CHAPTER TWO

He was not alone, and that was the trouble. Demons chased him: ax-wielding peasants, empty-eyed children, howling wolves and banshees and armies of dead men. They stalked him, railed at him, struck at him wherever he went. They outwitted him, but only by knowing his own thoughts even as he came to them. They could hear inside his mind—or his thoughts were leaking out of his head, spilling over in the darkness like a storm that comes in the night, pushing streams over their banks. Only with the dawn would the devastation truly be known.

But he could find no dawn, no respite. Tied tightly across his back, the Demon Blade weighed a hundred times more than it should have, and it had begun to glow with a cold, unnatural light that radiated through his robes, acting like a beacon, shouting out to all and sundry where the Demon Blade was—where *he* was—luring them closer. He pulled at the bindings until his fingers were bloody but they would not loosen or break.

Then a moment of relative calm, the demons busy

elsewhere, perhaps. But now he heard a familiar voice call to him. *Imadis . . . ?* He saw the other as he turned toward the sound but it was only Imadis' head after all, sailing along in the darkness like a bird adrift on the winds. He listened more closely and decided the voice did not sound like Imadis after all, not really.

He watched the head sail closer and noticed it wasn't even the entire head, only two thirds at most. The rest—well, the rest had been destroyed.

"Frost," the voice said again, chasing away shapes in the darkness and replacing them with pain, with light.

"Frost."

Frost opened his eyes and daylight stabbed into them. He winced at the brightness, tried to focus on the shapes of shadow, and finally decided Rosivok was hovering over him. He blinked, tried again, and saw that this was not the Rosivok he recollected. This one was gaunt, pale, shaking. His cheeks were hollow, his eyes surrounded by black circles. Sharryl stood just beside him, her own face like a skull covered with only the thinnest veneer of flesh. Much of their hair had fallen out. *Like living dead,* he thought, less than pleased.

Now Cantor came into view looking only slightly better than the two Subartans, holding one arm and bleeding from his hairline. The blood had left a trail down his left cheek, then soaked into his richly tex-tured tunics. A different man, Frost saw. The vaunting aplomb, the wry smile familiar enough to make Frost self-conscious of his own, all of it was gone, replaced by the look of a man suddenly cut off from every-thing he had ever held dear. He stared fix-eyed and slack-jawed at Frost, body trembling. Silent. *Well,* Frost thought, *there is that at least.*

He lay still for a long moment and decided he must look much the same as the others, perhaps worse.

Which was indeed a pity. He had been this way before, and hadn't liked it. Not to mention the weeks it had taken to recover, the pain and effort of restoration and recuperation, the monumental inconvenience, the vulnerability. He closed his eyes and thought about what must come next with the expectations of a man who has just upset a hornet's nest. Then he took a deep breath, and tried to move.

The Greater Gods took a hammer to his body, sucked the wind from his lungs and set off a chorus of thunders in his head. His chest still hurt the most, though barely. Frost relaxed the effort and struggled to draw breath again.

"How bad?" he heard Sharryl ask him, speaking each word separately, faintly.

"I . . . live," Frost said, hearing his words come out in a hoarse, barely audible whisper. He saw Rosivok and Sharryl nod.

"Is that what you call it?" Cantor asked.

Frost managed a nod. *For now*, he thought, *that will have to do*. He sipped water from a pouch with the help of both Subartans, then he lay back and closed his eyes, and didn't try to get up again for a very long time.

Hours resting, he guessed, dozing now and again, though he did not dream through any of this. Which suited him well enough. When he finally tried once more to move it hurt precisely as much as he'd expected. Nearly as much as before. *Nothing to be done about it*. This time, he raised his head high enough to look about. Two emaciated Subartans moved toward him, got their arms under his and helped him to a sitting position; where he remained, resting, breathing slowly, waiting for some of the pain to subside while he carefully scrutinized his surroundings. Cantor was nowhere in sight, but there were larger problems.

He was at the bottom of the ravine, but it had changed. The rocks that had comprised the top of the ridge where he'd stood during the battle lay broken all around and underneath him. Many appeared misshapen, their edges and faces smeared as if volcanic heat had begun to melt them. Still others had been splintered like crystals, exploded from within like steam-shattered rocks left too near a fire. Off to the right lay the remains of Imadis' soldiers—pallid, dried, twisted husks that barely resembled human forms, their flesh withered until it had torn, their bones crumbled to dust, no meat or blood at all.

He raised his eyes to the next ridge. Nothing substantial enough to identify remained of Imadis, or even the ridge itself. But unlike the side where Frost had stood, nearly the entire far summit had melted, then apparently solidified once again where the rocks had run and gathered in streams and pools that shined in places like so much colored glass. Directly ahead a massive crevasse had opened in the mountain's face, wide enough at the top to pass two wagons side by side. Many more cracks, cut deep and jagged, ran down the remaining face of sloping, twisted rocks and vanished into the earth—though as he turned again, Frost noted that those same cracks raced through what remained of the rise behind him as well.

He took comfort in a part of this; after all, the desired result had been achieved. But the rest was disturbing, and would require a great deal of reflection. The Blade had become the focus of Frost's concocted vampire spells, just as it had once before, but far more had happened here. On the battlefield in Ariman the almost instantaneous result had been the deaths of thousands of soldiers, and the second had been the removal from this world of the demon prince Tyrr, but that had been his precise goal, so he had accepted the magnitude of the devastation in kind. Here, against so few ordinary men and one surely mortal sorcerer, even an exceptionally talented and clever one, he had intended nothing so . . . extensive.

He looked at himself as he tried to move his shoulders and arms. The Blade itself was still in his right hand, the hilt clutched tightly in his stiff fingers. In fact, he could not let go.

"For a time, we thought you had died," Sharryl said as she and Rosivok knelt beside him in the rubble, helping him stay upright while they leaned on him at the same time. They were quite as weak as he was. He'd nearly killed them, while nearly killing himself and destroying half the mountain on which they stood.

"For a time I thought the same," Frost answered.

"What . . . what happened?" Cantor asked, appearing once more.

Cantor clearly sensed how tender the question was, Frost gathered, as they considered each other. The merchant likely knew the answer well enough. Frost considered his response—something he expected to be doing for a very long time to come—and said, "Far too much. It is one thing to call forth a terrible storm, but another to control it."

"We were not prepared," Sharryl said.

"We thought—" Rosivok began, but he did not finish.

"I was not prepared, not truly, or I did not listen to my own doubts," Frost said. His particular prowess with aging spells had been the final key to creating the difficult and concocted means to exploit the Blade, and he had used the Blade as he believed its creators intended. But here, all his talents and experience as well as the knowledge he had gained from using the Blade against the demon Tyrr proved not nearly enough.

"What you seek will take time," Sharryl said by way of support.

"I am not so sure," Frost said wearily. "I am a blind

man who attempts to understand a mountain by touching a single stone."

"Ah, yes, or a sailor who has learned to make use of the oceans but has no defense against their fury," Cantor said, sounding rather proud of himself. "It got away from you."

"Something like that," Frost replied.

"We will be rid of the Blade, one day," Rosivok said, resolute, and clearly as much for Frost's comfort as his own.

"One day," Sharryl echoed.

"Aye," Cantor said, pendulous, turning slowly in place, apparently gathering in the scene all around him as if he'd missed some part of it.

Certainly that was the plan, to determine the identity of the Blade's true heir, its Keeper, then deliver the sword to them. The last Keeper, old Ramins, had known the succeeding Keeper's name, but he had died without telling anyone and Frost could not be sure there was anyone else alive who knew. The Council of Wizards that created the Blade in concert with priests and the Greater Gods were all long dead, as were many of the demons that had nearly come to rule the world of man in that time—until the Demon Blade. Yet even when the Blade was no longer needed, it had continued to exist, as the Greater Gods required for some reason, one assumed. The Blade remained a terrible weapon, a terrible secret, closely guarded for generations. But a secret no more.

"I have reason to hope," Frost said. "There is someone who may know the true Keeper, a very old friend and more, one of those we go to Worlish to meet, but I cannot be sure what we will find."

"That is why you travel to your homeland?" Cantor asked, as he tried to get comfortable on the rocks underneath him; he wasn't having much luck.

"Yes, one of the reasons," Frost replied. He took a very deep breath, put his palms, fingers in, on his knees, and tried to rise. Sharryl and Rosivok moved to help him, then Cantor as well. Wobbling, they all succeeded. Once he was stabilized in the standing cluster Frost raised the Demon Blade, then reached back and slowly slid it into its scabbard. Rosivok helped him get his fingers loose. Sharryl found the wrappings and gathered them up. Cantor, wisely, kept his distance. In a moment the Blade was safely tucked away, strapped to Frost's once-broad, now shrunken back.

"There," he said, when they had finished, "is where the Blade must stay. I will not use it again."

"Truly?" Cantor asked, tipping his head. His look was part fascination, part consternation. Frost wondered if he should tell the man anything at all, then decided it was probably essential.

"I have come to believe that it may not be possible for one man, one mind, to comprehend the Demon Blade's full nature, or to use its powers without great risk not only to one's self, but to . . ."

Frost didn't know. Others? Realms? The world? Perhaps no one knew. But right now, this day, he felt that learning the answer might be much like learning what the afterlife was like—the knowledge could eventually be his, but the method and consequences left something to be desired.

"To whom?" Cantor asked.

He wanted Cantor to know the truth, the impossibility of it. "Never mind," Frost said. "But mind this: until I can say otherwise, we must be sure that this day is not repeated. We must be sure."

He let his voice trail off. These were not words he wanted to speak, not the thoughts he wanted to have nor the fears and possibilities he wanted to face.

And by the Greater Gods, not anything like the kind of day he'd intended to have, he told himself, mentally trying to shake off the daze he felt himself falling into. *Not ever,* he asserted. *And certainly not twice.*

"The Blade may be hard to control, it may have a mind of its own, but it obeys your will when you wish to attack," Sharryl said.

Again support, Frost knew, as he looked at her. She didn't smile, but something like that was implied in her pale expression. "I wonder at that," Frost replied, feeling weaker again, very tired.

"It is true, isn't it?" Cantor said. "We have all seen as much. What is more, when you were satisfied, you *were* able to make the Blade stop."

"This time," Frost replied.

"You will be the Blade's master again," Cantor said, clearly trying to sound reassuring.

"No," Frost said, pausing while a chill shook his body. *They need to know, all of them*, he thought. "No," he said. "I do not think so." He sank to the ground again and rested on the rocks.

Both Sharryl and Rosivok were silent after that. Even Cantor seemed to hold his breath, as if he was afraid to let it go. Frost found the silence a comfort, and made an effort not to disturb it for the remainder of the day.

Near sunset they made their way back down to the trail below. They found the mule easily enough— it hadn't wandered very far and had escaped the destruction—then they spent the night huddled under blankets and the clear, cold stars. Their packs held enough food stores to last a few more days, enough perhaps to get through the remainder of the pass and into the province known as Calienn.

In the morning all of them, shaky as new-born calves, tried to set out walking again, but it proved too much too soon for Frost. So the best part of the day was spent resting. The day after was better, and a little at a time, pausing as frequently as they dared, they slowly made their way down toward the lowlands beyond the mountains.

The third day brought hunger, deep and abiding, as the bodies of Frost and the others began to long for a thorough replenishment, but they had to make their food rations—the remaining flat bread, dried beef, fish and cheeses—last as long as possible. The Subartans were in no condition to hunt, Cantor had never hunted a day in his life, and Frost dared not try any sorcery, not even a whim, so depleted were his bodily reserves. He might kill himself before he knew what he'd done, or in his withered delirium he might well get even the smallest spell cast wrong and do more harm than good; but besides all that, it hurt. It hurt to breathe, to walk, to talk, even to think, let alone do magic. Frost was not the least fond of pain or discomfort. He'd struck the notion of magic from his mind as completely as possible.

And he walked on.

Each time they began again after resting, the struggle was evident in the others' faces, and in his own, Frost knew, but none would allow themselves to give in or falter. Even Cantor was so far proving himself to be made of sterner stuff than Frost had given him credit for.

Still, they were only human, as was he, and while sheer grit would see them through the Greater Gods' own fury, even this had limits. By the third night, Frost was all but certain they would not survive without some remarkable happenstance, some act of providence. None was forthcoming, yet somehow they managed another day, then one more, as the trail began to descend—a hopeful sign, if not too late.

After six days, their rations and strength truly gone, they managed one final rise where the trail passed between two grass-covered hillsides, and found themselves looking down into hope.

A valley filled with forests broken frequently by freshly cultivated fields met their gaze, and through it went the road ahead, straight and solid, not washed out as Frost had expected, things going as they had. Not very far, only halfway to the horizon, there were signs of a fair-sized village.

"We will go?" Rosivok asked, as guardedly as a Subartan was capable.

"Of course we will!" Cantor said, shaking his weary head; but then he turned to Frost and asked, quite pleadingly, "Won't we?"

Rosivok's question took risk into account, of course, and there was reason for concern, especially in their current and vulnerable conditions, but the chances of being accosted by Blade-hunters were less here than in the lands they had come from, or so Frost presumed. More importantly, their physical needs outweighed other factors.

Frost wasn't even certain they could trek the distance to the village. But by all the Gods that had ever been, they would try.

"We will go," Frost said in answer. The others nodded weary agreement, then Sharryl took her turn tugging the mule into motion again. She let the beast all but drag her along after that.

By day's end they were near the village, but each step had become so grievous a task that they all had taken to leaning on the mule, which slowed everything down even further. Then the mule stopped altogether, and would not budge. *It has come to this,* Frost lamented in silence, leaning on the backside of the mule while flies buzzed about his nose, no strength left even to cuss at the beast.

"Ho!" a voice called from behind. *A young man,* Frost thought as he waited a moment, gathering the strength to turn about.

"Ho there!" another voice repeated, a woman this time.

With a breath, Frost pivoted. The others turned as well and both Subartans gripped their weapons, but they did not make any threats. They were in no condition to fight anyone, though that would never have stopped them trying.

Fortunately conflict appeared unlikely. A mother and her son, Frost guessed, though the boy was nearly a man. They stood at the edge of the road where they had emerged from the woods just behind Frost and the others. Frost turned a bit further and rested what remained of his weight on his staff, then he tipped slightly to one side by way of counterbalance, and waved a limp arm over his head at them.

"Good day!" he called out, his best effort, though the words didn't seem to carry very far. The two figures came up the road all the same, each one carrying a muslin bag in front of them, heavily stained, with straps that went over their necks and shoulders. *Berry picking*, Frost thought, and his stomach ached.

"Wait, we would walk with you!" the woman said.

"Friendly, aren't they," Cantor observed, as the two drew nearer.

True enough, but normally strangers had a habit of approaching Subartans with particular caution. Not these two. Then the truth of it came to him. "They must have seen many travelers before. This is the only road into this part of Calienn."

"I am Taya, and this is my son, Lan," the woman said as she drew within range, a weathered but apparently fit woman, and still young enough to be of child-bearing age, Frost estimated, though not by much. The lad looked like her, dark hair and olive skin much like Frost's, rounded features, but slim, and with a good frame. *He might be fifteen*, Frost thought. They were both lively of step, something two Subartans, a merchant, one sorcerer and even the mule could only imagine just now.

Frost introduced himself, then Rosivok, Sharryl, and Cantor. Taya seemed to smile excessively at this last.

"You have traveled far of course," she went on, even more cheerful now. She examined Frost and the others with far greater scrutiny than her pert smile and balmy tone implied. She seemed intent on every detail, in fact.

"Yes, from the provinces beyond the mountains, perhaps as far as Kamrit or Neleva," Lan said, clearly hopeful, his own grin a fixture now. "You will have many fine stories to tell I'm sure."

"Lan dreams of adventure as all boys do, and tales well told, but I can see you are all much in need of rest and good nourishment," Taya said, frowning a bit as she considered them further, then she began to nod in advance agreement. "You will want to stay on a few days in our village, of course. There is a very fine inn, with good beds, good food, good company. All the very best hospitality will be yours if you stay there, I assure you."

"You are the innkeeper," Frost said.

"I will not deny it," she replied.

"Are you ill?" Lan asked, still looking the newcomers over as well.

"Yes, in a way, but it is nothing to concern others," Frost said.

"You were not robbed in the pass, were you?" Taya asked further.

"We are well, and sound enough to pay," Frost answered.

"Of course you are!" She chuckled, then showed her best grin to everyone. "There is nothing Lord Cantor cannot afford. Follow along, then, won't you?" Frost and his Subartans were staring at Cantor now, a bit leery. The merchant shrugged. "In Kamrit, you are well known, but in Calienn, *I* am well known," he said.

"Clearly," Frost said. "We will follow you," he told Taya. "But slowly. We are . . . weary from our long journey."

"As all can see," said Lan, shaking his head a bit, which earned him a scowl from Taya. Then she smiled at Frost and the others again. "Forgive him," she said.

"I have," Frost answered. She'd meant Cantor. He nodded. She nodded back, then she and the boy held their bags open and everyone sat right there in the road, feasting on the berries before they set off again.

Taya began chatting about the village as if duty bound her. Acklandar, it was named, for the lord that had owned it all before he had granted a charter, making it the only place of trade in the region and himself much richer. She told them all about the two ice storms they had suffered during the winter months, and the sickness that had taken eleven of the village's older folk, including Taya's father, which put the fear of plague in everyone before it left of its own accord. Babies had been born this spring. The weather had been cool and dry. None of this was terribly interesting or new to Frost's ears, but the listening made the walking possible, the pain and exhaustion more bearable.

"Then you run the inn yourself?" Frost inquired.

"I do, though my son is the reason I am able to."

At a bend in the road Frost stumbled on the roots of a large old maple and each Subartan grabbed one of his arms to steady him. All three nearly fell, but managed to recover in time. Cantor made a gesture as though he was about to step in, but somehow he managed not to get that far.

"Your friends say little, but they are heedful," Taya remarked.

Frost nodded.

"Aren't you supposed to say thank you?" Lan said, earning him yet another scowl from his mother.

"We must all rely on others," Frost said. "In that, some of us are indeed fortunate." He seldom gave proper thanks to Rosivok and Sharryl; they were doing what they'd been born to do and being paid well enough for it, after all. But over time he had begun to feel that bits of occasional praise were in order. He knew better than anyone how hard it was to find good protection; that they were good companions as well was all to the better.

The two Subartans said nothing for their part, Frost hadn't expected them to, but he noticed Taya glancing over her shoulder curiously at them. "They do speak," Frost assured her. "When they have something to say."

Taya nodded. For several moments after that the silence was broken only by the sounds of birds busy in the trees. Then another bend in the road revealed the low stone walls of a village of moderate size, its gates open wide, and inside a glimpse of clustered houses and buildings. This part of the valley was broader and flatter. In every direction patches of cultivated fields were all up in green, leafy sprouts.

"Home," Lan said, grinning, picking up his step and now leading the others.

Taya let him go. "Such as it is," she said, though the smile on her face meant it was well to her liking. "Tell me, what lands do all of you come from?" she asked. "You to begin with," she said, looking at Frost. "Your look is like the men from my husband's province."

Frost said nothing at first. Taya seemed to grow concerned. "He was a fine, good-looking man," she hastened to add. "Died three seasons ago from illness. Worlish was his home."

"And mine," Frost said. "You are right."

"Ahh, of course! Such a fine thing."

"As you say," Frost answered.

"How long have you been away?"

"Many, many years," Frost replied.

"We often have travelers from Worlish at the inn, especially now that the roads can be traveled."

"Soldiers sure enough, if no one else," Lan said, grumbling.

"There are always soldiers," Frost said in kind.

Sharryl and Rosivok quietly nodded.

They entered the village at last and found it only a fair walk from end to end. It consisted of a collection of the usual tradesmen's shops and clumped-together homes of mud bricks, mostly one-story buildings with wooden roofs. The small square featured a drinking well and little else, though there was room enough for market fair tables and booths, which Taya said would come in just a few weeks. The inn stood not far to the right of the main gate, the largest building in sight, larger even than the guild hall, though it was small by most standards.

"Everyone will want to meet you," Lan said.

"Not quite everyone, but many," Taya corrected.

"After . . . we have rested," Cantor said with a weak but authoritative voice. Frost nodded agreement, then he stumbled over nothing at all, his Subartans caught him, and the three of them finished in a heap on the hard-packed earthen road. Cantor's hand was out, but once again he had somehow missed making contact with anyone.

Taya and Lan helped them up. "Right," she snapped, "let's get you all inside."

The dreams were interrupted by a man whose voice was familiar, as was his name—which was given, but Frost could not make sense of it. He felt warm, wet, awful. He tried to move but the world insisted on spinning in all directions, this way, then that, and he felt the urge to vomit. He reasoned that if he'd had anything of substance in his stomach he would have done just that, but as it was, his efforts produced nothing worth noting.

Someone was there, however, he decided, as he tried to look up through the haze of his fever at the shape that hovered over him. The man was telling him to rest easy. Then the man was telling him good-bye. A man he knew, though he could not remember the name. At which Frost began to wonder which one of them was leaving. The next thing he saw was a woman's face, and things began to look much better again. Relatively.

"Your stew," Taya said, taking a rag in one hand and wiping at the deeply stained wooden surface of the table, then setting the bowl in the other hand down.

"Thank you," Frost said, thinking himself much too kind lately; he seemed to be saying such things in one manner or another at a regular pace. Yet thanks were in order. He inhaled, drawing deeply at the rich aromas. Taya was a fine cook, and she ran a proper inn. She'd raised a fine son in Lan as well, a hard worker, honest, and smart enough to know when to leave one alone, most of the time. Frost had long found this last to be a rare trait, especially among the young.

Though Lan's interest in who Frost and his companions were, in what they had done, the places they had been was surely acute. He asked constantly, and was greatly entertained by the smallest tale of battles or sorceries. Which, to one degree or another, was to be expected of such a boy in such a place. Frost had not been a boy in ages, but he remembered that much.

He gazed about the room. Though this place was smaller, it reminded him of the inn where he and Hoke and Madia had first spoken all together. Dark tables and sturdy benches cluttered the worn wooden floors, twin hearths warmed the room from either side. Just enough daylight came through the windows to see what you were eating by day, replaced by sufficient lamps at night. Best of all was the frequent presence of those most delicious smells; meaty stews and soups, cooking porridges and baking breads, and some very fine ale of a familiar recipe, made by Taya herself, an art she had apparently learned from her husband who had brought the knowledge with him from Worlish, years ago.

As the thought crossed his mind, young Lan set a tankard of ale down next to Frost's bowl of stew. Frost sipped at the stew first, savoring the hot broth, then slurped a chunk of cabbage and a few tender bits of meat into his mouth. A long pull on the ale came next. He looked up to find Sharryl and Rosivok gulping their food down at a typically frightful rate. After only two weeks spent as Taya's guests, the improvements in those two, and in himself, were quite significant. They were mending, physically and in other ways, though they were all still too thin to fill out their clothing.

Cantor had vanished after their third day here while Frost was sick with fever. He had apparently said good-bye, or it had been a dream, Frost wasn't sure. He found Cantor's departure curious at least, but whether it was cause for worry or not, he had yet to decide. In his youth he had been a very poor judge of the character of others. He had remedied that failing in the decades since, or so he believed. He saw Cantor as the type who liked to get what he wanted, but on his own terms, and he had seen Cantor's eyes that day in the pass. The merchant had not mentioned the Demon Blade since that day. Not once. Frost saw this last as a good sign, but he knew it didn't mean that Cantor was gone for good.

"More salt," Sharryl said, and the boy went to fetch the bag.

"Pie too?" Rosivok asked, with a look of rapt desire that Frost almost didn't recognize.

"Strawberry, if you don't mind the same twice," Taya said with a nod, then a grin as she saw Rosivok's reaction.

"Until they discovered your pies, I had only seen a Subartan so intense in the heat of battle," Frost chuckled.

"You eat two pieces for every one of theirs," Taya scolded him. "But I will say the three of you have appetites I have never seen the likes of."

The Subartans nodded as they emptied their bowls and belched mightily, almost in unison. They were seldom heard to give proper thanks as well as Frost, at least not in words, but they seemed to get their message of satisfaction across in every other way possible.

"We will leave in a few days, but I will pay you the week," Frost said between his last few spoonfuls. "And I will see what I can do for your friends as well."

Taya's neighbor, the smithy's wife, had been by several times complaining of a swollen jaw on the left side, a bad tooth, and the past two days it had put her in misery. Frost had no spells to raise teeth from bone, but a simple tool her husband could fashion from two gently curled strips of iron, flattened and joined in the middle with a nail, would work to grab hold of the tooth and pry it loose. The pain, well, Frost could help with that, at least for a day. He couldn't remember how many times in how many villages he'd done the same. Usually for whatever amounted to a reasonable fee in those lands, of course. He would have insisted on being paid this time as well if it were not for the way Taya had looked when she'd asked, as if agreement should follow the way summer follows spring; that, and those pies . . .

"You'll only pay me what you owe me," Taya said.

"We'll see," Frost replied. Then he asked the same question he'd asked nearly every day for more than a week now. "Has anyone new come along, perhaps from Worlish?"

"None you should bother with," Taya said. "I told you we will get them and whatever news they bring, just be patient. In the meantime I can likely tell you stories enough if you'd care to listen."

"I do," Frost said.

"You don't. Most of the time you barely hear a word I say, as if you are in some world all your own."

"My thoughts tangle sometimes," Frost said.

"That must be it, then. But tell me, why do men only seem to pay attention to a woman when she's calling him for food or love?"

Frost opened his mouth to respond, but realized he had no immediate reply to that.

"I thought so," Taya said. But she wore a grin now that Frost was fairly certain meant only one thing. It was an idea he rather fancied, in fact. He tended to have little interest in women when he was at his peak weight, a condition that made him feel less attractive to women to begin with, conscious of the possibility he might present a danger to anyone he inadvertently rolled over on; but now, recovering from his ordeal, he was at least one hundred pounds lighter than he had been only last month. He felt urges deep within, a stirring in his loins that only strengthened as Taya leaned closer to him, put her lips near his ear, and whispered, "I see I have made my point."

"Perhaps. It is a topic worth further debate, I think."

"Indeed," Taya said. "But it might be prudent to go where others won't hear."

Frost nodded, ready as could be, and finished his ale, but before he could rise he found another one being set down in its place. Lan left again but returned a moment later with butter and a fresh loaf of dark bread, which Frost and his Subartans set straight to work on.

Frost tried to think of something else, anything else. "I am curious what you meant by your answer about travelers," he said after a time. "You say there is no one I need bother with, yet anyone from the north might be . . ."

"She means the skull-wagers," Lan said, darkening.

That meant nothing to Frost. "Tell me more," he said, chewing at one last bit of bread crust then bringing his full attention to bear on his ale.

"You must know what Worlish was like, but I tell you that vassal we have on the throne of Calienn is near as bad," Taya said.

"Commlin?" Frost inquired, recalling the name of Calienn's Great Lord just then, surprising himself. *Perhaps it has not been as long as I thought . . .*

"Commlin has been dead for some years," Taya said. "Killed, most say. Calienn has not been a sovereign province for as long as Lan has been alive. It is more a part of Worlish, an agreement won without a fight by way of treaty, or what some call a treaty. Commlin's young brother Torlin rules now, but only in name. He had too many vassals to count, and had divided Calienn into smaller and smaller manors until most of the lords could not live off them. So they tried to live off others, where and when they could. Even Worlish soldiers opportune our lands, and they do not respect anyone's sovereignty. But Cantor has been putting pressure on Torlin, and he has begun reforms. Worlish is under no such pressure."

"We pay taxes so often, and often to men we do not even know," Lan said.

"Skull-wagers?" Frost asked again, still curious.

"Yes," Taya said. "They are from Worlish, they wear padded gambesons dyed all in a dark color, except for a single white stripe down the front and back that grows broader at the bottom. Pear-shaped, really. But on horseback, riding away, the shape looks rather like a skull, and if the horse is at a walk, well, you see—"

"I have seen them," Frost said. "Two days past, walking their horses to the stables. Are they staying here?"

"No," Taya said, almost too quickly, perhaps nervously. Frost wasn't sure whether she was lying; she had no reason to and the boy was taking no particular notice, but if so, she wasn't very good at it. Still, he let it drop.

"These men come to collect which lord's homage?"

"Borger's or Adeler's, who are lords of nearby fiefs, or even in the name of old Acklandar, who has the only right beyond the king himself."

Frost had heard every word, but what he was hearing didn't make much sense. Worlish and Briarlea were rich lands and should have no need of what amounted to robbery in a sovereign ally's villages. "Soldiers from Worlish are doing this?" he asked, clarifying.

"Aye, now and again, and they take their share of whatever else they want for themselves," Lan said, clearly displeased with the arrangement. "Cantor is the only friend we have, and he has yet to prove much of that."

Frost nodded. It was a familiar circumstance in other lands, and usually there was nothing to be done. The local vassal was weak or lazy or both, the noble to whom he owed fealty was only slightly more attentive and had more men of arms, but no stomach for war; so the taxes from grains and ale to craftsmen's work to coins, and sometimes laborers were collected as needed wherever they might be found, especially where one manor bordered another. Here, that practice had been taken to the level of principalities. There was no recourse, other than to start a revolt, become a vassal, or take to the road . . . as Frost had done.

"When I saw these men about in the village, they seemed as interested in me and my Subartans as I in them," Frost pressed. "Tell me, why should I not speak to them?"

"Their type is quick to act and hard to predict," Taya said. "They have stayed away so far. I wish that to continue."

"I hear they killed a man and his wife in Attaus just four days past," Lan added, "and all because the poor fellow had not enough food to get them supper."

"There are always stories, people love to tell them," Frost cautioned, "and stories always grow as they travel."

"Frost is right," Taya told her son. "You'll do well always to keep that in mind. But so is Lan," she added, turning to Frost. "If they were worthy soldiers, I dare say someone in Worlish would have better use of them. Instead they wander here. Such men are best left alone."

"Then they should leave others alone," Frost said.

"That is what I say," Lan muttered, mostly under his breath.

"Lan would be a knight and save the world, bless him," Taya said with a soft smile. "But the inn will not do without him."

"For now, I will heed your advice," Frost replied, leaning back, his belly filled to satisfaction. He had no desire to start trouble or make news here. "Meanwhile, I will accept your offer," he told Taya, gazing at her, "and listen to your stories. I predict they will be most . . . delightful."

Taya made a grin that held an enticing hint of sin as Frost stood up and held out his hand. She took it, and led him out the door, then around back of the inn to the small house that joined it, using part of the inn's roof and one of its walls. It had two rooms, the smaller of them arranged with two storage chests, a small table that held a washbowl and one spindly chair, a bed made of a sturdy frame and a well-stuffed mattress, and a chamber pot. They ended in the bed almost right away, then set about pulling each other's clothes off.

Frost laid his robes and tunic on one of the nearby chests, then he unlashed the scabbard and set the

Blade, still wrapped tightly in cloth, on the floor next to the bed.

"What is that for?" Taya asked, eyeing the obvious shape of the thing, and especially the hilt where it protruded from the bindings.

"Have you never heard the tales, that sorcerers cannot perform without a proper . . . aid?"

"I'll believe no such thing of you, Frost."

"No?"

"No, not that, though sometimes I do not know what to believe when it comes to you. Still, the learning is fun."

Frost hid his smile. "And why is that?"

"Because even weak and starving and ill, there is something remarkable about you. I know you are a man of magic, considered wise by many, perhaps talented, and certainly cocky as any man I've known. But I have known many men, tradesmen, warriors, a wizard or two. None were quite as you."

"No doubt," Frost said.

Taya wrinkled her brow at him and he grinned.

She grinned back, then held him. He brought his lips to hers, his hand to her breast. He had not been with a woman in nearly a year. Then it had been Sharryl, who lacked nothing with regard to mastery, strength or enthusiasm, but who was nowhere so soft as Taya was everywhere.

"You never did tell me about that sword," she whispered as if the topic were sensual somehow. "It is special in some way?"

Frost tried not to let himself fall out of his mood, which he was finding enjoyable. "Why do you ask?"

"You act as though it is quite valuable."

"Perhaps. But it does not concern you."

"Then it won't." She pressed against him, and neither one said more for nearly an hour.

When they had finished they lay in each other's arms for a time, listening to the sounds of people talking as they passed by on the street and breathing in the rich human scents of their conjugation. In a few weeks Frost would be much heavier, far less interested, and leagues from here. That didn't matter now, not to either one of them.

"What will you do when you get home?" she asked, leaning up on one elbow and looking at him. A wistful look, one Frost found curiously hard to read.

"To start, I will see what remains and what has become of the place, and of those I knew."

She sighed. "I say very little really changes."

"Yes, but as I said, I have been gone a very long while."

"Where, Frost?" Taya asked, practically getting on top of him again. "Tell me, where have you been?"

"All those lands you mentioned earlier, and many more."

"Are they the same as here?"

"Vassals argue, peasants pay, people have children, they grow old and die. And they are everywhere fond of wars."

"You see, nothing changes. Though we have had no wars in years, thank the Greater Gods," Taya said, laying her head on his chest.

"A peaceful land?"

"Mostly. Far to the north, there is the Grenarii Empire. The king is known as Kolhol. He has won or seized the lands of all the Grenarii tribes and united them, and he has built an army that worries even the Worlish king. Some say he has made threats."

Frost shrugged at this. "Kings are always making threats, they always will. Tell me, who would this Worlish king be?"

Taya paused at they reached her door. She looked at him. "Lord Andair, of course. I should think you would remember him, if all you say is true."

Frost felt his insides harden, felt the stew backing up. "Is anything wrong?" Taya asked, as she tried to put her arms around him and found his body rigid.

Frost realized what he was doing, then realized he wasn't breathing. He drew a breath and blinked his drying, staring eyes into focus. "Lord Andair?" he asked, finding it difficult even to speak the name. "The old king's banished nephew? He is not dead?"

"The same," Taya said. "And no. Do you know him?"

"I do," Frost said, feeling the full weight of this news settle upon him. "I did."

"Frost." Taya used her hand to turn his eyes to her. "Will you say what's wrong?"

It was not her fault, of course, and she had every right to be concerned. "It is Andair," he told her. Again he tasted the rancor in his mouth as the name touched his lips and tongue. "He is the reason I left."

CHAPTER THREE

"I wish to be your third Subartan. I will learn," Lan said, standing stoutly before Frost and holding a very old and battered sword.

"What have you told him?" Frost asked Rosivok, finding the Subartan with a steady eye.

"It was me," Sharryl confessed, before Rosivok could say. "The boy was curious, we talked a few times. But we did not talk for long."

"Enough to get his mind filled with foolish ideas," Frost said. He turned to find Taya coming out of the inn to join him and the others in the morning sun. She wore a light tan dress decorated with brown and green embroidery along the sleeves and collar. *Quite a handsome woman*, Frost thought, reaffirming his earlier assessment. "You will have your hands full, now," he told her.

"I already do."

"Now he will be worse."

"Why are you so sure?" Taya asked, smiling.

Frost gave her his most sober look. She needed to take this seriously. "He has been asking about

Subartans, and mine have been telling him stories. He has asked to be my third."

"What third?" Taya asked, growing more anxious.

"I am one Subartan short, but for now I will remain so." Frost turned to Lan. "You are much needed here, boy. Understand that you will do your mother and your village more good than you could do for me or these two. I have lost two Subartans already, and while your heart and mind may be ready and willing to meet the task, I fear your skills would make you my third loss. You serve no one dead."

Lan seemed to wilt with every word, and hung his head with this last. His mother moved to comfort him, but the boy tried to shrug her off. "I have never even been to Worlish," he said. "Never been anywhere, but I am ready. I practice almost daily with this," he added, brandishing the sword.

"You already are somewhere," Frost said. "As good a place as any, I promise you, and with better folk than many. Do not give it all up so easily. As for your fighting skills, they may be needed here one day, by your mother perhaps, or your own family. A war might start and conscription follow, then your fighting skills would help keep you alive. Almost nothing in life is wasted, but if you go with us, your life might be. Do you understand?"

Lan just stood there for a time, thinking, looking the visitors over. Frost tried to imagine the sight through the boy's eyes. Here was a mysterious, eccentric sorcerer in a colorful floppy hat and tunics and leaning on a dark, polished wooden walking staff carved with strange runes, and there were two Subartan warriors, tall and powerful, well armed, wearing their own, only slightly less ornate tunics and linked, leather armor dyed in red and brown. All images well fitted to the ambitions and imagination of a young boy such as Lan. He wanted adventure, stature and proof of the man he had nearly become.

Frost could not blame him, he knew what that was like. But at what cost? And to whom? That was the kind of mistake that could ruin one's life, and the lives of others, which was something Frost was even more familiar with.

"Yes," Lan said finally, barely speaking. He looked away, toward the old wall at the edge of the village and the wide-open gates. "I am glad Sharryl told me a few stories at least. I will still have them when you are gone."

Sharryl gave him a nod.

"It would be an honor to fight at your side," Rosivok told the boy. "One day, perhaps, but not this day."

"Frost," Taya said.

He turned to her and found her look had changed again, a dark expression Frost hadn't yet noticed on her face.

"You are leaving?" she asked.

"Today," Frost said. "I must go to Worlish."

"Can your need be so important?" Taya asked. "You are still weak from your journeys, you need more rest, a few more days. And I—"

"Indeed, my needs are more important than you can imagine," Frost said, stepping nearer. They had spent the night together and now he was going. She had known he would; he had made no promises to her and she'd asked for none. Still, a word . . . "I left something of myself there, a part I could not face, and I must return for that part now."

"If you need someone to listen, I would like to hear that story," Taya said.

"I know." Frost felt a peculiar tug somewhere deep inside, a feeling he could barely remember how to experience, from a circumstance he tried to forgo at every turn since—since leaving Worlish, no doubt. *What has gotten into me?*

"We will need supplies," he said, changing the

subject. "I trust a good meal can be found at your inn a bit later this day, to start us on our way."

"Of course, a wonderful meal," Taya said. "And—"

"Thank you"—Frost took her hand and held the softness for a moment, then he took up Lan's hand as well—"both." After a moment he let go and started down the way, the Subartans in tow, toward the smokehouse. They had already moved their few possessions from the inn to the stable where they waited with the mule. They would still need to purchase provisions enough to keep themselves fed on the rest of their journey. He needed more bulk, and plenty of it.

"I meant no harm," Sharryl said as they walked.

"I know," Frost said, "but you must keep in mind the many reasons why a young man might want to follow you to new lands and be part of your tales of battle and feats of magic."

"I have," Sharryl huffed. "I thought it was better he talk with me than letting him talk to the soldiers."

Frost paused in the street only two doors from the smokehouse. "He speaks with the soldiers?"

"They have been near the inn, but they do not enter. The boy is so far intimidated by them. I do not think he has approached them yet. Though he might at any time since his mother speaks with them without hesitation."

"Taya?"

Sharryl nodded.

"When did she speak to them?"

"I have watched the innkeeper closely these past few days, and she has spoken with them twice."

"There," Rosivok said, nodding toward the inn. Four men in light armor and short, shiny helmets, each wearing a dark gambeson with a single white stripe, front and back, strode out from behind the inn's far corner and continued up the street as if they'd been walking all along. At least one of them glanced over his shoulder at Frost and the others.

"They have not come past us," Rosivok said.

Taya emerged around the same corner a moment later, then went straight to the inn's front door and disappeared inside. Frost felt the breath catch in his throat. His mind suddenly began racing back over the last two weeks, retrieving every memory of what had been said or seen.

"I will learn what she has told them," Sharryl said coldly, each word stated clearly.

"No," Frost said. Then he puzzled at that. He would have let Sharryl do exactly as she said in the past, at almost any time in the past, yet he had said no. There was rational justification, after all, not just personal; Taya couldn't know much, only his name and that he carried a hidden sword, all of which could be learned by anyone persistent enough. The loss was not tactical. Yet in another way it was more severe. Madia had earned his trust, but it had taken many months and a war that had nearly destroyed them both to come to that. *Yet I have given my trust to this woman so easily . . .*

A mistake good only to learn from, Frost thought, growing cold inside, placing his resolve between his heart and his mind. "It would appear I was wrong about her," Frost finally said. "It will not happen again."

"We will go and learn from the soldiers, then, and stop them from taking their news to anyone," Rosivok said.

"A plan that has always yielded far too much attention and far too many efforts thereafter," Frost said. "Dead soldiers make for quite a story, one that will travel on the very winds. If we let them go about their business, weeks may pass before the troubles they bring return, and those troubles will come from fewer directions."

"As you say," Rosivok grumbled, clearly displeased, though he said nothing else.

Frost watched a silent exchange between the two

Subartans. He wanted the soldiers dealt with as much
as they did, and Taya as well, but . . .

He tried to set that thought aside. "Finish gathering our provisions and collect our goods and the
mule. If the soldiers return to Worlish they will tell
Lord Andair only what he will know soon enough in
any case—that Frost has returned."

"Then what?" Sharryl asked, for both warriors, from
the looks on their faces.

"A question that does not yet have an answer—
though it shall."

"Should we meet you at the inn?" Rosivok asked.

"No," Frost said. "I will not return there again."

By late afternoon the trio had taken to the road
again, unnoticed by most, though not by all. The
soldiers followed. They were being careful, staying
out of sight, but they were there. Which was something Frost had expected. The only question was
what the soldiers would do along the way, if anything. There was no sorcerer among them and the
odds were plainly poor, even to the most dense of
mercenaries.

"We should eliminate them," Rosivok said, as night
approached. "It aids the sleep."

"Not yet," Frost answered. "We are all headed in
the same direction. Until that changes I do not expect
them to risk direct contact."

"Unless they are fools," Rosivok said.

Sharryl scowled at him. "Of course they are fools."

"Then we will sleep lightly," Frost said.

"Can we at least go and throw rocks at them while
they sleep?" Sharryl asked, grinning coldly. It was a
game she wanted, verbal sparring in place of the other
kind. *Good,* Frost thought. It would help keep their
spirits up, and their edge, and his as well. Something
their stay in Worlish would surely require.

"Just be sure to hit them in their heads," Frost
required.

"But that is the only part they do not use," Sharryl said.

"Aye," Frost said, feeling better already.

After three days' walking and without any sign of trouble from the soldiers tracking them, Frost and his two Subartans crossed the border into Worlish, and made their camp for the night. The skies had blown crystal clear on a late day wind that had faded with the sunset. The season had not yet arrived for the hypnotic chirping chorus of crickets, but the silence had its own soothing effect.

These nights did not grow so cold as those of only a few weeks ago. The air was moist and full of the smell of bark and earth, of spring flowers and the rich dampness of the Lengree River, which flowed down from the Spartooths and arced its way through Calienn. Just beyond the Worlish border the river divided, the forks continuing through East and West Worlish, then into the vast northern lands beyond, known as Grenarii. The best road into Worlish followed the river and was heavily populated, and heavily traveled. As before, Frost thought it wise to stay away from the villages and the notice of their barons; no need to invite extra trouble, but here in Worlish that would be difficult.

So be it, he thought with tight resolve. He had not journeyed so far to hide in the bushes, and he could not do what he had come here to do without drawing attention. Lord Andair notwithstanding. *So be it . . .*

Camp this night was just off the road, a hollow in the woods where a great old oak had fallen. Frost sat with his back leaned up against the old tree's dead trunk, having slid the Demon Blade around to his side and positioned the sword just so. He let the stars and the crescent moon fill his eyes, as he tried to imagine what the days ahead might bring. He found the effort a difficult task. He shook himself loose of those thoughts and focussed on Sharryl and Rosivok, who were apparently quite focussed on him. They did not avert their eyes. Which meant there was an issue of some kind begging resolution, or clarification, though neither of them thought it proper to bring up the subject.

"Very well, what is your question?" Frost asked.

"There is more we should know," Rosivok said plainly.

"More?"

"You come here seeking the rightful Keeper of the Demon Blade, but it is clear there is more, another reason why you must travel to your homeland."

"You need not say, as is your right," Sharryl said, "and we will serve you no matter, but if the reason is important then perhaps we should hear of it. Knowledge always brings an advantage."

This was true enough, and he hadn't told them much; perhaps now was the time. He had been putting it off because some of the reasons he was here were not that certain even to him, and because others were still too painful to touch. That was part of what had brought him here, the need finally to face that pain, but that task had grown more complicated than he could have imagined. He hadn't expected that the focus of his most painful memories would wear the crown of King of all Worlish.

"You are right, of course," he said. "You should know as much as I can tell you. In order to prepare."

The question was where to begin. "I have no friends and little family left," he said, getting that out of the way. "My father was a powerful sorcerer in his own right, though I barely knew him. He was killed in a battle, far from home. I received word of my mother's passing some years ago, even before my travels to the Kaya Desert. Perhaps I will learn what her dying was like, now that I am home, and whether she suffered, whether she was alone. These are things I have wondered many times."

He tried not to think such thoughts even now; that was a trap sometimes, one it had taken him years to escape, if he ever truly had.

"She was well when you left home?" Rosivok asked.

Frost nodded. "She was, but much else was wrong. I tell you this because it has everything to do with Lord Andair, whose path it seems we are bound to cross. He was not a king then, but nephew to the king, as was his cousin, Lord Wilmar. I knew them both. Their uncle, Weldhem, was Lord and King of all Worlish. We lived in Briarlea, a collection of closely tied fiefs that includes most of eastern Worlish. The Weldhem I knew was the third king of that name to sit on the throne. The walled city that holds the castle he ruled from is named for them.

"But the king had no sons, leaving Andair and Wilmar as equal heirs to his throne. Weldhem had sought my father's services and advice on occasion, our families shared many times together, but after my father's death my mother moved out of the house he had built and went to live at the city's eastern edge with my aunt, Shassel."

"You have spoken of her before," Sharryl said.

Frost did not recall doing so, but he was not surprised.

"Yes, a sorceress," Rosivok stated, "and your mentor."

Frost nodded. "All those things. She is the one I seek, the only one I can think of who might know the true keeper of the Blade, or might know who would know. Though I am not certain she still lives, I believe as much. Had she died I would have sensed it, I am certain of that."

Frost paused again, collecting his thoughts, and rearranged his haunches on the moss-covered earth so as to improve the circulation in his thigh. There had not been a day since the first one spent in Shassel's house when he did not think of her in some way, sometimes many ways. She was in every measure her brother's equal, save in size. She had never acquired the weight needed to make her truly powerful, but no one mindful of magic or heedful of a woman's proper wrath dared any less than respect for her.

Shassel had instructed a very young Frost in the ways of sorcery in her brother's stead, had taught him all the things his father would have. Perhaps more. Frost had gleaned from her other things, confidence and forbearance among them, and an abiding dislike for men of moral compromise for another, and all of this with the blessings of his mother.

His mother and Shassel had been very close, and neither woman had ever suffered fools gladly, which was where Frost imagined he had gotten the trait from. In the end that had been part of the problem, part of the reason he had gone away, and left behind his family and his home.

The memories grew difficult once more, as they had for years, but he needed to tell his Subartans, his protectors, what concerned them most. Frost took a breath.

"When I was still a very young man," he said, pressing on, "quite convinced that I knew precisely how the world should be, and sure that my own place in it would know no limits, I had already learned more than someone of that age should have. This was not all Shassel's fault. I was a very fast learner. I had even managed to decipher Shassel's own binding phrase, which she used with every spell to make them hers and make them true. I spent many years developing my own phrase, as I knew I must, but for some time I borrowed hers. She never knew."

Frost used both hands to rub his face as the plundered phrase stuck in his mind, *Tesha teshrea, tesha teshrea.* A memory much like a nursery rhyme, unshakable once recalled, yet far more penetrating. Using the binding phrase had been like wearing someone else's clothes, someone older, someone bigger, though even then Frost had been a bit larger physically than Shassel. He'd been wrong to use the phrase at all, but for a time the knowledge had given him means far beyond even his own lofty expectations.

"I commanded great powers and an ardent desire to use them. A desire fueled by the hot blood of youth. Andair gave me just such an opportunity. I was his friend at the time. Wilmar was the quieter of the two and kept to himself, leaving many to wonder and make gossip about him, though I took none of the nonsense seriously; not until Andair came to me one night, and explained that I should.

"He had been quarreling with his cousin, Wilmar, for years, but I was unaware of the depths of their differences, their rivalries, and was surprised to hear of the conflict. Truly, I was unaware of the depths of the darkness in Andair's heart as well. He convinced me that Wilmar was a ruthless scoundrel."

Frost took another deep breath, let it out with a sigh, and went on. The details were many, and Frost recalled them all for his Subartans: the attempts made on Andair's life—each only two weeks apart—the dagger found on the walk just outside Andair's manor house bearing Wilmar's family crest, the clearly forged deed that documented the transfer of considerable land and holdings from Andair to Wilmar, and finally the curse, set by some unknown adept at the hire of Wilmar, and the cause of Andair's persistent, worsening illness. Taken all together they had been very convincing.

"I will spare us all the torture of the entire epic," Frost said, "but Andair managed to enlist me in what

I believed was his fight for survival against his increasingly ambitious, treacherous cousin. Together, with the help of my magic, Andair and a troop of his allies confronted Wilmar. A battle took place, one that Wilmar lost. He was not killed; in the end I would not consent to that. Indeed, it is the one thing that has given me solace in the years since. He managed to flee the province with his wife and little else, leaving his lands and holdings, his serfs and his remaining family in the accepting hands of Lord Andair.

"I was well rewarded, and with the departure of Wilmar the trouble stopped. Even the curse was lifted. But . . ."

Frost felt the weight of his guilt try to grip his chest, a feeling that was familiar enough. This was the most difficult admission of all, even after three decades and all he had been through and done. The reality of the past could not be reasoned away or taken back.

"Andair tricked you?" Sharryl asked, bringing Frost's eyes into focus on the two Subartans.

"Yes."

"Yet he lives?" Rosivok asked next.

Frost felt the pressing weight within him grow. He nodded. "So it would seem. My aunt, Shassel, had been an adept who lived deep in the Hubaran Forests. When she returned and learned what had happened, she began at once to cast doubt on the story. I did not want to believe; I would not have listened at all had it been anyone else. But Shassel . . ."

He let her name fall through the darkness, into the small fire that smoldered at his feet, and mouthed his own binding phrase, then hers once more, for the first time in years, "Tesha teshrea." The embers flared into small, yellow-orange flames then died back down an instant later. That was why he believed Shassel still lived. Her name, her magic, still held power.

"She used images drawn in a pool of water," he continued, "much like the vision I used to entertain the leshys in Golemesk swamp, though hers were from the past, not a possible future. They were all very real. I saw the Lord of Lies, Andair, send thieves to steal Wilmar's dagger for Andair's use, saw him pay the men who faked the attempts to kill him, saw him pretend to be cursed by sickness. I was not the only one fooled, he had convinced even the king, but that made little difference."

"And yet he lives?" Sharryl said, repeating Rosivok's invective.

They had not known him then, Frost thought— he had barely known himself, which had been a big part of the problem. He balked at the thought just as his Subartans did now, but hindsight always had that advantage, and at the time, he'd had almost none.

"Not by my grace," he said. "I swore revenge, swore to right the wrongs I had helped visit upon so many innocent people, but Andair learned that I knew the truth, that I was seeking justice and Shassel was sworn to help me. He persuaded the king entirely to his side, though his soldiers had orders only to detain me for questioning.

"They found Shassel, and took only her message back with them. When the king learned that Shassel was seeking answers and justice, he called his men off, for the time being, until more could be learned. Andair grew frustrated at this, and hired a handful of mercenaries to kill me. A final gambit. It failed, but they succeeded in buying Andair the time he needed. He told those close to him that I was mad to kill him, that everything I claimed about him was a lie. Some believed him. They may have hidden him or helped him in other ways. Soon after that he fled, but with a considerable fortune. I vowed to search for him, but my first concern was to find Lord and

Lady Wilmar and make amends. I . . . did not succeed."

Frost remembered clearly the days that followed. He found it difficult to face all those who lived in the collection of fiefs that surrounded Weldhem, known as Briarlea. Harder still to face his mother, or Shassel. Alone he was left to face himself, which proved hardest of all.

"I decided I had much to learn, and that I would be no good to anyone until I did. I thought it might still be possible to learn all that, but not in Briarlea, and I still needed badly to learn what had happened to Wilmar, and to find Lord Andair. So I left. I took to the road."

"They let you leave without quarrel?" Sharryl asked.

"I never brought myself to say good-bye," Frost said.

"I left without word. I did not intend to be gone for long, a few months at most." He paused, holding half a breath in his chest. "I have never been back."

"Now Andair is king of Worlish," Rosivok muttered.

Frost met his eyes, and nodded. There was no need to say more.

"You are a different Frost now," Sharryl said.

"We shall see," he replied, then he scuffed at the dirt near the last glowing remains of the fire. The bugs would be at them when the fire died, but their bedrolls were light and large enough to allow them to wrap their entire bodies up, heads and all, so as to escape most of the attacks. They had each nearly accomplished that very task when a brief sparkle of greenish energy lit the trees some thirty paces away.

Frost had set up the warding spell as a matter of routine. Comprised of few resources it could do no damage to even the insects, but intrusion by anything larger than a sparrow caused its luminous collapse and sent a sharp quiver through Frost's body, enough to make him flinch. He sat up, and found both Subartans already rising with him. In that instant they were on their feet.

"Visitors," Frost whispered, while Sharryl and Rosivok melted to either side, then vanished into the darkness.

CHAPTER FOUR

A man yelped, then another began shouting only to have his shouts cut short, and his throat by the sound of it. Frost heard horses after that, hooves beating on the hard surface of the road. Two men went yelling after them, their voices fading quickly up the road. *Running full out*, Frost thought. One of the voices suddenly grew faint and stopped. The other began to yelp like a frightened dog. He kept yelping, kept going up the road.

Then Sharryl and Rosivok reappeared. *Too quickly*, Frost thought at once. Something was not right.

"Someone comes," Rosivok said, making room. From behind him, a moment later another figure emerged into the firelight. No, three figures. Two of them were soldiers. Frost recognized the hat and jerkin of the other—Cantor.

"Good evening, my friend," Cantor said. "My compliments to your Subartans. My men are still alive this time."

Frost threw another branch into the fire, watched it catch and burn on the glowing embers. The men with Cantor were splendid by any means, each one dressed in fine jerkins and polished armor and helms. Well paid, well fed and fresh, that was clear. He would have expected nothing less from Cantor.

"From what I heard, someone is short a few men all the same," Frost said.

"Soldiers," Cantor said. "From Worlish. We found them prowling about, eyeing your camp. They have been following you."

"We knew," Frost said.

"Of course." Cantor stepped closer to the fire. "My men killed three of them and cut their horses loose. One caught his horse just as they were running off. You will miss them?"

"Not at all," Frost said.

"The other one will not return," Rosivok said.

"I can track him a ways," Sharryl said. "Do you want him killed?"

"No," Frost said. "Stay. Let him go. I will conjure the warding spell back, and we will get our rest. We all still need to mend. We have a few good days' walking ahead of us before we reach Briarlea, and there is no telling what awaits us there. Though . . . I could cast the stones, and consider what they tell me."

Rosivok and Sharryl were quite silent. Even Cantor seemed suddenly preoccupied with the leaves on the trees.

"Tomorrow, perhaps," Frost muttered. "I am not sure they work at night."

"Doubtful," Cantor said, and the Subartans nodded.

The flames at their feet were already dying again, allowing the darkness to creep back into the clearing once more, surrounding them. "What brings you here?" Frost asked Cantor. "Or can I guess so easily?"

"I tell you as you might guess wrong," Cantor said. "I came to warn you. News has already spread of your coming. Many will seek you out, for one reason or another. Andair is sure to have his own designs on—"

"And of Andair," Frost interrupted. "Why did you not tell me he was king of Worlish?"

Cantor seemed taken aback by the sudden harshness of Frost's tone, but he shook his head and shrugged easily enough. "You did not ask. You would know him of course. Old friends?"

"I have sworn to destroy him," Frost said.

Cantor's brow went up. "Indeed. He is my best customer, you know."

"As will be the next king, no doubt."

"No doubt," Cantor said, smiling at that.

"You waste your time just as before if you hope to bargain for the Blade again," Frost went on. "No matter what you say of your purpose here tonight, I find it hard to believe otherwise."

"You are mistaken," Cantor said. He clasped his hands behind his back and began slowly to pace back and forth in front of the fire.

Frost could almost hear the wheels turning in the man's head and as he turned to the fire, he could see the depth of deliberation in the man's eyes. This was not Cantor at his best and both of them knew it, but Cantor seemed bent on seeing this through, no matter. Frost waited until Cantor paused and looked up again.

"I was there, in the mountains," the merchant said, biting nervously at his lower lip as he considered his next words. "I saw what happened. I felt it. I have traveled to a good many places in this world, seen a good many things strange and wonderful, been in the company of sorcerers, kings, conquering armies."

Again he fell silent and began pacing, though this time his hands were held up in front of him, fingers flat against each other, prayerlike, as if he were asking the Greater Gods for help, and his eyes were cast downward. "I know enough about magic to know . . ."

Cantor turned abruptly and faced Frost, fingers locked together, eyes set, and took a breath. "Ten times the greatest sorcerer in all this world could not have done what you and the Demon Blade did in that battle and I saw what it did to you as well. Why you still live is beyond knowing. More troubling still is this notion I have that what I witnessed was only a small part of the terrible darkness the Blade can touch, a power more terrible than—"

Cantor closed his eyes and rubbed them with his fingers, gently at first, then harder. "I have come to tell you, Frost, that I no longer want the Blade. I do not even want it or you in Calienn, and as long as you are in Worlish I will not sleep well at night. The Blade is far too dangerous for any man to have, therefore, every man desires it."

"Except the one who has it," Frost remarked.

"Unless that one is a fool, and I suspect you especially need not be told of the troubling number of fools about these days. No, I wish you as far from here as possible, you and that Blade. I will pay you to go. No reasonable price will be rejected. Even the unreasonable will be considered. Go, Frost, leave this part of the world. Find a land where no one dwells, where you can hide the Blade forever or devise a means to render it harmless or give it back to the Greater Gods if you will. If you can. Whatever you need I will see you get, but go. On your own if you can, with my help if I must. I see your dilemma, perhaps more clearly than you. Worlish will bring you sorrow and war on some scale, or troubles unknown. Your quarrel with Andair only makes matters worse."

"It is not that simple."

"Then it must be made so. Alone you would have only your own fate to worry about, but your fate is bound to that of the Blade, and that is something the living and perhaps the dead as well need fear."

"You are a curious sort of friend," Frost said, "but I do understand your concern. I will make my stay as brief as possible, but I will stay for a time at least. I must. I can promise you only that I intend to be rid of the Blade first, and Lord Andair second."

"A small comfort," Cantor said. "I will be watching you most carefully. I bear you no ill will, Frost, but trust that I will ally myself and all my resources with anyone I must in order to save the home and the life I have built."

"Would you?"

Cantor nodded.

"And all the innocent ones, of course," Frost concurred, with a slight bow of his head.

"Yes."

Both men looked into the fire for a moment.

"Well then, tell me what you need," Cantor said.

"For now, nothing, but I will let you know. Truly, I will. For now just be on your way."

"You would send me out into the night?" Cantor asked, as though surprised. "You too are a curious sort of friend. I thought we might talk a while, you and I." He added a faint grin to this, an offering of sorts.

Frost shook his head. "You have threatened me, Cantor. There is nothing more to it. You have yourself intact, your men too, your advice well taken; now, accept all that and leave."

Cantor drew back as if buffeted by this last. He just stood there for a moment staring eye to eye with Frost, reflecting. His gaze slowly narrowed, as if his thoughts were weighing down the lids of his eyes. Finally he nodded once. "For now," he said with a bow, then he turned and motioned to his men, and without another word they were gone.

The road into southern Worlish was wide and level and in many places laid with flat stones, some of them worn smooth, others worn to ruts. This road dated back to ancient times and had been built by a civilization that hadn't existed for a thousand years. New roads had been added. Frost left the main way and trailed off to neighboring fiefs and holdings. Most of what Frost could see did not impress him. The lot of Worlish's serfs and peasants had not improved notably in his absence, and in places looked like it had declined.

As Frost walked along he noted that work was being done by the crown in places: at the split in the road that would take a traveler eastward into Briarlea or west into Treserlea, he saw a marked difference— the eastern road had been recently repaired, and many of the holes and ruts filled in. The other road looked much the worse for wear, however. The flow of trade clearly favored Briarlea.

Treserlea was a collection of fiefs similar to Briarlea, but the region had long been considered somewhat less blessed. Two rivers, the Rosha and the Worl, ran north and south through Worlish, essentially splitting the country into three pieces. Between the rivers lay a deep, lush valley many leagues across. Beyond Rosha, the more western river, the land grew hillier and rocky; it was a poor land for farming or traveling, and sparsely populated. Over time the region had become like a separate province whose lords still owed fealty to the Worlish crown in Briarlea, but who seldom had any more to do with the eastern fiefs than that.

Good only for taxes and in time of war, Frost thought. Even when he was young, some of the nobles in Treserlea made no secret of the fact that they would sooner drop all association with the rest of Worlish tomorrow, and might even be willing to fight for that end; but the odds did not favor them to start, and fealty to Briarlea meant the same in return—an attack on Treserlea by the Grenarii or anyone else would bring all the resources of every part of Worlish to their defense.

Frost considered making that trip first. He might find allies among the hills, but the effort might just as well turn up nothing worthwhile, and he was too eager to get home.

He took the eastern road, steady along, letting the mule set the pace and letting his body continue to heal along with those of his two Subartans. *Andair must be doing well*, he thought, *to keep such a fine road*. But Frost found this no surprise. Andair was not the type to allow wealth to slip though his fingers; that had been true since they were boys. Almost nothing else about the new king of Worlish could be taken for granted, assumed, or even believed. Frost had made that kind of mistake once before.

His thoughts kept straying back to those times as he walked, to the worst of his memories. No matter how often he tried to redirect them to the better ones, to his mother, his aunt, his life in those days, so full of grace, expectation and discovery—his mind strayed back. To a time fouled by the fates, by indiscretion, and tragedy.

By the time he'd gotten his mind arranged in reasonable order it was nearly dark, and they began looking for a place of sanctuary for the night, and thinking about food. They had entered into the southernmost edges of Briarlea. Here peasant villages and the sprawling manors of local lords were more common, but no more prosperous. Most village inhabitants were more than willing to give whatever they could spare to travelers who could pay. Food and shelter would not be a problem until word of who he was, and what he might possess, reached into the countryside. At least that had not happened yet, so far as Frost could tell. No one they had spoken to on the road seemed to know him.

"There," he said, "that will do." It wasn't much, a small, haphazard manor surrounded by fields of spring wheat and barley and rows of cabbage. A clutch of peasant huts stood down a gully a little way from the road. That would have been Frost's first choice before; no one bothered him in such places save the occasional Reaver, and they were most often easily bought. Now, so close to home and already approached by soldiers and merchants, Frost saw less value in keeping to cover and some advantage to knowing what the smallest of Andair's barons knew.

An older man answered the door, a squire who told them to wait while he retrieved the lord of the manor. He returned in only a moment with an even more aged fellow, fairly well dressed in a dark, reddish brown tunic decorated with intricately woven detail at cuff and collar, and well made shoes. *Slim for a lord*, Frost thought, but then this man was old enough to have passed on some years ago. He had graying hair and roughly half his teeth, which became evident as he smiled at his guests, and greeted them. "I am Burrel," he said, looking his visitors over with an increasingly judicious eye. "What do you call yourselves?"

Frost made the introductions truthfully, then waited for a reaction. He got none. Anticipating the next question he added, "We are journeying to one of the northern fiefs, and seek a night's comfort in your home."

"Have you good stories to tell in return?" Burrel asked, clearly hopeful.

He did, stories this lord who had surely spent his entire lifetime in Briarlea could hardly imagine. Frost however was in no mood to spend the best part of the night drinking too much ale and telling endless tales, and his Subartans were far less garrulous than he. "We have gold," Frost said instead.

Burrel's spirits seemed to sink more than a little, though he recovered quickly and set a most reasonable price. Frost took the pouch from his sash and counted out the necessary coins. "Now," he said, that out of the way, "we are very, very hungry."

Burrel sent his squire to see to dinner, then he showed his guests where they would sleep. "Tell me, if you will," he said to Frost after that, as they stood in the manor's small but warmly appointed great room eating chunks of brown bread while the meal was prepared. "Would you be the one I have heard all the stories about, the sorcerer come from Ariman who carries the legendary Demon Blade?"

Frost nearly choked on the bread as he swallowed. He forced the bread down his throat. "Whatever gave you that idea?"

Burrel shrugged. "To have such a great adventurer and mage as my guest would be quite a rare luxury," he said, clearly hopeful, and showing no signs of fraud or deceit.

"What if I was, and I was not prone to kindness toward those who speculate so loudly about such things?"

Burrel's expression turned grim. "You have that potential, I can see that. But I meant no harm. I am not the young and steadfast champion of the crown I once was. I will tell you that I do not fancy Andair greatly, or many of my neighboring lords. A vicious lot, all but one or two. The first surprise of each day is that none of them have come and killed me while I slept. One by one, most have crossed or swindled me over the years. No, Andair and his favorites will be all your problem, and none of mine."

"You are keener than you look," Frost said.

"I am not at all sure of that, but these days I feel I have been a fool often enough already. If you are who I say, certainly Andair will look for you and find you, but whose purposes that suits does not concern me. For now you are here in my home, and I am curious about a great many things that you might know. All I wish is to chat. Nothing more. You have nothing to fear from me."

"Nor you from me, as it stands," Frost said. "After dinner we will talk, but only for a while, as I am in great need of good rest." Burrel nodded swift agreement. Then he turned without another word and headed toward the table.

The meal was simple yet satisfying, much as Frost found the manor and Burrel himself. They ate more breads, a rich vegetable stew, and a great amount of cooked fish taken fresh from the river and some sort of small bird or other, of which there were more than two dozen. Everyone ate in relative silence, though even Frost began to grow uneasy with this; while pleasant, it was unnatural to have a meal in another man's house without conversation, and he had offered, after all.

"I will tell you one story," Frost said when they had finished, and tankards of ale had been set about. "About a meeting I had with a dead warrior mage in the depths of Golemesk swamp, and the leshy creatures that share his realm.

"Go and gather what serfs and squires you might."

With that, Burrel nearly leaped up and instructed those present to do as Frost had said. Then he excused himself and went to help see to it personally.

Frost had done more for many—removed a curse, aided the ill, or tipped the balance in quarrels between men and armies, or the demons and the gods themselves. Trying to make amends. Trying to make sense of things. Yet this was more than an aging lord, a survivor, could hope for, a tale of mystery and magic from a faraway land, something he could remember and retell again and again, for as long as he lived.

Frost sat back as he waited for all to gather, and found himself in a curious light—he had never fancied himself such an altruistic fellow . . .

Perhaps you are losing what is left of your edge, he told himself. Or he had left this land too long ago, left too much unfinished business to ever return.

"Can we bring you anything else before you begin?" Burrel asked, as he reappeared with a handful of others.

"Nothing."

"We will have visitors tomorrow, I think," Burrel said. "Perhaps you can stay and be my guest at dinner once more?"

"I have only a two days' walk ahead of me before I reach my home, and I grow anxious."

"I see," Burrel said, his eyes drifting toward the heavy tabletop, his hands looking for something to do. "You know, now that I think of it, I do remember a man named Frost, son of a great sorcerer, nephew to another. The stories were told for years. You are the same man, I say. And Shassel would be your aunt."

Frost eyed the lord more carefully. It seemed he truly could not be taken at face value. He was certainly old enough to know of Shassel and much more. Frost was in no mood to play a guessing game with someone known to withhold knowledge. After all, that was his own domain, not Burrel's. "What kinds of stories?"

"Some good, some bad. There are always stories."

"Indeed."

"Can I ask why have you come back?"

"I have my reasons."

"I would be happy to honor your stories with a few of my own, which may interest you," Burrel said.

Frost nodded. "Fair enough."

Burrel smiled at that. The others were seated about. It seemed time to begin. Frost regretted agreeing to this telling already; he had little interest in old tales, even the good ones, in this place where the past met future. But it was too late now. He started with the tale of Madia's fall from grace and expulsion from Kamrit, then realized this was too much and skipped ahead to the events in Golemesk swamp and the finding of the Demon Blade itself. When he had finished he discovered every mouth in the room hanging slightly ajar, every eye fixed upon him. No one so much as blinked. He allowed himself a satisfied smile.

"Now," he said, looking to Burrel. "You spoke of Shassel. What do you know of her? Is she well? Where can I find her?"

"Find her?"

"Yes," Frost said, noting the tension in Burrel's voice.

Burrel look stricken as he took a small breath. "I-I am sorry, truly I am, but I think she is dead."

CHAPTER FIVE

He hated horses, and this gelding was no exception.

Their spirits were too strong which, short of cruelty, required constant negotiation. Stubborn and moody when they wanted to be, and not always as trustworthy as many a horse lover might have the rest of the world believe. Frost much preferred the reliability and pace of his own good two feet to being jostled and jounced, and to listening to endless equine complaints about his weight. That, and he needed the exercise. Nevertheless, right now he and his Subartans needed the speed only three good mounts could bring, and Burrel had insisted on supplying them—for a fair price.

He kept a vigorous pace, prodding the horse to a slow lope as often as he dared. His Subartans matched him without comment. Even nightfall didn't slow them at first. But ultimately, good sense and their horses' obvious fatigue combined to form a convincing argument for rest.

Once their mounts had been fed, watered and

secured for the night, Frost and his Subartans ate cold
provisions and made no fire, so as not to draw attention. He still did not believe Shassel dead. He had
felt no sign of this as he was sure he would; and the
words of a minor lord with uncertain motives, a man
old enough to have slipped some of his senses, were
not the sort of thing one took to heart. But there was
a chance . . .

No matter. He had to learn the truth for himself.

He lay awake that night on the hard ground,
wrapped in his bedroll, staring at the crescent moon
and countless stars darting in and out of great dark
cloud banks that passed slowly overhead. As he had
on too many nights in countless places just like this
one, he allowed himself to stew in the broth of his
burdens until his brow began to sweat, despite the
coolness of the air. He needed to face Andair once
more, to find Shassel, to see his stewardship of the
Demon Blade through to whatever end the Greater
Gods intended; and he needed to learn what going
home again held in store for him, a thing less certain than he had thought it might be when he set
out on this unusual journey. Yet part of him wanted
nothing to do with any of that. Part of him wanted
to walk away and keep walking, just as he had so
many years ago. Busy himself with whatever amused
him or distracted him. Yet it wasn't that easy any
more. In truth, it never had been.

All of this, he thought, not for the first time, *I
never intended* . . .

He fell asleep finally, he wasn't sure when.

At first light they pushed on once more, resting
only in spots. Hardly a word passed between them.
Frost was in no good mood, something the others,
even the horses, easily sensed. And the hardest part
of the journey lay just ahead. Late in the day, as he
knew it would, the road came round the forest's edge
and over a low hilltop, and Frost found himself in

sight of Weldhem, the most noble city in all Worlish—
and within its walls, the battlements of the castle that
held the Worlish throne. This was the heart of the
land of Frost's father. The land of Andair's father. Now
Andair's alone.

The city had overgrown the old walls and was
spread out across much of the shallow valley. Fields
covered up in rows of spring plantings filled the rest
of the valley and gave way to stands of woods only
on the higher ground to the south and east. Frost
stood in the sunlight just beyond the edges of the
trees. A gentle breeze from the north lapped at his
robes and hair and face, carrying faint traces of gloriously blended scents from wood fires and cooking
and baking all mixed with the somewhat less allur-
ing smells of refuse and human and animal waste.
Still, the smells and sights combined to bring back
a flood of memories. Not all of them good.

The lands that had once belonged to Wilmar lay
just to the west. Frost had no desire to see them
again. His own home of many years was further east.

"It is . . . nice," Sharryl said, then she busied herself with snatching a fly out the air as it circled about
her head.

"Hmmm . . ." Rosivok added, folding his arms
across his chest as he surveyed the scene. "Yes, nice,
but we have seen many cities like this one. It is but
one more."

He meant no slight of course. He was trying, in
his way, to help. Frost realized how furrowed and
frowning his mouth and brow had become. He
decided he must look utterly confounded, just as he
felt.

"It is good to be back," Frost said, filling his lungs
deeply, exhaling slowly and evenly in an effort to bring
himself around. It felt good to say such a thing, at
least. He let himself feel buoyed by the moment,
though another side boiled just beneath the surface.

In truth he wanted to rush into the city and seek out people he remembered, to visit the streets, markets and homes he had visited with his mother and aunts and uncles as a boy—and later as a young man. Most of all he wanted to storm the throne room in the castle itself and confront Andair, Lord of Lies, Lord of Pain. He wanted to exact all the justice and vengeance he could—just as he had imagined doing countless times.

But he could not. Not yet. Not while the Blade was his, and so much else remained unknown. He had waited decades, and those decades had taught him a great deal. Now, he must wait a little longer.

"One day, soon, we will pay this city a visit," Frost said, as he turned and focussed on his Subartans again. He felt a twinge of amusement looking at them; even at a glance, they presented a perfectly subdued combination of tension and boredom. It helped to further break the trance Weldhem had set.

"As you say," Rosivok replied.

Sharryl nodded. "As you say."

"First we will go east, to my family lands," Frost went on. *And learn what has happened in my absence*, he added in silence. "We will find a village along the way to stay in for tonight, any one of them will do. There is something else I must attend to."

They waited until dusk before descending the gently sloping hillside toward a village set beside a small wellspring, and far from the sight of Weldhem. Frost led the way slowly, making no threat, letting the peasants notice the unusual strangers entering their midst. In only a few moments nearly the entire population of the village had gathered around. Frost put them at ease with words at first, then gave everyone a copper coin.

"You will eat, and tell your best stories," one of the older men said after that. "But we have little to share. We should fetch the lord of the manor."

"No," Frost said. "We need not bother any barons this night. What you have will do well enough."

He ate lightly, just enough to stave off the hunger for tonight, then waited while everyone gathered to share his company. Frost tried to be more engaging than usual. He told his stories, careful not to choose the ones that might be too provocative just now, then he began to ask questions.

These people were poor, that was clear; Andair took all he could from the land and its people. Few of these men stood any chance of one day buying a bit of land of their own, and ultimately becoming freemen. The king had seen to that. It seemed he needed the land and what could be gotten from it to maintain the throne and keep his mercenaries. Andair had apparently seized great parcels of land in order to grant fiefs to the vassals who had come with him from other lands, and to men who swore fealty to him since them.

None of this surprised Frost in any way.

He asked about his family next. No one knew anything more. Finally he bid them all good-night, though he did not go to sleep at first.

After everyone had gone to bed, Frost went to the edge of the village and stood facing in the direction of the city of Weldhem. He closed his eyes and began reciting the words that would renew the spells he had used in the Spartooth Mountains to learn what he might of the men who followed them. Tonight he focussed on one man, the one his memories recalled so well. He needed to know better what sort of man Andair had become, needed to taste the bitter waters, and know his enemy anew. This was something he had not possessed the ability to do in his youth, a talent that might have spared so many so much.

The spells began to draw energy from him, to work as they were intended to, but when he felt a sudden presence of another mind he knew at once it was

not Andair—the king for all his sin and pretext had
no skills as a sorcerer, and this other did. A powerful mind, and already aware of Frost's probings,
awakened by them, already looking back . . .

In frustration Frost ended the attempt. *Gentaff,* he
thought, recalling the name the merchant Cantor had
used for the sorcerer which Andair kept. A formidable
opponent, perhaps, but Frost had no intention of
testing him just now. There were too many variables
once that road was taken, and already too many
reasons he must wait. *One victory at a time,* he
counseled himself. First he needed to go the rest of
the way home. And soon.

Even from so brief and intangible an encounter,
Gentaff would no doubt guess more than Frost
needed him to know. "We must leave," he told his
Subartans, waking them. "At once."

"It was him," Gentaff said, standing in the dark in
the king's chambers, a voice from nowhere.

Andair sat up and dug the sleep from the corners
of his eyes, then he pulled the bed curtain back. He
still couldn't see a thing. His oil lamp had apparently
gone out, and the fire in the hearth had faded almost
to nothing. Which meant most of the night had
passed.

"You could bring a fresh lamp," he said.

"I know," Gentaff's voice replied.

Andair frowned. He loved melodrama, this sorcerer, to the point of fault. But even a monarch had
to make do now and then, and Gentaff had more
than enough redeeming qualities to allow his eccen-
tricities to be overlooked. Most of the time. Though
Andair particularly abhorred the man's occasional
habit of posing absolutely still and closing his eyes
and keeping them closed when someone was talking. Even when Andair was talking. As if the topic
was not interesting enough to warrant all of the great

Gentaff's attentions; as if he were off, somewhere else.

He always returned, and always seemed to know where he was in the conversation, but that didn't lessen the implied aspersion. Nevertheless, this was the one man he must deal with. Especially now, with the Grenarii king and his growing army threatening Worlish's northern borders, and more immediately, with the remarkable news of his old confederate's return.

"You are sure?" Andair asked.

"Yes."

"What of him, then?" Andair prodded, pulling on bed shoes and a robe. "How should I feel?" He looked more closely at the hearth. Scarlet embers still smoldered in the heaped gray ashes. Andair got to his feet and lit the wick, then set the lamp on the table beside his bed.

"Hard to say," Gentaff replied. "I was barely aware of him, and then only for a moment—though he was aware of me, and possibly you. I have waited in meditation for hours, seeking him, but there has been nothing else."

"What does that mean?"

"He is not far, but he is very good at going unnoticed. I believe he is moving away from here, at least for now."

"Curious behavior," Andair said, fixing his gaze on the shadowy figure that appeared in the candlelight, still near the door. "Frost has come all this way, come almost to my very doorstep, yet he does not enter. For years I have considered this day and all its possibilities: Would he seek to destroy me; would he oppose me publicly in hopes of provoking an uprising? Would he fear me, and seek an arrangement? I would have thought any of those likely. But to stroll past without so much as a greeting?" Andair smiled to himself. "Perhaps he fears me more than I'd hoped."

"He protects the Blade," Gentaff said.

"I am sure," Andair answered him, frowning now. "But then why come near Weldhem Castle at all? He must know I am king. Why come home again after so long unless he intends to use the Demon Blade to complete his revenge?"

"Do you fear him?" Gentaff asked, offering nothing in his tone that might reveal his design.

Andair swallowed back his first thought. Not even Gentaff would ever be allowed that kind of currency, even if fear were shaking him to his bones. He had long known how to read the hearts and minds of others, then use what he found to his best advantage. He would not allow others the same advantage over him. "No," he said flatly.

"Then perhaps you should be," Gentaff said. "The Blade is powerful, and so is Frost. Perhaps we are no match for him."

Again no emotion showed in his voice, but Andair had come to know this wizard well enough in the past two years to guess that this was mostly a hostile statement. Gentaff believed no man and perhaps not even the Gods were truly a match for him; and for all Andair knew he was possibly correct, at least where sorcery was concerned. As to cunning, Andair was not willing to make any such concession. Gentaff was both wise and powerful, but any strength could be used against a man, as well as any weakness. Granted, this sorcerer's weaknesses were few, but Andair had discovered at least one. . . .

"If you are frightened, good wizard, you may wish to leave while it is safe to do so," Andair said.

"A generous offer," Gentaff replied, "but I will wait until I have good reason."

"When will you know?" Andair said, pressing.

Gentaff kept his demeanor, though Andair could sense the venom. No matter. Despite his age Gentaff was taller and stronger than Andair, and known to have considerable skills with weapons of every kind. Andair had not let himself go, but even without his great talents, Gentaff would prove a challenging opponent if it came to that. Which was part of the appeal of taunting him now and then, or pressing a point until it made the old wizard flinch. Gentaff needed someone like Andair with his stronghold, his army, his wealth. It was just a question of how much, a question Andair was willing to wager against again and again.

"May I speculate a little about this Frost," the wizard said, not a question. "He is not the unpracticed fool you deceived and defamed those many years ago."

"Then what is he?"

Gentaff moved closer, until the candlelight illuminated his face, stout yet angular features, a short-cropped beard still mostly dark in color but going silver in streaks, deep set eyes. He loomed over Andair. Was he taller than Andair remembered? Of course it was not possible, so he discounted it.

"I will know. There will come a time. He moves away for now, but if he comes to us again it will go differently. We will each learn a great deal, and quickly. As will you. Of course, we could go to him. Go after the Blade."

Andair balked at the notion, but he made an effort not to show it as he allowed the idea in his mind, and gave it brief audience. Chasing Frost, getting things out in the open, getting on with the inevitable and perhaps even gaining the upper hand against his old friend-turned-foe again—all this had definite appeal. The chance that they might devise a means to acquire the Demon Blade in the process was especially delicious, and especially dangerous. Perhaps too dangerous for now. "We should not be hasty."

"The Blade is the key," Gentaff said. "To everything."

Andair tried to assess the amount of melodrama in this last. For centuries men had sought the Blade, and here was Frost bringing it from halfway across the world like a gift—which was unlikely. *He brings the Blade to destroy me,* Andair thought, but if that was true, why hadn't he done so this very night? What if Gentaff could somehow turn things around, somehow take the Blade away from Frost and wield it as Andair required, then no realm could stand against them.

He was in no hurry. For now there were too many unknowns—not the least of which included the Blade itself.

Even Gentaff seemed to have no idea what its powers were or how to control it, let alone how to counter its powers if Frost should attempt to use it against them. Andair only assumed Gentaff had a plan in mind. Gentaff had never actually claimed any such thing.

"We should wait and see what he has in mind."

"Is it caution or cunning that guides you this day?" Gentaff asked. "When he has finished his reconnoiter he may decide to journey north to Grenarii and join your enemies."

That was a more immediate worry, and one Andair had already considered. He had spent years securing his throne, building fealty and hiring soldiers, assembling an army that could challenge anyone in the world—the Grenarii in particular. Kolhol, the Grenarii king, had amassed an even larger force, and though they were reportedly ill-trained, Andair did not like the implications. Such an expensive and unwieldy tool could have only one ultimate use, as far as Andair was concerned. He had no desire to allow an alliance that might cost him half his own army or perhaps all of Worlish in the end. But nothing was ever that simple.

"If I fall, Worlish falls, and it is Frost's home as well as mine."

"If that matters to him. Has he any family left?"

That was a tender subject. "Shassel is his aunt."

"The old sorceress?"

"Yes, but she has been quiet these past few years, seldom seen. I do not bother her, and she does not bother me. She knows what is good for her I think."

"No one else?"

"There may be a few others. Some friends, perhaps." *Wilmar in particular*, he thought with some consternation. He didn't want Frost making amends with Wilmar, though that was most unlikely. He doubted Frost even knew Wilmar was alive and living in Worlish again. Then there were the twins. "Something that bears watching," Andair conceded. "For now, leave all of that to me and let us consider other possibilities. I hear Frost is known to appreciate a generous payment from time to time. It could well be that he has come here to sell me the Demon Blade in exchange for something—gold, his family lands and more, or a share of the throne after all. It is safe to say that I am one of the few men alive who can afford to bargain with him."

"Or he will kill you with the Blade, then take all you have and sell it back to your heirs," Gentaff said, and Andair though he saw a grin touch his face in the dim, flickering light.

Andair drew a deep breath. "Very well. I will send someone, a messenger. Whatever we learn will likely be of use to us. All we know is that Frost and the Blade have arrived in Briarlea, and have taken to cover among the trees and peasants."

"A puzzle wrapped in a mystery," Gentaff said.

A favorite saying. Another quirk that annoyed Andair. "Only for now."

"I agree. If your messenger does not return, then?"

"I will send another and another. I have many."

Gentaff turned to one side as if examining something, though there was nothing there. When he turned back he said, "You should send your messenger, and we will sit idle and wait. But be prepared to learn that this may all have been a waste of time."

The conversation was becoming a waste of time. Gentaff apparently believed himself the only truly capable one under these or any other difficult circumstances. His sort always did. It had been the demon's own job, but after several tries Andair had finally gotten rid of the last court wizard while he was out hunting—and for similar indiscretions. Of course, he hadn't told Gentaff any of that. He'd taken the head off the spike only two days before Gentaff's much heralded arrival. To be safe he had kept the dried head, hidden of course, as they were known to possess residual powers that could one day be most useful.

"No matter the Demon Blade, and no matter who and what Frost has become," Andair said, "I managed him once, and I will again. After all, I am not the same man I was then, either. You need take that into consideration."

Gentaff's shoulders formed a shrug. "I have."

"You are not impressed?"

"You have made the manipulation and exploitation of others your hobby, perhaps your life's work. To that extent I am impressed. However, there is more to this."

Andair noticed Gentaff's eyes had closed. He did it to annoy, Andair was almost certain of it. "You may go," Andair said, "to prepare for the time ahead."

"As you wish."

Andair watched the dark-robed sorcerer disappear through the chamber doors into the darkened hall beyond. The heavy wooden door seemed to follow him closed, and as the iron latch struck the catch the lamp beside Andair's bed flickered out. Melodrama, Andair scoffed, shaking his head.

He was still tired. He wanted to pull the warm

covers up and go back to bed, but he knew that wouldn't do. He lit the lamp again and summoned his aides instead. In a very real sense he welcomed the end of the waiting and the exhilaration that came with it, the chance to get on with the challenges he knew would come to him one day, and with it the chance to triumph again—once and for all. That was the way to look at all of this, the only way.

In the third village Frost passed through and less than half a day's ride from the lands that had once been home to him, an old couple turned up, minstrels until their legs and fading health had forced them to give up the traveling, though they were lute players still. Everyone Frost asked said they would know of Shassel if anyone did. He paid the villagers to tend to their horses and went looking for the couple. He found them waiting outside the hut that was their home, a large enough place, but only one room and that shared with the cow on colder nights. They eagerly accepted Frost's meager payment for their time.

"We remember you and yours," the old man said. "Hard to forget such folk. No one is left to welcome you home, though, not that we know of."

"Save maybe those twins," the woman said.

Frost tipped his head. "Twins?"

"Living further east last I knew," the woman answered, looking to her husband for accord.

"Driven out?" Frost asked.

The old man paused in rapt concentration, picking at a hole where a tooth had been, then nodded. "A brother and a sister born of a cousin, one of yours, but the land did not pass to them. They might be gone by now, somewhere far."

"If you do find them, they will know of any other family about," the woman said.

"Shassel," Frost said, watching their eyes. "What do you know of her?"

"We remember her," the husband said, uncomfortable with something about her. "We don't know what might have become of her."

Frost believed them, but there was more. He decided it would serve no one to menace them into saying what it was.

"You are welcome to stay in our house tonight," the woman told him.

"A fine enough offer," Frost said, "but we must go."

He turned to do just that and drew up short, greeted by the sight of two fully armored soldiers on horseback and one young man, perhaps a troubadour of some sort, dressed in lavish, ruddy colored pleated trousers, a feathered leather bonnet, white blouse and a striking gray and black vest. The trio approached at a leisurely pace and paused finally when they were only a dozen paces away.

Sharryl and Rosivok stood ready, each exactly two paces to the front and one pace to either side of Frost, weapons up, but making no movement.

"I am Jons, at the service of his lordship, Andair, King of Worlish at Briarlea," the troubadour said, addressing Frost but examining the Subartans all the while. "If you are Frost, I have a message for you."

"Does Andair seek audience with me?" Frost asked.

The man had a narrow face that hid nothing, including his momentary disdain, though he seemed to overcome it abruptly. "No, he does not," Jons said. "Not unless it is absolutely necessary."

"I can imagine," Frost said, watching the messenger's eyes and manner. He was young and pretentious, and as sure of his sponsor as any fool could be. Andair would have many like this—all incurable.

"He bids you greetings, commends you on recovering the Demon Blade, and wishes to acquire it. What is your price?"

A familiar question, Frost thought. "Bring me his head," he answered.

The young man's brow went up, then a smile crossed his face. "Of course, a joke. I have heard you knew him once, long ago."

"I did, and I made no joke."

Jons glanced at the two men-at-arms on either side of him but got no reaction. His brow furrowed in thought, then he seemed to set those thoughts aside. "He is willing to pay you extremely well."

"I will see him pay, I assure you."

Again Jons paused. *He is beginning to catch on,* Frost thought, which was bound to limit what little amusement the conversation still held.

Jons adjusted himself in his saddle. "As you say. Can I tell him your terms?"

Frost rocked back on his heels. "How are you so sure I have the Blade?"

"You do. Everyone knows it."

"I may already have sold it. A very rich merchant in Calienn offered me a fortune for it."

"Gentaff says you have it. I will ask once more, what are your terms?"

Frost raised his walking stick and pointed it at the troubadour which, to Frost's satisfaction, caused the young fellow to flinch—an action followed by crossbows being raised. The soldiers intended to protect Jons from harm without question, which meant they were fairly well trained—these few at least.

"Attempt to harm me and we will defend ourselves," Jons said, lowering his voice. "If you insist, we will kill you and take the Blade from your corpse."

Sharryl and Rosivok stood calmly, unmoving, while the others focussed on them intently.

"Yes, yes, of course," Frost said, waving the stick three times. "I am sure you believe all that, but let me tell you what you must accept, like it or not."

The strange and sudden distress among Jons and his protectors was increasingly evident. They began blinking furiously, then shaking their heads, then waving hands and crossbows about as if bees were hovering. Groping, in fact. They did not cry out, though the urge to do so was evident.

Frost waved his stick about three times more. "Better?" he asked.

"I can see again!" Jons said with no small amount of relief, but that expression was quickly replaced by one filled with indignation. "Enough, wizard. Your magic has failed. If you think in your crazed little mind that—"

"You should be concerned with your own thoughts, and who controls them," Frost interrupted. "As well as your fate, you see, because I choose it. If any of you finish this day alive it is because I choose it. Andair and his sorcerer still live only because I choose it. Leave me in peace and go unharmed. Tell your king as much. I cannot promise to keep that bargain with him for long, but I will offer nothing more, other than to tell him this: The Demon Blade will never be of any use to him, or to Gentaff. Tell Gentaff it will destroy him if he attempts to prove otherwise. That is the truth. There are no terms—there is no price. Now, go."

Frost lowered his walking stick, eyes locked on Jons' eyes for just an instant. This fellow was basically sound, he was just an ardent, misdirected young herald, largely an empty vessel, easily buffeted and driven off course. Frost had known too many like him, enough to grow weary of them, of trying to teach them something of rules and strategy in a game they barely realized they were playing. He let this one go. He turned and walked away, passing between his Subartans and walking on while they remained where they had been.

"Where are you going?" Jons called after him. "Hold where you are!"

"Take his advice," Rosivok said. "Go."

"Andair will have his say!" Jons shouted.

Frost moved on, the focus of the entire village's attentions until he passed between the cottages and disappeared from Jons' line of sight. He waited just upwind, near a small shed built to shelter the village hogs. In a moment Sharryl and Rosivok joined him.

"They have gone on their way and lived," Sharryl said. "Their direction is toward the city."

They will be back, Frost thought, *or others much like them.* Though the nature of their mission was bound to change. He decided there was nothing to be done about it. Not until he had completed his journey, and learned the truth.

CHAPTER SIX

"Come in," the girl said, stepping aside and pulling the door wide. For a peasant's dwelling it was nearly extravagant, three rooms in all—though the third was small—with two windows in the front, both with heavy shutters. The house was not in the village proper either, which sprawled substantially just north of the eastbound road, but was set off by itself, several hundred paces further north and east. Behind the house stood a thick stand of woods that swept up a low hill and blocked the horizon. A herb garden of some size made up much of the front yard, save the space penned in by a wooden fence and containing a family of pigs, two goats and a few small hens. A well worn earthen walkway connected the house and the village.

Frost steeped over the threshold out of the sun and into the dark interior, where he waited for his eyes to adjust to the scattered light from the windows. A large hearth, a table and chairs, a long bench, sturdy shelves and a collection of storage chests of various sizes made up most of the room's furnishings.

Herbs were hung in small clumps near the fire from strings for drying, and a rocking chair, well made and well padded, rested nearly below them.

"Welcome," said the other person in the room, a young man in his mid teens, same age as the girl. "I am Dorin," he added, standing back and keeping his distance as Frost was followed through the doorway by Sharryl and then Rosivok, who had to duck to make the opening.

"Dara," the girl said. As his eyes grew accustomed, Frost could see the resemblance easily. The boy's sister. Fraternal twins, but twins nonetheless. Both were near as tall as Frost, both fit and orderly in appearance, though their clothing was simple peasant's garb, linen tunic and pants, a linen dress.

The girl's hair was long and straight and very dark, the boy's a bit shorter. Their olive skin had a healthy look, and their features were broad like Frost's, yet fairly well proportioned. An attractive pair indeed, Frost decided, save the boy's nose, which had a kink in it where a break had healed. Either he was prone to accident or he'd been in a brawl or two.

The girl drew nearer, eyes darting, as she made her way around her new guests and joined her brother. Side by side Frost noticed another resemblance, though more subtle, a part of the past.

"I am told by others that the two of you are second cousins of mine, the son and daughter of my cousin, Shalee."

The twins glanced at each other but didn't say anything.

"Well?" Frost prodded.

The twins nodded.

"What became of her?"

"An illness many years ago," Dorin said, gurgling a little at first, then clearing his throat. "We lived nearer Weldhem then. But you have yet to say your name."

"I do not give it out so readily. Tell me, how did you come to live here?"

The twins looked at one another again, then began mumbling. They seemed to arrive back where they'd started. Frost thought to rephrase the question. "At least tell me whose house is this?"

"It is our great-aunt's," Dorin said. "We have been here since our mother's passing."

"And what say you of your great aunt?"

"She is wise, and very kind," Dara said.

"Not uncommon family traits," Frost remarked.

"Why are you here?" Dara asked, as if she couldn't hold it in anymore. "What do you want with any of us?"

"For now, only to find my way, and perhaps to help you find a part of yours," Frost said. "You have nothing to fear from me. If you are the children of the same Shalee I knew, then you are all the family I have left. Except for your aunt, of course. My name is Frost. Now tell what has become of your aunt? Where can I find her?"

"Frost?" Dorin blurted out, as if he thought it some minor revelation.

Dara turned suddenly pale, then the twins began looking at each other quite conspiratorially and taking turns glancing sidelong at Frost.

"Then you know of me?" Frost asked.

"We . . . we have heard of you, that you might be coming. We did not believe it," Dorin said, more nervous now.

"Tell us what you want with us?" Dara asked again, trying to sound a bit more stern and doing a fair job.

"Answers to questions. Your aunt calls herself Shassel, correct?"

Again neither twin spoke, though between them their eyes sent a flurry of messages. Then Dorin nodded and turned once more to Frost. "If you must know, yes."

Now it was Frost who stood fast. He had traveled for weeks and through many lands to find her, or at least someone who knew of her, and here, now . . .

He glanced first toward Sharryl, then to Rosivok in a silent exchange. He had the feeling something was about to go wrong. He hadn't had the time or opportunity to pay attention to the signs and omens around him these past few days—hadn't so much as scattered the augur pebbles from his pouch. "I hear many things of her," Frost said. "Mostly, I hear rumors that she is dead."

"There are always rumors," Dara and Dorin said precisely at the same time.

Frost caught Sharryl and Rosivok in a telling nod; if there had been any doubts that these two were relatives of Frost, or that they knew Shassel, they had been dispelled.

"She is well?" Frost asked.

The twins each nodded.

Frost breathed an audible sigh, and with it felt the tightness in his neck and chest begin to loosen. "Take me to her," he said.

After another glance: "Why?" Dara asked.

He moved forward, and drew up less than an arm's length from the twins, then set his walking stick standing up against the table. Now he reached out and took one of their hands in each of his. "You must take me to her."

"Why should we?" Dorin asked again, narrowing his gaze, trying to pull his hand away. "She has taught us to trust no one, no matter what, though in your case she need not have taught us at all."

"Dorin!" Dara glared at her brother and he made no attempt to continue, though Frost was not entirely certain why. He understood Dorin's tone, however.

Both of them tugged, trying to free their hands.

Frost held his grip. These two had more spunk and muscle than many at their age, which Frost was pleased to note, and they were bright enough, but they seemed less than charmed by his presence. "Tell me because you must. Is there something I should know?"

"Nothing you do not already know," Dorin said, that tone surfacing again, incensed, tenacious.

"Really," Frost said, more curious than before.

"Perhaps he is right," Dara said, though she sounded less than pleased about it. Her animosity toward him was as real as her brother's, though she was better at keeping it covered up.

"Perhaps," Dorin repeated.

Frost studied them, waiting. He let go of their hands. "She has spoken of you often and always," Dara said at last, to Frost at first, but then she turned to her brother. "She will want to see him."

"I know," Dorin said, looking down, but then he met Frost's gaze and his eyes rose again.

"Tomorrow?" Dara asked.

"Tomorrow," Dorin said, "we will take you to her. You can stay with us here tonight. If you must."

"Of course he must," Dara said, though not so much scolding him as perhaps thinking out loud.

Frost decided he would learn what the problem was later on. It was no doubt foolishness in any case. For now he let a smile of satisfaction find his features, then turned to his Subartans and raised his hands, priestlike. "This is at last a good day!" he said. "The first good news I have had in far too long." He turned again and gave his expansive torso a loving pat. "We accept your hospitality," he told the twins. "The road has been long and hard. Now tell me, what have you got to eat?"

Dinner included a honey sweetened bread and a thick pork stew full of carrots and cabbage, and afterward, bits of bread boiled in lard and rolled in sugar, a treat Frost ranked with those made by the finest royal bakers. At least just now. The ale was thin and slightly sour, but not so bad as to force one to put it down. As they rested after dinner the conversation began at last to flow. Small talk at first, the past few seasons' weather, the villagers' never-changing lives, the burden of taxes, the sickness that had taken many of the cattle three years ago before it stopped of its own accord, or by the will of the Greater Gods. Frost listened, gracious and patient as he could be, then he pressed his own needs—he had a lot of catching up to do, a lot he needed to know.

"What has Shassel told you of the past?" he asked, when the topic, or something close enough to it, arose.

"Bits and pieces," Dara said, looking away from the table toward the darker corners of the room.

"Can you offer a little more detail?"

"We are young, you see," Dorin said. "Most of the past happened before we were born, so we tend to forget a lot of it." He kept a straight face as he and his sister exchanged a knowing glance, one Frost read as dark.

"Fine, just what you remember, then," Frost went along. "Tell me how Andair came to the throne, and of his reign."

"That is easy, you left," Dorin said.

"To find Andair," Frost replied. "He made a fool of me, he betrayed me and many others. He owed a great debt."

Dorin scowled. "You could not have looked very hard."

"He returned some years later, I'm not sure when," Dara said, "but in time to befriend his old and fading uncle."

"Lord King Weldhem," Frost clarified.

The twins nodded.

"But dear Uncle Weldhem knew nothing of Andair's deceit, as Shassel tells it, or he never allowed himself to believe it," Dara said. "So when Andair returned swearing he had done nothing wrong, he was able to convince the king of it."

"Convince him that his only rival, Wilmar, had conspired with you to make him seem the villain," Dorin added. "Weldhem never could bring himself to proclaim Wilmar a criminal, or even banish him, but when the king finally died, Andair was in place to assume the throne."

"He has been a poor king," Dorin said. "The taxes and fealty are bad enough. Now there is talk of tolls on the roads! But he does nothing to solve any of our problems. It is impossible for even many of the smaller barons to get an audience."

"Perhaps Andair is interested in other things," Frost said.

"Aye," Dorin said. "He now occupies his time with hunting, counting, women, and preparing for war."

This was something else Frost had wanted to discuss. "War with whom?" he asked.

"The Grenarii Empire to the north," Dorin continued. "They say Kolhol is their greatest king. They say he has designs on all Worlish, but Briarlea first of all. He has an army more than adequate for the job and Andair takes that seriously enough. He has been busy building his own loyal army of late."

"With fiefs granted to his chosen lords and riches taken from the land or his uncle's coffers," Dara huffed. "And with magic."

Dorin nodded. "He has a sorcerer as well, known as Gentaff, very powerful and hired at great expense. They have been keeping the Grenarii at bay, at least so far."

"And what of Lord Wilmar?" Frost asked. "Has there ever been any word of him?"

"Wilmar returned as well," Dorin said. "Though he grows old and sickly before his time. He has a son our age, Tramet. Dara spent much of her time with him before we came to live here." He tipped his head toward her. "They got along very well." Dorin's smile was positively mischievous.

Dara looked about to blush, though Frost guessed it would take more than romantic innuendoes to accomplish that.

"Shassel was once a close friend of Wilmar's wife," Frost said, moving along. "Are they still?"

"His wife never lived to see Worlish again," Dara said. "Wilmar and Tramet are but serfs now, one of the many families who have lost their lands, and whose sons have been forced to swear fealty to Andair."

"I am surprised Wilmar would yield to such a thing," Frost said, sitting back in his chair and finishing off the cup of ale before him. "A pity."

"Wilmar and Andair confronted each other, years ago, not long after Wilmar's return," Dorin explained. "No one knows what was said, but Wilmar was granted a serf's land and hut—a small part of the lands that were once his—which Shassel said was preferable to a swift beheading. But he and Tramet are forbidden to set foot inside Weldhem."

"So is Shassel," Dara said.

"So are we," Dorin said.

"Is that so?" Frost asked, not terribly surprised.

"We were given like treatment," Dorin said. He swept the air with one hand. "This is all the land left to us. The rest was taken."

Frost felt disturbed by all of this, but by one as yet unanswered question in particular. "Shassel allowed all this?"

"She was not here for most of it," Dara said. "She left for a time, not long after you did, but she does not talk much about it. We know she went east, deep into the Hubaran Forests, perhaps even beyond. After some years she came back. She has done much good since her return."

"Yes," Dorin said. "She took us in, and she has

helped countless others to survive, even to resist Andair and his young lords when the need was there— there was a time when they warred against each other, and many peasants were caught in between."

"She helped keep Andair hemmed in as well," Dara said. "He may be a dishonorable wretch in every way, but he is no fool; I think he knows he will have to face Shassel if he goes too far."

Frost nodded. "She has that effect."

"Still," Dorin said, "Andair seems always ready to press her limits, to test her. He knows she is growing old and frail, and now that he has Gentaff at his side, many have warned her that the two of them are plotting to finish her. Briarlea is not a safe place for her these days, yet without her, it is not so safe for any of us."

"Does she show herself in Weldhem at all?"

"No," Dara said. "Not since she was barred from the city—though that seems to suit Shassel well enough."

Frost smiled. "I have no doubt." He missed her now, not only because she was all that remained of the world and family he had known, or because he still hoped she might be his best chance of determining the true fate of the Demon Blade, or even because she might be an ally in a world filled with far too many who were against him, or could not be trusted. If nothing else, Taya had provided bitter reassurance of that during his stay in Calienn. He could not even trust Dara and Dorin completely yet.

All those things mattered, some greatly, but he missed her the most because of who she was, her spirit, her soul. His own father had been the royal court wizard, and had died in some far-off land in fulfillment of that duty. It was Shassel that helped Frost's mother raise him from a tender age, and showed him the truth and ways of his own born abilities—showed him the things his father never had the chance to. Many things, though not all. Sorcery was a thing taught best by those closest to you in spirit and body, mind and blood.

But magic, Frost was sure, was not the only thing a boy learned from his father, or shared with him . . .

"What of your father?" Frost asked. "You didn't say."

"No, we did not," Dorin said.

This time the exchange of looks between the twins was clearly troubled—an old wound of some kind, one that had left scars that never completely healed. Frost waited, but it was as if the subject was so large and burdensome that they could not begin to come to terms with it. Their look was familiar to him, much like the mix of pain and guilt that had marked his own reflection for so many years. A disturbing thing on the faces of the young.

"I would hear of it," he said.

"We grow tired, it's late," Dara said, breathing a wearied tone into her voice.

"It is important that I know," Frost encouraged her.

"You would be wise to let it be," Dorin said, looking sage as a man twice his age. Whatever had happened, this part of the past had shaped him in some way.

Frost folded his arms across his broad chest and cocked his head to one side, sagelike in kind. "I have never been much for letting be, especially when doing so deprives me of something I value. I am willing to help you in whatever way I can, but I need your help, and your trust."

"Trust?" Dorin said, venomous now. "And what good has trust in you done any one of us? What help did you give when we so needed it? Shassel speaks of the great Frost, so clever and so powerful. It makes a fine story for children, like tales of the Demon Blade or the Council of Wizards, or the news we hear of you and your great battle with a demon of the darkness. Many others are fool enough to believe such things, but perhaps they have always believed in myths and fables. I have learned other lessons, and so has Dara."

"Your brother seems upset," Frost said, attempting to sound sanguine, yet sympathetic. "But tell me, has he a reason?"

"Good reasons," Dara said. "Our father for one."

"Enough!" Dorin snapped, leaning nearer, seizing Frost's attention again. "Where were you? What kept you away so long? What do you want from us?"

"I went in search of Andair, and in search of answers to some of the very same questions I see in your eyes," Frost said. "Then I would have been no good to you in any case, but now . . ."

"So you say, but I am already tired of your tales. You left by choice. You could have stayed and taken your place in your family—wherever that led, whatever that meant. No matter what else had happened, you could have helped. You would have been here when Andair returned instead of leaving all that to women and children, or men without the gifts you were born with. Everything might have been different if you had!"

Dorin held a breath for an instant, emotion lending a jittery nervousness to his hands and a redness to his face. He knew he was losing control.

"You might have saved our mother," he went on, attempting to measure his words more carefully. "You could have kept us from making the mistakes we made, and our father might still be alive. But now we will never know."

"Never know what?" Frost asked, as the boy's assertions buffeted him. So many of them, in fact, that it was hard to know where to begin to argue them. "You still have not explained."

"You could have shown us the magic," Dara said, now only slightly less provoked than her brother.

"Shassel has tried her best, but for her it is difficult, especially these days, and early on she had no idea that we—" She cut herself off, and sat biting her lip, clearly struggling to hold something back that was perhaps much bigger than she was. Abruptly she looked up at Frost again, and he could feel the grasping pain in her heart as though it was his own. "You could have warned us, Frost," she said, as a tear slipped free of her eye and pooled, then ran down over her cheek bone. Anger took her expression again. "We didn't know! We thought—we thought we were doing right, doing what we had to do! But you—you chose to leave like your father did. You never got yourself killed, but enough others have died in your place."

"You do not know enough about me, nor I about you," Frost said, though he still wasn't sure precisely what was going on. He was missing too many parts of the story. "We should start over. I am curious what you would learn of magic, and what you already know. And I must explain a great deal. Then you will explain, and all before this goes any further."

Dorin stood up and tossed the chair away. It tumbled along the floor and struck the wall. Dara stood up and put her hand out toward him in caution but he ignored her.

"It is true!" Dorin said, spitting the words. "All truth, as we have always believed." He aimed a finger at Frost. "You know it best of all. I can't think what Shassel ever saw in you, because you do not deserve her respect, or her trust. Or ours. You never earned them, yet she gives all that and more to you even in your absence. I'd wager that some of us find it easier to live with guilt than others."

"Dorin!" Dara snapped, glaring at him, though Frost caught no hint of sympathy for himself.

Dorin glared at her for an instant, then he turned and went round the table, where he pushed out through the door and slammed it shut behind him.

Dara turned to Frost and simply stared at him—or through him, perhaps.

"Now you," Frost said, and Dara's eyes refocussed. "Yell all you like. Then, perhaps, you can bring yourself to talk with me and help me understand."

"I am sorry," she said, "for all of us. Even for you. Nothing more." She moved past him and followed her brother outside.

Frost sat in the quiet room for several minutes, glancing from side to side, exchanging one contemplative glance with Rosivok, then another with Sharryl, who had remained completely silent throughout the exchange. It had not precisely concerned them, after all.

"I am curious to see what might happen next," Frost mused, trying to sound calm, though he found it a struggle to put any starch in his voice.

"They will come back, I think," Sharryl said.

"They do not know you," Rosivok offered, saying so much with so few words, as always.

"And I do not know them," Frost replied. "So you see, they are right."

Now it was Frost who stood up and went outside. The twins were nowhere about, but they had likely not gone far. To the village of course. To friends, perhaps. People Frost had no wish to face this night, and the good sense not to try. He didn't know the details, not yet, but he knew . . .

He knew enough to let it be.

The sun had just set leaving a sky filled with fading orange light. Smoke curled from fires burning in the nearby village, spreading a sweet roasted-wood scent on the still evening air. He was tired, and so were his Subartans, but what he felt was more than fatigue. For the first time since leaving Ariman he wondered why he had come here, what he had hoped it would be like?

"We should fix our bedrolls," he said, turning and

throwing his voice through the open door behind him. Then he went back inside.

The two warriors made their beds on the floor. Frost lay awake in Shassel's bed watching the fire burn to coals, thinking, dozing but not sleeping, until the twins finally returned sometime during the night. They said nothing and went straight to their own beds. Frost fought the urge to speak to them. They had gotten something out of their systems earlier this night. The rest would come, given time. Finally he drifted off to a restless sleep, until a ragged scream and the clash of iron brought his eyes open wide.

CHAPTER SEVEN

Another crash, and someone else shouted. Frost didn't recognize either of the voices, but when Dara yelped he knew well enough. Shapes moved all but unseen in the darkness. Frost shook himself alert and spoke to the lamp that had rested at the center of the table. A flame sprang from the wick and revealed the lamp's location in the far corner of the room, where it had tumbled to rest after the table had been knocked aside.

Frost counted three men, though one was already quite dead and lying on the floor just behind Rosivok in a growing pool of blood. Another fought with Rosivok still while the third cornered himself with Sharryl and the twins. Both intruders brandished swords, but the one in the corner had seen fit to bring a studded war club as well.

"I can't get to my sword!" Dorin shouted, eyes dancing back and forth between the attackers and one of the storage chests along the wall near Frost.

"Or my dagger!" Dara chimed. "Frost, there! That one with the sewing coming loose!" She thrust a finger at one of the storage chests.

Frost drew a breath as he slid his legs off the bed and set his feet on the wooden floor. These were not trained soldiers any of them, not dressed in simple commoners' clothing and without so much as a shield for protection. Which would be their undoing. "There is no need," he said.

"But Frost—"

Dorin's protest was cut off by a howling scream that sounded of rage first, and death just after that. The man attempting to advance on Sharryl and the twins dropped club and sword at the same time and tried to run toward the door. He nearly got to it before he collapsed, holding his middle in a failed attempt to keep his insides from sliding out through the fresh opening Sharryl had rendered in him.

All eyes focussed on Rosivok and the remaining intruder—who had picked up one of the chairs near the table and was using it to bat and block. It was obvious that already his arms were getting tired, and he had begun to swing the chair lower, had begun to let his sword arm droop.

Rosivok swung the subarta almost from behind him and struck the chair with force enough to crack the wood and send splinters scattering. The attacker rallied, dropped the broken framework and lunged, striking ahead with his sword. Then he dodged left, bobbed and came in again. A competent parry, but one Rosivok sidestepped, then used to his advantage as an opening presented itself. The next blow opened up the man's right thigh just below his hip. When he staggered, Rosivok drove the steel of his subarta forward once more, and finished him.

Frost gestured toward the hearth, and the fire crackled up, adding more light and warmth to the room—though he knew cold was not the reason Dorin and Dara were both shaking so. They stepped away from the corner and Frost saw the blood on Dara's arm. He came to his feet at once and met her at the center of the room.

"Let me see," he said, and she raised her arm. The blow had done more damage to the sleeve of her tunic than to flesh, but it was near the elbow and deep enough to leave a scar, and still bleeding. Frost closed his eyes and held his hand over the wound. He could not undo what had been done, but he could help, he could stop the bleeding and ward off infection, then let nature do the rest.

He wiped her blood off his hands on his own tunic when he had finished. "Wrap a clean cloth around it and let it heal," he said. Then he turned to his Subartans. "They were nearly killed," he said of the twins.

"We did not allow it," Rosivok answered.

"You allowed too much."

Sharryl and Rosivok only nodded.

Frost sighed heavily as he stood and looked about the room. "Mostly, I am troubled by the necessity. Nowhere is safe, and no one is safe around me. I should never have come here."

"I had hoped you'd changed for the better while you were gone, but I see you haven't." Dara snapped at Frost. "What new crimes have you committed? What did those men die for?"

Dorin moved closer to Frost, confronting him. "Answer her," he said.

The boy showed more spunk than sense, but that was all too common among the young. *Of all men, you should not forget that much,* he told himself. "I have done nothing, and it was their idea to come here asking to die," he said. "They were fools whose greed outweighed the value of their lives. I will show you."

Frost drew closer to the twins, who were gathered at the center of the room, and removed his robe. He worked at the harness fastened about him next, then tugged at the linens, unwrapping them, until sword and scabbard were revealed. Finally he reached with his left hand and withdrew a sword. Its blade was short and flat, its edges sharp, the hilt dark and meaty and smooth. A well-made weapon, but unremarkable in most respects. He held the sword straight up before him. "This is what they wanted."

"They had swords," Dorin said.

"Not like this one," Frost said.

Dorin snorted loudly. "Next you are going to tell us that is the Demon Blade. Don't think we have not heard the rumors that you have it, that you used it to save the world, destroying demons and armies alike. Stories fit for small children and perhaps one old woman, who has surely let her feelings and her memories get in the way of common sense."

"Common sense has little to do with the Demon Blade, I promise you," Frost replied. "But everything you have heard is true. That, and more. Which is one of the reasons I came back. It is also one of the reasons I needed to see Shassel—though not the only one."

The twins stared at the sword in Frost's hand as if it had just bitten them and might strike again. "I still don't believe you," Dorin said finally, shrugging free of his daze.

"Neither do I," Dara said, though she seemed less resolute.

"Believe what you will, but it changes nothing," Frost said. Perhaps too sternly, but he had good reason, after all. He knew he ought to grant these two some leeway, yet he had feelings too, and knowledge they lacked; he would not suffer as their fool, at least not without end. He thought to further test one thought of his own while he tried to change another's. "Tell me of your gifts," he said.

This drew two silent stares.

"You condemn me for not teaching you of magery," Frost went on. "Therefore you must both possess at least a glimmer of the gifts Shassel and I possess."

The twins glanced intently at one another, and Frost knew he had touched on something dear. When they turned back to him Dara asked, "What of it?"

Frost considered his reply. Where to start? "Best to begin with the matter at hand," he said. "I have learned a great deal about the Blade since it came into my possession. More than anyone since the first Council of Wizards, I suspect, but I have a great deal more to learn. More, perhaps, than can be known by any one man, or ever should be. But I am certain of this: an adept of any measure who lacks proper knowledge and understanding of the Blade risks death, merely by touching it. Even forewarned, the Blade will teach you a lesson not soon forgotten, a lesson I learned several times over, and each time too harshly.

"These are not stories or lies, only the truth. I have managed nearly to kill myself more than once, as well as those unfortunate enough to have been on hand at the time."

He glanced at Sharryl and Rosivok as he heard both of them groan quite softly, just under their breath.

"How so?" Dorin asked, clearly for himself and his sister. "Tell us . . ."

"Better to show you," Frost continued, stepping forward until he stood within arm's reach of the twins. "I want you to do precisely as I say. The Blade has a powerful aura, it is enticing and exotic, irresistible to many. No doubt you have sensed it already, but you have convinced yourselves it was not real, a touch of fever perhaps, or the rush of the fight. Feel it now, and believe what your heart and mind are telling. But resist the urge to test its depths. Resist your desires, and the bitter-sweet seduction of the Blade. Resist the urge to use your magic in any way. Ward yourself against it as best you can. Then use only your left hand to touch the sword."

A considerable moment of hesitation followed. But then, with the sharing of a glance, they reached out together with their left hands, just as Frost knew they would, and gave in to the desires and curiosities that must be turning them mad.

Frost remembered the feeling well. He watched as their fingertips touched the flat steel of the blade, as they closed their eyes as if in ecstasy, as their bodies began to tremble ever so slightly. He waited for the rest—for what he knew would come despite all his warnings and advice. A thing learned only the hard way; though his words would never leave these two once they had been wedded to the experience, his advice probably would save them now.

It took only an instant for the looks of anxious rapture on the twins' faces to change to sudden, contorted agony. Their voices formed a sour harmony as the pain displayed itself through their vocal cords in a low growl at first, then rising, twisting, and finally hurtling toward the heavens. When Dara's body began to jerk and snap, Frost called to her, and she seemed to understand, though she also seemed powerless to do anything about it.

Frost pulled the sword away. As if tied to the motion the twins rocked, then collapsed on the floor in front of him, moaning softly, both of them clutching left arms with right hands. It was several moments before they could so much as focus their eyes again. It was some time after that when they finally managed, with help from Sharryl and Rosivok, to get up again, only to sit in chairs. By that time, Frost had slid the Blade back into its scabbard and wrapped it away from sight.

"Well?" Frost asked, brow raised, waiting.

"It's—it's true," Dorin said, though it came out as more a gasp.

"Yes, true," Frost said. "Only the Demon Blade could have such an effect, and only on a true adept.

It draws from you, from every part of your body, and then from your soul if you let it. The means with which to safely employ the Blade without devastating yourself in the process still escapes even me. Though not for lack of trying. I have come close, I have even succeeded, after a fashion, though luck has surely played a part. And that is not all.

"I have come to believe that the last of the Blade's secrets may not be knowable by any one sorcerer, and to believe that those secrets are far greater, far darker, than anyone can imagine. Perhaps even the Council of Wizards that created it did not know its full potential—or the Blade's powers have grown in the centuries since that time, until even the Greater Gods might wonder at it now.

"But short of that knowledge, the Blade can wreak havoc. It can bring a most grisly death to thousands, and to those who would use it. It can even reshape the land, as I have learned. But without having felt its touch the two of you would never have accepted these truths."

"Frost," Dorin said, his voice still thin and rasping. "I believe you." He closed his eyes and rubbed his arm once more while he fought to keep himself upright in the chair. There was no way to describe what had happened, he was coming to that now.

Dara had apparently arrived at a similar conclusion. "We didn't know," she said, trailing off.

"I will accept that," Frost said almost jauntily. "Now, perhaps you will tell me how to find Shassel. I need her."

"You want her to help you learn more about the Demon Blade," Dara said, trying to finish Frost's thoughts for him.

"No," he said. "It is my hope that she can help me find the Keeper of the Blade. Old Ramins held it for ages, but he died without naming his successor. There is only one, and such things are known from birth.

But Shassel may know the one I seek . . . or someone else who does. That is why you must take me
to her, and quickly, before others try what these men
have."

"Who were they?" Dara asked, observing the bodies
again. Frost shrugged in unison with his Subartans
as they all followed her gaze to the bodies.

"Not soldiers," Rosivok stated.

"No, but Andair has already offered to buy the
Blade from me," Frost said. "Now that he knows I
will not sell it, he has surely put a public price on
it, and likely on my head as well in hopes of bargaining with a new owner. So you see, it does not matter who they are. They came, and there will be
others."

"We don't know where Shassel is, not exactly," Dara
said, recalcitrant.

Frost looked at her first, then Dorin, and waited
for an explanation.

"It is true," Dorin said. "She has seldom wanted
us to know, and has made that fact known about, so
that we would not be in danger from anyone who
came looking for her."

"A good strategy, but it has drawbacks," Sharryl
noted.

"You cannot warn her of someone looking for her,"
Rosivok added.

Frost nodded wearily. "So, you never visit her?"

"We have," Dorin said "At a small cottage she
keeps in the forest. We travel by night, mostly. It takes
two nights, and she is not always there. She knows
of many others in the region, many places where
friends welcome her whenever she visits. She could
be anywhere."

"A pity," Frost said, shaking his head. He was in
no mood to hunt all over half a province looking
for her.

"We don't know exactly where she is," Dara said,

"but we know someone who might. We can take you to him. He will take us to her."

"Who?" Frost asked.

"A friend," Dara said.

Frost nodded. "Very well, when?"

The twins exchanged a brief, defining nod. Then Dorin said, "Now."

Lurey stood beside his cart wearing a full beard, a hat to rival Frost's, and robes sewn in vertical colors, most of them shades of blue, green and brown. A rather smallish figure, not terribly stout and not daunting in any way, though there was a definite flare in his aging eyes, a guileful look that grew more persistent through the wrinkles around his mouth. He was more weathered than old, more peasant than prince, though he was far better dressed than anyone in these parts. Frost judged him to be between forty and fifty, but it was hard to tell.

The draft horse hitched to the cart was a splendid animal, healthy and able enough, like its owner. Lurey was a muslin peddler and by all appearances a successful one. His house was the largest and finest in the village, as was the building next to it, used to store Lurey's goods.

"This is Frost, nephew to Shassel," Dorin said. "And this is an old friend, Lurey."

"I am, that I am," Lurey said with a bow, though he never lost a wisp of the craftiness in his eye, nor his focus on Frost. "Good to meet you, nephew of Shassel."

Frost bowed in return.

"A moment," Dorin said, and the twins took the peddler aside so as not to be overheard by the villagers in the huts nearby; then, while Frost waited silently, they explained all that they could have of what had just happened. They got most of the story right, but told far too much of it for Frost's liking, though there was little to be done.

"You look well," Lurey finally said, turning again to Frost.

Frost nodded. "As do you."

"A fine day," the peddler said. "It is," Frost agreed.

Lurey simply stood staring at Frost after this. Frost had no difficulty staring right back. Then Lurey chose to step forward, until he'd removed all distance between them, save a hand's width. "Dara and Dorin say you are their trusted friend," he said under his breath.

Frost didn't budge. "That is true."

"And Shassel's?"

Frost nodded.

Lurey grinned. "You know, so am I."

"Why?"

Lurey grinned some more, in spite of Frost's stance and tone, and the subsequent gathering near of his two Subartan warriors that had followed Lurey's movement. "I see you are truly concerned," Lurey said.

"It is not worth testing," Frost replied.

The smile on Lurey's face remained. "I have been their friend for years. I am a widower myself. I have no children of my own, you see, and for all the luck I have with women it is possible I never will. But I have always wanted some. These two have generously offered their services in that regard, and I offer them mine, from time to time. We see to each other's needs that way. Shassel is simply someone it is much too easy to like."

"I should consider them all fortunate," Frost remarked.

"I would agree," Lurey said with a hearty chuckle, the sort that might put anyone at ease—the sort that might have been intended to do so. Which gave Frost pause, though only briefly. Too harsh a judgment would serve no one, least of all the twins. They trusted him, and apparently so did Shassel, which meant Frost should at least attempt a neutral stance for now.

"Perhaps I should let you live, for now," Frost said.

Lurey hesitated, then he broke into laughter again.

Frost managed a smile as he realized how Lurey had taken the statement. *So be it,* he thought. "These two tell me you can take us to Shassel?"

"They are correct. We can go tonight."

"We can go now."

"No, no," Lurey said, shaking his head with vigor. "We would be much too easy to follow by day, and if you carry the Demon Blade with you, we will be followed for certain. There is the matter of my promise to Shassel that I would not allow others to know the way. If we bring a crowd . . ."

"If we are followed I will know, and steps will be taken. It is more a question of how many will follow us, and the longer we wait, the greater that number. The rest does not matter."

Lurey seemed a curious fellow, a mix of vagabond, rogue, and favorite uncle all rolled into one. Despite Frost's doubts, especially lately, he felt he could give the old fellow a chance. A small one.

Old fellow, Frost repeated in his mind, allowing himself a mental shrug, *the man is only a few years older than I.* Frost stepped back, allowing the peddler some room.

"I understand," Lurey said in time, then, adding a grin, "I will defer to your wisdom on the matter. However, and I am embarrassed to say this, truly I am, but I have a small wagonload of goods to load and deliver, and the payment to collect, which I am in need of lately, you see. Leaving right away will likely cost me, or at least . . ."

"How much?" Frost asked, waving come-hither at Lurey.

Lurey seemed to ponder the answer as though it involved a whole day's calculations; then, with sudden relief, he held up four fingers on one hand, and one on the other. Frost dug in his pouch and produced the coins. Lurey snatched them up and whisked them from sight.

"All well and good," Lurey grinned.

"I expected no less," Frost said. "Let me know as soon as you are prepared to leave." Then he turned with his Subartans and walked away.

The journey took three days. Lurey and the twins usually rode in the peddler's cart; Lurey's horse could easily manage the load since the cart was not heavily laden with muslin, but two Subartans and a most substantial wizard thrown in were out of the question. So they traveled in a loose line, taking turns walking in front of or riding up on the cart, while Frost's mule plodded along behind.

Lurey, for his part, helped the journey seem to go more quickly by treating one and all to a seemingly endless string of stories from his travels. Though an unusual number of them tended to find Lurey himself the hero of the day—if often reluctantly, or so he said. At first he told tales of things familiar, nearby places and minor adventures, from catching a thief in Calienn to following a herd of sheep out of the mountains into Camrak one late autumn, when the snows had caught him unawares.

Soon, however, the stories grew too fanciful to believe—especially the second day, when the drudgery of trekking through the sparsely populated woodland trail began to set in. The forest itself was old, with a thorough mix of thick, tall trees that let little sunlight in, which in turn kept the underbrush thin. Visibility was good, a virtue to wary travelers, but cover would be difficult to find. The weather had turned sunny and hot, but the coolness of the forest's shade made the walking comfortable, and the dryness that had come with late spring this year had kept the bugs to almost bearable numbers, as long as one kept moving. All in all there was little to complain about, other than boredom.

Which made even Lurey's most dubious stories welcome, no matter, like the spice trader with wives in three different kingdoms, a man who came to life sounding curiously like Lurey himself, save the spices—though of course he denied all implications. Or the court wizard in Grenarii who had attempted to cure a most conspicuous wart on the face of the realm's young prince, and instead created a plague of warts that covered the prince's entire body for weeks.

"The king only spared the wizard's life so that he could devise a cure, and only spared it after that because there was no one else to fill the wizard's position," Lurey said.

"I was not aware you traded with the Grenarii," Frost said, which caused Lurey to grow nervous for a moment.

"Yes, well, of course I used to," he said, "sometime ago, when the lines between sovereigns were less strictly drawn. I have not been there in ages."

Then he quickly moved on to a fresh tale about a hedge witch in a province no one had ever heard of, a woman who had the means to cloud the eyes of others so that she could walk unseen in their midst. "Quite useful for picking pockets at festivals and such," Lurey said. "No doubt she is rich by now."

"I do not think even Frost has ever contrived a spell such as that," Sharryl said, teasing Frost. But while he had built his ego into one of his largest features over the years, it had been resized in dramatic fashion in Ariman a year past, and remained manageable. The story was sheer nonsense of course—at least the part about clouding so many minds all at once . . . .

"Perhaps I lack the necessary imagination," Frost said, and showed Sharryl a surly grin.

"Or the experience," Rosivok added.

"Or the body mass," Sharryl said, turning and walking backward just ahead of Frost and making a show of sizing up his girth.

"Outshined by a hedge witch," Frost said, shaking his head. "I must spend more time with such women, I think, acquiring skills."

"Perhaps, but he has managed an impressive trick or two, now and then," Rosivok said in a slightly mocking tone.

Frost sketched a bow. "We all have our moments of luck and coincidence," he said.

"As Frost says, so say I," Dara said without cheer from her perch on the front of Lurey's cart, where she sat beside the peddler, taking her turn.

"I don't doubt it is luck," Dorin agreed, sounding much too dour.

"I believe they see no humor in our argument," Frost said of the twins.

"Let me," Lurey said, waving one hand and grinning. "They were joking," he told Dara and Dorin. "Understand?"

"No," Dorin said.

Lurey's brown went up. "No?"

Dorin narrowed his gaze. "No. The Blade has great power, I have felt it. But what of Frost? He claims he left so many years ago to look for Andair, yet now he finds Andair on a throne not rightfully his, and still he does nothing. Perhaps Frost left because he knew one day Andair would return, and there would be nothing he could do about it."

"In the attack at our cottage he did nothing," Dara said, less acerbic but equally sincere. "A trick with the lamp, nothing more. These two fought the battle," she added, waving fingers toward Sharryl and Rosivok.

"That is our purpose," Rosivok said bitterly, his

expression severe—though his tone had more effect, as this look amounted to no great departure from his regular one.

"A lucky thing for Frost," Dorin said.

"For us all," Dara said.

"I see," Frost said solemnly, as he walked beside the cart. "Well then, think what you will."

"I'd say you have hurt this big fellow's feelings," Lurey said, tipping his head to the twins. They refused to humor him.

"It is all right," Frost said. "They will believe what they want." *And say only what they want,* he thought, certain there was more they were not telling him. Though he was just as certain this was not the time to press. They were in no mood, and neither was he, come to that. *You are getting used to taking their abuse,* he told himself. Well, he could tell himself all he wanted.

"That is true of everyone, I think," Lurey chuckled, lightening the mood somewhat. The subject was dropped after that.

The rest of the day went quietly. The twins and Lurey managed some idle chatter among themselves, as did Frost and his Subartans, but no conversation included them all. Not even that night when they made camp on a rocky knoll at the edge of the woods.

Sharryl and Rosivok took their usual turns standing guard through the night. The absence of any sign of trouble or anyone tracking them was itself a cause for worry of a sort, though still preferable to being under siege, Frost decided as he lay in his bedroll, thinking. But no one knew where they had gone, or why, to the best of his knowledge. And anyone who did might as well expect them to return all by themselves. Then there were those who might guess they were seeking Shassel, and would not follow for that very reason. Who would risk angering Shassel and Frost together?

Fools, Frost answered himself—something the world always seemed capable of creating in vast numbers.

The next day saw slower progress as the forest floor became more hilly, bringing with it greater caution and fatigue. But by midafternoon, after crossing a small stream and combining their efforts to push the cart up a sharp rise textured with roots and rocks they came upon a cottage, small and in poor repair, a place that had plainly been abandoned for some time. Or left to look that way. Frost knew the latter was the case. He could sense another within, and knew without a doubt it was Shassel.

CHAPTER EIGHT

"What is it?" Lord Andair said, as he was joined by Gentaff in the hallway.

"Frost has gone into the Hubaran Forests," Gentaff said, matter of fact. The two men continued walking a few more paces, then stopped before a narrow wooden door. "Surely he is searching for Shassel. He goes with two others, the twins who live in Shassel's old cottage, Dorin and Dara. I'm told you know them, that you knew their father."

"True," Andair said, leaving it at that.

"Together, they will be harder to follow. Even without the Demon Blade that would be so."

"I know, but in a way my mind is eased," Andair said, more pleased than he had once thought he might be at such news. The waiting, the not knowing what Frost was up to, he liked that least of all. As for the twins, well, he remembered all that well enough, nasty children playing at curses and such. The whole family was a bothersome, defective lot, but he'd taught them a lesson—those twins and their father. He would teach Frost a similar lesson at least before he was through.

He entered the giant storage room and watched while a barrel of barley for the alewives was rolled near and opened for his inspection. This was the receiving room, just above the castle's main storage rooms, and the place where all Andair's private goods were accounted for before being lowered through the large, square hole in the floor. It was not Andair's job to assess the goods, but he was often on hand. He enjoyed the task, and it tended to prevent a good deal of loss in general. He'd had his eyes opened the first day he happened along and looked things over—a little digging beneath the grain had turned up not more grain but rocks, and had necessitated having two stewards put to death. No one had tried to cheat him since, and he had every intention of keeping it that way.

"We both seem so confident," Gentaff said, almost singsong in his tone. "One wonders if it is all justified."

Andair took the other's meaning in stride. "I never doubted this day would come, it was only a question of when," Andair said. "But we do not even know if Shassel is still alive, and if so, is she well enough to help Frost? They have the Blade, but I have you, and Weldhem Castle for another. They are not the type to wipe out the thousands of innocent people and soldiers that inhabit this city just to smite me. So we have some leverage to work with as well as a great many uncertainties that could be problems as well." That was the troubling part, or one of them anyway.

"You have a plan?" Gentaff asked. "No, but of course you do."

"Perhaps."

Andair grinned. "Then we'll do that."

"What you do next may decide the future," Gentaff said. "What I do will come after that."

"Of course," Andair said; then, thinking to turn the wizard's words back, "Which is why we'll hear what you suggest." He glanced over and found Gentaff frowning, which on his moody features tended to make one think of unpleasant things. Andair was unfazed. Having seen his own frown in the mirror times before, he had the confidence of superiority.

"But you are king," Gentaff deferred.

A *lively game*, Andair thought. One they were both good at. But Andair had traded heavily in countermoves over the years and was especially devoted to letting his opponent lead, which usually allowed for any number of advantages. "And you are Counsel," he said.

Gentaff put a great deal of stock in himself, his intellect, his powers of sorcery, his own goals and his ability to combine them with others. Andair understood this well enough to make it amount to one of Gentaff's few weaknesses.

"Very well," Gentaff replied with a grunt. "I favor the easiest path to our goals. You concern yourself with the day when you might be forced to confront Frost once more, you fear retribution for past deeds, and now that he has the Demon Blade you worry that even I will not prove Frost's equal. You also worry he will use the Demon Blade against you, yet you worry as much that he will keep it forever from you."

Andair wanted the Demon Blade for many reasons: It was priceless for one, but more importantly, in Gentaff's hands it would make Worlish the most powerful realm in this part of the world. Instead of worrying about the Grenarii, their great King Kolhol would fear for his throne's survival instead, and for good reason. Andair liked that idea very, very much. He'd already imagined what it might be like, imagined prolonging for a long time the pleasure of watching Kolhol and his great kingdom dangle on the end of that tenuous string, waiting for the inevitable . . .

"You make yourself clear," Andair said.

"There is only one way to be done with all this worry and speculation. Invite Frost here. Alone. Tell him to bring the Demon Blade. He must want something from you, and perhaps from me. We should know what it is, then bargain."

"What could he want from you?"

"I have information he is no doubt interested in."

"What kind of information?"

"Very old, but it does not concern you," Gentaff told him. "What matters is that we hear him out face to face, after which you will attempt to make him a fresh offer that will be acceptable to everyone. Failing that, we will take what we must ultimately take anyway, no matter. I can be most persuasive. I suspect, given the right incentives, he will come to reason."

"What if he won't listen, won't reason, won't make peace? What if all he wants is vengeance, and he will not rest until my head is splayed on a spire before the city's gates, and yours along with it?"

"You see, you claim we have leverage, yet you worry over what might be. We must learn what is and worry about that instead. We must take the lead."

"Then you suggest we let him enter the castle unhindered and negotiate in good faith," Andair said, "and go again as if he were a bard passing through. This is not like you, Gentaff, or me."

"I suggest no such thing. We will employ every trap and trick imaginable, and use every means so that no matter what happens the outcome will favor us. Whatever magic he commands can be countered, if it is done carefully. That will fall to me. You must be prepared to do the rest."

Better, Andair thought with a small sigh of relief.

More barrels were opened, these filled with finely woven cloth for the castle's tailors. Andair had some of the material brought to him so that he could examine it more closely. "Well and good," he said,

waving the servant away. He liked to find fault with
even the finest merchandise to keep the tradesmen
working at their best, but this whole business with
Frost and Shassel and the Demon Blade, not to
mention the cursed, growing Grenarii threat on his
northern boarders was keeping him sufficiently distracted these days. All of it required too much inspection on its own. A frustrating situation he was at pains
to remedy.

"Agreed, then," he told Gentaff, as barrels of spring
wheat were hauled through the doors, then rolled on
edge and set before him. "Get hold of that same good
fellow again, what was his name? The one who fan-
cies himself twice the nobleman of any of my nobles."

"Jons. He is a troubadour by trade."

"Yes. A most ambitious troubadour, eyes on the
court, though not so great an entertainer as I recall.
We'll try him at this again. Frost did not kill him the
first time, so he may not again. And if things go badly
his loss will not be so great. I will call my captain
as well, and have the two of them come to see me."

"Agreed," said Gentaff, clearly pleased with the
whole idea.

"But there is one trouble with all this: We can
invite Frost here, but it is likely he may refuse."

"Then we will need a means to insure that he will
come. Especially, one that will give us more leverage. I have some ideas. Perhaps we can discuss them."

Andair smiled. He had some ideas of his own. It
pleased him that Gentaff was thinking along the same
lines. "Meanwhile," he said, "we should prepare some
plans that do not rely so heavily on magic. Those are
the kind that worked so well on Frost once before.
The kind that work on almost everyone. I must know
how to find Frost's weaknesses, and use them against
him."

"That is your excellence, Excellence," Gentaff said.

Andair turned and glowered at the old wizard, who

chose to ignore the expression. That sense of humor again. But Andair knew to let it go—for the time being at least. He watched Gentaff leave, then went back to the business at hand. Wool for weaving was being brought in. Lots of wool. He wished there were someone to do the job for him, someone he could trust. But he was resigned to the fact that there was no such person. He'd never kept a wife or had any children for much the same reason.

"That third bale," he instructed, and two men set about untying it. All proper and accountable he learned, to his satisfaction. Or was it? He had found so few crimes committed here during the past year that no punishments had been required, not so much as a flogging. Nothing to take his mind off his troubles . . .

Now Frost had made his troubles worse by leaps. He decided to let the rest of the stores tend to themselves. If Frost was coming he needed to prepare, he and Gentaff needed to talk in private, the army had to be notified.

At last, a step toward progress, and the end of waiting.

She met them at the door, shorter than Frost remembered, or it was the fault of her declining posture, and she was thinner, as many an aged mage tended to be. But it was Shassel. Her face, with finer features than his even when she was young, had grown almost sharp-edged, though there remained a subtle, crafted kindness about it that even the wrinkles of age had not debased. Her eyes were dark, puffy bags beneath them, but they were blue and keen as ever, endlessly deep and mystifying. Her thick dark hair had been long enough to sit on when last Frost had seen her, but it had been cut to just below her shoulders and was turning mostly white.

She looked much as Frost had imagined, including

the part he had imagined most—the smile that lit her face as she laid eyes on him, and opened her arms to embrace him.

"You look splendid!" she said in a smooth voice that was still the envy of any minstrel, though in a lower key than it once had been. He leaned forward and put his arms gently around her as she hugged him with surprising strength. He felt like he was ten years old again, like he ought never to let go.

"I am a bit lean, I fear," Frost said, standing back again, "but I am determined to fix that. You on the other hand look perfect."

"Do not perjure yourself," Shassel scolded. "I am an old hag at best."

"A looking glass would convince you," Frost said, "but alas, I brought none. I think it best that you return with us to Briarlea at once, so that we can find a good one and settle the issue."

"I may have one about, somewhere."

"It will not do, I'm sure."

"You have things all figured out already, I see," Shassel replied, just grinning.

"Only this part of this day," Frost said. "Everything else is a jumble of bits."

"I thought I taught you to leave jumbled thinking to others?"

"I have come to let you finish the job."

"Indeed," Shassel said, the smile a little bigger now. "I see you found my two latest projects," she added, greeting Dara and Dorin by way of a nod. The twins greeted her in kind, silent and looking utterly tractable.

Frost witnessed this in amazement. "No flip remarks?" he asked them. "Nothing to say?"

"Good-day, Shassel," Dorin said.

"We brought sweetened bread," Dara said.

"And myself, of course," Lurey said, stepping into the doorway, standing back of everyone else. He raised one hand above heads to wave.

"Lurey was kind enough to drop everything and bring us here, as Frost asked," Dorin explained.

"How much did it cost you?" Shassel asked, raising one eyebrow to Lurey.

"Enough," Frost said, to which Shassel gave a nod.

"We trust we did the right thing," Dara said.

"Polite, respectful, and thoughtful," Frost observed, shaking his head as he listened to the twins. "They seem to have undergone some sort of transformation. Most remarkable. You must teach me the spell," he added, turning again to Shassel. "I have never seen the like."

Shassel was grinning like a girl now. "Sometimes I hardly know them myself," she said. "Now, everyone come in. Your warrior friends as well, Frost, if they like. We will finish our introductions over some fresh soup, and that bread of course."

She turned and the others followed her inside. The room was small and sparely appointed, but it looked a little better on the inside than it had outside. Shassel had hung plenty of linens over the two small windows, over gaps in the mortar of old walls, even on much of the earthen floor. Lurey had apparently been generous, though Frost imagined Shassel had been generous in kind. A large stew pot was hung in the hearth, and the smell of soup heavy with greens and spices drifted freely from it. By the time the soup was in the bowls and on the table, everyone was properly acquainted, and the talk had turned from small to large.

"These past few years have been difficult," Shassel said as one by one the bowls were slowly emptied. "With the twins getting older and bolder of course, and Andair suffering much the same fate, and all of them taxing me to the point of distraction."

Dara and Dorin had been saying as little as possible while the two old friends began the task of catching up; they said nothing now, though the looks on their faces were easy enough to read. They knew they were not the easiest pair to deal with, especially for a woman of Shassel's age, which left them short of excuses for themselves, depending on the details. Shassel told several accounts of mischief, the sort common to all children, and everyone managed a laugh or two—especially Lurey; the peddler was quick to humor by nature, but especially so where Dara and Dorin were concerned. He even managed to embarrass them with a tale about secret plans to visit Wilmar and in particular Wilmar's son Tramet, whom Dara had apparently gotten to be rather good friends with before Shassel decided it might be better for everyone if she and the twins relocated, further east.

"They asked me to take them and I said no, not without Shassel's approval, which I knew they did not have, so instead they tried to steal my horse that night, which—"

"Borrow," Dorin corrected.

"—which I knew they very well might do, so I decided to sleep with the horse, which was how I was awakened by the two of them tripping over one another and me in the darkness, and caught them in the act!"

"It was a year ago, and we have made it up to Lurey many times over, which is the only reason we've never told you," Dara assured Shassel, who had fixed the two of them with a cold, merciless look.

"We will speak more of this later," Shassel assured them, and they lowered their heads like scolded puppies. "But I have heard a great many things about you, Frost," she continued. "You've made quite a name for yourself."

"What sort of name?"

"They say you are a rogue, a sorcerer for hire, if you approve of the task and those who require it. Which fits you, I think. Though some of the stories are quite fantastic, and some of the fees they say you have garnered for your services must be exaggerated. That, or you are more wealthy than a king."

"There are many kinds of wealth, I have learned that much," Frost said. "And I have been fortunate to acquire a great deal of most of them."

Shassel smiled gently, then she cocked one eye. "Of course there is the story I hear most these days, of you and the legendary Demon Blade—of a battle for half the world fought against a terrible demon and an army of thousands, and all of them left lifeless and destroyed by your hand alone. Surely there is a bit of embellishment in all of that, as is common."

Frost folded his arms across his chest and leaned back. "No, that more or less sums it up."

"Remarkable."

Frost bowed his head. "Many would agree."

Shassel wrinkled her nose at him. "Such bragging of mastery I have never heard, yet I could more easily believe that you have forgotten how to cast even a simple sleeping spell."

"That is possible," Frost said. "Though I will wager you have forgotten a thing or two as well, you being so much older than I, and probably a little absent-minded, as is common."

Shassel was undaunted. "Absent-minded, you say?"

Frost nodded.

"Lurey?" Dara said, collecting everyone's attentions to the peddler; he who was seated comfortably enough in his chair, hands folded neatly across his abdomen, eyes closed, snoozing quite soundly. When he did not respond Dara reached over and shook him. Slowly, he began to come to.

"Still a streak of imp in you, I see," Shassel said. She held him in her gaze. "Dara, go, bring me a small piece of firewood."

Dara nodded once, then got up and went straight to the pile of split logs stacked beside the hearth. She picked one up and brought it to Shassel.

"Give it to Frost, he hasn't had enough to eat," Shassel told her. Dara held out the log, which as much to Dara's surprise as anyone else's, had somehow managed to become a loaf of bread.

"I am quite full, in fact, but I expect a chilly night," Frost answered her. He spoke the base phrases of the spell he needed, then he used Shassel's own binding phrase, loud enough for her to hear, "Tesha teshrea." Then he told Dara to put the "bread" on the table. By the time she did, the loaf had turned back into the piece of maple it had been.

Shassel looked a bit unsettled, or as close to that as Frost hoped she might. "You had forgotten I knew," he said, and saw that she understood exactly.

"I was testing whether you still remembered," Shassel corrected. "I am satisfied."

"Without a doubt," Frost said wryly.

"He is here about the Demon Blade," Dorin said. The stubborn look on his face was clear, the lack of indulgence, though wisely he had stopped short of directly chastising anyone.

"We have at least one in our midst in the mood for serious business," Lurey said, still not fully alert but getting there, and perhaps more anxious than most just now to see the two sorcerers move past their game of magical tit for tat.

"Very well," Frost said, settling his gaze on Shassel once more. "I have a question to ask you."

"No, I do not want the Blade," Shassel said flatly.

"Neither do I," Frost replied.

"Have you ever considered selling it?" Lurey asked, sheepish.

Frost shot him a bitter look, and Lurey put his arms up, palms out—hands off.

"Then what do you want?" Shassel asked.

"You knew many of the mages who were present at the last council during the time Ramins was chosen as the Blade's Keeper. But he was already old and

others are always chosen to take the place of the
Keeper, when the time comes, though it changes
according to who is born to whom. The succession
is intentionally hard to follow from outside, but I
must. I seek to find the next, chosen Keeper, so I
can be rid of the cursed thing."

"Some would not think it a curse," Shassel mused.

"Death follows the Blade everywhere, and it will
only get worse," Frost said.

"Which is why I do not want it," Shassel said.

"Then help me. As much as I would be rid of it,
I cannot allow the Blade to fall into the wrong hands.
I have learned many things since it came into my
possession. Enough to know that the consequences
of a mistake would be far greater than anyone real-
izes; even you, Shassel, perhaps even me."

They sat looking at one another in silence. No one
in the room made a sound. If Shassel knew anything,
she had surely sworn an oath never to divulge the
information to anyone, under any circumstance. But
these were not "any" circumstances, Frost insisted,
and he was not "anyone."

"I do not know, I wish I did," she answered, letting her eyes wander as if looking for something other
than what she knew was there. "But as you say, I
knew many who were part of the last council. I know
of only one, though, who remains. One who would
know. He is aging, like me, yet still quite powerful."

Frost let a sigh of relief escape his lips. He had
come so far to hear these words, never knowing until
just this moment whether he ever would. "Do you
know where I might find him?"

"Indeed, he is not far. But he may as well be."

Frost tipped his head. "Why?"

"The one you seek is Gentaff, court wizard of
Andair."

Frost closed his eyes. It seemed always to be this
way with the Demon Blade, each step forward carrying

with it a step backward, each instance of relief involving a modicum of pain. On the face of it, this situation seemed to have no solution. "Then I must find someone else."

"That might be impossible," Shassel said.

"Then we have to find a way to make Gentaff talk!" Dorin spoke up, trotting out the bluster he seemed to be increasingly fond of.

"Dorin's right," Dara said.

"Even if that were possible," Frost said, "anything Gentaff said would be suspect. He has no reason to cooperate and at least one reason not to."

"There are ways of being sure what he tells is the truth," Shassel said. "Though none of them easy," she added with a shrug. "Especially with the likes of him."

"And what is he like?" Frost asked. "You must know well enough to say."

"You would not like him. Big and oftentimes bold, always arrogant, far too talented and cunning, and concerned largely with sport and profit these days—"

"Nothing at all like me, then," Frost put in.

"—and the wishes of Lord Andair, of course," Shassel continued without pause. "Which I happen to know are many. Gentaff has changed, or he has left behind the masks he once wore. He was always a cold and greedy man, mind you, but he has gotten worse in latter years. He never spent time in this part of the world, largely because he knew I was here and would disapprove. But I am older than he, and no match for him anymore. Perhaps no one is. Even you."

Frost shook his head. "No one can know that. But short of finding out, he may be willing to listen to reason."

"Even you doubt that already, I can see it in your eyes," Shassel said.

Frost thought it over. "True."

"Let me think on this, and you as well," Shassel told him. "You have all had a long journey, and I grow tired of simply sitting on my haunches these days. In the morning, we will talk further, and come to something. You cannot both keep the Blade and be done with it at the same time, after all, and I rather doubt it can be destroyed."

"Destroyed?" Lurey asked, though Dara and Dorin both said it too, half a beat behind him.

"They do not understand as I do," Frost said. "I doubt anyone can."

"Sounds impressive," Shassel remarked.

Frost nodded.

"Can I see it?" Shassel asked. "Before some high-wayman pries it off your big dead body?"

"Of course," Frost said, "but you should consider carefully. If you seek the Blade with your talents in any way, it will draw from you immediately and endlessly, until you force an end to the bond. If you can. If not, without the corpulent reserves of your youth you might die."

"Interesting," Shassel said, turning quite serious. "I had imagined something much different."

"As did I, but the truth was a painful lesson for me, one I have yet to fully learn."

"Keep your Blade for now, then. We will talk more of this, too, in the morning," Shassel said with a long sigh. She looked from one to the next about the table and everyone seemed in agreement. Frost could see the fatigue on her face.

Sharryl and Rosivok got up without a word, though two quick hand gestures communicated all that was necessary between them—who would stand first watch, who the second. Then Rosivok went to get the bedding.

Frost said good-night to Shassel with a kiss on the cheek and laid his head down on a mound of linens Lurey had fetched from his cart. He found it comfortable enough, but thoughts of what to do about

Andair and Gentaff kept him awake as they twisted together in his mind, and refused to unwind. He closed his eyes and waited for morning. After a time, he wasn't sure how long, he was rudely awakened.

"I think he's asleep," Dorin said in a faint whisper, when Rosivok stepped outside for a moment and moved into the trees; his task would not take long, Dorin knew. They had to work quickly.

"He isn't snoring," Dara said. "I'm not so sure about this."

"No doubt snoring is too undignified for him. He has probably devised some means to prevent it. But he is not the only clever mage hereabouts, though he thinks he is greater even than Shassel."

"I think you are right," Dara whispered back. "And he has no remorse, not for anything that's happened."

"Except for when Andair made a fool of him."

"True."

They sat side by side in their bedrolls on the floor watching Frost. One oil lamp burned, turned down low, but it was enough to see by.

"What do we have in mind?" Dara asked.

"There," Dorin said. He pointed to Frost's walking stick which stood leaning against the wall near the wizard's head, in the small space between Frost and Shassel's bed. There was no way to get to it without stepping on Frost. Which was the idea. "Frost seems quite fond of it. There may even be more to it than just wood."

"A talisman of some kind?"

"Yes. Who knows what means or charms he may have invested in that stick over the years. Countless hours' work, all gone, just like that. And he will have to come to us to get it back again."

Dara smiled. Dorin smiled with her. He liked the sound of that. And they would give it back, but only when Shassel asked them to.

"When he wakes in the morning and finds it gone, he will be a little less smug, I think," Dara said, putting her hand to her mouth to blunt a snicker.

"Probably furious."

"Probably a mess," Dara said. And then, sobering, "But how furious do you think he will actually be?"

"It doesn't matter. He would not attempt to harm us with Shassel here, and anyway, I am not convinced he is so much more powerful than we are, especially if we stand together."

She nodded, but Dorin had known she would understand. He had felt it first many years ago, the special bond he and his twin sister seemed to have from time to time—something they had spent great efforts developing since then. The sense of what the other one was thinking, where the other one was, or wanted to be. But there was more. It didn't always work, but more often than not they could use the same spell, with the same binding phrase, and pool their energies. The process had never been tested against another mage—save that one time, some years ago, when it had failed. But they had successfully managed more than a trick or two since then.

"We have to hurry," Dara said.

Dorin nodded. Without another word he took Dara's hand and began to recite the spell. The spell started drawing from their inner reserves, converting their physical energy into magical energy, then he directed it with their binding phrase. Together they commanded the stick to leap into the air, over Frost, and come to them on their side of the room.

Something went wrong. The stick jumped up, but then it instantly leaped away with at least twice the force they had applied to it, as if it was terrified by the touch of their influence. With a loud clatter the stick found the wall farthest from the twins and proceeded to bash and clatter against the wood as if it was trying to break through and escape to the world beyond.

"Stop!" Dorin shouted, letting go of Dara's hand and severing the flow of energies from within himself, then letting the spell discharge. As the cottage door burst open the stick rattled to the floor, where it lay still again. Rosivok stood in the doorway, poised and ready as he scrutinized the room. Dorin looked from the Subartan to the others, heart pounding, blinking in disbelief. Everyone was awake and trying to gather wits enough to wonder what had happened. Dorin found Frost looking straight at him and Dara, as was Shassel. They already knew. . . .

Frost raised his hand above his head and the walking stick drifted up from the floor, then crossed the room, floating just high enough to miss Shassel's bed; it ended in the grip of Frost's still raised hand. He placed it precisely where it had been against the wall.

"It is nothing," he said to one and all. "An experiment by Dorin and Dara that did not go as planned, I think. A bit more training, perhaps. But they need their sleep as much as the rest of us. I think Shassel will agree that enough is enough for tonight."

"Agreed, more than enough," Shassel said, with a look in her eyes that Dorin could read even in this dim light, the one that meant he and Dara would be smoldering footnotes in the fables of history if she did not love them both—or if they tried anything else.

"We," Dara began, stumbling, "we were only, um . . ."

Dorin took a breath and tried to help. "We were just going to—to, um, I mean, we thought . . ."

"Say good-night," Frost said.

"Now!" said Shassel.

"Good-night," Dorin repeated along with his sister.

Dorin heard Frost mutter something after that, and saw Shassel's lips moving along with his. He couldn't hear the whispers. He lay down and closed his eyes, and kept quite quiet and still. The next thing he knew it was already morning, and Lurey was shaking him awake.

"Come, eat your breakfast," Shassel called as he got to his feet. He found his great-aunt sitting at the table with Frost, Sharryl and Rosivok, eating porridge and grinning quite slyly at him and his sister.

"And when you are done," Frost said, "we will talk."

Dorin looked at Dara and saw a familiar flash of panic in her eyes, though like him, she tried to quell the obvious signs almost immediately. They pulled on their boots and ate as they were told. When the meal was ended they put away their bedding and joined the others outside.

"You may find this hard to believe, but there is much you do not yet know—about me, about sorcery, about the world," Frost said.

"There are not many teachers about," Dorin said, despite thinking he ought to keep his mouth shut just now. "And we lost some of those we did have, no thanks to you."

"Enough," Shassel said.

"It is all right, for now," Frost said. "I'm not sure what you were trying to accomplish last night, but I can tell you why you failed. I maintain a simple yet most reliable reversal spell on my staff—one which causes any new spell cast upon it to work in reverse. A useful precaution, thrifty, versatile, quick, and it has always seemed to come quite naturally to me. One of the few spells my father tried to teach me before, and which Shassel helped me perfect. We will teach it to both of you."

Dorin felt a mix of frustration and relief; here, finally, was the mentor he had always imagined, yet coming so late he felt betrayed by it all—or by himself if he accepted Frost now, if he forgave him for not being there before, and for the terrible price that had been paid in Frost's absence.

"You and your magic were never here to help us," Dorin said, using the words he had recited in his head for years, awaiting this day. "We do not need it now."

"But you do!" Shassel said. "All of us do. And Frost will need us as well to face what is to come. You have not told him, have you?"

Dorin shook his head.

"I will," Dara said. "I will."

"It will serve no one," Dorin said.

"No," Shassel stopped her. "You are wrong. But now I think it will be better if I tell him." She turned to Frost and took a deep breath. "To begin, you should know their father had no trace of the gift, but he was a good man, a good teacher, and he understood well enough."

Frost nodded sympathetically. "I wish I'd known him, but what has he to do with me?"

The twins grunted at this. Shassel cleared her throat and continued. "When Andair took the throne, many in Worlish were angry over it, and with good reason. He took so much land, the easier pickings first, but he got round to the rest when the time was right, including nearly everything that had once belonged to our families, and Wilmar's. He and his army grew too powerful too quickly, until even the worst of his misdeeds went unchallenged.

"It is as much my fault as anyone. I was away at the worst possible time, a time when Dara and Dorin were just beginning to realize their nature and their potential."

"Some five years ago," Lurey said, "when they were just eleven, they started trying little sorceries. I remember because I had just been to their manor for the first time that year."

Shassel nodded acknowledgment. Dorin stayed silent, and let her go on. "They managed a few spells," she said. "They taught each other, and became charged with the enthusiasm one feels at such a time—though much more so than they should have. With the taste of their newfound powers fresh in their minds and our lands clearly next in Andair's sights they decided to take matters into their own hands, and teach Andair the lesson he needed to learn. The kind of lesson they believed their blood required of them. The sort of task that would have fallen to me, had I been here."

"Or to me, had I been here, but it fell to them," Frost said, nodding.

Dorin went to open his mouth, but the glare from Shassel make him close it again.

"Yes," Shassel said. "We lived closer to Weldhem then. They were able to slip away from the family I had left them with and go to the city on their own. They got into the castle and past many of the guards to the great room, where they attempted a heraldry spell on Andair, one intended to transform the king into a goat. The spell did not work, by all accounts, but it worked well to the advantage of the court mage Andair was keeping at the time. A buffoon, that one, but he was able enough to sense the twins' location, and they were captured instantly."

"He would have a time of that now," Dorin insisted.

"No doubt," Shassel replied. "In any case, they were seen publicly as a bad joke, but I suspect privately Andair took them much more seriously. They are your blood, and mine, and Andair knew as well as anyone what that implied. When their father came to see to them, distraught and angry, he too was arrested. They were made a public display, and as an example to others, Dorin, Dara and their father were all beaten in the city's northern square. It was supposed to be a punishment, not an execution, but Andair's soldiers went too far.

"The twins survived, but their father became wild with anger, and was ultimately beaten to death for their crimes. So you see, they do not blame you for the mistakes you made with Andair; you were not much older than they are now, and they have made their share. They blame you for your absence since that time. They blame us both, but you most of all."

Dorin kept his tongue. She had said it all, even though he had expected her to flag at the very end. Dorin felt a weight, very old and heavy, lift off of him, or a part of it at least.

"I didn't know," Frost said, turning to the twins. "I wish I could tell you everything that is in my heart and unburden yours, but proper answers are not always easy to come by."

"Yes, we know," Dara said.

"I cannot change the past, but the future is a different matter," Frost said. "Andair will pay for all he has done, I promise. He will pay most dearly."

Dorin heard the words and tried to set them aside, but he could not. He felt drained by all that had just happened, and yet . . .

There was something about Frost—a dauntless nature that spoke to something deep inside Dorin's soul, a roguishness that seemed not quite familiar, yet destined to be. He wasn't sure whether Dara felt it, though he guessed she might, a little at least. And the feeling was growing despite no desire on his part to allow such a thing. None of that could put aside the rest—the cowardly way Frost had abandoned his home, his family and his pride. The trouble was, Frost was not the haggard, shallow, sorry husk of a man Dorin had expected, and as he had spoken those last words Dorin saw the unmistakable gleam of unrequited hatred and vengeance in his eye.

"You'll have your work cut out for you, Frost," Shassel said, "just getting on with these two. But I can already tell you have grown enough these many years to make a fine mentor for them. Perhaps even an example, though that may take more time."

"A mentor?" Frost moaned. "Such a generous offer."

"One you should think about carefully before accepting," Dorin warned. "It may be too little, too late." He looked to Dara for support and found her lost in her thoughts as he had been, though she hadn't yet snapped out of it.

"I have a talent for bringing people together," Shassel said. "You will all get along, I'm sure. In the meantime we must return home. Whatever Frost decides to do, I grant that he did not come all this way simply to hide in these woods indefinitely."

"I suppose not," Frost said wearily. "At least not . . . indefinitely."

"I do have to get back to work," Lurey said, breaking his silence only now, though he was careful not to sound too worried. "My goods do not peddle themselves while I am sitting here enjoying your company, and I have many places to visit this month."

"Good," Shassel said. "Then we can leave this afternoon."

Dorin turned to Dara, who was focussed now, though she did not look well. He decided he must look at least as bad. "What is it you plan to do?" he asked Frost, though he avoided the sorcerer's eyes.

"I will tell you," Frost said, "on the way."

CHAPTER NINE

"Your son is here to see you," Enrude said, the
oldest of Kolhol's squires, and the most trustworthy,
which was why the king kept him around much of
the time. "He says it is urgent."

"Of course he does," Kolhol said. He let his pages
finish dressing him, wrapping him in a thick saffron-
hued tunic that helped with the chill of early morning,
then he came out of his chambers and proceeded
down the hall. The pages and Enrude followed. His
son, Haggel, mostly kept to his own part of the keep.
It had been that way ever since Haggel's mother had
died, just about the time when Haggel was becoming a young man . . . of sorts. She had doted over
Haggel. "Probably along to tell me he is finally doing
well at his lessons."

"Anything is possible, my lord."

That was part of Enrude's charm—he understood
the difficulties, and so the humor. Kolhol grinned only
a little, then sobered as he entered the great hall
where his son was waiting. Some mornings they
missed one another—Haggel liked to sleep late, unless

he had something big and, most often, disagreeable on his mind—that was surely the case today. *A fine day already*, Kolhol lamented, as he took to his chair.

Kitchen servants had put out breads and cheeses, and were just entering with a bowl full of freshly scrambled eggs. A handful of Kolhol's other servants and their families mulled about at tables along the right side of the room. Kolhol dismissed everyone and told them to wait in the gallery. Everyone but Enrude.

"A good day, my liege," young Haggel said, as he sat across from his father and began the morning feast without delay.

"A little chilly, but beyond that, I have not had a chance to notice," Kolhol said, noting the "my liege" instead of "Father."

"You need to get out of this old dark castle now and then," Haggel said around a mouthful of eggs. "It's bright and sunny outside. Just the sort of day that makes a man feel anything is possible. Anything at all. Tell me, do you ever feel that way anymore?"

Not a big man, Kolhol thought, taking a bite out of a thick slice of buttered bread, sizing up his son. The boy's proportions were at best average. Which was odd, since height and a strong upper body tended to run in the family—for that matter in most Grenarii families. Kolhol himself had a stout frame and good height, and he was still as robust as most men years younger. Kolhol's father had been even more intimidating and his father before him. And all of them wearing fine manes of thick brown hair.

Yet here was Haggel, built wiry and dark, even his hair, like one of the western barbarian tribesmen— the sort Haggel's mother had thought so intriguing once, long ago . . .

He has good teeth, though, Kolhol thought, watching him bite through crust and tear away chunks from the wheat loaves. Kolhol had lost several of his teeth, which made meals more difficult to enjoy and the choices fewer. But fewer choices and age seemed to go hand in hand—that was the kind of revelation in which no man took comfort.

"I feel different things on different days," Kolhol replied finally. "Then do whatever I please. This day, for instance, when I get around to going outside and having a look for myself, I might send for my bird and go hawking."

"No greater ambitions?" Haggel asked, studying his own bread now instead of his father's face, examining it as if it were a puzzle.

Kolhol was not eager to reply. He knew where this was going. As he knew well that his son had been waiting to broach the subject for weeks. He'd hinted around and had even been blunt about it a few times, as he was about to be now. Kolhol would have preferred getting into such an argument over dinner, when plenty of ale was on hand. But he liked to keep away from the ale at least until midday as it tended to make a man sluggish and lax. "I am in no hurry to invade and conquer Worlish."

Haggel's features twisted as if he'd eaten something foul. "Why not?"

Haggel glanced at Enrude before answering. Enrude made no expression at all. He would keep silent all the while his king and the young prince were speaking, as was expected. That usually suited Kolhol well enough, but just now he would have welcomed a grunt, or a roll of the eyes. "Because it is not yet time."

"When will it be time?" Haggel asked. "When will you be ready? During all your glories in these lands no one sat about telling you to wait. Yet now that it comes my turn, you keep me from—"

"From running off and getting yourself killed, and half my army in the bargain."

"Our army is more than adequate for the job. We have half again as many men as Andair, and all of them well trained. Perhaps they suffer from a lack of leadership."

Kolhol tried mightily to hold his temper as he looked across the table. Haggel was eyeing him back, showing more backbone than was common for the boy. The same kind of unfounded self-righteous rot his mother was so capable of.

Haggel's full head of hair and short-cropped beard made him look more daunting—Kolhol had taken to shaving these past few years—but lately everything had gone to his head. Haggel seemed to think he was ten feet tall, and no one else in the world knew quite as much as he. Kolhol tried to remember if he had been that way at that age, but that had been nearer to thirty years ago than twenty, and near the bitter end of a war against the Thackish barbarians to the north, a war that had gone on for more than a decade and cost his father his life.

Kolhol had built a great kingdom from the ruins, and conquered all lands now known as Grenarii. He'd plundered lands to the north as well and extended the kingdom even further. But he had known war all his life, and seen defeat as well as victory. Haggel, having only been alive for seventeen years, only knew of victories, then relative calm.

"I will not be so easily provoked," he told his son, and perhaps himself. "What I see here is a boy turned to a young man who has ambition enough, but lacks experience and the wisdom that comes with it. I did not prevail against all our barbarian cousins and their allies by running off and getting men killed. It takes a good head as well as might. I used both, and still it was only luck that carried the day more than once."

"It was not luck that won the day," Haggel said. "And not might or cunning alone; it was the relentless pace you kept, never giving quarter, never letting up, never waiting or hesitating."

The boy had been filled with far too many stories

told by noblemen, freemen and soldiers alike. True,
Kolhol had never minded being known for his ruth-
lessness—those he had fought against had been the
enemy, and they would have shown no mercy had
they been the victors, he was sure—but even through
the most ale-soaked memories he still knew it was
the grace of the Grenarii gods that had seen him
through, and he no longer wished to rely on the
providence of gods, or luck. He'd been much more
willing to die for his cause in those days as well, for
the goal of conquering all Grenarii and uniting the
ancient tribes. He was less eager to die for the sake
of conquering Worlish. Or even continue discuss-
ing it.

"You will stop making stupid plans," Kolhol said
harshly, through with bantering. "I made mistakes in
the past, then learned from them. I can only hope
you will one day do the same. The trick is to keep
your mistakes from getting you and your army killed."

"I will crush any who—"

"Shut up and listen!" Kolhol howled, pounding the
table with one fist. He waited till the words echoed
back to him from the walls of the great hall. He took
a long, deep breath. "Our army grows by the day, I
am pleased with their training, and I have had my
eye on Worlish for a very long time. There is little
doubt it will be mine one day. *Ours*, one day," he
corrected with a groan. "That day is not far off, but
for now I lose nothing by biding my time and making my plans, by sending spies to look for weaknesses,
and looking for a sorcerer who might even the odds.
Andair has a powerful ally in Gentaff."

Haggel boiled at this, as Kolhol expected he would.
"We have Tasche," the boy insisted. "A match for any
man of magic!"

"So he is fond of saying," Kolhol muttered, shaking his head. He had suffered a run of charlatans
these past few years. The rewards, protection and

celebrity of being court wizard was lure enough for many a trickster. But more than tricks would be needed against one such as Gentaff. The boy had no idea. And for some reason known only to the gods, Tasche and Haggel got along. In fact they'd become inseparable. Kolhol looked at his breakfast and decided he wasn't hungry at the moment. Though he could see when he might be. Just after Haggel had gone.

He took no pleasure from the fact.

"Andair's wizard, Gentaff, is twice Tasche's age and has twice the reputation," Kolhol said evenly. "Men like him do not suffer fools gladly." He leaned over the table and glared at his son. "Neither do I. Do not underestimate Andair's army either. He has a large one now, with many lords who have sworn fealty to him. And mercenaries, more each day. As I said—"

"Which is why we should attack *now!*" Haggel interrupted. "Before he gets any stronger!"

Haggel was sweating. He sat with his jaw set, lips pursed, breathing like a bull in heat through his nostrils while he balled his fists on the table in front of him. He had small eyes set too close together. Kolhol didn't. *An unintelligent look*, the king thought; he had killed dozens like that in battles too many to count. Though possibly not enough of them . . .

"I will take Worlish when I am ready, and you will be a part of it. If you live, you will have lands enough for any two men. But first I must know in my heart that we will win. That we can crush them swiftly. That it is their blood, not ours, on the ground when it is done."

Haggel pounded his fists on the table with a double thump. "I have no doubts, not one, that it will be so!"

"You make that clear, but know this—when you invite trouble it is usually quick to accept."

Haggel's expression grew pained. "That makes no

sense." Kolhol stared at Haggel just long enough to realize the boy was serious. He glanced at Enrude again, who rolled his eyes this time. Kolhol had all he could do to keep a straight face. "Do not trouble yourself over it," he told Haggel. "And do not trouble me with more talk of war this morning—I wish to finish my meal in peace!"

Kolhol snarled smugly to himself at his choice of words, then stuffed eggs into his mouth, and promptly bit his tongue. He winced, then looked up and decided Haggel had missed the point anyway.

"One day," Haggel muttered as if to himself, but loud enough to be sure he was heard, "I will do as I will."

"And I promise to bury you proper after you have," Kolhol grumbled back.

Haggel finished his meal in two gulps, then stalked off. When he had gone, the squires and servants that had earlier been about were summoned to return.

Amid the bustle of this, Enrude approached and bent to his lord sovereign's ear. "I did not like the look of him today," he said, while attempting to sound as respectful as possible. "More so than usual."

"Nor I," Kolhol said.

"Your son grows more restless by the day; it has been that way since early spring. He spends too much of his time among your best warriors, and all the more consorting with lords of every rank, usually over plenty of ale and roasts."

"They appreciate good food and my best ale when it is given," Kolhol said.

"The more generous Haggel is, the more inclined to him the lords become."

"But they owe no fealty to my son. He is a joke to most of them, which brings me no pleasure, but I will lose no sleep over it."

"He spends the rest of his time with Tasche," Enrude went on, apparently not the least dissuaded.

"They speak in whispers and behind closed doors, and often leave the keep together. They disappear into the countryside. Sometimes for days at a time. I have been having them watched, as you instructed. They visit with the heads of families that once held power before you defeated them, and they are not above engaging freemen or pages. Even some of your court squires have been found in their company, cloistered away in some corner or other. Most are only playing the game, as you say, letting whatever grace might fall upon them fall—or they are planning for the future, one in which young Haggel might be ruler. But some, for reasons of greed or ignorance, are loyal enough to Haggel himself, I think, at least on the face of it."

Kolhol had already suspected much of this, but now he was faced with it, and it left a very bitter taste in his mouth. "Keep a list. When I grow tired of all their plotting, dreaming and scheming, I will have a few of them chained, killed and hung from a gibbet for the crows to pick at. That will quell the rest of them. Sometimes I think Haggel is still irked over the fate of his good friend—what was his name?"

"Indem."

Kolhol nodded. The princely son of one of Kolhol's largest and loudest nobles, and always with Haggel. But his father had fought bravely and well for his king and his lands until the day he died, with honor, fighting a wound that finally would not heal. Indem, though at least the size of his father, had little control over his temper and even less good sense. On a winter hunt two seasons past, an argument had erupted, and Indem had seen fit to challenge Kolhol at sword point. Kolhol had thrown his own blade aside and grappled with the prince hand to hand. Indem had made the error of picking up a fair-sized rock and pitching it; it struck Kolhol's arm as he tried to block the impact and opened a gash just above the elbow. While Haggel watched, Kolhol, driven by anger and blood-lust, had leaped at Indem and broken his back in an instant. At his own request, Indem's squires had killed him after that.

Kolhol regretted the incident, but it was Indem who had picked the fight and then made it a dishonorable one.

"Haggel was indignant after that, but Indem's death marked the end of their friendship," Enrude said. "Dead, he could serve Haggel no more. Why would Haggel ever consider him again?"

Kolhol knew as much, but it was hard for him to remember such ethics. Friends and enemies were each worth remembering. Only a fool . . .

He stopped himself. "I see your point," he said.

"It is Haggel's closeness to Tasche that troubles me most," Enrude said, whispering even more quietly now, as if the walls themselves had ears. Enrude was even older than Kolhol and perhaps a bit too apprehensive these days. Age did that to a man. Which was why Kolhol still fought in tournaments and went on the hunts, and still spent the night testing his stamina with a maiden or two on a regular basis. One day age would defeat him, but not without a fight. And one day Haggel might be king, but not without proving himself, which seemed less likely than ever. As for Tasche . . .

"Tasche?" Kolhol scoffed. "There you worry too much."

"It helps keep us well."

True enough, Kolhol thought, but still he shook his head. "Tasche is a toad at best, a fraud at worst!" he said in a raised voice certain to be heard. He couldn't be sure what rumors were circulating, what amount of poison had been spread to the ears of his court by Tasche, his son, or others who might have reason. Then he lowered his voice again, and turned his head to Enrude's ear. "He and Haggel deserve each other, but I doubt the two of them could rout a clutch of angry children without taking casualties."

"Your son is your problem, but it would grow smaller if you were to have Tasche beheaded in the meantime."

A proper solution, Kolhol thought, but without any court wizard at all he lacked an effective deterrent against every hedge witch, alchemist and apprentice mage that lurked in the shadows. *Tasche is at least better than nothing*, Kolhol thought. Though in truth even that small wisdom was becoming hard to accept. Kolhol belched eggs and bread and gulped down the smoked herring that had just been warmed and set before him. When he was finished, he summoned the servants back and waited while the table was cleared.

Next the king sat back while one of his barons and a steward approached the table, bringing news of renewed flooding in his region—a problem in eastern Grenarii this spring, but one Kolhol had thought was passed. He promised to send men to help in any way they could.

Others waited to see him next, the day was off to a good and rolling start.

But it got no further before a young page came running into the hall with news that the scaffolding had given way on the new tower, and most of the masons had fallen to their deaths. A tiny fish bone stabbed at the roof of Kolhol's mouth, punctuating the report. He winced, then he spat on the floor. *A truly fine day already*, Kolhol lamented, for the second time. "Ale!" he shouted to the servants nearby—perhaps it was close enough to midday after all.

"The old bastard!" Haggel snarled, kicking at the chair nearest to him as he strode into the upstairs counting room, where Tasche sat waiting. No one else was about. Haggel spent a moment examining Tasche, the table, the floor, letting his blood boil down, then he sat with a thump.

"Your father is well?" Tasche asked, boorishly. He pawed at his beard, which was thin below his chin from constant wear.

"The fittest fool in the land," Haggel snorted. "By the time he decides he is ready to take Briarlea, he and Andair will be dead of old age, and I will be too old to care."

Tasche laughed, though it was not a sound Haggel particularly enjoyed, so breathy and hollow, and especially odd coming from a man whose head seemed a bit small for his body—a body that was most distinctly a plump blob. Haggel shrugged off much about Tasche. He wasn't much to look at or listen to, but he had other traits Haggel found valuable.

"You can laugh, but I cannot. I am more than ready to take my place at my father's side, and Grenarii's army is past ready to crush whatever forces Andair can put to the field. Wait, and one day they will come for us instead. Yet he sits, and he waits."

Tasche kept grinning, a small grin on a small, round face. "Which is why we are not!"

Haggel nodded. Well, that was the plan. A plan that was nothing short of extraordinary, and one he and Haggel had been hatching for more than a year now. It involved a spell that Tasche had been working on for many years, as far as Haggel knew. Something that was sure to put an end to his father's stranglehold on progress, one way or another. Haggel didn't care which way, not anymore. He had feelings for his father, probably at least as many as his father had for him, but if conquering Worlish and seizing the glory that would come with it could only be had by sending his father to his well-deserved rest among his ancestors and the gods, well, that was his father's choice. And the will of the gods, no doubt.

"You will be well rewarded," Haggel said, grinning back at his accomplice, "if you can do what you say."

To which Tasche grinned all the more, until his eyes seemed to close. "I am nearly ready," he said. "As soon as we can find someone who is fitting, I will be able to begin."

"I am less worried about my father and even Andair than I am about Gentaff. Are you sure we can stand against him?"

"You worry too much about him."

"My father fears him too, I think."

"I am Gentaff's equal," Tasche scoffed, pulling nervously at his beard again. "I am eager for the chance to prove it."

Haggel nodded. "There is much each of us will prove to those who doubt."

Tasche grinned again.

The cost would be high, but acceptable. Soldiers were trained to fight and die, after all. Even while Gentaff was reputed to be one of the world's great mages, it was hard to imagine him being much the better of Tasche. Haggel had seen him work, and before Tasche he had known several others, court wizards to his father. Tasche was easily their better, and no doubt Gentaff's. The spell Tasche had been building to ensure their victory against all who opposed them, including Andair and his famous sorcerer, was more incredible than any Haggel could have hoped for.

"We must give Grenarii a leader with the will to lead," Haggel said as he got to his feet, to no one in particular, to everyone in the world.

"It so happens, I know precisely who that is," Haggel said, as the two of them stood together, then turned and left the counting room. They headed toward the spiral staircase at the end of the hall. "The only question had been *when*. A question that will soon enough have an answer."

So be it, Haggel thought. After all, his father had enjoyed a good and glorious life—hadn't he? How many times had the king himself said that nothing of value comes without some kind of payment. Which, Haggel accepted, meant *someone* had to pay, though he recalled no specific mention of *who* had to pay. . . .

"I have knowledge of a man," Tasche said, still pulling the tips of his beard as they walked. "He wishes to meet with us in secret, but I am told he can be relied upon to provide what we need, for the right price."

"Just the man we have been looking for."

"I think so. He travels everywhere. It is said that if anyone knows where to find the sort of person we are looking for, it is he. With your leave, I will send a messenger to him."

"A swift messenger. I have a strong hunger for action, and I do not wish to wait to satisfy it, or wait and miss the best chance we have."

"You are young, my prince," Tasche said, though he bowed respectfully as he spoke. "Even if . . ."

"And you are old," Haggel said, sneering long enough to be sure Tasche would see. "Are you making excuses already?"

"I am not sure what I meant," Tasche yielded.

"Forget it. Let me know the instant we are ready."

Tasche bowed again and tried to let Haggel go first down the stairs. But as Haggel started down it occurred to him that there was no sensible reason for him to go first.

"After you," Haggel said.

"No, after you, my lord," Tasche said.

Haggel thought he was probably making something out of nothing, but that was preferable to taking chances. After all, if a father could not trust his only son, who could the son truly trust?

"I insist," he said, and held there until Tasche nodded and went ahead of him instead.

With his mind at ease again, Haggel reflected further on the messenger idea, and managed to turn the whole idea around in his mind, where it presented him with a more appealing possibility. "Tasche, I was just thinking, why wait for a messenger to go?" he said.

"Why not?"

There was barely enough room in the hallway for the two of them to go side-by-side, and Tasche had a way of swaying and tossing his bulk with each step as he walked, causing one to be bumped intermittently by undulating flesh. Haggel opted to continue walking half a step behind.

"It will take a long and boring time, which I have had enough of, that is why. We will have to decide many things once he returns in any case, after which we will have to decide what to do, then perhaps what to do after that."

Tasche stopped in his tracks and pivoted enough to display a completely puzzled look. Haggel shook his head in frustration. "Where can we find this informant of yours?"

"He is a traveler, which is what makes him valuable, but he can often be found in a village in Worlish. The messenger we chose—"

"All the better."

"Better for what?"

"We will need sufficient gold, proper clothing, a few men who can be trusted and then a false reason for our absence." Haggel let a grin find his lips as the idea bloomed and grew enormous in his mind—and showed its many shades of danger, exhilaration, glory!

"What are you saying?" Tasche asked.

Haggel focussed. Tasche looked ill. He would get over it. "Forget the messenger," Haggel said. "We are going ourselves."

❖   ❖   ❖

Enrude entered the bath followed by two pages, both carrying large painted pottery jugs filled with hot water. Once the water had been poured carefully around the king into the stone bath, further warming the water already there, the pages were sent away.

"What is it?" Kolhol asked. "You have that look on your face."

"What look?"

"The one that means you've got something worrisome to tell me."

"Very well, I thought you should know that Haggel and the wizard Tasche have taken leave of the castle. They took only a small guard with them and left no word as to where or why they left."

"I can think of very few reasons why this might matter to me or anyone else, though I suppose it should, and there are those few."

"I wondered whether you wanted them followed?"

"Unnecessary," Kolhol replied, waving his wash cloth dismissively. "He has been his own man for some years now, and gone off on his own often enough. If it was an honorable mission he would brag about it, tell me at least, but he does not."

"That proves nothing."

"Perhaps. Be sure I am told the moment they return. While they are gone, I intend to interrogate some of my lords and squires, so as to know the lay of things with them. If Haggel and Tasche are up to something, there will be those in their camp who will run to ours once confronted."

"Do you worry that Haggel may be forging too many alliances?" Enrude asked.

"No," Kolhol said. "Though I will ask. Yet there is a greater question. Perhaps in spite of himself the boy is right in one thing: I do want to take Worlish. It must be done, sooner or later, but I do not want to send half my army to their deaths in the effort. So I have been waiting until I could field a force large enough, all of them well trained and able to do what they must, and for a sorcerer who I am sure will be Gentaff's match. Yet I may never find such a mage, and if I wait too long my army will grow overready and become a hazard to itself."

"As you say," Enrude replied.

No fool, that Enrude, Kolhol thought, not for the first time. "One other thing."

Enrude waited attentively.

"See if you can find that wench I spent the night with four days past. I fear she is in need of a bath as well."

Enrude kept his visage in order as he nodded, bowed, and swept back out of the room.

Tasche led the way as they crossed the border on horseback well to the east of the Lengree River. Under cover of darkness they entered the northernmost province of Worlish, part of the region known as Briarlea.

The four men Haggel had brought along were well-armed and loyal to their prince, and the sort that seldom asked any questions, which was something Haggel prized. He would have preferred to go alone—just he and Tasche—but a few good swords would be needed if all went as planned, and they could be handy to have about in any case. Haggel was eager to fight, but not the least bit eager to die like a fool.

As they walked the road beneath the overcast sky, barely able to see, Haggel grew anxious over the thoughts that kept running through his head. So many choices, chances and possibilities. But how could he choose a path without knowing where it might lead? He knew what he wanted, and he had every confidence in himself for when the time came, and that would be enough. But that still left him with nothing to do in the meantime except plod along on horseback while thinking about it all, until . . .

His horse stumbled in an unseen hole in the road. He feared it might go lame, but it began walking again without any apparent problem. "Are we there yet?" he asked, not for the first time. But it had been a while.

"No," Tasche said. "Must I repeat myself? It should be nearly sunrise when we meet him. Until then, I suggest we each keep quiet. The horses' hooves make more than enough noise without any help from us."

Yours in particular, Haggel thought. The rather presumptuous Tasche was mounted on one of the king's strongest horses, yet even that brute gelding seemed to be having a time of it carrying Tasche's ridiculous weight. The man practically spilled over either side of the poor animal, and his legs were twice as thick as the horse's. He thought to levy an insult or two, but restrained himself under the circumstances. He didn't want to get into a pissing contest with a sorcerer in the dark of an enemy's lands. Not that Haggel was afraid of who might overhear them, but again, why tempt fate? "How far off would you say sunrise is?" Haggel asked.

"Not far," Tasche said dryly.

The walking went on for what seemed a very long time. Haggel thought it might go faster if they could talk, but without any real exchange required; idle chatter, at least for now, was probably ill-advised. So instead he daydreamed, and mumbled to himself a little, until they rounded a bend in the road and Haggel saw a small fire burning a little more than a hundred paces away. No one was about, but just behind the fire stood the remains of a cottage—three walls and a mostly fallen in roof.

"There," Tasche said.

"It's still dark," Haggel muttered.

"It doesn't matter," Tasche said. "We have found him."

CHAPTER TEN

The fire went out, kicked over with dirt, leaving
Haggel and everyone else straining to see even vague
shapes in the dark.

"Rather a secretive one, aren't you?" Tasche said,
a distinct air of mockery in his tone.

"I am, that I am," the other replied, almost chuckling.

Already he sounded too arrogant for Haggel's tastes
and he didn't like the look of this. He could tell the
stranger—the informer—was not young and not a
brute, and apparently alone, yet despite being outnumbered six to one he didn't seem worried. Likely that
only made him a fool. But you never knew about these
kinds, these supposedly clever kinds. You never knew
what they might be thinking or plotting. Although, you
could always ask. . . .

"Why go to the trouble? What are you afraid of?"
the prince asked.

"It is for the best," the informer answered. "Best
for all, that I remain a stranger. As for being afraid,
I am afraid of the usual kinds of things, I suppose,
but what can be done?"

"How can we trust information from one who will not trust us with his identity?" Haggel countered. "And another thing—what makes you think we won't just take you prisoner until we learn who you are?" *Just the right question,* Haggel thought, smiling to himself at the informer's silent pause.

"If you do that, you will not get the information you want. But if you simply pay me, listen to what I tell you, and then we go about our business, both our needs will be met, and you will learn soon enough that what I tell you is the truth. For now, you can call me Friend; I am the closest thing to that you will find in this land."

"Very well, Friend, let us do our business," Tasche said, cutting Haggel off before he could respond again. Which he was just about to.

"You offer a great price," their Friend said. "What would you know in return?"

Haggel stood silent, sorting things out. He still didn't know how to take this one. But this might go on all night unless they moved on. "Tell him, Tasche," he said.

"I was about to," Tasche said sharply. "We are in need of an adept," Tasche continued. "Not a trickster, mind you, but one with a true born talent. But not one so powerful or so well guarded as to be unreachable, or uncontrollable. We are prepared for most anything, but I do not want this to be any more difficult than it has to be."

"And what would you do with this . . . adept?" the other asked.

"That is none of your concern," Tasche said.

"It is if you want me to hand you such a person. I must know what is to become of him. I need to know if this person you seek will come to harm. I trade throughout the land, and I do not like to lose customers, or their mages. Besides, gold spends much better on a clear conscience."

Now he was talking nonsense. Haggel drew his sword and stepped toward the informer, and the four soldiers with him quickly followed. He extended the tip of the blade until it hovered near his new Friend's chest. "If you want to live, you will tell."

"No," Tasche said, waving at Haggel. "He is right, if we kill him we may have the gods' own time finding another like him; it took long enough to come up with this one. I can persuade him without damaging him too badly, I think. And I believe he knows that."

"Indeed, I do, that I do," said the Friend. "But I am not being difficult, only sensible. You could do just the same, and answer my questions, while I answer yours."

"You're saying I am not being sensible?" Haggel huffed, pressing the blade even closer. He was not about to be put off by a knave who hides in the dark.

"I did not mean to."

"No," Tasche said, waving at Haggel again. "The mage will not be harmed. I need a mage to use as a channel, an instrument, in a very complex spell; it is one I have waited years to complete, and the future of all Grenarii may depend on its success. Grenarii, and Worlish. I have even gone to the trouble to prepare another spell that will allow this mage to sleep the entire time; once we have returned the mage to the place where we found him, he will awaken again in good health, and have no memory of what happened."

"Incredible," the Friend said.

"It is, I know," said Tasche.

"Then this mage need not be very . . . cooperative in nature?" the other asked.

"That does not matter," Tasche said.

Haggel didn't like the hesitation in the informant's voice. He stood back and leaned to Tasche's ear. "He's up to something," he whispered.

"So are we," Tasche replied.

"That's different," Haggel snorted. Then he felt Tasche lean closer and gently rest one hand on his shoulder. "Please, my prince, a moment."

Haggel decided the wizard was trying to get him to back off. Which still didn't seem like the best idea. He went along anyway, though he instructed his soldiers to stand where they were and keep a careful eye on the shadowy figure.

"It shall be, then," the shadowy figure said at last.

"Very well, your gold," Tasche said.

Haggel was in charge of that. He untied the leather bindings and pulled the bag from his waist, then held it out. The dark cloth was invisible in the night, but it was clear his hand was holding something. "I would count it out for you, but some fool has doused the fire," Haggel said.

"I understand," the Friend replied as he took the bag. He dug his hand inside, then withdrew, and set the bag in his lap. "There is a mage, an old woman who was powerful in her day, but that day has long since passed. Still I will warn you, she may prove a handful. Her name is Shassel. She is not easy to find, she moves about and is away often, but she has just returned from the Hubaran Forests a few days past, and can be found not far from here. If you do all as you say, we are both well served. But there is a catch. Or . . . several."

"What sort?" Haggel asked, his hand tightening on the hilt of his sword again.

"There is another mage with her, a substantial, most forbidding fellow named Frost. Quite powerful as I understand it. He has two warrior guards as well, a dangerous pair, the equal of a small army. She also lives with her great-nephews who have been known to try a trick or two as well, and the two of them, like Shassel, must not be harmed in any way. Can you promise that?"

"None of them will be," Tasche said. "Tell him, my prince."

"Yes, yes, yes," Haggel said, nodding in the dark.

"Even by herself, Shassel will be a challenge," the Friend said. "I suggest you try to win her to your cause, and enlist her help willingly. She has been known to favor many such as yourselves, though I would not attempt to lie to her."

"Are you saying we are lying to you?" Haggel protested.

"Yes, yes," Tasche said, waving at Haggel yet again. "We will do that. We will try. How do you suggest we go about it?"

"It will be best to wait until they are not all together, until Shassel is alone. You must bide your time. Then you can approach her openly, and tell her what you need. If she does not agree, use your sleeping spell, but be sure you do not—"

"Yes, yes," Tasche said. "We won't harm her."

"Tasche can see to Frost," Haggel said, growing tired of the conversation, thinking about other parts of it.

"I have heard of him," Tasche said. "You may be right."

Haggel thought Tasche was agreeing with *him* at first—then he realized the reply was meant for the informer. Which was troubling, since Tasche billed himself as one of the most able sorcerers in the known world, and since he had been insisting all along that he had everything well in hand. Not that Haggel believed such claims entirely, but he believed enough to have come this far. Any sign of doubt . . . "Does the presence of this Frost and the others concern you so much?" Haggel asked, probing.

"Not only them, I have also heard of Shassel. She will be perfect for our needs, but she was indeed powerful once, and may still pose a challenge. If we must contend with her and Frost at the same time we could cause ourselves undue hardship."

The informer chuckled quietly at this. Haggel frowned. "Is it at least possible that you could manage them both?"

"Yes, but why not choose battles that are easily won?"

Haggel thought about that, as he strained to see the wizard's face and failed. Tasche was old and well traveled enough to know quite a bit. It hadn't been easy, but Haggel had learned to at least listen to him now and then—just as he tried to listen to his father sometimes, though he often had poorer luck with that. "I see," he said. "I just don't want to spend too much time in this province."

"Of course not," Tasche replied. "Now, Friend, where can this Shassel be found?"

The weather held and good speed was made the next two days, though not a minute of it proved pleasant to Haggel. He felt sore and stiff from so much riding, though he was certain Tasche must be worse off, having twice as much weight to carry on a frame not much bigger than his own. But Haggel was determined, and he tried to make the best of things; in his youth Haggel's father had made greater journeys and—as was told him time and again— suffered far greater pains only to reap great triumphs. *It will all be worthwhile*, he kept telling himself. *It will all be glorious* . . .

They kept their horses off the road whenever others were coming, at least as much as that was possible, and made small talk about the spring weather and the remarkable health of bug popula- tions. Dressed in proper tunics and caps instead of armor and velvet, they could have been any minor lord and his squires. Haggel rather delighted in the role, though at every meeting along the way he had the greatest urge to tell both freemen and peas- ants alike that these lands would all be his one day. A day not far off. Then he would be their lord and king.

The only thing that bothered him was Tasche's silence; not that this alone was unwelcome, but it was unusual.

"We need to know exactly what we are going to do once we find this old adept," Haggel said, taking Tasche aside as they approached the region in eastern Briarlea where the small village they were seeking was supposed to lie, at least by Haggel's best estimate.

"We are going to wait for the right opportunity, I think."

"Yes, yes, and then what?"

"We will take her."

"Yes, but what if something goes wrong?"

"Now you are asking me to see the future."

"No, no," Haggel snarled, growing frustrated. "I want to be sure this Shassel will not turn us all into toads . . . or worse."

All four soldiers, who had been riding silent for the most part, began to mumble in unison at this. Tasche paused to glare at them. Haggel glared at Tasche. The assembly drew to a halt.

"I have prepared warding spells," the wizard said. "They should protect us. But they take good time and energy to construct, and they will only last a short while. So we must determine the best time and place to make our move. Then, once I enact the spells, you and your men must do all the rest. Grab her, bind her, and so on. I will be busy maintaining my spells and watching our flanks."

"From a safe distance, I'd guess," Haggel said bitterly.

"I will require as few distractions as possible, of course, but I will be right behind you," Tasche replied.

Haggel frowned and shook his head. Aside from

himself, Tasche was the only man he knew who could mix duty and apparent sacrifice with self-serving conceit so well. Though that was one of the few things Haggel actually liked about Tasche; it helped him see himself in a more justifiable light. Anyone could lead a charge, after all, but to stand aside while others charged valiantly to war and still be revered as the hero—that, to Haggel's mind, was an art worth perfecting. Though just now, Tasche had beaten him to it.

Before he could ruminate on the subject much further, another troop appeared on the road, all on horseback. Soldiers, perhaps, though they were still to distant to make out details. Regardless, the woods looked better than ever. Haggel ordered everyone to cover, hoping they had not yet been seen by the approaching riders.

"Keep the horses still, and behind the trees," Haggel ordered the soldiers.

"Shhh . . ." Tasche said, after everyone had done their best to comply.

The riders passed at ease. A well-dressed man led the way, a nobleman. Four men accompanied him, soldiers in Lord Andair's army, as was made clear by the style of their light armor and the royal coat of arms, plainly visible on the shields that flanked the horses behind their saddles. All five kept riding, and never cared to glance this way.

"I am eager for battle, but not here, not now," Haggel whispered, as he crouched behind a tree and watched.

"Oh, agreed," Tasche said from behind a neighboring tree. "We will choose the time and place."

The riders finally passed out of sight. Haggel waited just a bit longer, then he ordered everyone to follow him out again.

"If our Friend was right, the village lies just around this next bend, on the left," Tasche said as the horses walked. "Shassel's cottage will be set against the woods to the right of the clearing, beyond small rows of cabbage. That is the one we look for."

"I was about to tell them that," Haggel said.

"I waited," Tasche replied. "You said nothing."

"I guess I wasn't paying attention," Haggel said, then he let it drop. He'd been thinking about other things. There had been women working in the fields along the road earlier in the morning, several of them young and, for peasants, well, not altogether unpleasant to watch. . . . He wondered if he'd have better luck with the women of Briarlea, once he conquered it, than he'd been having at home.

As the village came into view Haggel found it was much to be expected, quite unremarkable, about two dozen huts surrounded by planted fields and pastures, a few cows about, too many sheep and lots of chickens scattered here and there. The hut that Haggel thought must be Shassel's was exactly where it should have been, and one of the larger structures in the area, though not much finer than a barbarian hut in the northern ends of Grenarii. People could be seen in the village, a few small children and fewer adults; most were out in the fields. No one stirred at the cottage by the trees.

Haggel had been ready for this. "We should ride on past, as if continuing; then, before it begins to get dark, we can make our way back and find a suitable place to wait, and watch all the goings on," he said.

"Before we get too close I must shield myself, or Frost and Shassel may sense that I am near."

"You can do that?"

"Of course," Tasche said.

Haggel saw that look on Tasche's face, the one that passed for intense concentration but somehow reminded him of a man suffering from extreme constipation. Haggel narrowed his gaze. "Are you sure?"

"Of course I am sure!"

He isn't sure, Haggel thought. But it was that way with all great wizards; Tasche had explained this long ago, when the topic had come up one evening. "Nothing is certain in magic," he'd said. Which made it rather like sword fighting, as far as Haggel was concerned. He had spent many nights practicing, making use of the finest swords in the land and his father's most reliable teachers, honing his skills until he was sure he'd become the best swordsman in all Grenarii.

Even so, when it had come time to spar with one of his father's warriors, the other had bested him completely. Devastating at first, but Haggel had since reasoned that no one could be that much better than he was, that luck and the prevailing will of the gods must play a crucial role in such things. In any case, he'd improved since then.

"Do what you must," Haggel told Tasche, then to his men, "Keep the horses close, just in case."

With the soldiers' acknowledgment they kept riding until the village was out of sight, then they turned and picked their way back into the trees, with Haggel leading the way and Tasche coming along behind.

"It may be possible to meet with Gentaff alone, and not Andair," Frost said, picking up the topic once more as he walked with Shassel along the road. She had been eager to say hello to people she hadn't seen in some weeks, old friends and neighbors, and had insisted Frost come along. He had little patience for that sort of thing, but could not refuse Shassel her wish. Almost everyone had been delighted to see her, but that came as no surprise to Frost. Now, with the day's light and their energy both starting to fade, they had decided to make their way back to Shassel's cottage.

"Possible, maybe, but unlikely," Shassel said. "Even

if Gentaff was a decent and reasonable man, and he is neither, he would have very little reason to go about meeting with you in secret. He has nothing to gain."

"If he knows the true-named Keeper of the Demon Blade, he might well want to see the Blade delivered into the proper hands as I do, even though Andair may not. A private meeting would separate the two and allow him to speak his mind, and to hear mine."

"All for nothing. You don't know him. Even if he bargains he will not bargain in good faith; it is something he and Andair utterly lack."

Frost believed her and stopped short of further debate; he hadn't even convinced himself. Had this been any other situation he might never have had this conversation at all, but it wasn't that simple. As long as the fate of the Demon Blade remained in his hands he could not act as he would, but rather as he must— no matter the personal cost, or how small the chance of a proper result. With a sigh he said, "I should give him the opportunity, even so. I feel I have little choice. Not if there is to be any chance at all that Gentaff might cooperate. Once I am rid of the Blade I can exact retribution on Andair, in full, but not until."

"Tell me, when you confront Andair, on whatever terms, will you kill him?" Shassel asked matter of factly.

"It is . . . possible."

"Then I must tell you something else. As appealing as that prospect is, even to me, there is a reason I have not been plotting to rid Worlish of him these past few years. One you should consider as well, before you act."

"Go on," Frost said, slowing his pace a bit.

"The military balance would be sorely affected. Kolhol, the Grenarii king, has had his eyes on Worlish since fighting in his own lands ended almost a decade ago. He has a large, well-trained and well-supplied army, one that could be successful, I think, under the right circumstance. If Andair and Gentaff were removed, then much of their army would effectively be removed as well; many are loyal to him, or to his wages. There would be confusion, at least, for a time, long enough to leave Briarlea open to an almost certain invasion from the north. The rest of Worlish would fall easily enough after that."

"Might this Grenarii king be persuaded not to act? A solid argument could be made, a messenger sent."

"He has a son with an eager sword as well, or so I am told and the Grenarii army is much too big to sit on its hands forever. No, I doubt Kolhol would be persuaded even by the great Frost and his Demon Blade."

She'd said this last half in jest, but the thought had crossed Frost's mind. "The Blade, perhaps," he said. "He has no doubt heard of it like everyone else. A cautious threat might be arranged, to at least buy time . . ."

Shassel looked at him. "But?"

"But I believe it would be ill-advised. If I am to go to Kolhol and threaten them with the Blade, I must be prepared to use it, and I am not. Thousands might die. I might die. Besides, we have no reason to believe the Grenarii know that the Demon Blade has surfaced, and I have no desire to tell them. Men and nations enough are looking for it already."

"So, there seems no easy solution," Shassel said.

"No, but I cannot simply do nothing. If I have to, I will find another way to see the Blade safely delivered into proper hands, then come back and see to Andair and the Grenarii in my own good time, by my own best means."

"I will help."

"I know," Frost said, and glanced up as a boy of about fifteen years came by at a trot, heading the same way they were, toward the village. He looked ruddy-faced and tired as if he'd been running a long way and looked like just the sort Frost was going to need if he was to do as he'd said—like it or not. "You, boy, hold!"

The boy stopped, chest heaving. Sweat soaked his brow and made his hair stick to the sides of his face and the back of his neck. His clothes were faded and frayed, but his eyes were bright enough. Frost asked, and the boy said his name was Muren, though he sounded uneasy. He seemed to recognize Shassel, but that apparently provided him little comfort, and Frost was clearly the reason.

"One of your neighbors?" Frost asked Shassel.

"Not everyone understands me as you do you," she said with a nod.

Frost nodded in kind. Shassel had helped the peasants countless times with sick children, beasts or crops, and her presence in the region had helped to keep the worst of Andair's troops and others less savory from taking greater advantage of them. But sorcery was something most folk feared, even in the best circumstances. Like the weather it could turn against you without warning, and there was no defending against it. They knew Shassel, they didn't know Frost.

Frost leaned toward the boy and held his gaze. "You have nothing to fear from us, boy. Only the king and his wizard need have those worries. Which is who I want you to see. I need a messenger to go to Weldhem, and I suspect you need a few good coins."

Muren's frown lasted another instant. Frost held out the coins, and the boy's enthusiasm blossomed.

"How can I serve you, my lord?" Jons asked. He'd worn a freshly laundered green and blue tunic, new taupe pants and his best boots—all tailored precisely to his liking—to his audience with Andair and Gentaff in the great hall, and he felt every bit as daring and colorful as his clothes. What the king thought of him was possibly more important than what the king paid him. Jons could see himself serving no one of lesser stature in the future.

"We have another mission for you," Andair said from across the center of the table. Only a chalice was set out on the table in front of him. He picked it up, sat back, and took a sip of its contents.

"Refresh my memory of your meeting with Frost," Gentaff said. He was seated as usual to Andair's left, an empty table before him. Jons recalled the earlier meeting for his lords, including something of the warning Frost had issued. He couldn't help forcing a thick gulp down his throat as he finished with the worse of it, and waited to learn whether his choice of words had earned him any censure.

"Ah, yes, Frost's warning," Gentaff said. Jons blinked as he noticed that now Gentaff was holding a wooden device in his hands, small blocks hooked together somehow. He moved them about methodically. "What was it he told you—precisely?"

Jons was anything but eager to repeat the exact words, but he saw little choice. "That it is by his grace that Andair lives, and that the Demon Blade will never be of use to either of you."

"And that I would be destroyed if I attempted to prove otherwise?" Gentaff added.

"Y—yes," Jons said, growing even more nervous. He didn't like being the bearer of bad news. Though, unfortunately, he was not quite done yet. "He said also, I believe, that no price could be set." At least that arrived on a slightly less personal note. He waited, trying to look as penitent as possible without looking pitiful as well, while Andair and Gentaff exchanged unreadable looks. Then Gentaff got up and made his way slowly to Andair's side, where he bent to the sovereign's ear and spoke too quietly for Jons to hear.

The king nodded several times, then muttered something in return. Then he focussed again on Jons.

"We had a visitor just this morning. A boy from an eastern village. Shassel's village, I believe, or thereabouts. He came to see Gentaff on Frost's behalf to arrange a meeting between the two of them. A private meeting, somewhere else, so that they could discuss the Demon Blade among themselves. Of course Gentaff came to me just afterward. We decided to send the boy back with a reply. But not alone. You and a small guard will go with him and see that our message is heard. We are inviting Frost to come here to Weldhem, and guaranteeing his safety, so that we might hear him out."

"He may not accept," Gentaff said.

Andair nodded. "It is unlikely he will."

"So we must force him to come here," Gentaff said. "We have worked out a plan."

"Which is why you will be followed by one of my captains and several of his best men," Andair said, while Gentaff turned again toward his own chair. "They will know what to do when the time comes, but I want you to be the one to give the order. You have a talent for following, observing and speaking with Frost, all without getting killed in the process. Not many can say as much."

"Not many," Gentaff added. Jons tried to swallow again. It wouldn't go down.

Andair leaned forward, a look of deepened concentration on his face, then he clenched a fist and thumped it heavily on the table. "Frost must come to us, but *we* must make the terms. Only then will he bargain . . . umm, correctly."

"And there is *always* a price," Gentaff said, looking at Jons but speaking more to Andair, as far as Jons could tell. "Just as there is always a cost. The trick is knowing what they are."

Both men nodded at the same time, and Jons felt something churn inside him—though it was a momentary discomfort at worst, probably explained by a lack of breakfast. He straightened, grinned, and bowed at the waist. They grinned back, first at him, then to one another. He had worked hard to gain Andair's notice and elevate himself to a position worthy of his own talents. *This is an opportunity for everyone*, he thought. For himself, this was only the beginning.

He tried to match the haughty grins on the others' faces; it would take practice, but he was more than willing. "What would you have me do?"

CHAPTER ELEVEN

Dorin tossed a ball of freshly wadded bread to Dara, whispering to it as it sailed free, and Dara caught a ripe, red apple an instant later.

"Good," Frost said. The trick was to fashion a piece of edible fruit, and not simply a lump of something that had changed color and consistency. "Take a bite," he told her. Dara examined the apple briefly, then bit into it. She nodded approval as she slurped and chewed.

Frost stepped forward, away from the shade of the cottage and the trees that stood tall behind it, and took the apple from Dara's hand. He held the loaf of bread out to her next. She dug into the bread with her fingers and came away with a fistful.

"Your turn," Frost said. She made the toss and spoke the phrases precisely as Frost had taught her, and Dorin caught an apple of his own. Without being told he took a bite. His glowing expression said the rest.

"Now, the other way, Dara first," Frost said, handing the bitten apple back to her.

She threw her apple at Dorin and watched it become a wad of bread once more. "Now, you try," Frost told Dorin. His apple spun through the air, bright red, turning pale brown as it went. Just as it reached Dara it turned red once more. She caught the apple's unexpected weight awkwardly.

"I don't understand," Dorin said, while Dara held the fruit up for their mutual examination.

They both turned at the sound of Frost's chuckle. "It was me," Frost said. "I changed it with a spell of my own, as I knew precisely the spell you had used. But even if I had not, I might have guessed at the spell closely enough and contradicted it all the same. Both of you need a true binding phrase, one that will make the spell your own and fixes it, so that it cannot be altered or undone. I have my own, as does Shassel. But it is not so simple as choosing a word or two. First, you must each find the phrase that is right for you. That will be a beginning. Over time you will strengthen it, layer upon layer, until no power on earth can violate its truthfulness. It will take years, but both of you can do it, and you must start now. I will help you."

"Why hasn't Shassel ever shown us this?" Dorin asked without charity. The same question appeared on Dara's face.

"There is much I never showed you," Shassel said from the cottage doorway. She stepped outside, still in shadow, but did not come further. "You were young and foolish, both of you, at least until something like a few days ago, I think. And since your father's death I have been afraid of what you might do if you thought you had true sorcerer's powers. You hardly knew anything when you ran off and tried to teach the King of all Worlish a lesson."

"That was different," Dorin said.

Shassel scowled at him. "Was it?"

She stopped short of blaming the twins for their

father's death, but the implication hung in the air between them. After a moment the silence began to make Frost uneasy.

"There is more to it than that," he said. "Part of the problem is that she is old, tired and cranky, and spends too much of her time alone in the forest, where only trees and birds stand to benefit from her wisdom—" Frost looked decidedly down his nose at her. "—or suffer from it."

Shassel had venom in her eyes as she focussed on Frost. "Yes, something like that," she muttered, and then she stuck out her tongue.

"Ah, yes, and she is rude as well," Frost said. "But we try not to notice."

"Or set a better example," Shassel replied.

"But we saw you use Shassel's binding phrase at her cabin in the forest," Dara said, moving past the banter.

"Yes," Frost said. He favored her with a smile. *She is keen enough*, he thought, *as is Dorin*. Which was making his attempts to teach them much more enjoyable than he might once have imagined. "Understand," he went on, "I have known her binding phrase for almost as long as my own, and while it does not suit me well, I can wield it if I must. As with anything, time and practice are the keys."

Dorin and Dara nodded, satisfied.

Good, Frost thought. *A good day*. Though this was only the start. The task of teaching these two to be capable, responsible mages within whatever limits they had been born to seemed completely enormous in Frost's mind, something that should have taken place one step at a time over a dozen years or more. But it had not, and neither of the twins had any reservations about telling him as much whenever it came up, which was often enough. He had a personal understanding of what it was like to lose your father and go begging to learn from others. That thought alone outweighed any bitterness they would show him.

"You are setting a different example there, Frost," Shassel said, pausing until she held his gaze once more.

He hated to ask. "How?"

"You say you are good at using what resources you can find, but you do not care whether you have any right to them." She made no attempt to hide her evil grin.

Frost grinned in kind. "You taught me well."

Shassel eyed him narrowly. "Perhaps I need to teach you another thing or two."

"I fear it would tax you unduly."

"How considerate."

"Someone is coming," Dara said.

Frost found her gesturing toward the road beyond the village. He recognized the boy who jogged toward them: Muren, the very one he'd sent to Weldhem to speak with Gentaff just a few days ago. The boy had made good time. Frost pulled at the bag slung from his shoulder and fished inside. His hand came out holding four copper coins, the rest of the boy's payment, as promised. He held the coins out as Muren fetched himself up in front of Frost and the others. Muren snatched the coins eagerly, then bent over and placed his hands on his knees while he tried to catch his breath.

"Take your time," Frost said. "Then tell me everything you can. Leave nothing out."

"I have returned with . . . another," Muren said, still gasping too much. "I did as you asked. I gave Gentaff your message. He sent me back with a young lord . . . and his guard. He is called Jons."

"And where are they?" Frost asked, glancing up the road but seeing no one.

"Waiting," Muren answered. "I, that is, he . . ."

"Very well." Frost placed one hand on Muren's

shoulder to calm him. "I believe I know this Jons. What did Gentaff tell you?"

"Nothing. Jons has his reply, and that of Andair, I think."

Shassel stepped closer now. "How many soldiers has this Jons brought with him?"

"Only four," Muren said. "He says . . . he wishes to meet with the sorcerer Frost, but only in open fields, where no traps can be set by either of you. He said he will wait for one full day. By dusk tomorrow he will return to Weldhem."

"Which field?" Frost asked.

"Near Greldon Manor, half a day's walk," Muren said, pointing back up the road, west, toward Weldhem.

"If we leave now we can be there before dark," Frost said. The boy nodded.

"Frost," Dorin said, turning quite serious. "Let him come to you. We owe Andair nothing, at least nothing good or fair, and we owe those who serve him even less. As for Gentaff—" He paused, then he cleared his throat mightily, leaned to one side, and spit on the ground.

"All true," Frost replied. "But this has little to do with things right or fair, or even what is owed. There is much more at stake."

"You should not go all the same," Shassel told Frost. "Such an offer is not to be trusted."

"If Gentaff is with them I will sense it, and face the challenge. If he is not, then Jons and his men are the only ones who need worry."

"If you insist on going, I am going with you," Shassel said.

"Jons asked about you, and said you would be welcome," Muren said. "He said some of what his lord and Gentaff wish him to say will be of great concern to you."

"Then you should *not* go," Frost said.

Shassel frowned at him. "Why not?"

"As you say, nothing that comes from Andair or Gentaff can be trusted. You should suspect his motives now more than ever."

"Oh, I see," Shassel huffed. "You are somehow special, and I am to be coddled. Poor old woman. Well, that may be true in part, but I am going."

"There is no need," Frost assured her. "My Subartans will be with me. They know this kind of situation well, and so do I."

"They will be with *us*," Shassel said, serious now.

"We are going too," Dara said, stepping nearer her great-aunt and great-uncle. Dorin wasted no time in moving to stand in solidarity with his sister.

"No!" Shassel commanded. "Not you two."

"Absolutely not," Frost agreed. "I will have more than enough to worry about."

The twins began immediately to protest. Shassel silenced them. "You both will stay, and wait, and leave this to Frost and myself, and that is the end of it," she said, with a fury Frost had not seen in ages, though the memory came clearly to him now. "You are being selfish," she added. "Frost is right, we should not divide our attentions between those we must face and those we must protect, no matter your will. More than that, *think*! If no one stays behind, then who will come after us if we do not return? If something goes wrong, what hope is there?"

Dorin and Dara considered her words with obvious weight for a moment, then they exchanged a brief and troubled look.

"Say whatever you both are thinking," Shassel insisted.

"Shassel," Dara said, biting at her lower lip.

"I'm listening."

"If you do not return, you and Frost and the Subartans, we fear there will be nothing we can do."

Shassel nodded. "Exactly true. I wondered whether you would say as much. But that changes nothing.

There is hope, and the lack of it. So long as you remain, there is hope."

The twins slowly nodded, and Frost felt a twinge of relief; beyond seeing the truth, they had each been sobered by the seriousness of things, instead of brushing it aside. There was hope indeed.

"You must swear by the Greater Gods that you will not follow," Shassel insisted. Solemnly, Dorin and Dara did just that.

"Good," Shassel said. "If we are finished chatting, we can be on our way." She turned to Frost. "Where are those two Subartans of yours?"

"Out hunting," he said. "But I can call them to return. I have a way."

"Another trick I taught you, as I recall," Shassel told Frost.

"Teach us that as well?" Dara asked.

Frost sighed. "Why must you insist on taking credit for every good piece of sorcery I command?"

"Do I?"

"Yes."

"Either one of you, teach us," Dorin insisted.

"We will, when we return," Shassel replied.

"And much more," Frost promised. "As you will see."

The twins agreed, somewhat crestfallen, and Frost followed Shassel inside.

Captain Trellish felt his knees crack as he knelt in the brush among the trees and peered into the distance toward the cottage. Sitting still like this, the bugs had been fierce; he'd already worn his arms slack swatting at them, waiting while the boy delivered his message. He much preferred a straight-ahead task—confronting a quarrelsome baron or two or even going on patrol along the Grenarii border—to all this sneaking about and hiding. Frost and the others were far enough away that Trellish found it hard to tell exactly who was who, and what was what, but he dared not get any closer. Dared not tip his hand and take a chance on failing his mission. Trellish didn't abide failure in himself or his men, but Andair bore it with even less grace.

Not that Trellish hoped for better. What monarch was not imperious? What pleasure was there to be had from being lord over other men, if lives did not hang on your word and whim? If men did not fear you? Andair had always been that way, flitting from one idea to another, one game to another while never growing fond of losing at any; and since the sorcerer Gentaff had come to Worlish, Andair had gotten worse. But in his place, Trellish would have been no different, that was sure. Regardless, he was master of soldiers, one of Andair's most favored captains, and that was close enough.

He slapped another insect, a bloody one he saw, as he pulled his palm away from his neck. As he watched the large fellow, the one he'd decided must be Frost, and two older youths who must certainly be Dorin and Dara, he saw them joined by an old woman. Muren, the messenger boy sent by Frost and since sent back with Jons, arrived just as they had planned, soon after that.

Trellish motioned to his men once more to stay quiet. He'd brought twenty soldiers in all, and keeping them still and out of sight these past two days had been no easy task. Now they grew restless, between the bugs and the first signs of progress since leaving home; he knew exactly how they felt.

He watched intently as the boy talked with Frost and the others. Soon they all disappeared inside the cottage. By the time they emerged once more they were joined by a pair of formidable looking warriors and a close discussion took place. Trellish found himself waiting again, watching, swatting. Finally most of the group took to the road, headed west, though two of them stayed behind. . . .

Trellish waited still longer to be sure which two, squinting to see, then nodding to himself as he concluded that they were the two younger ones, the twins Andair and Gentaff had sent him for.

When he was sure Frost and the others had journeyed far enough away so as not to be a threat, he breathed a double sigh. Things were happening, and going well. The old sorcerer Gentaff had worked his magic on Trellish and his men, some kind of spell intended to make them difficult to notice whether by magery or, somehow or other, simply seeing them on the road. It was not foolproof, more like lurking in shadows even when you were not, but the peasants they had encountered on the journey here had seemed quite confused, as though they weren't sure whom they were talking to, or where, or even about what.

Trellish didn't particularly trust sorcery; it was a strange, unfathomable thing that seemed often to do more harm than good, a thing more easily corrupted than a two-coin mercenary. But he was certain this odd bit of spell-working would prove more useful than most, especially if the twins were any sort of minor mages themselves—which, according to Andair, they apparently fancied themselves.

He motioned his men to him. "The two we want have gone back inside the cottage," he said, as they gathered closely about, careful not to batter one another or the many tree trunks with their swords and armor, so as not to clank. Trellish turned two men out of the ranks and stood them aside. "You two follow Frost and the others," he said. "If they turn back, you must get here ahead of them, so that we will be warned. When they meet with Jons, you are to stay close by. If the meeting goes badly, you will lend your swords, but only if you are needed."

The pair nodded and saluted their captain, right arm extended downwards, then back, and rushed off through the brush as quietly as possible.

"The rest of you will circle with me," Trellish went on. He pointed. "That way, until we are behind the cottage." *Now is as good a time as any,* he thought. They could not wait for dark, but most of the villagers were in the fields right now. If he and his men were quick they would not be noticed. If they were noticed . . . "You are to kill anyone who comes near."

Trellish received their silent nods, then he gave the word, and led the way.

The fields Jons had chosen were part of one of the largest fiefs in Briarlea. Rows of barley mixed with weeds and wildflowers stretched away over rolling hills to small, distant clumps of woods and greater tree lines. The villages that were home to those who tended the grain lay well beyond the hills to the south. Today, no one was about.

"The baron of this manor, Greldon, is devoted to Andair," Shassel said as they walked. "We might expect anything at all."

Frost made no reply other than to nod. The sun was lower in the sky now, making long pools of shadows on the eastern sides of the trees. Frost did not trouble himself with peering into them in search of movement; he left that task to his Subartans and concentrated instead on preparing a handful of minor spells that might prove useful, should anything go wrong. He expected something would, and so did Shassel. She hadn't said anything more on the subject since they had taken to the road, but Frost knew her mind, and that look in her eye, as she constantly assessed the way ahead.

"There," Rosivok said, pointing toward a field that became fully visible as the four of them topped a long, low rise. Only a few hundred paces ahead five figures stood along the side of the road near a stand of young pines. Their horses waited in the shade. All five began walking out onto the road as soon as they saw they had visitors.

"I sense nothing wrong," Frost said. "Yet."

"Nor do I," Shassel answered. "But that is not enough."

"I know." Frost started forward again, whispering to himself as he went. Shassel did the same beside him, helping him build a layered warding spell that would protect his Subartans against at least one assault, and perhaps another before it collapsed. For Rosivok and Sharryl this had often proved more than enough of an edge. Shassel finished her work just as Frost did—as they drew within earshot of the others. Quickly they each went about building one more warding spell, intended to protect one another. Shassel's wardings were thinner and more frail than Frost's, much as she was, but probably sufficient all the same. Frost went forward with confidence enough.

"Jons, isn't it?" Frost asked, coming to rest some twenty paces from the others. All four soldiers were well armored considering how far they had traveled. Each had their crossbows held at the ready. Jons himself carried only a sword, and that still in its hilt.

"Yes," Jons said. "You are Frost."

"And this is Shassel," Frost said with a nod in her direction.

"Good to meet you at last," Jons told her.

"No, it is not," she replied. "It is a troublesome thing at best, and likely a waste of everyone's time."

Jons smiled haughtily. "No need to raise your hackles, old woman," he said. "I come directly from the throne in Weldhem, and I have good news. You should be glad I am here."

"That will depend on the news," Shassel replied.

Frost planted his walking stick in front of him with a thud. "Which you will be kind enough to render," he said. "At once. But heed this warning: do not let your tongue get ahead of your backside while speaking to Shassel again."

"Is she so in need of a protector?" Jons asked, grinning and glancing back at his soldiers.

"I am not trying to protect her," Frost said. "I am trying to protect you."

Jons studied his opponents a moment. *Weighing as much as he can comprehend*, Frost thought. In fact it was more of an effort than Frost would have given him credit for.

"Very well," Jons said, pressing on. "You sent your messenger to Gentaff to ask for a meeting of some kind. Andair has sent me on his and Gentaff's behalf. They act as one, and want first that you understand that much. Next, they remain interested in the Demon Blade and are willing to hear any reasonable offer. Perhaps even an unreasonable one, depending on the circumstances. They also have many questions for you, I think. Not enough is known about the Blade . . . apparently."

Jons had added this last on his own, but he'd gotten the idea somewhere, Frost was sure of that.

"Go on," Frost said.

"Andair says he bears you no ill will, Frost, you or Shassel. If you come with me to Weldhem it will be under Andair's full protection, and only to talk."

"A day in the castle," Frost said loftily.

"Exactly," Jons said.

"I will not go," Frost said, losing his smile abruptly. "As my messenger no doubt told your king, I will meet with Gentaff, and Gentaff alone, and only as we are meeting now, somewhere in the open—here, or further west if he likes. A place where no traps can be set and no tricks can be played."

"I was told you would say as much, and told how to answer thus: They do not trust you. The king will not risk such a meeting. He doesn't know your mind

these days, or Shassel's. No, you must go to them.
And I must take you."

"Still the same self-serving coward he always was,
eh?" Frost said, and heard Shassel snort her approval
from just behind him.

Jons seemed displeased.

"Ah, you are actually fond of him?" Frost asked.

"So it would seem," Shassel said, scowling at Jons.
"Fortunately, I had a low opinion of you in the first
place."

Jons boiled a little hotter. "I will have your answer,
and your regard!" he snapped, grasping the hilt of
his sword tightly enough to turn his knuckles white—
though he did not draw the weapon. The soldiers with
him held their places as well, each with a firm two-
handed grip on their crossbows. Nervousness showed
in their eyes, the kind Frost had seen often, and taken
advantage of nearly as much.

Sharryl and Rosivok remained where they had
positioned themselves, just forward and to either side
of Frost and Shassel, their subartas held ready, their
eyes and senses utterly keen.

"You have my answer," said Frost. "I will not set
foot inside Weldhem, so you may as well run along.
Go back and tell your lord and that old and wretched
sorcerer of his that you have returned as you left—
empty-handed as well as empty-headed."

"But be sure you remember to tell him of Frost's
offer," Shassel said, "to meet as we are now. It is the
only way."

"You are the fools here," Jons snarled, clearly
wounded by the words pelting him.

"And just how would you know?" Shassel asked.

Jons looked about to explode. "Listen, old
woman . . ."

"Go, or regret what happens!" Frost said, fixing
Jons with a hard glare. "Enough is enough. Go before
your pride is not the only thing wounded."

Jons drew his sword at this, which prompted the guard nearest him to loose an arrow from his crossbow. Too quickly to follow, Rosivok's subarta flashed in the late day sunlight, deflecting the arrow before it could do harm. He'd read the soldiers correctly—and so had Sharryl, who leaned away from the shot to give Rosivok the room he needed. Then she bobbed forward. She stood directly between both groups now, subarta raised, legs spread apart, eyes locked on Jons'. Waiting for him to stir while Rosivok watched the others.

No one moved.

"We will go," Jons muttered, turning slowly only halfway around as he began backing away toward the horses. "No one was supposed to die here today, and we have our mission to complete. I have said all there was." He kept backing up and his men slowly followed, one eye over their shoulders as they put distance between themselves and Frost.

"I thought they'd never leave," Shassel said, watching the others reach the trees.

Frost looked to her and found her grinning. She'd enjoyed this, and quite a bit, judging from the naughty little-girl look on her beautiful old face. Frost smiled back. "It is time we did the same," he said, and they turned to head toward home.

He hadn't accomplished very much; in fact he'd succeeded primarily in learning that Shassel had been right about Andair and Gentaff all along. But that was something in itself; he knew where he stood. So he knew better how he must proceed.

The walk back was a slow and silent one, leaving Frost with a good deal of time to think. It wasn't until they were nearly there and walking in darkness that Frost suddenly began to wonder at Jons' last words, and to worry that the fears spreading through his mind might be all too real.

"Again, we are followed," Rosivok said evenly, and kept walking steadily, calmly.

"I have seen them, too," Sharryl said.

"How many?" Frost asked, hearing the harshness in his voice only after he'd spoken. It wasn't Rosivok or Sharryl; he was annoyed that anyone could be so coarse as to trouble him while he already had so much to concentrate on, so many grim possibilities to consider.

"Not many, one or two," Rosivok replied.

"I will circle," Sharryl offered.

She would kill them, whoever they were, and catch up in a little while. Frost did not want even that distraction just now. "No," he said. "Keep notice of them and let me know if they draw near. I may need them." Both Subartans nodded, and continued walking.

"What's wrong?" Shassel asked him, and he knew she sensed his mood completely.

"I'll say nothing yet, but we should walk more quickly, I think."

He saw her eyes. She'd guessed it, too, just then, but did not say more. The pace picked up considerably. It was dark when they arrived back at the village; Frost had considered going on ahead or sending one of his Subartans, but he was going on nothing more than a hunch, and he didn't want to worry Shassel if there wasn't a need, or add vulnerability by splitting everyone up.

As they approached Shassel's cottage, Frost could sense something wrong—not a function of magic or anything he could see—just a feeling, a hunch. The glow of light from within the cottage was always visible against the woods surrounding it, but this night the window that faced the road was dark.

"Go," Frost said, sending Rosivok at a jog into the village to collect torches while he waited, silent, with the others. Her hand reached out and gripped his wrist, and she held it tightly until the Subartan rejoined them holding one lit torch in each hand; Frost took one and handed the other to Shassel.

"It is too quiet," Shassel said thinly, haltingly. "I know," Frost said, and started forward.

"The door is open," Rosivok said as they neared. He stood peering into the darkness past the fluttering light of the torches. Sharryl joined him and they flanked the doorway.

Shassel started after them. Frost quickly leaned one arm in front of her. "Wait," he said. "Let them."

She nodded, and remained with Frost.

Cool moonlight blended with the light from the torches, highlighting the heads and shoulders of the two Subartans and reflecting off the polished flat metal of their half-raised subartas. With no detectable word or glance between them, they suddenly rushed into the dark interior, one after the other. A silent moment later Sharryl poked her head back out. "Come, look," she said.

Shassel went rushing past her. Frost found Rosivok lighting the oil lamp as he looked in. The room was a mess. Stew had spilled from the kettle, which lay on the floor near the darkened hearth. One leg of the table had been broken off leaving the table down on its corner. Two of the chairs lay splintered nearby. The chest where Dorin had kept his sword was open, empty. As for the twins themselves there was no sign.

"Frost," Rosivok said, kneeling near one of the beds. As Frost came to his side he held the torch low, illuminating the floor. Frost dabbed his finger in the pool of dark liquid there. He knew it was blood even before he raised the finger to his nose and took a whiff.

"I know of no way to tell whose blood it is," Shassel said, and Frost realized she was standing over his shoulder.

"I knew a mage of limited wits once, an enormous woman whose girth nearly prevented her from walking, but she had a spell useful on such occasions. A number of dyes were involved, as I recall, with the result that a sample of blood could be matched to its owner, provided one had a known sample to match it with. She also claimed ingesting the dyes and blood brought her visions."

"I am fresh out of twins' blood," Shassel grumbled. "And appetite."

Frost nodded, then he stood and turned to Sharryl. "What of the ones that have been following us?" he asked.

"They are there no longer," Sharryl replied.

"Soldiers," Rosivok said. "I saw a glimpse of armor as the sun was setting."

Keeping an eye on me, Frost thought. But why? And whose soldiers were they? Andair's, probably, but if not his then whose? The answer would wait. Or it was already here, somewhere.

"Sharryl, go into the village and ask anyone you find if they saw anything, if they know anything," he said. "Rosivok, take a torch and search the woods and rows for any sort of sign. Shassel and I have work to do here, until you both return."

The two Subartans nodded and disappeared out the door. Frost gathered two of the remaining chairs and got Shassel to sit on one of them while he settled on the other.

"We will call to them," he said. He took her hands in his and they began to chant, slowly, melodically, sharing their strength, building a spell that grew ever larger with each repetition. They used both their binding phrases, but nothing came of the effort. Such spells were limited no matter what—by time, by distance, by the condition of those being sought. Wherever the twins had gone, they would not be found by mind and magic alone.

"Frost."

Rosivok stood once more inside the doorway. "Come with me," he said. "I have found something."

They cleared their heads and followed. Rosivok led them around back of the cottage and into the woods, not very far, going just slowly enough to keep the torches from flickering out. Even in the dark it was clear that some of the underbrush and saplings had been recently trampled. The trail weaved its way through the trees until, just over a hundred paces out, Rosivok stopped and held the torch at arm's length. A body lay facedown on the ground in front of him, a soldier, one of Andair's "tailwaggers," Frost saw. Blood covered his left hand and forearm, which stuck out and back at an awkward angle. More blood had pooled beside the body on the mat of dead leaves and moss that covered the ground.

"Dead a while," Rosivok said.

"Unfortunate," Frost said.

"Yes," Shassel agreed. "He might have told us something."

"The other one," Rosivok said, stepping over the man's body and waving his torch at a thicket of berry bushes just a few paces further ahead, "the one that crawled in there, is still alive."

Frost could see him now, a shape too dense to be part of the bushes. The figure was hunched low to the ground, and wasn't moving.

"I will get him," Rosivok said. "He bleeds from the head and arms. He can go no further."

Frost nodded as a rustle from behind told Frost that Sharryl had joined them. She helped Rosivok fetch the dying soldier. They left a trail of blood as they pulled the man near and laid him out on the ground beside his fallen comrade. Even now blood ran down his nose, cheeks and neck, and soaked into his clothing. The damage was extensive. His flesh had been peeled away in bits and chunks from his head, his arms, anywhere his armor did not cover. The look on his young, ravaged face was one of horror and shock, and it only worsened when he saw the other soldier.

"We cannot save you, you are dead already," Frost

said. "But you can help us. If you do, I will ease your pain. And you have your place in the afterlife to think of. Tell us what has happened here."

The man stuttered, then gurgled, then swallowed as if he'd had something enormous in his throat; none of which seemed to help. Frost closed his eyes and touched the soldier with his fingers, then he spoke over him, choosing the words that would give him the precise control he needed over his own body, and the others'. He felt energy being drawn from himself, being metabolized, drained—enough to make the magic work, though such spells as this required more than most. He could not heal the soldier, there was no power known that could do that, but as the man's pain began to ease he could see the terror draining from his face. After a moment Frost withdrew, and asked his questions again.

"Ravens," the man said, closing his eyes. "So many . . . so many of them."

"Birds is what did this to you?" Shassel asked, perking up just a bit.

The man nodded. Then he glanced at his comrade's butchered stomach. "That is from the boy's sword. We should have killed him, but—but we could not."

It wasn't anger but regret that fueled these last words, Frost saw, watching the soldier's eyes. Orders, he guessed.

"I taught them that," Shassel said. "Dorin and Dara are both good with creatures, especially certain ones. The ravens of course, dogs as well, and there's the hawk that frequents the cottonwood tree in front of the cottage. I don't know what else, but they have been practicing."

She went suddenly silent and stood staring at her feet. Thinking about the twins, certainly, just as Frost was. Though she had known them all their lives . . .

"Dorin's sword arm is not to be overlooked either, it seems," Rosivok noted.

To which Frost nodded. Then he turned his attentions back to the soldier. "What have you done with them?"

This, the soldier would not say, but now Shassel came forward and knelt with him, and spoke to him. She began to tell him about Dara and Dorin, what they were like, how hard it had been for them, growing up without their father, and how much they meant to her; then how the Greater Gods, she was certain, were as fond of them as she, and would likely show true kindness to anyone who helped right the awful wrong that was the taking of them. While she spoke he began fading in and out now, not enough blood left in him.

Frost had nearly given up when the soldier drew a haggard breath and said, "Andair."

"What of him?" Frost asked.

"Andair and Gentaff want . . . them . . . for barter."

"Barter for what?" Frost asked, though he already knew.

With his dying breath the soldier said, "The Demon Blade."

CHAPTER TWELVE

"I'm going with you this time as well," Shassel said, fists balled and firmly planted on her hips. "I must."

Frost had seldom seen her so determined, or so concerned. He understood. Dara and Dorin must be rescued, and quickly. Shassel felt she needed to be part of that. "You should not chide yourself for leaving them here alone," Frost said. "It was the sensible thing to do, all things considered. They are more than old enough, even for uncertain times. They have been for years."

"Yes, of course, I know," Shassel muttered, shaking her head in frustration, then muttering something else that escaped Frost's ears. Apparently his assurances had fallen short.

"Taking too many chances will help no one," Frost pressed on. "If you were to take ill or become injured or worse in the course of things, how would Dara and Dorin feel then? And just as we told the twins, who will come after me if you come along with me?"

"I will not just sit here while you go off alone. I would worry about you as much as them."

"No, you would not," replied Frost. "I have no wish to argue the point with you. The journey is long, the danger is great, the means to our end uncertain. I will have to make something up as I go, or change my plans at an instant's notice, perhaps invent a surprise for the Greater Gods themselves. It will be difficult enough without taking you into account. You would be a great help, but I care too much about you. I cannot let you jeopardize yourself—and through my heart, myself along with you. I will get the twins back, you will remain here. If I need you, you will know, and then it will be up to you."

"I'm still going," Shassel said again as firmly as before, though perhaps not as enthusiastically. She was getting too old for this sort of thing; she knew that better than anyone, Frost believed. They had done a fair amount of traveling these past few days as it was, and that had taken a toll on her. If she went now, like this, she would be too weak to be of any real help against the likes of Gentaff or Andair's army.

Shassel shook her head. "I still think our greatest strength lies in combining our talents."

"Perhaps, but I cannot allow it, and neither can you," Frost said.

"We will protect Frost," Sharryl said, stepping into the argument. "But without a third Subartan it is at best a difficult job. Do not hold us responsible for your safety as well."

"She is right," Rosivok said. "You should not ask any of us to enter so difficult a battle with such a burden."

Shassel looked visibly wounded, though she tried to hide it under a glare she levied on both Subartans. "Who are you to call me a burden?"

"They are my Subartans," Frost said, "and they are right, as you well know."

Frost could tell her mind was not in the fight any more, only her heart; she knew what Frost and his

Subartans were saying, but Frost could not imagine a day when he would be willing to admit such a thing to himself, that he was not the menace he once had been—let alone admitting it to others, and especially when the fate of family was involved.

"I know of other reasons," Frost said. "Dara and Dorin will need someone to come home to, if I fail to return. And even if I do."

"You will not fail," Shassel said, looking down for an instant, then finding him with her eyes again. "But if you do, *I* will not fail . . . in your place."

"Find Lurey, tell him to stay close; pay him if you must. I will give you the gold," Frost told her. "Before I go we will form a link, you and I. If I need you, Lurey can bring you to me."

Shassel seemed reluctant to accept even this, but Frost saw the look of weary capitulation in her eyes. He would talk to her some more, but nothing would change. Then, the Greater Gods willing, they would eat, and finally they might sleep a bit. Sometime just before dawn, they did.

In the morning, before he left, Frost went searching in the forest. He emerged carrying a very young oak sapling, pulled from the earth roots and all. He brought it into the cottage where he sat with a knife and peeled away one very long, thin strip of soft, green bark. He wrapped one end around his right thumb, then let Shassel wrap the other around hers, and together they spoke the chant. The young bark turned brown as the chant was repeated. When the two mages whispered their binding phrases, a curl of smoke rose from the middle of the strip between them, and it came apart. Each of them finished wrapping their piece around the thumb.

"Just so," Frost said as he looked at Shassel with satisfaction. Almost no energy was required, nothing else was needed, and the spell would not have to be renewed unless the bark was somehow removed. Yet nothing else would have been more effective: If anything untoward were to happen to either of them, the bark on the other's thumb would smolder, perhaps even catch fire, something that seldom escaped one's notice. Shassel let a small sigh escape.

She still hadn't given him her blessings. He looked to her now in hopes she would.

"There is much you will need to know," she said, putting her hand on top of his. "I have spent a good deal of time in Weldhem. I will tell you what I can before you go."

The Castle of Weldhem at Briarlea was well designed to thwart any head-on assault. Built by one king and finished by another nearly a century ago, it seemed both sovereigns had gone to lengths to indulge a healthy dose of paranoia. Frost stood on the road less than half a day's walk from the city's main gates and gazed into the distance, watching storm clouds gather and feeling the first moist breezes of a change in the weather tug at his hair and cloak.

From here he was just able to make out the city and the small mountain of stone that stood at its western edge: the castle, wedged into the top of the spacious valley's only true hill. Behind the castle the hillside fell away in a steep cliff to the river below. Elsewhere the city, now grown well beyond its original walls, spread out on all sides.

Frost remembered much of the city and the castle, but not the sorts of details he'd needed to know. Shassel had helped with this; though her knowledge was several years old, little changed in such places. Nevertheless, nothing in their conversation had emerged as good news. The only way in was through the main gates of the city, then through the central streets and squares and straight to the castle gates themselves. Once inside the outer courtyard, the odds only got worse.

What Frost needed was a good plan, yet as of this moment he had none. He would keep his favorite spells at hand of course, and the layered warding spells he and Shassel had constructed around him and his Subartans before he left. But taking on an army and a sorcerer in their own castle required . . .

Well, much more.

He felt the weight and breadth of the Demon Blade where it rested on his back, wrapped and held snugly in place by the harness, then the cloak that covered it. Such thoughts had walked with him at every step this morning, but each time he had tried refusing them, as he did now. The sensible thing would have been to leave the Blade somewhere safe, to hide it or give it to someone else to hold while he went to Weldhem, but the Blade's aura was too easily detected by creatures and folk with even the slightest magical nature, and there was no telling how many eyes watched him lately.

It could not be hidden for very long, he thought, and he would not have wished even the most temporary possession of the Blade on anyone. Especially Shassel.

No, it had to stay with him, though he had taken steps to disguise the weapon, a small bit of cleverness he hoped Gentaff was exactly smart enough to believe.

"We may be able to find support in some of the villages," Rosivok said. "A small army could be gathered."

"And if they die so that my kin might live, then what have I done? Farmers against soldiers is bad at best. I cannot ask them, not yet, the odds would be too great against them. Though there may come a time."

"We will wait for dark?" Sharryl asked, eyeing the morning skies as Frost had.

"No," Frost said. "It will do us no good. My first hope is to negotiate. Failing that, we will use whatever comes next to our advantage, as we so often must."

Both Subartans nodded. The three of them would be hidden from the eyes of most as they entered the city and crossed into the castle itself, but Gentaff would surely be aware of them, and able to use resources of his own to allow his men to see as well. After that he needed something grand and unexpected, at the very least.

Crumbling walls and towers made a fine diversion, but the energy and concentration required for such a feat were too great, and Weldhem's stone and mortar walls too sound. Illusions of fire and smoke were best, but with the weather building dark and the winds gusting and damp from the west, he thought he might not be able to rely on any of that.

Which left him to face Gentaff sorcerer against sorcerer, sword against sword in the castle's outer courtyard, if they got even that far. And on Andair and Gentaff's terms. All quite hopeless of course. Frost started out along the road again, muttering to himself.

"Something else?" Sharryl asked, prodding him.

"I'll let you know," Frost muttered.

He didn't say any more until they were nearing the outskirts of the city, where he paused to activate the spell that would help keep them from being too closely watched. True invisibility was much too difficult and taxing a thing to attempt even for the best reasons, but a certain vagueness could be easily won, a muddling of perceptions that left most passers-by completely uninterested. An old and common trick, as many of the best ones were.

When he had finished, he collected himself and they walked into Weldhem, through the outer streets, through the main gates and past narrow streets lined with foul gutters and an assortment of two- and three-story houses; past inns, bakeries, tanners, blacksmiths' shops; past guild halls and small, noisy squares filled with merchants' booths and the heavy aroma of fish and pigs and spices. The aromas were what seemed most familiar: tannic acid from the tanners, breads baking, and a blend of hot metal and horse manure as he passed a small stable. He had smelled these scents before but somehow this seemed different, this was home.

The city filled his mind, more familiar than he might have thought, though less comforting, at least just now. As they passed an inn with tables under a roof out front he paused to sit, then ordered food and ale for all three of them. A good meal and something to wash it down certainly would not hurt, and might even make a difference.

"The soldiers do not notice us," Rosivok said, apparently pleased. "Or they do not want to."

"So few soldiers," Sharryl said.

"Too few, I think," Frost agreed. "So as not to scare us off." He looked up at the castle, so close now, so massive and imposing on its hilly perch, its high walls, towers and parapets reaching skyward. . . .

The sky itself had grown even more menacing, he noticed, as he felt the wind gust even here on this narrow, sheltered street; it stole the smell of the stew as an old woman put steaming bowls before them. He worried they might not have time to eat and still reach the castle before it stormed.

"The rain will be our ally," Rosivok said, following Frost's gaze.

"Perhaps," Frost replied. Rosivok was speaking only as a warrior, one that had trained and fought in every kind of weather. Andair's troops were not likely to have that advantage, small though it would be against such numbers. But from a sorcerer's point of view the storm would be an obstacle all the way around. Which favored Frost on the face of it, but Andair was sure to have surprises in store, and bad weather would likely only mask . . .

"What is it?" Sharryl asked.

Frost realized he'd been staring at the sky, entranced, watching the black, towering anvil clouds building toward the heavens. *A violent storm, surely*, he thought, *and close*.

"Nothing," Frost finally answered. "Or . . . something. It is hard to say." He looked about but didn't see what he wanted, so he got up and went inside. Momentarily he emerged with a long, cylindrical clay bottle in hand. He paused, eyes closed, reciting a careful phrase, then he raised the bottle to his lips and gently breathed into it. A cork fitted into the opening. Frost secured the bottle to the front of his cloak with a leather thong and left it there, in very plain sight.

"But it has the *feel* of something," Sharryl said, coy for a Subartan.

Frost nodded. "Possibly," he said. Then, "Come."

But just after he'd started toward the castle again, he ducked into a smithy's shop. The man at the forge was young and strong, and eager for the coins Frost had to offer. In only a few minutes Frost emerged again, this time carrying a straight iron bar about a man's foot in length, with a four-sided point on one end. This he put in one of the two long pockets sewn on the front of the cloak.

Just ahead, the outer walls of the castle stood waiting for them. The entire length was protected on this side by a moat. Spring fed, Frost recalled, though the water looked dark and turgid now.

The bridge across the moat was wide enough so two wagons could safely pass on their way in or out of the main courtyard. Today, none did. In fact there was no one at all, riding or afoot, coming or going. Frost kept walking past the massive metal-faced gates and through the archway, until he emerged to face a squarish, medium-height wall designed to force traffic to the right or left. Frost chose the former.

Positioned along the top of the wall he counted a dozen archers, all standing at ease. They watched Frost and his Subartans as one watches passing livestock. Frost knew his spell was a good one, but not that good. Andair and Gentaff, whatever they were up to, had no intention of stopping him yet.

Beyond the wall he found the main courtyard in much the same condition as he remembered it. A large livery area for stabling horses occupied the right side, along with the castle blacksmith's forge and a storage area for goods to be unloaded before they were inspected and moved elsewhere into the castle. On the far-facing end of the courtyard two ramps set wide apart led up to a broad marbled terrace and, at either end, two of the keep's main entrances.

The larger set of doors on the right side was designed for goods and processions, while the smaller, left-hand door led to the living areas of the king, his servants and their families. Both were guarded by four soldiers each, and there was no easy way to get to them uninvited. Each of the ramps had been built to incorporate a pair of zigzags, where intermediate landings had been located. More stairs led to a parapet that rose above the terrace. One lone, large figure stood atop it. Frost knew it was Gentaff.

"More that way," Frost whispered to his Subartans, and they all trailed further right, past the stables. Dust clouded around them, stirred up from the wide strips of dirt that lay between the flat stone that covered parts of the yard. Soldiers began appearing now along the terrace and parapet and the battlements that surrounded the courtyard.

Frost made certain he did not slow or hesitate in any way, so as not to appear too cautious—a sign, however subtle, of weakness or worry. As they passed a pile of freshly raked dung and straw, he waved his hand in front of his wrinkled nose and spoke as if commenting to his Subartans on the odor.

Once they'd cleared the buildings he wandered nearer the courtyard's center. He stopped when a horn sounded from somewhere high above in the castle's keep.

Only Rosivok turned to look as a commotion arose behind them. When he kept watching Frost turned as well. Doors set into the walls on either side of the main gates stood open now. Men poured out of them, more than a hundred, filling the yard behind Frost.

"I recall no storerooms beneath the walls in my time here," he said. "Andair must have added them."

"A useful enhancement," Rosivok said, nodding approval.

"Indeed," Frost said. Then he turned his attentions forward once more and found a growing troop of soldiers gathering in close order at the base of the wall, three dozen or more. Above, Gentaff stood precisely where he had been, unmoving, waiting on the parapet in a voluminous lavender robe, hood back, grayed hair and short graying beard showing. From here Frost could just make out some of the intricate carvings on the staff held in the sorcerer's right hand, could see the lines of age on his seasoned face, and almost, the look in his eyes—though this was felt more than seen.

Behind the keep the skies had grown even darker. A visible line that hung like a black curtain across the heavens marked the leading edge, and was nearly over the river now. Lightning flickered and arched at a furious pace across the length of the storm front, followed by growing rumblings of thunder that echoed through the heavy air in the valley and shook the ground beneath Frost's feet. Thick gray mist hid the distant hills along the valley's western horizon, and had begun to creep downward.

Frost closed his eyes briefly, gathering strength, then he opened them again, raised his own staff and spoke to the heart of the storm, completing the warding spell he had been charting. A spell similar to most wardings, but changed, adapted so that it could be projected away rather than near, as he had seen Imadis do to protect his men during their battle in the mountain pass.

As he focussed on Gentaff again, it was clear the sorcerer's interest had peaked. Frost stared up at the other, waiting for his reaction. This would tell him something about the man he faced. To his credit, Gentaff seemed to treat the incident correctly, and did nothing.

"Worried about getting wet?" Gentaff called out, his voice carrying clearly in the stillness that had suddenly grown to envelope them all, as if time had stopped. Even the soldiers kept still, or nearly so.

"Yes, I am!" Frost shouted, his voice echoing back to him from the courtyard walls.

"Perhaps I have underestimated you," Gentaff returned. "Here you are, come to me preceded by tales as tall as mountains, a legend of a man, too much to believe. Yet you do not hesitate to spend your time, your thoughts, your strengths, merely to hold off the rain. Were I you, I would not be so wasteful."

"Why would I need to conserve such things? I have come only to talk."

Gentaff let the notion stand between them for a moment. Then, "What have you to say?"

"I have much to say, but would speak with your Lord Andair as well, and I would have back the two young ones you have taken, Dorin and Dara."

"The king has decided to await word of our meeting in the privacy of his chambers. As for the others, they are right here."

"Where?"

Gentaff waved his staff about. Frost watched as two pallets were carried into view by four men each, then laid on the stone and propped at an angle, front down, back up. Dorin and Dara lay on their backs on the pallets, hands and feet tied with ropes. They did not appear to be conscious.

"Are they harmed?"

"No. They needed rest."

"I would test this myself."

"As you wish," Gentaff replied, bowing only slightly. "But do so from where you are. It should be a simple thing for one of your talents."

Frost returned the bow, then cast a gesture at the twins. He paused, as if listening to some inner voice, then made an effort to grow visibly frustrated and nervous. He tried the gesture again, then once more.

"Do you need any help?" Gentaff asked, clearly amused.

Frost shook his head and fought back a grin. He glanced at his Subartans only briefly, then he turned back to Gentaff. "They—they do appear to be alive, save whatever spell you have chosen to make them sleep."

"It will wear off."

Frost came ahead a bit further, until he stood some forty paces from the wall and the soldiers in front of it. The larger contingent of men behind him advanced along with them, though they kept a fair distance. Instructed to do so, certainly. Their purpose was to cut off any attempt at escape, and to discourage such ideas to begin with.

"You want these two back, and you may have them. They were detained for questioning after rumors of their intentions to harm the king were circulated. These rumors may have been false, as I believe. If so, they will be released . . . eventually. But the whole process, and Andair's good will, might benefit greatly from a gesture of good will on your part. I understand you have something I want, and which Andair is willing to compensate you for, quite apart from the release of your kin."

"The Demon Blade."

"Yes."

"Compensate how?"

"Something reasonable."

"It is worth far more than two children."

"Agreed, but while I do not see what that has to do with anything, Andair, for sentimental reasons so far as I can fathom, is offering you gold as well, and a generous portion of land in the far western provinces. All in return for the Blade and your promise to go, willingly, and not return."

"A reasonable offer."

"Andair is a reasonable king, and the Blade will be in good hands, Frost."

"Andair is a thief and a coward, much like those he associates with, I'd wager, but there is nothing to be done about it. Therefore I will agree to your terms. I have the Blade here, strapped to my back. I will get it for you."

Gentaff watched intently as Frost reached behind, under his cloak, and pulled the Blade's scabbard around in front of him.

"All your knowledge of the Blade will be required as well," Gentaff added. "But that will not take long, as I am a fast learner, and likely you know little more about it than I do already."

"I can tell you, with the Greater Gods as my witness, that the Blade is a fearful thing to me."

"Your honesty impresses me, Frost," Gentaff said. "But is it honesty, or deceit? I do sense something, an aura that is surely that of the Demon Blade, but such a thing can be mimicked. A false aura would allow the truth to be corrupted enough to make possible a lie. No, the blade you have is not authentic, just as Andair expected. We are not foolish enough to think you would bring it here, knowing we would be waiting for you."

"I am capable of no such thing," Frost said.

"You have fixed the weapon on your back with an aura like that of the real Demon Blade, but I can sense that it is not quite true as surely as I stand here."

Frost bit his tongue, then took a breath. "I assure you, Gentaff, it is the Blade."

Gentaff laughed, an unhealthy sound, more like coughing. "Your assurances mean little," he said. "You think yourself clever, but you have more than met your match this day. What do you think of that?"

What I think, you do not want to know, Frost thought. Thunder shook the earth as the breeze began to move again. Frost looked up at Gentaff and the frenzied lightning that framed the keep as it crossed the sky behind them, releasing pent-up energy as the binding began to fail.

"I will show you the Blade," Frost said. "You will see for yourself."

"No!" Gentaff shouted down. "Not yet. We will proceed as I say, one step at a time."

"That is what I am doing," Frost explained, and he began by removing the leather thong and bottle from his neck. "It is time," he whispered. His Subartans began to retreat slowly from their positions to either side of Frost. "And you are correct," he added. "I am wasting too many of my strengths. A little weather might do some good after all."

He gestured to the storm, releasing it fully, then he held the bottle up and pulled the cork. The skies surged forward almost as if they had sprung from a catapult. A thunderous clap sounded, and the world was suddenly ablaze with lightning and awash with wind-swept rains that burst from above. Gusts blew strong enough to stop a large man's charge or knock a smaller one down.

Between the rain and wind it was all but impossible to see anything, but Frost did not need to see with his eyes. He raised his staff in one hand and the bottle in the other, then reached up with his mind into the high anvil cloud that was the heart of the storm and felt the swirling of the winds, the clash of warm and cold. He spoke to the storm once more, bringing all his strength to bear, and he began to pull the central winds down, toward a joining with the earth and the bottle below.

When he opened his eyes he was greeted by the sight of a dark and spinning funnel dropping earthward, then touching down, where it instantly began to grow wider and stronger—and nearer. It threw a spray of stone and wood up in all directions as it hopped the castle walls and crossed over the keep, tearing up the roof, before descending to the parapets below.

Frost tossed the bottle to the ground and used all his will and concentration in a single effort to keep the storm funnel aloft just long enough to let it skip just over Gentaff and the twins. It landed straight ahead of him on the courtyard floor, making instant victims of the soldiers still gathered there. The deafening roar of the funnel hid the first screams, but as the darkness consumed the rest of the men, they raised a chorus of panic and fear heard even above the storm.

Nothing in the courtyard was staying put—with the notable exception of the stables. Frost's warding was holding there—the one he had placed while feigning annoyance with the fumes—as was the other, he noted, turning and looking up to the parapets. Gentaff himself was holding on for dear life, arms wrapped around stone, trying to survive long enough to get his bearings. But the twins rested nearly untouched. Frost had not let go of the warding he'd used to hold back the storm, but had repositioned it around the twins instead.

Good, he thought, then he reached into his pocket and withdrew the iron rod. He turned and ran, back

toward the rows of soldiers blocking the way out—
soldiers who were having problems of their own with
the intensity of the storm, but not so great as to
disable any of them. When he had run just far enough
he crouched and drove the pointed end of the rod
into the ground, then he bent the other end toward
the soldiers, and left it. He began to retreat and the
soldiers came after him, slow and low to the ground,
braving the winds but making progress.

As the troops overran the metal rod, Frost released
the charm he had placed within it, a simple enhancement of the metal's natural properties. The rod became
an irresistible magnet for the storm's limitless fiery
energy. Dozens of lightning bolts leaped down out of
the clouds, then dozens more, searing air and earth
and shearing the furious winds within the courtyard.
Torrents of soaking rain turned instantly to steam as
deafening thunderclaps followed each flash in rapid
succession, like the galloping of the Gods' own horses,
shaking mortar from stone and teeth from bone.

Despite the wardings, Frost raised his arm to shield
his face against the blistering heat that struck in the
instant that followed. He strained to shore up the
wardings—on himself and his Subartans, on Dorin and
Dara, on the stables nearby—but even this was not
enough to keep the heel of his exposed hand from
registering the pain of the burn. He felt his strength
fading under the stain of so much effort. Too much
for any man, but he could not let go just yet.

He turned away while the lightning rod was consumed, then looked again to find no soldier still
standing. Their charred and burning remains were
strewn in gruesome heaps across the courtyard
between Frost and the main gates. Rain pelted the
bodies and formed pools around them, mixing with
blood and sizzling on those that still smoldered.
Already the frantic, swirling winds were filled with
the wet stench of scorched air and burnt flesh.

Frost turned once more to Gentaff and found the other thoroughly absorbed in the task of staying put long enough to use his talents to gain some level of control over the storm and its deadly funnel. What few soldiers remained had reached the farthest corners of the courtyard, where they huddled behind their shields and clung to each other as the wind flung debris and sheets of rain over them. Even the men on the walls were gone, pulled to their deaths by the winds or gone to cover.

Gentaff and the twins were alone on the parapet.

Then the storm funnel began to lift back up toward its source overhead. Gentaff had found purchase on it. Frost watched the other, gauging his grasp of things. Gentaff was visibly straining, using all his strength and abilities to contain the funnel and drive it away. But succeeding.

The moment had come.

"Now!" Frost shouted over the roar of the storm. His Subartans came to his side and clasped his arms, one each, then together they leaned forward, eyes nearly closed against the wind-driven rains, and made their way to the steps—then started upward.

"I would have a word with you, Gentaff!" Frost howled as soon as he was certain he was close enough for Gentaff to here. He had let go of the storm completely now; he barely had the energy to stay on his feet, but Gentaff didn't know that.

"I know you well, Frost!" Gentaff shouted back. "You have given me what I needed. This day will not come again!"

"Once is enough!" Frost answered, but he knew Gentaff was right, or half right: they had learned a great deal about each other, enough to make another contest between them infinitely more difficult.

"Wait where you are and we will end this here and now."

"No—but soon, and differently," Gentaff said,

finally taking his eyes off the storm as the funnel vanished into the sagging black clouds. The heart of the storm seemed to be passing, moving on.

"You want no more?"

"In good time."

Frost blinked—and lost sight of Gentaff. No vanishing act, more likely a quick retreat through a door held open by guards at one end of the parapet. A door that would be barred and heavily guarded by the time Frost reached it. But Frost had no desire to go after Gentaff or to search for Andair. He had only Dorin and Dara on his mind.

He reached the parapets and the twins a moment later. Sharryl and Rosivok cut away their bonds and threw them one each over their shoulders, then all started back down.

The thunderstorm was clearly moving off now, taking the worst of the winds and rains with it. More soldiers would be arriving soon, reinforcements for those few that dared venture out from corners and from behind walls. "The stables!" Frost commanded, and headed toward them at his best speed. A handful of guards were holed up in the stalls along with the stable workers, but none of them tried to interfere as Frost and the others entered. Rosivok laid Dorin down on a bed of straw and went about collecting three horses while Sharryl, still holding Dara over her shoulder, raised her subarta and kept it well in view of the men crouched nearest to them.

"If you keep still, you will live," Frost said.

No one seemed to doubt this. Rosivok reappeared with the horses and he and Sharryl got the twins draped over two of them. They mounted one each with the twins, holding them in place, while Frost fought to hoist himself onto the third horse. His strength was nearly gone now, but he forced himself up, calling on the stout and powerful muscles he kept hidden beneath his robust form, using up his last reserves. A wave of fatigue hit him as he tried to sit upright on the gelding. His vision blackened and he felt the world spin just a bit, felt himself nearly slip off.

"Frost?" Sharryl said, nudging her mount nearer his and lending an arm for a moment.

He breathed deeply, eyes closed. "I will be all right. We must go."

He clung to the horse as they rode out, picking their way through the destruction and carnage in the courtyard. Every building other than the stables had been dismantled, leaving goods and splintered wood strewn everywhere among the ghastly wreckage of armor and bodies. One of the main gates stood nearly closed, and the men who had closed it were busy working on the other. Frost hadn't the strength left in him to deal with them in any proper fashion. Instead he did what little he could, the least taxing thing he could, using the only resources at hand. He created the vaguest of illusions all drawn on the drifting clouds of steam and smoke swirling from the courtyard and the light rains that still fell from the gray clouds overhead.

Only twenty ghosts, Frost could conjure no more than that, all supposed to be the spirits of the dead soldiers trying to leave the battlefield as far as the men at the gates could tell. Or so Frost hoped. As the men at the gates abruptly scattered he saw that his trick had provided the desired result. When they crossed the bridge over the moat, two archers appeared on the split wall behind them. Both loosed their arrows. One went wide. The other struck Sharryl's subarta as she reared her horse and swatted at it, nearly spilling Dara. She managed to snatch a handful of tunic in time, and dragged Dara back onto the horse.

Before the archers could fire again, they had reached the city's streets.

"They will come after us," Frost said. "But it will be a while I think. If we hurry, we will stay ahead of them."

Both Subartans nodded. Rosivok took the lead, and set his horse to a trot. The jolting made holding onto the twins much harder, made holding onto the horse at all much harder on Frost, but the pace got them through the city and beyond without any sign of trouble. Though trouble, Frost knew, was not far behind.

Andair stood leaning against the solid oak of the massive table behind him and stared into the darkness at the tall, hooded figure that approached him. The great hall was lit only at this end and completely empty, save these two. As Gentaff emerged fully into the light and put back his hood, Andair folded his arms and tipped his head to one side. "You are well?" he asked, before tipping his head the other way to await the answer.

"I am," Gentaff replied.

He came to rest a full ten paces away, this man who usually crowded Andair to fill his ear with fertile whispers. Not now. Not this night.

Andair thought to get right to it. "My men tell me our first encounter with Frost was a perfect catastrophe."

"For a few of them, yes."

"More than a few," Andair corrected. "Over two hundred dead, almost as many wounded, and workers will be weeks repairing the damage. Oh, yes, Frost has the twins back as well, and he still has the Demon Blade. Then there was that inspiring moment at the end when what was left of my First Guard looked up to you and saw you running away. Have I left anything out?"

Gentaff's expression was stolid. "I learned what I needed to know of Frost. I turned the storm, I ended its rage, and—"

"And piqued mine!" Andair boomed, standing erect, clenching his fists as he took a step forward. "If you were one of my commanders you would be dead already! I will remember everything about this day, sorcerer, when next we make plans together. I will remember that I listened to you instead of myself!"

"Remember too, my lord, that kings also may die," Gentaff replied, closing his eyes, though this time his teeth came together, the jaw rigid.

Andair had never seen him do that. He'd been shaken, there was no doubt, but he was not the only one.

"Do you threaten me now?" Andair asked, getting that out in the open as well.

"I have no wish to be a king," Gentaff replied, eyes open once more. "Only to own them."

Andair boiled at that, but he fought not to let it show.

"You have no idea what happened out there today," Gentaff went on, "aside from the limited view of a few dull-witted soldiers and stable hands."

"Ahh," Andair said, nodding while he began slowly to pace back and forth in front of the table, which seemed to help calm him slightly. "Yes, I see. There is much you are aware of that the rest of us are not."

"Exactly," Gentaff replied.

"Enlighten me."

"I would have preferred that Frost was destroyed today, but from the beginning I understood that possibility to be remote."

"You never said that. You said given your magic and my men you could trap him and take the Blade from him."

"Yes, but not this day." Gentaff closed his eyes. Andair stomped his foot on the floor in frustration. "Enough games! I am not in the mood."

Gentaff looked up and nodded. "Think of this, my lord: Neither of us had any true knowledge of Frost's powers, his limits, his mind, his magic, until this day. It had to be learned. One hopes the learning is quick and reveals a solution right away, but more often the learning leads to solutions later on. The twins were the perfect bait to lure him here, a trap with the means to make him perform under pressure and with maximum effort."

Andair pondered the other's words as he paused. "Why didn't you tell me all this in the first place?"

"You might not have risked what you did."

"True, but now that we have, was it worthwhile?"

"I learned a great deal. More important, he did not use the Demon Blade, which means he either did not have it with him or he is hesitant to call upon it, even when trapped and outnumbered. My guess is that his reputation with the Blade is exaggerated and that he is afraid of it, he as much said so. Perhaps it is too powerful for him . . . that is also quite possible."

Andair nodded. "All the more reason for us to have it."

"Yes. And we shall, you and I. Henceforth we will have no secrets. I will see to that."

Somehow that assurance didn't made Andair feel any better. "What is next?"

"We must have him back."

"What?" Andair sputtered. "Have him back?"

"Yes, my lord, and soon. But not too soon."

"I see."

"Good."

With that Gentaff turned and walked away. Andair felt about to burst as he followed Gentaff out of the room, but he followed in silence. For now.

CHAPTER THIRTEEN

"This way, follow me," a voice from the shadows said, as Frost and the others passed the crook in the road just east of the city. Lurey emerged from the trees mounted on his draft horse, minus the wagon. He wore a simpler-than-usual tunic over his other clothing, a dark brown color that blended well with the woods, particularly at dusk. He pointed. "You should go north, I think, there. If they are following you, they will likely stay to this road, thinking you are headed home."

A small village lay within sight of them, a place where the road intersected with another that ran north and south. An unremarkable village and crossroads. "Why here?" Frost asked, as the peddler eased his mount into line with the others. "And why north?"

"You have friends that wait to help you."

Frost nodded. "Who?"

"It is best to wait and see. That is their request. How are Dorin and Dara?"

The twins remained unconscious, draped one each over the withers of Sharryl and Rosivok's mounts.

Frost had a fair idea of what he needed to do to revive them, but that would take a few moments and a second wind, both of which must wait till later.

"They will be fine," Frost answered. "Have you seen Shassel?"

"No," Lurey said, still looking away, up the road. "No, not for days. I have been traveling. But when I heard you were on your way to Weldhem, I guessed you might be in need of an ally. No reward is necessary, of course. I do this out of concern for my friends, no matter the cost in lost business. Which has been dear."

Frost held his frown in check. Lurey seemed an amiable sort, but he tended to put his purse ahead of everything else; although, that could provide a handle by which to wield such a man.

"I insist on giving you a reward, all the same," Frost said. "It is important to me."

"You are much too kind."

"I know," Frost muttered. "Something I intend to work on very soon."

Lurey looked and sounded a bit nervous as he chuckled at Frost's remark, then his eyes got busy as new thoughts grew behind them. "You look most tired."

"I am."

Lurey nodded. He said nothing else as the horses drew to a halt at the crossroads. Then, "I was wondering . . ."

"Yes?"

"How did you fare with Andair and Gentaff?"

Frost thought first to brush aside Lurey's questions about the rescue of the twins; the details were none of his business, and Frost was just weak and weary enough from the ordeal to make talking and riding too great an effort when combined. But he found another part of himself eager to talk about what had happened. The part that had confronted Andair's army

and his great sorcerer Gentaff on their own terms—
and won. "I fared well," Frost said, indicating the
twins.

"But what was it like?" Lurey asked. "Tell me, and
leave nothing out."

Frost smiled, took a breath, and turned his horse
northward with the others. "Very well," he said, allowing himself a grin. "It was most . . . extraordinary!"

Wilmar rushed to greet them, followed in close step
by his son, Tramet. Frost recognized him immediately,
though as they drew nearer one another he saw that
the years had not been so kind to Wilmar. Memory
recalled a striking young man full of vigor, but here
walked a man whose face was dark and weathered,
his hair thin and graying beyond his years.

Tramet, on the other hand, reminded Frost of his
father precisely, right down to the gait and the grin
the boy showed as he sprinted ahead of Wilmar to
greet everyone—Dara in particular.

"The one I told you about," Lurey said, grinning.
Frost nodded, relieving any doubts.

"Welcome!" Wilmar shouted out. "Welcome, old
friend!"

If Wilmar had come charging up the road with a
weapon in his hand and cries for death-born retribution on his lips, Frost would have accepted it.
Would even have expected it, up until this very
moment. In choosing sides with Andair against Wilmar
all those decades ago, he had made the biggest mistake of his life. Yet here was the man he had wronged
and ruined loping up the road, shouting welcome and
apparently offering sanctuary. Which only made Frost
feel the worse for misjudging him so completely back
then, for being such a fool. *Andair's fool* . . .

"We are grateful beyond words!" Frost called back.

"We expected you sooner," Wilmar said as he came
well within earshot and stopped to catch his breath.

They met on the narrow dirt road in a low and drifting cloud of dust stirred by the horses. Tramet went straight to Dara and Sharryl's horse, nearly bouncing as he walked. Frost had managed to awaken them, but barely.

"It has been a very long day, old friend," Frost said in reply, still half expecting Wilmar to dispute the phrase.

"A successful rescue against such great odds and adversaries makes for such."

Frost nodded again.

"Are you all right?" Tramet asked, gazing up, eyes completely full of Dara—who had certainly noticed him but had made no attempt to react.

"Dara and Dorin were deep in trance," Frost explained. "It took much too long and proved a most draining task to revive them. They are only just coming around."

"Gentaff's spells," Wilmar said, shaking his head. "He has that reputation. As word of your march on Weldhem spread there was great speculation about the outcome, but I can tell you that almost no one thought you would succeed. And yet you have. Now, no one in all the land will speak of anything else for weeks." Wilmar smiled, though there was a shrewdness in his eye.

Frost decided to set the record straight from the start. "The spells Gentaff used on the twins were more layered than I would ever have expected. Which only adds to my assessment of Gentaff. The rescue went well, though thanks to luck as much as skill, and the storm in particular, which I was able to plunder. But Gentaff quickly managed to control the storm's worst fury, and he gave up much too easily after that. No, Gentaff is an even more formidable and dangerous opponent than I had expected. Just as Andair was so many years ago." *And may yet be* . . .

"I hear much the same about you," Wilmar said, adding a wink—or was it only the dust in his eye?

"I have learned a thing or two, though perhaps not enough," Frost said.

"So say we all," Wilmar replied, and Frost sensed this was meant to put an end to the subject, or at least dissolve the darkened heart of it.

Frost could not let it go so easily, though whether it was guilt or regard or some pairing of the two that compelled him he could only guess. But he heard himself say, "I never meant to allow so much wrong to happen. I searched for you, and Andair, for years. I do not expect your forgiveness, or your son's, for what . . ."

"Then forgive yourself," Wilmar said. "Shassel told me most of what I needed to know, long ago. I will not tell you I wasn't angry for a very long time; I was. I lost everything. But so did you. And none of it was all your fault. The blame lies with Andair. He is the one who took away the future, the kingdom, the friendships, the life that was mine to live. Now that you have returned, perhaps we can pay him back in kind."

So that is Wilmar's mind on the matter, Frost thought, seeing it now, feeling a chill of relief and satisfaction touch his spine. *Good.* "Perhaps," Frost said, allowing himself a smile, one he had no will to censor. "Perhaps we shall."

The chill melted into flush. He closed his eyes and was nearly overwhelmed by the darkness and dizziness yet again; finally he opened them. He was still on his horse, but Wilmar stood beside him now, both hands reaching up to prop Frost up there.

"They need a meal and a good rest," Lurey said, coming around to the front of the group now, bending from his mount as if confiding in Wilmar.

"We will hide you in our home," Tramet said, his voice sounding much that of a man's—his father. Dara was coming around a little more, apparently inspired by Tramet's considerable attention, though she and Dorin still relied mostly on the able arms of Sharryl and Rosivok to keep them from falling.

"It is near," Wilmar said. "You will all come."

"You may bring misery down on your heads by this," Frost told him.

"Andair's soldiers won't find you there, not for a time at least," Wilmar said. Then, "But if they do, we will all live or die together."

"Together!" Tramet called out in echo.

Wilmar smiled. "My son is perhaps too keen, but his heart is willing."

"Which counts for much," Frost said readily.

"I will be along later on," Lurey said, as he turned his mount back the way they had come. "I have neglected my business much too much these past few days. I must tend to it."

Frost nodded, followed by Wilmar and Tramet, who both wasted no more time in turning about and leading the way.

"A visitor so late?" Lord Andair grumbled. He had just retired to his chambers for the night, having spent much of the evening in conference with Gentaff, and taking little joy from it. He liked being in control, liked being the one orchestrating others' troubles, not suffering with his own, and here he was mired in difficulties with his fate resting all too heavily in the hands of another.

But it was Gentaff, after all . . .

"He says he has vital news," the page said from the doorway. "He says you must come at once."

"Tell him to leave his news with you and I will tend to it in the morning." He'd had a little too much ale and much too trying a day for anything more.

"He will not do so, I have already asked," the page replied. "He is speaking with Gentaff even now."

By the Greater Gods, Andair thought wearily. But if Gentaff thought it important enough to hold an audience with the man, then . . .

He considered his options. He had just finished changing into his bedclothes and dismissed his squire. He sighed, then began pulling them back on himself. Nothing ever seemed to happen at midday, for some inconceivable reason. "Very well, I'm coming. Now get out!"

He tugged at his shoes, then he followed the page. He arrived in the Great Room to find only Gentaff and the visitor, a rather short and unimpressive fellow just older than Andair himself, neatly dressed, though his clothing was not that of a nobleman, especially the drab tunic he wore.

"A merchant?" he asked, gruff, as he strode toward the main doors where the two men stood—where Gentaff had apparently met the visitor, and kept him.

"I am, that I am," the man said.

"You will introduce yourself," Andair ordered.

"A loyal citizen, a friend," the visitor replied.

"He wishes to remain nameless, for now," Gentaff said. "Though I can force him to reveal whatever you wish."

It probably isn't worth the trouble, Andair thought, *and it is bound to take too long in any case.* He glared at his visitor instead. "Let us get straight to it. I have no intention of dragging this out any longer than we must. You have information? Information worth risking imprisonment for?"

"That I do."

"He does," Gentaff echoed, and for the first time Andair took his visitor seriously.

Andair nodded. "I would have it then."

"If what I say proves valuable, I would not be averse to some sort of . . . compensation."

Andair watched the merchant's eyes. He didn't like what he saw, but he understood it perfectly. "Yes, of course, I pay very well when I am pleased. But so far I am not."

"It concerns Shassel, Frost's aunt."

Andair felt the name as if struck by it. A reaction he had every intention of eliminating soon . . . one day. "What of her?"

"Shassel has been taken captive by Haggel and Tasche, the lord prince and court wizard of your enemy, Lord Kolhol of Grenarii."

"I know Tasche. I doubt he is any match for Shassel," Gentaff stated.

"No doubt, but they intended to capture her this very day, and by now they may have her. They plan to take her home with them."

"I do not enjoy the lords and mages of other realms prowling about my lands uninvited, snatching citizens," Andair said, "but in this case I may make an exception. Regardless, I fail to see why this should be of immediate concern to me. Unless they decide to bring her back."

He glanced at Gentaff with this last to see if the sorcerer would endorse the humor. Gentaff looked unaffected. Entirely.

"If you will, one moment," the sorcerer told the merchant, then he touched Andair's arm and walked with him to the center of the room, where he lowered his voice to a harsh whisper Andair found discomforting.

"It may be that the Grenarii intend to use her to bargain with Frost for the Demon Blade," he said. "Tasche and Kolhol and the army they command are already threat enough, but give them the Demon Blade . . ."

"No!" Andair blurted, then he glanced over his shoulder at the merchant waiting patiently near the door. "No," he repeated at a whisper. "That will not do at all."

"We should first learn whether this information is

accurate," Gentaff said. "If so, we must use it to our advantage."

This was sorcerer sophistry, Andair knew, yet another annoyance that seemed inescapable with Gentaff's kind. They made much of their great cleverness in always finding ways to use the momentum of enemies, forces or circumstances to empower their magic and help them succeed, which added insult to invention. But they spent their lives training their minds to think that way. Andair could do nearly as well on the spur of the moment. Nearly. Though now and then it paid to listen to his sorcerer all the same. Andair let out a sigh, then bent to Gentaff's ear. "Of course. What do you suggest?"

"We steal their deeds. We make it known that we have taken her, not Kolhol, and are holding her, but elsewhere, not here at Weldhem. Frost will know she is not here in any case, he has the ability. If he goes to Shassel's cottage, which he likely will, he will only find her gone. He will then be forced to come back to Weldhem and bargain with us, instead of Kolhol. If he wants to see her alive again, he must give us the Blade."

"He will be *most* unhappy when he learns we have her. But far, far more unhappy if he learns we do not actually have her," Andair said, glee in his voice at first, though he was not so sure it was warranted.

"True," Gentaff replied. "But it will not matter. When next he returns we will be better prepared to meet him, no matter what he does, and we can always claim that Kolhol raided the spot where we had taken her—he killed all your men and took her prisoner, back to Grenarii."

Andair stared at Gentaff for a moment, a bit awed with the plan, then he nodded enthusiastically. *Perfect.*

"We need only learn where he and the twins have gone, or where they are going," said Gentaff.

"I have sent men to search for them, but it will be tomorrow at least before we hear anything."

"Perhaps, in anticipation of your royal generosity, I can help with that as well!" the visitor piped up.

"You have remarkable hearing," Gentaff told him, turning to him.

"A gift," the merchant replied.

Gentaff nodded once. "Yes, but some gifts are poison."

The visitor said nothing. Andair started toward him again, with Gentaff right behind. "Very well," the king said. "We will see how useful you can be." He called out into the hallway. A page and a young squire appeared almost instantly. "Fetch the gold, the red bag," he ordered, and the two disappeared again. Andair faced his visitor once more. "Now," he said, drawing close, "you will tell us where they are."

"And then you will see that they get our message," Gentaff added.

"I will," the merchant replied, "that I will."

The sound was that of breathing, several men breathing loudly and clearly in Shassel's aging ears. The warding spell worked that way, a fine spell that required almost no energy at all to function and no tending whatever, unless it needed to be redone. One she had taught young Frost, so many years ago. It did not shimmer or repel or bring any forces to bear, it simply gathered sounds and brought them to her— specified sounds, whatever remained after weeding out unwanted others. Breathing was chief among them.

She sat up in bed and drew her walking stick near. In the event of just such a hazard she had prepared two of her oldest and most reliable spells. One of them made considerable use of the nearby forests, and was by far the most complex of the lot. The other was merely a trick of the light, and was already in place.

Closing her eyes, drawing carefully from within herself, Shassel spoke the words that would give life to the spell she would need, if her concerns about her visitors were correct.

Before Shassel could finish the door burst open. Blinking to see detail in the aura of moon and starlight she counted five armed figures as they rushed into the room. They seized just inside the doorway as they found themselves face to face with what Shassel knew to be three wooden table stools.

"Wolves!" she heard them yell—or curse—it was difficult to tell. "Three wolves!" another voice shouted. In the near darkness, their minds already prone to absurdities of woodlands and magic on such a visit, these were not difficult false glamours to create in a stranger's eyes.

"They are trained!" a third called out. "Look, they do not move. They wait to strike."

"They await my command," Shassel said from across the room, buying just a little more time. Shassel spoke the final words under her breath, then added her binding phrase, "Tesha teshrea." She glanced up as the commotion ahead of her drew her attention. The men had drawn their swords and were advancing. They grew suddenly busy, hacking away at the three chairs. Shassel grinned slightly, but kept concentrating on the work at hand. The forest teemed with life; it grew on every surface, on every fallen tree, the surface of every still pool of water—life that came on the air and settled in a bowl of porridge or fruit to change it into something else again. Shassel could not create such life, but she could attract its attention easily enough, could bring it searching toward her, hungry, avid—then, she could guide it on its way. Dampness was the key; she had already planned for this, but there was more than enough water in the rain barrel at the corner of the cottage to supply what she would need.

As they finished battling the chairs and came toward her, she fed the spell all she could manage. She couldn't see the rain barrel, but she could sense its level dropping, just as she could sense with slightly less certainty the sudden sogginess of the intruders' clothing. The rest of the task came easily after that.

The men stumbled a little, shrugging and tugging, scratching and pulling at clinging clothes, then they began to rub their eyes, to wheeze, and sneeze, and cough. One doubled over and heaved whatever he had eaten last onto the cottage floor, then another did the same. Already they were starting to smell like muck dredged from the bottom of a marsh . . . or worse.

"Leave," she said to them, in her harshest tone. "Leave this house or suffer greatly."

One of the intruders barked a command, and they all tried to come at her again, but their ills were clearly getting the better of them, and the effect was increasing. They would be mildewed, moldered and going to rot both inside and out in another few moments if they did not turn about and leave. Away from here the spell would wear off eventually, and they would slowly become less enticing to the tiny creatures infesting them now. Shassel felt a moment of relief as she watched the men stumble, then take to their knees and begin to crawl away, their forms just visible in the open doorway. She breathed a sigh. The effort had tired her considerably, but the worst of it was behind her, and it was a good sort of tired, like climbing a hill for a magnificent view. She felt quite pleased with herself.

Then the doorway filled with darkness as a huge shape the breadth of the opening, though not quite its height, appeared. The man's head was round and topped by a wide-brimmed hat. At first she thought it might be Frost, but no, the hat was different and even Frost was not so large a man, not nearly so big around. In the same heartbeat she knew this was an adept, one capable of hiding his glamour from her until he had stepped into her presence. Shassel had nothing substantial prepared for this.

Instead she attempted to wrap the spell afflicting the soldiers around this new intruder too; she spoke the extra phrases as best she could imagine, then drew all she could from herself, more than she should. The effort seemed to succeed at first, but then she felt the energy of the spell—all of it— suddenly dissipate, like pushing on a door that's jammed and having it abruptly opened. The other had used a warding spell of a different kind, one capable of deflecting, of shedding magical energies like a well-oiled cloak shedding rain. It had been well constructed over time, and quickly adaptable to whatever the wizard encountered, though that required substantial personal resources. Clearly, this big fellow had the capacity. Shassel could not hope to match him toe to toe.

The men on the floor were getting up now, urged on by the mountainous mage.

"Who are you?" Shassel called out to him. "Why do you come here? I have nothing you want."

"I disagree," the man in the doorway replied, raising his hands and shouting an undecipherable phrase. Shassel felt the other's binding spell take hold. Her hands would not move, and neither would her feet. Another solid piece of magery, another this wizard had no doubt spent considerable time on. He was maintaining the spell directly, keeping it well supplied with energy from his considerable reserves.

Shassel tried, but she did not have the mass or the strength to free herself. Or the tools—not just now, at least. She tried to speak but her throat locked, bound as well, though not as tightly as her limbs. Only a muffled, wheezing whisper came out. Certainly not a voice to be used for casting spells.

"You have her?" said yet another voice. A much, much smaller, younger sounding man appeared in the doorway just as the colossal sorcerer moved inside and came a little closer.

"Yes."

"Good as your word."

"Who . . . you?" Shassel got out, though she barely recognized the words herself.

"I am Tasche," the wizard said. "You have heard of me."

Shassel tried. "Y—y—"

The wizard waved a hand, and Shassel felt her throat ease a very little bit.

"Yes."

"Of course."

"Though . . . nothing good . . . I assure . . . you," Shassel said, straining but happy to do so.

"Just quiet her again," the one in the doorway said.

"I can feel you trying to undo my bindings," Tasche said, ignoring the one behind him. "It will not work, but you are welcome to exert yourself all you want. It will only make things easier."

Tasche reached the table and waved, lighting the lamp that rested there. He looked quite wicked in the dim light flickering up from the table in front of him. All jowls and shadows. Deep-set eyes. A tent of a cloak.

Shassel struggled, but she was forced to let up. "The Greater . . . Gods . . . curse you," Shassel growled, angry enough to have screamed, if only she could.

The bastard was right, that was the worse of it. She was too frail to force him loose of her. Better to bide her time and use her wits, something Tasche likely did not have in proportion to bulk.

"Ah, much better," Tasche said, as he felt her ease her struggle against him.

"Who . . . is he?" Shassel asked, nodding in the direction of the door.

"Prince Haggel of Grenarii, of course," the man in the doorway answered for himself. "And one day, king. King of Grenarii, and more."

"So . . . sure," Shassel said, closing her eyes. She had heard enough of the prince as well. She had expected nothing more than this. But one could hope.

"I am sure, yes," the prince replied. "And you are going to help."

"Yes," Tasche said. "You are indeed."

"How?" Shassel asked.

"It is the most wonderful idea," Haggel began, sounding very keen as he took one small step forward. "Tasche has been working on a spell that will allow him to draw forth—"

"My prince!" Tasche shouted, cutting off the younger man. "She does not need to know."

"Ah, of course." Haggel turned to his men, who were all gathered near him, coughing as quietly and politely as possible and apparently trying to stop their shivering. "Get her," he said. "So we can leave. We have been in this land long enough . . . for now."

Shassel had never met either of these men, though she had heard enough about them to know that even King Kolhol himself was not terribly fond of them. "For now?"

"I will be King of all Worlish soon enough, old hag. Pray you live to see that day."

"Perhaps . . . *one* of you . . . will be king," Shassel answered, getting her voice in slightly better order.

"*I* will be!" Haggel snapped, then he seemed to calm himself. "Me," he added, all the same. "Me."

"I live only to serve," Tasche said with a minor bow.

Shassel shook her head. Now she knew what she was up against. In her youth these two would have been the most glorious of playthings. She cursed the march of time. Then she left that thought, and began important new ones.

Two days didn't seem like very long, but it had been long enough to allow Frost to get his wind back, if not all the bulk and stamina he had spent like a drunkard's coins during his battle with Gentaff. He was still recovering from his battle with another wizard in a mountain pass, and had not been fully back to normal in the first place, but he had done well for himself, he was sure of that. And he liked the idea.

Almost as much as he liked the idea of breakfast, which Dara had insisted on cooking for everyone, though especially for Tramet. Frost feasted on eggs cooked with cheese and thick hot porridge complemented by fresh bread rich with lard and spread with honey. Tastiest of all were the pieces of well-smoked and salted pork that lay in a shrinking pile in the center of the table.

"She has not stopped looking at Tramet since we arrived," Frost said, pausing from the meal, raising a thinned yet still corpulent hand and speaking behind it to Wilmar. He was back to consuming the rest of his generous portions by the time Wilmar had swallowed and said, "And he her. But it was so even years ago, when they were only children. It seems time and ripening has only deepened their fondness for one another."

"And absence, perhaps," Frost added.

"She's making a fool of herself," Dorin said, careful to keep his voice down as well. He sat close to Frost's right and opposite Wilmar, but right next to Tramet— who had taken his elders' remarks in good stride, but now seemed to take exception to Dorin's.

"I suppose that means I've made a fool of myself as well," he said, eyeing Dorin pensively.

"Actually," Dorin said, "yes."

"Is that so?" Tramet said, rising from his chair as if to challenge.

"Sit down!" Wilmar commanded, and the boy did as he was told, reluctantly.

"He is the one who started it," Tramet protested. "He is saying that—"

"Are you defending your honor, or Dara's?" Wilmar asked.

"Both," Tramet said.

"Then you have a job ahead of you," Dorin said with a wicked grin.

Tramet seethed, but as he looked to his father, he found the other shaking his head slowly, side to side, warning him. Tramet calmed himself slightly, took a breath, and turned to Dorin once more. "Life would be simpler if I were more like you, and simply had little honor to worry about."

Now it was Dorin whose features grew gnarled.

"A fine parry," Frost said, placing his hand solidly on Dorin's shoulder. "But that will be enough, I think. Anymore and this wonderful meal would be spoiled."

As Dara returned to the table and sat, everyone was absolutely silent.

"What's wrong?" Dara asked, as she looked up.

"Not a thing," Frost said.

All heads nodded in accordance.

"You weren't talking about me, were you?" she pressed, apparently not convinced.

"About how good the food is," Tramet said, glancing hopefully at Dorin.

"And I was agreeing," Dorin said.

Wilmar grinned privately at Frost, then at the boys, who had gone studiously back to eating. *Not so serious*, Frost thought, looking at these two young men who had known each other for most of their lives. They were too alike, if anything, and good friends. A bit of testing was to be expected, especially where Dara was concerned.

"If you are up to it, we have much to talk about, you and I," Wilmar told Frost, as even Frost finally admitted his unwillingness to attempt another helping.

"I intend to right some very old wrongs," Frost told him, even though he had said as much the day before.

"I know," Wilmar said. "And I am counting on you to do just that. I have waited too many years for this time. But there are many new wrongs as well. We also will work on them."

"Yes, we shall," Frost agreed.

"If we can truly count on Frost to help," Tramet said, making sure not to look anyone in the eye.

An awkward silence filled the room for a moment. Frost had expected this from Wilmar and his son. "You can," Frost assured him.

"It is not your place to say such a thing," Wilmar said. "With all I have told you, all you have been told, there is much you still do not know."

"Dorin and Dara have told me more than enough already," Tramet said, though as he sat there under the disapproving glare of his father, he seemed to grow less confident.

"There are always two sides to a story," Wilmar said.

"When did they tell you these things?" Frost asked, turning to the twins—who for their part looked suddenly as if the Greater Gods had only just created them, wide-eyed and innocent of the world.

"It was long ago," Tramet answered for his friends. "When you left, you cleared the way for Andair and all the misery that has followed. I don't know if you were scared, or shamed, or both, but Dorin and Dara—"

"I know," Frost said, loud enough to stop the boy. "They have told me, and I am sorry. This comes to mind too often, but I cannot change the past. I am working on the here and now, however. Andair and his sorcerer did not have their way this time around. Dorin and Dara are here as proof of that."

"But for you, we would not have been taken," Dorin said, not angry, but not entirely forgiving either.

"Of course, you are right," Frost said, and nothing else as the two stared at one another.

"We should clean up," Wilmar said.

Frost set his spoon back in his empty bowl. Three pieces of pork remained. He reached for one, but dropped it again as he heard someone at the door, knocking. Tramet went to the door and opened it.

"Good to see you again," Tramet said.

Lurey stood grinning at him, looking a bit flustered. Tramet let in the peddler.

"Back so soon?" Wilmar asked, rising to greet his visitor.

"I came at once," the peddler replied, all out of breath. "There is a herald from the king," he said. "He walks about asking questions and speaking of our friends here." He looked straight at Frost. "He asks that any who know of you or might come across you convey the king's message."

Frost nodded. "Which is?"

"He claims Andair has taken Shassel in place of Dara and Dorin, though she is not at Weldhem."

Everyone stood up at once in a clatter of wooden chairs on wooden floorboard. "Shassel?" Frost said, repeating the name out loud as Dorin and Dara gasped in unison. They all looked at one another, stunned.

"While you were busy rescuing Dorin and Dara, it seems Andair and Gentaff were busy working the second half of their plan," Tramet said, clenching his fists as he spoke.

"Still clever enough," Wilmar said, his voice shaking with rage.

"Surely, he will want the Demon Blade in exchange," Lurey said.

"As surely they have planned things differently this time," Wilmar added.

It is a lie, Frost thought, looking down at his hand.

But then he froze. "Shassel," he said again, only a whisper this time, though it drew the others' attention. Sometime during the night the thin strip of bark twined around his finger had smoldered and blackened. Weakened, exhausted, famished then fed, he had apparently slept through it all.

Frost looked up. He took two steps forward, grabbed the peddler by the arms and held him dead in his gaze. "He said she was not at the castle?"

Lurey nodded.

"We will begin at the cottage," Frost said. He turned to Dorin. "Find Sharryl and Rosivok at once. We have to leave."

"Perhaps it would be best if Dorin and Dara stayed with us," Tramet offered, taking Dara's hand, holding it tightly.

"They are safe here, and if there is any sign of trouble we can move them—move all of us—to some place safer."

"He is right, I think," Wilmar said. "You don't know where you might have to go, or what you might face. And Andair has already taken them, already tricked . . ."

He stopped short. Frost looked at Wilmar, feeling the truth of the other's words rest hard and heavy in his gut. It was true. He nodded. He didn't like the idea—every time he left someone somewhere lately, they disappeared—but it did seem like the best course for now.

The twins began to argue at once. In the end, they lost. Before the sun had risen to the middle of the sky, Frost and his two Subartans were on their horses, and on their way.

CHAPTER FOURTEEN

Frost approached the cottage unseen as he made his way nearer, staying to the trees. He noted he was not the only one to do so. Even in the late daylight, it was clear the woods had been trampled by a good many footfalls and horses hooves; twigs had been snapped, holes had been dug as makeshift privies, meaning some visitors had stayed for a time.

Sharryl and Rosivok went ahead. When they were sure there was no one inside, Frost went around and entered through the open doorway. He was greeted by two stools and a chair that had been hacked and broken to pieces, and the damp, musty smell of the forest during the rains filled his nose as he breathed.

Shassel, Frost knew, drawing another breath as he looked about, noticing the faint smell of rot mixed in. She had been taken, but not without a struggle of some sort, which meant she was aware and able when they made the attempt, which meant it should have failed. Even old and frail she was resourceful, and a match for any troop of brigands.

Frost found little in the way of clues as he searched

the room, aided by his Subartans. Especially, he found no fresh blood, which was some small comfort. Of great discomfort was the thought of Andair and Gentaff holding Shassel somewhere, making her suffer. She would not be asleep as the twins had been, she was much too valuable awake. The king and his sorcerer would be interested in anything she might be coerced into saying.

"Frost?"

He spun with his Subartans; it was the boy, Muren, the one he had used twice now as messenger. He entered gingerly, glancing about as if something—a Subartan or worse—might jump at him from the corners.

"Stop there," Rosivok said.

The boy did. "She is gone," he said.

Frost nodded. "So I see."

"What will they do to her?"

He'd asked the question evenly. The boy apparently liked Shassel well enough to be concerned, but he was reluctant to show it fully. *Habit*, Frost thought, *to show only the most tentative attachment to those who worked magic, or who might, as they were usually more curse than blessing to have around.* It was not a baseless fear, after all.

Frost turned and went to examine Shassel's bedding for anything unusual, but found nothing. "She will be ransomed, no doubt."

Now the boy nodded. "Oh."

"But they must keep her alive to do that," Frost said. "Andair and Gentaff are many things, but neither of them is stupid."

"Andair?" Muren said, looking about nervously.

"Yes, and Gentaff," Frost repeated, still looking about on the floor, in the corners.

"But they did not take her," Muren said.

Frost looked at him. "That is what I have been led to believe. Are you sure?"

"Yes," the boy replied. "I saw them; they came in the night, but I recognized the markings on their horses."

"Who?" Frost asked, suddenly impatient.

"They were Grenarii."

Frost felt rage taking control of him as the words faded in the air between them. A flood of thoughts rushed in, all falling into place. If the Grenarii had taken her it was possible Andair had somehow known about it, and simply used that information to his advantage. Had simply lied. Such was not unusual for Andair. *He has tricked me yet again!*

Sharryl and Rosivok stood close to Frost now.

"The Grenarii have made a grave error," Frost said through gritted teeth, as he turned to look from one Subartan to the other. Both nodded.

"Are you going after her?" Muren asked.

Frost felt an urge to kick something, to destroy something. He fought it. "Yes."

"I saw the road they took. I followed as far as I could, but they had horses, and . . ."

"Yes, boy, good. You may show us."

"Will we return to Wilmar's holdings first?" Sharryl asked.

"It would be wise," Rosivok agreed. "If Andair and Gentaff know of this, they are sure to expect you. If they learn that you have fled north after the Grenarii instead, they may abandon their plans."

"And attempt new ones," Frost added.

Rosivok nodded.

"The twins," Sharryl said.

"It is impossible to know what Andair has in mind," Frost said, fighting hard to control his frustration. "I know only that the Grenarii have taken Shassel, and I will not allow that to endure. She must not come to harm. Wilmar and Tramet are charged with tending to the twins. They will have help. Dorin and Dara have been captured by Gentaff once already, so they will be keen to any fresh attempts at trickery, or force. We will trust together they are up to the task, at least for now.

"As for Andair, he has tried to make it known that he has Shassel. He would not spread such a dangerous lie unless he is prepared for me to visit him again, to bargain for her return, or fight for it. He must wait a little longer than expected. Then, he will get more than expected."

Frost stayed his own tongue. The taste in his mouth was sour enough to kill a man, and seemed to get worse as he spoke. Now, only the pain inside spoke to him. He stepped out of the cottage once more, then turned to the boy, Muren, in the doorway behind him. "Tell no one," he said. "When I return, you will be well rewarded."

"Shassel's return will be reward enough," the boy replied, stalwart as could be.

Frost nodded. "Good boy," he said. "I believe you may actually mean that."

"Once and half again," Muren replied.

Frost signaled his Subartans, and they gathered their horses to go.

"I bring you word, Lord Kolhol, of treachery and deceit, of a dangerous threat, but also unexpected opportunities! News that might save your kingdom, and yourself."

"Did I hear that first part right? Do you threaten me?" Kolhol asked, leaning forward and glaring at the smallish peddler that stood before him—an older man, not quite Kolhol's age, narrow eyes, weak chin, well dressed for traveling but properly disheveled, someone who had just made a long, hard and hurried journey on horseback.

"I would *never* do that," the visitor said. "I am here to serve you as any man of my means could. Out of conscience . . . and need. I have heard you can be a generous man, when the reasons are good ones."

Kolhol raised his brow and used two fingers to stroke at his short, thick, graying beard. "You think your news that valuable, do you?"

"I do, that I do," the other said.

"Then speak, and if I find this news to be as you say, you shall have twice its worth. If not—well, you will not like that at all." Kolhol smiled, but stopped short of a chuckle.

The visitor seemed undaunted. "We should speak in private, my lord."

The king frowned, considering the request, then he shrugged and waved the many in attendance in the great hall away from his throne, except for the two large and armored soldiers that stood guard on either side of him. They would stay. "Go on," he said, leaning forward.

The visitor leaned nearer as well. "It is not my place to ask, but I must, you see: Have you ever wondered at the ways of your son's mind? The truth of his heart? The goals he has set for himself?"

"Constantly," Kolhol said. This fellow couldn't know the half of it, and probably shouldn't. "Go on."

"And your court wizard, Tasche, have you ever—"

"More so. We each have our own ideas about things; many of theirs are wrong. I have my doubts about them both, but I wonder why I must discuss them with you?"

"You need not. I needed to know whether you trusted them."

Kolhol saw the look in the other man's eyes, a little too steady, too calculating. "And as I do not?"

"I would call you wise. I do not know all the facts, but it would serve you to wonder whether Haggel and Tasche are hatching a plot to do you harm—perhaps imprisonment, or even death. They have gone to great lengths to do whatever it is they are up to, even as we speak."

Kolhol sighed. He had known or guessed most of this, and the rest . . . "You mean you do not know their plan, either?"

"I do in part. They have captured an aging adept named Shassel from her cottage in Briarlea. They apparently intend to use her to help them with a spell designed to summon some powerful and most offensive creature or other, an ally from the darkness. Then they intend to send her back."

"I wondered where those two had gone," the king remarked. This was as good and foolish an explanation as any. "They were seen returning. But instead of coming here they have since traveled east, into the Maardre Forest. That must be where they plan to try this spell you speak of."

"You had them followed?"

"Of course."

"Then you do not doubt what I say, that they plot against you."

Kolhol shook his head. "If any of this was to benefit me, they would have told me about it, and they would be here, not hiding in the forests."

"My very thoughts," the visitor said.

Kolhol shrugged. He would deal with Tasche and Haggel soon enough, in one fashion or another. "You say there is more?"

"Yes. Much more. As luck would have it a man named Frost, a most powerful sorcerer to begin with, has returned to Briarlea after many years' absence, and he is in possession of the Demon Blade."

"The Blade?" Kolhol said, sitting forward. He had heard rumors, many rumors lately, but there were always rumors.

"Shassel is family, so it is not unreasonable to expect that sooner or later Frost will come looking for her. He might be a natural ally for you. He despises Andair."

Kolhol's mind was racing. "A powerful sorcerer?" The other nodded.

He might just be a fine replacement for Tasche, Kolhol thought, *if it should come to that.* Kolhol tried not to drool. "I am intrigued. This may be great news indeed."

"I must warn you, my lord, this Frost is a capricious sort, unpredictable, dangerous. Controls would be wise."

"Agreed," Kolhol replied. "But what controls such a man? Wealth, certainly, and power, but others can offer him that. What does he want?"

"Other than Shassel, and Andair's hide?"

"Yes, I see," Kolhol agreed, rubbing his chin once more; then he began to chew at his thumbnail. He stopped so he wouldn't accidentally chew it off, then sat back once more as satisfaction spread through his mind like the warmth from a fire. "If I were to capture this Shassel away from those two fools, Frost would be forced to do my bidding."

He saw a new and curious look in the visitor's eyes now, as if somewhere in the man's mind he was talking to himself in earnest. "Your thoughts?" Kolhol asked.

"You know best, of course, my lord," the other answered, adding a gracious bow. "But you might be better off *rescuing* her."

That did make better sense. He needed to think. "Pay him," Kolhol said, waving to one of the servants waiting at the back of the room. As soon as the gold had been counted out, Kolhol told the visitor to be on his way. He was gone an instant later.

"Call Captain Durret before me," Kolhol told the guard on his left. The soldier acknowledged the command and rushed out of the room.

Durret was an able soldier, a man Kolhol had fought alongside in the past and shared more than enough ale with, a man who got things done, and done right. He would have Durret take as many men as he thought he would need to collect this Shassel and return her to him, unharmed. He would have him collect Haggel and Tasche as well. No matter what that required.

"Isn't there some means to shut her up?" Haggel said, pulling at the door on the old keep at Maardre.

"There is, but not yet," Tasche answered, glaring at Shassel as two soldiers carried her in and laid her on the floor as quickly as they could. They wore strips torn from blankets wrapped around their hands to keep from being burned, a consequence of holding onto Shassel this past day and a half. Though the warmth, some of the men conceded, was partly welcome considering their general condition. While they continued to improve, the men looked abhorrent: their skin greenish-brown and mildewed, rotting clothing, snot running out of their noses between bouts of coughing and hacking, their hair falling out in clumps. All particularly unsightly, so far as Haggel was concerned. He remained eminently pleased that he had not entered the cabin with them that night, not until Shassel had been hobbled by Tasche's binding spell.

"We rest tonight," Tasche said. "I will need most of the day tomorrow to prepare. By the end of the day I will be ready to do all that must be done. Once the spell is completed, I assure you, she will be silent."

Not a moment too soon, as far as Haggel was concerned. She hadn't stopped riding, degrading and threatening him, his father, Tasche, the soldiers and every man, woman and child in Grenarii since they had left her cottage in Briarlea.

"There are ghosts here," she said now. "I will speak to them. They were wronged by your family, young fool Haggel. They will want your blood when I am through."

Haggel glanced up and about reflexively, part of

him expecting to see something in the shadows and corners of the large hall. The lord who built this place had been dead for years and the lands had gone back to forest. The walls that once protected the castle were but tumbled remnants now, though the keep still had a roof, or most of one, which made it suitable enough for their purposes. Haggel didn't know what had happened to those that once lived here, and he hoped he wouldn't have to learn.

"I will tend to any ghosts that bother us," Tasche said, haughtily. "I fear no such things."

"Fear comes either from ignorance or wisdom," Shassel said. "You lack the wisdom even to tell the difference."

Tasche's light brown face turned florid at this. He looked about to explode. Haggel shook his head in frustration. "This is all I need," he said. "If you fall apart, everything does."

"Yes, yes, yes," Tasche said, looking too much like a scolded child for Haggel's tastes; he'd been that too many times himself.

The two of them just stood there. Haggel thought it an awkward moment. He was nervous about absolutely everything: the spell Tasche was counting on, the very idea of defying and likely imprisoning his father—at least for a time, the idea of actually assuming the throne of Grenarii—as opposed to thinking about it. And then there was Shassel and her threats, and Frost, whom they knew almost nothing about. The one thing he didn't doubt was his own destiny to rule as no one had ruled before. Somehow. Soon. It was getting there that posed most of the difficulties.

"We need a good night's sleep," Haggel said finally.

"Not so likely to happen," Shassel said, adding a laugh that was more a cackle.

"A good night's sleep," Tasche affirmed. Then he added, "To forget about the old woman and her big mouth!"

"She will not forget either of you," Shassel told them.

Tasche was glaring again, turning red again—or still. Haggel had had enough. He shook his head and went to find a suitable place to lie down for the night. The lord's old bed was still usable, though fresh stuffing would have been nice. He lay down and fell asleep quickly, as he always did, though he slept uneasily, dreaming of ghosts chasing him. He woke up screaming when they caught up to him, then realized where he was. He peered into the quiet darkness but saw nothing, and went back to sleep. The third time he woke up screaming he gave up and decided to sit up the rest of the night. Which proved boring, so he woke Tasche a little early, and asked when the spell-working would begin.

"I want to watch," he said.

"There is not much to see," Tasche replied bleary-eyed, after grumbling that the sun had not quite risen yet. "A lot of concentrating, a lot of reciting and confirmations, a little testing, more reciting, more building, more overlaying, and so on."

Haggel shrugged. "What can I do to help?"

"It is a most difficult and dangerous task I am undertaking," Tasche replied. "You can see that I am not disturbed."

That was what soldiers were for, but Haggel only had a handful of those, and none was in very good shape. Still, out here in the middle of nowhere there were no distractions anyway, which made the job palatable even for a prince.

"Very well, get to work. I grow anxious."

"So do I, but I haven't had breakfast."

"You don't need it," Haggel said, making a show of sizing up the enormous proportions the wizard expressed.

Tasche frowned condescendingly. "Food is strength, and hunger is a distraction."

Haggel tried to think of a response but decided it was too much trouble. "Then eat!" he said, throwing up his hands. He left Tasche alone and went to awaken his men.

"Can we get on with this?" Haggel asked Tasche. "It will be dark again before long."

Tasche turned on him, clearly irritated. Haggel didn't care. The bugs in the forest were eating them alive, the fresh food was nearly gone, and he was bored silly; but mostly he was dying to get a look at Tasche's most powerful, incredible, boundary-crossing, sorcerer-snubbing aberration of darkness that was to come from this most difficult spell-working Tasche claimed to have spent so many years on.

"It goes well," Tasche said through his teeth.

"I am impatient," Haggel said. It was about time, and Tasche knew it. But now, as he studied it, Haggel wasn't sure he liked the look on the other's face— one he was not accustomed to seeing there. Concern? Consternation? Fear?

"What's wrong?" Haggel asked.

"Nothing, nothing is wrong," Tasche snarled, turning back to the staff laid before him on the floor and the smoldering earthen pots set one to either side, each the size of a man's head. Whatever was in them smelled horrible, like burning dung with some sort of sour plant, surely poisonous, mixed in. The smoke curled about Tasche and drifted through the poorly lit room keeping company with the echoes of Tasche's chants as he went back to him.

"How much more is there?" Haggel asked honestly.

"Indeed, we are ready, if that pleases my prince," Tasche said with venom.

Haggel dismissed it. "Good," he said.

Tasche got slowly to his feet, then instructed the two soldiers present to pick up the bowls. "Follow along," he told them. Then he nodded toward Shassel.

"Bring her," Haggel commanded, and the other two guards wrapped their hands, picked her up, and followed the others outside.

They walked well into the woods and away from the old walls and keep until they reached a large clearing, now knee-deep in brush and shrubbery, where grain had once been grown. The sun had just disappeared behind the tops of the trees to the west and the clearing was already cast mostly in shadows. When they reached the middle Tasche bid everyone halt. Then he had the two soldiers carrying the pots tramp some of the ground cover flat, an area oval in shape, eight paces across and six wide. Next they were told to place the pots at either end of the trampled spot, and Shassel was laid length-wise in the middle, head and toes pointed at the pots.

Now Tasche strode forward, placed the point of his staff in the earth beside Shassel, and began to chant once more. The chants went on for several moments, the same four, repeating. Haggel had no idea what the sorcerer was saying, the words were not familiar, but it sounded quite dire. Haggel guessed that was probably good. He tried to grin at the tension, then he jumped as he heard a yelp—from Shassel.

"What are you doing!" she screeched "Are you an idiot, or a fool, or both?"

"Silence!" Tasche shouted at Shassel. "Why?" the old woman asked. "I hear you well, and I cannot believe what I am hearing. Even I would not attempt such a thing. If you continue with this madness, you will destroy all of us, perhaps many more!"

"I refuse to listen to you," Tasche said. "You would say anything to save yourself and to change the course of this night. You have only your life to concern you. I look to the future of this realm and the destiny of its prince!"

Shassel coughed. "*Who* would say *anything*?"

"Tasche is right," Haggel said. He leaned over so as to spit on Shassel's prone form, but at the last instant thought again. "We expected you to try and save yourself. We did not expect it would be such a pathetic attempt."

Tasche sent Haggel an approving nod.

"You want to see pathetic, allow your half-witted sorcerer to continue," Shassel answered. "You will be sadly enlightened. He does not know what he is about. He has bits and pieces of the spells he needs to bring forth a creature of the darkness, but he does not know what sort of beast he will conjure. He is making much of this up as he goes, guessing, rounding, blundering. He does not have the mastery required to do what he is attempting, not on such a scale."

"I do!" Tasche howled.

"Do not!" Shassel snapped back.

"My skills are greater than you know!"

"Your eagerness exceeds your talent."

"Shut up!" Tasche boomed. "Just shut up!"

"You are insane," Shassel told him. "You don't know what the darkness holds, what beings you would conjure. You are like a boy groping with his hand in a murky pond. You might well catch something, but you will not know what until it is in your midst. That should worry you, Tasche, and you, Haggel, but I fear put together you have not the head to know it!"

Tasche made a clear and desperate attempt to collect himself. "I have been preparing for this moment for half my life," he said, to Shassel, as far as Haggel could tell. "I have everything I need."

"And I have been preparing to lead Grenarii for most of mine," Haggel added, supportive.

"The time is now," Tasche said.

"The time has come," Haggel said.

"Your time has run out unless you cease this

madness," Shassel said. "If you persist I shall have my revenge one way or another."

"No more from you!" Tasche boomed, eyes on fire now, obsessed, another look Haggel had not seen before. He growled the final phrases of the spell beneath his breath, keeping them from the ears of Shassel and Haggel alike. Then he raised his staff and raised his voice in a long, low moan that climbed until Haggel thought the sorcerer would strangle himself. Tasche went abruptly silent and the two earthen pots boiled over. They spewed rancid smoke and brown foam that rolled down the sides and steamed up in clouds over the grass.

A shroud of darkness emanated from the staff, growing to envelope Shassel, the pots, Tasche, and—before he could move away—Haggel and the soldiers as well. The darkness grew further until it was as tall as the forest's oldest trees and far enough across that Haggel could not determine its edge anymore.

And with that darkness came heat like that of a dozen summer suns; it flowed over Haggel on a harsh, dry breeze and made his scalp and spine tingle.

Haggel heard Shassel calling out—words garbled by the sound of the boiling pots and the hot wind and as it picked up, causing clothing to flutter and snap and the surrounding bushes and grass to bend. Tasche suddenly faltered as if he'd been struck hard in the gut, and his staff wavered. The darkness grew uneven, thickening here, thinning there, all of it mixing and swirling while the hot winds grew to violent gusts. Tasche screamed as if his voice were being torn from his throat, a sound unlike any Haggel had ever heard—the sound of rage, that was the bulk of it, but seared with something more disturbing, something akin to panic.

"There!" Tasche shouted, straightening and glaring down at Shassel as the darkness seemed to solidify and the winds again came in a hot and steady stream.

"Now I have turned your strength to me, your essence, your life!"

Haggel looked on in awe as Shassel died, glowing bright white for an instant, then turning a charred and withered gray before her body burst into flames. The brightness flowed to Tasche's staff, followed by the fire. Then the winds ceased, and the air grew suddenly cold.

Just beyond the pots a great and utter blackness existed now, surrounded by silence, a hole in the universe, and from it stepped the beast.

Tasche shook himself loose from the trance that had gripped him. His heart was pounding as he used his sleeve to draw sweat-soaked hair out of his face. Still more sweat dripped off his chins and ran hot down the rolls of fat inside his robes, making the cloth cling to him. His head was pounding, his hands were shaking, his eyes burned, but he had done it!

The creature materializing before him was more incredible than he could have hoped. A hideous thing that towered above him, easily as tall as six men, and broad as a building. It glowed like the coals in the heart of a campfire, smoldering black lace over molten crimson that flared ever brighter in dozens of spots as the winds swirled around the beast. Its limbs were massive, like ancient trees, and all four of them ended in claws that appeared more reptilian than any a warm blooded creature might have, and each talon had a dry, dull sheen like freshly fired iron.

Tasche turned to Haggel and found exactly what he was looking for, a face filled with awe, astonishment, and terror. This was the look that would find the faces of all those who sought to oppose them. The last expression for hundreds, perhaps thousands of fools.

But for now another task awaited. He must control the beast, and he had carefully prepared the spells designed to do just that. He need only . . .

"Tasche!" Haggel shouted.

Tasche felt a jolt of annoyance as he turned. "What?"

"What is it doing!" Haggel said pleadingly, like a child. Tasche winced at a stiffness in his neck. He didn't have time for this. He turned and looked as the smell washed over him, a stench like rotten meat thrown into a fire, but with it came the more familiar, more palatable aroma of a hearth fire, of wood burning. Tasche narrowed his gaze against the wind and blowing smoke and saw that the forest itself was on fire. And the fires were spreading.

"It is . . . moving," Tasche answered after a long, intense pause. He watched the incredible creature shift from one side to the other, pivoting its whole body to compensate for the lack of any neck. It had no eyes in the normal sense, only two great, blackened holes in its bulbous and glowing head. Whatever it was looking for, Tasche decided, it had apparently not taken notice of Haggel or himself. Not yet.

"Is this supposed to happen?" Haggel yelled even louder, shielding his face with his sleeve against the growing walls of flames that snapped all around them now.

"It is the energy from the creature or my spells combined with it that has gone slightly . . . er, awry."

"Awry? The whole forest is on fire!" Haggel shouted, backing away from Tasche, the beast and the center of the clearing, following his men.

"Not the *whole* forest," Tasche said. "A good deal of it, perhaps, but a few trees will not be missed . . ."

"All of them will be!"

Tasche tried to breathe and forget the cowardly prince. He had to concentrate. He tried to remember the spells he had so carefully prepared and memorized, yet now they somehow seemed to go missing in his brain. Or parts of them did.

Tasche watched the beast take several steps, getting its balance, then it began to wander about, apparently aimless. *The whole forest* will *catch*, Tasche thought wearily, working at the parts of the controlling spells he could recall. The rest was coming back to him, he just needed a moment. If only the fires would stay away long enough to . . .

To his sudden surprise, that was what happened. Indeed, the flames began to disappear. As the beast moved about, it was somehow absorbing all the energy from the flames its worldly birth had created. Then, like water down a hole, the fires rushed to it and vanished, leaving only smoke and smoldering remains in its wake. In moments the fires were all but gone. But the beast kept walking, wandering here and there.

"Is *that* supposed to happen?" Haggel asked. "Is *any* of this supposed to happen?"

Tasche forgot the next line of the spells as he watched wide-eyed with wonder. As the beast walked through unburned forest every living thing around it was turning brown and dying, as if all living energies were being absorbed. And Tasche had begun to notice another effect as well—the farther the creature walked, the larger it grew.

"It is . . . more than I expected," Tasche admitted, blinking as he racked his brain for the knowledge he had put there. More pieces came to him, reason overcoming the combination of dread and astonishment that sought to paralyze his thoughts.

"Do something!"

"I have the controlling spell at hand," he told Haggel with as much determination as he could manage. "It is not too late. We will have this beast at our beck and call!"

"Good," Haggel said, as Tasche raised his hands, waved his staff, and recited the four final phrases his spell required.

"At least it hasn't seen us yet," Haggel said, from

at least twenty paces behind Tasche, and still moving further back.

No matter, Tasche thought, as he added his binding phrase and initiated the controlling spell . . . *Soon enough now it—*

Tasche swallowed as the beast turned, struck by the controlling spell just as it should be, but not slowed, not still, as it should have been. It kept turning—toward its master.

"Well, it sees us now!" Haggel howled, clearly not as pleased by the result as Tasche.

Tasche repeated the binding phrase, which was surely the problem. "Do not fear, my prince, the spell is working!" he said. The beast took two giant steps toward them. "In a moment everything we have worked for will be realized," Tasche went on, holding his staff high before him and waving it again. Waving the beast to halt.

"Are you sure?" Haggel asked, still further away.

"Yes, I—I—" The words caught in his throat as the beast lumbered toward him, picking up speed. Tasche stepped quickly left behind a tree he knew was much too small. But in a related way the move was a good one. He watched as the beast reached out with one massive, black claw and snatched a screaming, writhing Haggel up off the ground instead of him. A hole opened in the beast's face, somewhere below its eyes, and Haggel vanished inside.

Tasche heard a fresh scream—a sound that seemed exotic and strange as it found his ears, as if it belonged to someone else—then he realized it was him, and he screamed again as the beast tore the tree out of the ground and stared down at him. Tasche felt his throat seizing up. He tried all the same to repeat the last two phrases of the controlling spell, changing them slightly, hoping . . .

It should have worked! he thought. He had done everything right. Had done all that was required. He should be in control of the beast by now, completely.

He repeated the spell and fed it everything he could. Felt the fat on his body melting off as he let go of any constraints and let the spell feed freely on his reserves.

The beast raged as it reared back. It howled with a sound that seemed to come from the earth itself, a sound like the ground opening up. *Yes,* Tasche thought, straining desperately. But then the beast came around again, fighting the spell off. It reached out, and Tasche felt himself swept away just as Haggel had been, felt the hot claws of the beast wrap around him and tighten unmercifully.

Darkness met searching pain for an instant as he was consumed, but suddenly the pain vanished. He waited, but the end Tasche expected did not come after that. He still existed, but where?

Then he knew. He felt himself a part of the mind of the creature—a dim seething mind much like its body—and though he could not remember much about whom or what he had been, he knew he still lived, somehow.

The spell! He remembered that much. *My spells were not a total loss,* he thought, gloating, aware of the spell itself still resonating around him. Some part of his former mind knew this was perhaps not the happiest of results, but he tried not to dwell on that. There was much to think about.

Already he found it difficult to tell which parts were of him, and which were of the dim consciousness of the creature itself, but that seemed to matter less and less the more he thought about it. The creature burned with strength and magic, it seethed with fire, with life and death. It called itself . . . Tasche? Yes, that was it. Or that would do. The thing had too little a mind and too vague an identity to argue. They were all and one, whoever they were. *Tasche will do!*

Tasche could not recall precisely who had summoned

them here, but they had been summoned to take life, all life, everywhere it could be found. Everything, every bit and breath. That was why they existed. And as long as they could find more life they would not die.

There had been another, though. A prince? The term meant nothing. That other's essence had been dismantled and made a very small part of the whole.

And yet—there had been another before that . . . hadn't there?

Yes. They remembered . . . a someone. Tasche remembered. Someone much larger.

Another whose voice Tasche could hear somewhere deep within the nether reaches of his consciousness. *But who?*

No name came forth, no true memory, not now at least. But a part of Tasche was sure this other had been there when they had been given birth from one universe into another. *This other, she is . . .*

A she?

Tasche's mind began to reel at the vastness of such thoughts. Tasche needed simplicity, needed to move on, needed to do what they had come here to do. A welcome distraction caught his attention, and he strode toward it.

CHAPTER FIFTEEN

Captain Durret's eyes were raw from rubbing them with his fingers. He couldn't help it. He couldn't believe what he had seen. Not to mention the smoke. Finding their quarry had not been difficult. Durret had asked about them, and travelers through these woods were rare enough that they were most often remembered. There were also few places his quarry could go where the eyes of others would not be about, busying themselves with everyone else's business. Durret expected Prince Haggel and Tasche would desire secrecy, whatever they were up to, and he had been right; it had taken him very little time to turn them up once he had the direction down. But then he'd come upon them . . .

Whatever they were doing, Durret was certain it was horribly evil. He thought it ever since he'd crept near, taking care not to be seen, and began to watch the strange goings-on in the tangled clearing, a place not far from the old castle's eastern wall. The onset of dusk had concealed too much detail at first, but then the burning giant had appeared, glowing deep red and spewing smoke, and setting the forest on fire. Durret had been ready to order a retreat when the giant suddenly began to suck the flames off the trees and ground cover, until all of it was gone.

The beast had wandered about after that, for a moment. Then, as Durret watched in astonishment, it had turned and gone after Prince Haggel and the wizard Tasche, snatching them up and popping them down its maw like so many grapes.

He wasn't sure whether his Lord Kolhol would be pleased or not when he learned of all this, but there was little to be done about it either way. Durret's mission had ceased to exist.

He would have a hard time explaining this, no matter what else happened. Kolhol had been counting on him. But what he was witnessing defied explanation. As he kept watch, Durret became fascinated by the effect the beast was having on the forest. Everywhere it walked, everything alive turned brown and seemed to die. He'd never seen the like, or the like of the horrible burning beast itself. The scene was mesmerizing. Until he realized the beast was turning toward them . . .

"Get out of here!" Durret commanded his troops. "Run!"

He turned and followed as the men scurried away to their horses. Then he led the retreat that began in a thunder of horses' hooves, but those sounds started to thin almost at once, replaced by sounds of men shouting out or screaming in terror. Durret looked back over his shoulder and saw the giant right behind his troops, loping along at an easy gait, methodically scooping up horses and riders and sucking them down. He heard the horses' shrill whines, heard his men call out as they were consumed. There was nothing he could do except keep riding, and hope the creature tired of the chase before Durret ran out of men.

In fact, to Durret's hysterical relief, it did. At last, slowed by the thickening of the forest or simply because it had changed its mind—to Durret it didn't matter—the creature fell back and stood on top of a long, steep hill, where it watched its quarry pick their way through the trees. Durret counted three men still with him. Three of thirty. Kolhol would be even less pleased than Durret might have once imagined possible.

But there was still more bad news. The creature might turn any which way—who could tell?—but if it stayed on the course Durret had clearly, and unfortunately, set for it, if it followed the road at the bottom of the hill, it would end up in Lord Kolhol's lap. The Grenarii kingdom, or most of it, would perish in a matter of days.

Durret reached the road and set off at a gallop. He kept pushing his mount, riding it to death. He had nothing to lose. Or everything.

Kolhol sat tightening his grimace as he listened to Durret try his best to recount what he had seen in the forest, and what happened after that. Kolhol had already decided no disciplinary actions would be taken against the commander—the man was white as a ghost and shaking so badly he was having a hard time speaking clearly enough to be understood—and the story he told was too incredible to be contrived, even by someone good at it, let alone a trusted, loyal, simple soldier like Durret.

Besides, the news wasn't all bad; he was finally rid of that poor excuse for a sorcerer, Tasche. His son was dead though, and that was something Kolhol had mixed feelings about. He was glad to be free of the worry over how traitorous the boy's heart truly was, and the disappointment at having already learned most of that answer. Haggel had been Kolhol's only son, after all. Which was a pity, in more ways than one.

"And what of the demon creature?" Kolhol asked. "Where is it now?"

"It is—uh, we think it is, uh, it could be—"

"Out with it!" Kolhol boomed, suddenly short on patience.

Durret hung his head. "It may be . . . on its way here."

Kolhol swallowed. *Here?* Durret nodded as if he had heard the thought.

"My lord," one of the royal pages called from the doorway. "A visitor is at the outer gates. He wishes an audience at once."

"Who is it?" Kolhol barked, in no mood for this, either.

"A sorcerer. He says his name is Frost."

By the Gods! In large part Kolhol had hoped for a visit from Frost at some point, but this was not that point. If everything his well-paid visitor from Worlish had said was true, Frost was here looking for his aunt, Shassel; and for justice to be dispensed upon those who had taken her. All of which was a very large problem, in light of what had just happened. Kolhol was not a great talker, he was a warrior by trade. But killing Frost, or attempting to, was probably unwise at best, even if half his reputation was true. He was too dangerous, and potentially too useful. Then there was the matter of the mythical, legendary Demon Blade he supposedly had . . .

No, there was but one course of action. *Lie.*

"Bring him here at once!" Kolhol commanded.

"What of the two warriors with him?"

"Bring them as well, if they insist."

"They will."

Kolhol nodded, then waited while the page went to fetch Frost. A few moments later the sorcerer and his warriors strode up the center of the great hall, and stood before the king. Frost was large but not slovenly, not quite the sort of bulk Tasche had supported, nor was there quite as much of it. No, muscle guided Frost's every movement, and an air of confidence Tasche could never have imagined. He was brightly robed and topped by a bright, floppy hat; he wore a dark, short-cropped beard and long dark hair that emerged from beneath the hat and fell nearly to his shoulders. He held an unremarkable staff in one hand and gestured a greeting with the other.

Kolhol was instantly envious of the two warriors, especially the female, tall, dark-skinned and powerful, clad in overlapping leather and metal sewn armor. The male was even larger and looked the equal of any opponent Kolhol could imagine. Each of them carried the most impressive weapons Kolhol had ever seen, certainly they were Subartans of the Kaya Desert.

"A fine palace," Frost said. "My compliments, Lord Kolhol." Frost's voice was large and assertive, befitting his girth and stature.

"I have heard many things about you, Frost, most of them good. They say you live by a code. So do I."

"One man's code need not be another's."

Kolhol moaned under his breath. He'd expected this would not be easy, but one could always hope for the unexpected. He cleared his throat and went on.

"I find myself in need of the services of one such as yourself. Would you consider, for the right rewards . . . ?"

"Many are in need of me. Many go unsatisfied. Some go in devastation. But you need not concern yourself with that. I have come here today for only one reason, the safe return of my aunt Shassel, who was taken here by your own soldiers. No doubt behind your back. Which does not speak well of you or your men, but for now that is only your misfortune, and I do not intend to add to it. No, this day I want only Shassel. Immediately."

Kolhol had no answer Frost would want to hear. He did, however, have two paths to follow as he saw it: He could order his men to attack Frost and attempt to kill him, even join in perhaps, and end up with a lot of dead and wounded—or he could do as he'd planned, and lie. Place blame where he could and leave it there. Yet he needed Frost's help as well. His life, perhaps the future of Grenarii, was at stake. He couldn't let Frost turn him down. He had to make sure that didn't happen.

Already he saw that such a course would require very big lies, dangerous lies. However, as he saw it, he didn't have much of a choice; and he could blend the lies with the truth, so as to make the mix more palatable. Kolhol smiled to himself and tried to feel a little better about it. A young warrior had only brawn and enthusiasm, but he had other weapons these days—his experience and his wits—a boast his son and that wizard Tasche could not make.

"I do have her," he said, trying not to wince as he did. "And she is—safe and sound. I will turn her over to you very soon, but first, I need your help. In fact, we can help each other. I cannot get to her, you see. My son, Prince Haggel and my own court wizard, Tasche, have her tucked away in an old castle in the Maardre Forest to the east. A great demon beast of some kind stands between them and us, a beast I fear even my great army may not be able to stop. It wreaks havoc in the countryside even now, causing death and destruction wherever it goes."

"There are always beasts, always troubles," Frost replied, shaking his head. "I am not concerned with yours, only my own. Deal with this trouble yourself and return Shassel to me, or the beast will be the least of your worries."

"Surely you can help! I will pay you very well, you will save countless lives, and you will get your aunt back. If we cannot reach her, how will you? What if the beast turns back toward the castle before we can stop it, what then?"

"It is you who brought her here, therefore it is you who must bring her to me. Unharmed."

Kolhol watched the two warriors; they stood straight, feet apart, breathing steadily, eyes in constant motion, muscles tense and ready but not strained. *Magnificent*, he thought. He would lose a lot of time and men trying to get past them to attack the wizard, and that would give the wizard time to visit all manner of vile magery upon him . . .

"It is not my fault!" Kolhol said, adding another truth to the lies, a painful truth. "My son and Tasche went behind my back. I have no idea what they think they are up to, snatching your aunt, demon creatures, hiding in the forests; but I am only too happy to deal with them as soon as I can get to them. We are both victims, Frost, and we can help each other. It is the only way."

Frost was clearly thinking things over, and Kolhol began to think he may have said just the right thing. Which would please him immensely. If he could get Frost to rid the kingdom of the beast, then Haggel and Tasche—who were apparently already dead—could be blamed for Shassel's death. Meanwhile, Kolhol could work on Frost a little more, try to find a way to win him over, to convince him to fight at Kolhol's side in the inevitable war with Worlish.

Frost said nothing. Kolhol felt himself falling prey to frustration and anger, and why shouldn't he? "My men are fighting the beast, they are dying even now," he said.

"I am reluctant to believe you, Kolhol," Frost said at last. "Though it seems I have little choice for the time being. But I must warn you, that may be a short time."

"Fair enough!" Kolhol shouted to the heavens, rising to his feet. The gods were smiling on him this day. And if they were not, he didn't need them anyway. He raised one fist in the air. "We leave at once!"

Frost did not trust Kolhol even within sight of him; all the same he had the king and his soldiers, more than sixty in all, ride ahead while he and his Subartans followed along behind. It was dark by the time they left, and several times the troops stopped to rest, even to sleep briefly. Frost did not protest. He had been riding horseback almost non-stop for days; he was sore, everything hurt, and he was extremely tired, yet even his sleep, when he managed any, was fitful and worried. But a little rest still helped, and would be needed if the task of dealing with the demon creature was to be a difficult one. He tried to redirect his thoughts, to concentrate on the coming encounter, and do his best to prepare.

He didn't doubt that he would prevail. Tasche, by Frost's best estimate, was not capable of the complex and exhaustive lengths required to extract a truly powerful creature from the darkness. But whatever he'd accomplished, controlling any order of dark manifestation would be the far more difficult part of his plan—though apparently Tasche had already found that out.

"What do you plan to do when we find the beast?" Kolhol asked, as the troops rested on a hilltop overlooking a small and peaceful moonlit valley.

"When we do, I will tell you," Frost answered. Kolhol took affront, but Frost made no effort to placate him. He had no intention of chatting with the king, of making "friends." Though clearly Kolhol was trying to move in that direction. The more time Frost spent around Kolhol, the less he trusted the man; not that Kolhol struck him as an evil sort, or a veteran liar, like Andair, but the sense that there was more here than Kolhol was letting on was unshakable. So

Frost shook Kolhol off and went back to his meditations, until the order was given, and they got moving again.

It was just after dawn when they came upon the beast.

The men at the front of the line barked the alarm as they crested a low knoll, but everyone, all the way back, saw the creature at the same time—a towering thing, tromping through the forest, smoking and glowing and leaving a trail of burnt, steaming, crackling woodland wreckage behind. Frost had expected a monster, but the beast before him now exceeded all expectations.

It had grown taller than the oldest trees and bigger around than the towers of Weldhem Castle—and it was moving along the main road, a path that would take it through Grenarii's most populated areas. Frost held fast on the knoll and watched, surrounded by Kolhol's soldiers; both were there to protect and aid the other, though neither drew comfort from the fact as their eyes had borne witness to what was happening.

"Kolhol, do you see that?" Frost said, pointing with the top of his staff and poking Kolhol's side with his elbow as the king drew up beside him. Kolhol did not so much as flinch, so dazzled was he by the sight. As the beast walked, everything before it burst into flames, but in its wake only faint trails of smoke curled up from the places where it had been. Kolhol did nod, however slightly.

"Your wizard Tasche has outdone himself, whether by accident or design," Frost said. "Containing that beast will be difficult and costly, if it is possible at all."

"But you have the Demon Blade!" Kolhol blurted out, as if his trance had suddenly been broken. He turned but stopped short of grabbing Frost by the arms. "You can stop it, can't you?"

Frost said nothing as he went back to watching the destruction drawing nearer. All around, beyond the reach of the flames and the blackened, smoky trail they left behind, everything that lived was dying. The circle of death extended several hundred paces from the demon beast, and the effect was almost instantaneous.

"The creature can absorb any sort of energy, and at an extravagant rate," Frost explained, "which poses a particular problem."

"What?" Kolhol asked, growing incredibly keen now. "What problem? Surely you can fight it."

Frost sighed and closed his eyes for a moment. It would take too long to explain to someone like Kolhol, but clearly, he must try. He took a breath and turned to the king: "Any attempt to use the Demon Blade against that beast might well backfire," he said. "It would come down to a contest between the Demon Blade's ability to draw energy from the creature, and the creature's ability to draw from the Blade—and from me." *If I do anything even slightly wrong*, Frost guessed, *the beast might outpull me, might drain me instead.*

"You are not making any sense!" Kolhol argued.

"And you are making too much noise."

"By the Gods!" Kolhol cursed.

"Your gods can help if they like," Frost said, annoyed at the way his attention was being divided. Kolhol seemed intensely frustrated—a warrior's rage barely contained—or the rage had flared to cover something else.

"Why don't you just strike it down?" Kolhol huffed. "What good is a magical sword if you can't use it?"

"The answer is complicated, but the power of the Blade does not work that way."

"But ours do!" Kolhol shouted, wild in the eyes now as his horse stirred beneath him and the beast lumbered nearer. He drew his sword, which brought a great chorus of ringing steel as sixty men drew theirs in kind.

We will need to do better, Frost thought, paying them as little mind as possible. He had few options, but the only one that came to mind was to combat the beast by pulling energy from another source, then using it and all the power he could draw from himself to create an intense, single pulse strong enough to destroy the creature. But if the beast absorbed the blast, it would grow much stronger instead, and larger, and then there would be no other means of stopping it. Not even with sixty courageous warriors.

"Wait," Frost said. "Hold your men."

"We have to do something, or it will keep growing and walking and growing, keep destroying everything until it has laid waste to half of Grenarii, and perhaps much of Worlish to come after," Kolhol said.

Quite correct, Frost thought. "I know," he said. "But tell your men to stay back for now. I have something in mind." With that he dismounted, and started ahead, toward the beast.

"It's about time!" Kolhol shouted after him, but Frost noted neither king nor soldiers tried to follow.

The stock remedy for an unsavory creature of preternatural heritage—especially when controlling the creature was not possible—was to construct a magical trap, and traps were something Frost had his share of experience with. The spell that had always worked best for him was a straight-forward one, though it came in five parts, each of which worked to form one side and finally the top of the magical "box." Size was all that mattered after that, along with supplying the trap with enough energy to maintain it against the usually violent attempts of whatever was inside to escape. In this case, the trap was going to have to be very, very big; indeed, Frost had never attempted to build one like it, and so far as he knew no one else had, either. He walked on, followed closely by his Subartans, until he stood as near as he dared. With each step he grew increasingly aware of the depths of the demon beast's powers, and he feared no trap or spell might work against it. *An almost irrational fear*, he thought, and probably due in some part to the creature's powers as well. Whatever Tasche had done, he'd done it huge, and blundered badly, that was certain. Almost as certain as his consequent demise, though that remained to be seen.

Summoning all his strengths, Frost finished the fourth, then the fifth segments of the spell, then added his binding phrase, and the trap began to take shape. A faint crackling of energies marked the outline of a rough and changing bluish-green cube that formed all around the beast and sizzled harmlessly where it came in contact with the leaves and branches of nearby treetops. The beast seemed oblivious to all of this, and made no reaction out of the ordinary— ordinary for it—until it turned and glanced downward and caught sight of Frost. For an instant nothing happened. Then the beast suddenly raged toward him.

Frost fed energy to the spell and the outline of the cube flared into a brilliant blue-white wall through which the creature could be seen—arms and black claws flailing, the gaping black hole that must be its mouth opening as if the creature was howling up at the gods. Frost heard and felt the sound, shrill, yet bone-jarring at the same time. It echoed more in his mind than in his ears, and he wondered if the others could hear it at all over the fierce crackling of the cage. Then he felt the onset of fatigue as the spell began to take from him more than he could give it.

He held on, trying to maintain the spell as long as he could, fighting the beast's best efforts. Abruptly the beast fell back, apparently relenting. But after only a moment it spread its massive, molten arms and hands out to either side, threw its head back and howled anew, a very different, horn-like tone. Before

Frost's eyes it turned an even deeper shade of orange-red beneath the black outlines. Suddenly the cage vanished into the beast, and was gone.

Frost stumbled back and fell. Rosivok tried to catch him but he landed sprawled on his haunches, one hand clasped to Rosivok's while the other clung to his staff. He tried to get his bearings, and realized the beast was coming toward him again.

Frost felt two pairs of strong arms grab hold of him just below the shoulders and haul back. Sharryl and Rosivok ran as best they could, pulling Frost along with them as if he weighed only half of what he truly did. *Well, I nearly do*, he thought, remembering that he was well below his physical peak these days. He felt inadequate, and decided in almost the same instant that he could not afford to be anything like that, no matter if he was . . .

"You have failed!" Kolhol said with venom as the Subartans drew up among the others again, then helped Frost get his feet under him. "You are no better than Tasche!"

"Your opinion is your own, but I would have you show me anyone who might do better," Frost said, almost as bitter.

Then he turned to his Subartans. "The beast could have digested the cage at any time," he said. "It did not. Not until it realized it could. It did not understand."

"It is stupid," Sharryl said, nodding understanding.

"Yes," Frost answered. "Go," he added, speaking now to Rosivok as well, "and circle around it. Take some of Kolhol's men, if you can get them out of hiding. Keep circling and attacking it with the slings, javelins, arrows, anything they've brought."

"How can we hope to harm it?" Kolhol demanded.

"The idea is to keep it thoroughly confused," Frost answered. "You must all do that, while I do what I must."

"You have another idea?" Kolhol asked.

"Yes."

The beast paused, clearly within striking distance, apparently taking aim. Frost accepted the nods of his Subartans—and Kolhol—then watched them fan out into the forest and begin their attacks. The beast turned as expected, this way, then that. When it was sufficiently occupied, Frost removed his cloak, pulled the harness around, unwrapped the cloth and drew the Demon Blade.

Frost! Tasche came to realize the name as they, as *he,* looked down at the figure that approached. The name meant nothing to the rest of his demon mind, but enough of Tasche responded. Tasche could not think straight, could not see well, could not move as he had always moved. Fire churned in his belly, smoke filled his lungs, darkness welled up immeasurably behind him—yet all this meant almost nothing when compared to the energy that coursed through his body like a river fed by countless tiny springs. Power, strength and energy beyond imagining was his to do with as he wished, and he wished . . .

He wished for more!

He had the greatest urge to laugh out loud, loud as he could, loud enough to render deaf anyone in earshot. He did not seem to have that capacity, exactly, but he could do other things, he wanted to do other things, needed . . .

He needed to destroy Frost!

Yes, that was answer enough to a host of questions. Tasche had played second to such as him for most of his life, had always been challenged to prove himself equal to them, had always fallen short.

No! he thought. *Now, here, it is different!*

Tasche—Demon Tasche, unstoppable, splendid in his burning, growing, stomping glory. He tried to remember his spells, that was what this Frost would use to try to save himself, but the memories proved difficult somehow. Then he understood he didn't need them. He could simply draw the very life out of Frost, out of any like him, out of anything that lived.

Men scurried about, attacking him in their pitiful way. Tasche killed a few, but only a few. Many more could be killed later, he thought, men who belonged to Kolhol, once Tasche's king, though soon he too would be no more. But their sparks were small, as was the task of extinguishing them. Frost's was large, and he was there, right there, just stepping out from among the trees. Up to something, but it would not work.

Tasche felt his own excitement and the excited rage of the beast unite completely as he surged forward, close enough that Frost could not escape. He howled like mad, even though no one could hear, and reached for his prey.

Frost heard the sound, the mad howling more like that of a man than the demon beast it had come from. He tried to ignore it as he rushed along, finishing the series of spells that would empower the Demon Blade to do his will—or most of it. Once again he changed the spell just slightly, experimenting, making yet another attempt to finally, truly gain control over the Blade and its effects—to finally learn how to use the Blade without damaging himself and those others he did not intend—not to mention mountains.

When he had finished the primary spells, he raised the Blade toward the beast—and saw that it was nearly upon him. All around him and within him, everything began to die. Frost sounded out his binding phrase, and let go his controls, and the Blade exploded to life.

Immediately he knew his efforts were once again flawed—that something in the series of complex and altered, bent and borrowed series of spells had not been quite right, and had not worked as it should have. The consequences of his error were swift and devastating. The familiar pain he had nearly managed to put from his mind surged through him, first his hand, then his torso, twisting him from the inside out, debilitating his mind, his senses, his body. He felt his knees buckle, then felt himself sinking. He began to imagine what destruction the Blade might bring to the earth and all who stood anywhere near. The idea was at least as terrifying as the beast itself.

But he was getting better at letting go, he reminded himself, trying to find a positive thought as he struggled to ease the agonizing drain of life energies from every part of his body and mind without losing all the work he had done. When he could again draw a breath and focus his eyes, he saw the beast before him, hovering, gloating at his obvious agony. *So unlike a beast of this sort*, Frost thought. So strange . . .

The beast straightened, fixed to lunge. Frost saw he had time for only one more attempt, one that might well kill him, but he was beyond holding back because of that anymore. The lives of far too many depended on what he did next, and the time for hesitating, for holding one's bets, had long ago passed. All or nothing, that was the only choice, the one truth he had learned in his battle with the demon Tyrr. He owed that much to Shassel, to Dorin and Dara, to his Subartans, to himself.

He recited the activating spells once more, then raised the Blade just as the beast came for him. It reached toward him with its great black and glowing molten arms before Frost could utter the spell's final phrase—before he could bind it. Long black claws lashed out suddenly and snatched the Demon Blade from him with a precision that took Frost completely by surprise.

He opened his mouth to yell at the creature, but

he learned just then that he no longer had the strength. From his own attempts to use the Blade or from the creature's ability to draw all life from anything near to it, he could not tell, but he had tried, and failed, and lost the Blade in the process.

The beast stood so near right now that the heat radiating from it caused Frost's skin to feel as if it was burning off. But he could not move other than to breathe scorching breaths of air and try to stay on his feet. *No, on my knees,* he realized, as he tried to take stock of himself.

Running would do no good even if he could. The beast would have him with ease.

Sweat dripped into his eyes, burning them, blurring his vision. He just managed to see the beast looming up straight, raising its great arms, and waving the Demon Blade about. It looking tiny as a sewing needle in the beast's clumsy claws, but the thing's enormous triumph was clear and complete. *It will tire of this momentarily, and finish the job of killing me,* Frost thought.

Then a terrible sound from within—like fear and rage all blended together rang out in Frost's mind and even in his ears. As he heard it again he realized there was something else as well, confusion, perhaps. It was difficult to tell, as Frost could not concentrate very well.

He heard a voice then, separate from the demon beast, like a thread unraveling, becoming visible apart from the whole. The voice of a sorcerer he did not recognize at first, though he guessed it must be Tasche. Or some part of Tasche. They were one, somehow, or they had been.

Then another voice! Impossible, but Frost was certain this was a third mind, different and distinct from the others. A voice that drowned out the one that must be Tasche. A voice that spoke to him in words that could not be understood, but that were somehow familiar—somehow so personal that there could be no doubt of it. The words repeated, and became even more familiar. Enough that it came to him in a rush exactly what they were. *A spell of some kind,* he thought, still not certain how he knew, but . . .

My spells! The spells he had used on the Demon Blade to bring it to life. But how could Tasche, if this was him, or the dull-minded beast have the knowledge and skill to wield the Demon Blade? How could they know exactly the phrasing he—?

No, Frost realized, beginning to shake with weakness but clearheaded about at least this much. *Not Tasche.*

Before he could wonder any further he heard the final phrase, and knew that it would almost surely work. That the spell would activate the Blade, and bring it to life. The beast, or Tasche, or whatever this great fiery anomaly truly was altogether, would wield . . .

But his thoughts seized as he heard the words of the binding phrase that came last: *Tesha teshrea!* Then he watched the beast raise its massive claw in the air, shaking as if wracked with a sudden pain, and plunge the Blade straight into the earth.

A deafening roar that came from earth and air and the beast itself drove into Frost's ears, hot spikes that brought his hands up, but instead he used them to shield his eyes from the glow, bright as a hundred lightning strikes, that radiated from the beast for an instant, before it suddenly began to fade, drawing with it a wind that rushed past Frost from all directions, bending tress and flinging a cloud of brush and dead and living limbs and leaves through the air. Frost threw himself on the ground to keep from being swept away, toward the beast as all the wind and fire within the beast flowed hot and brilliant down through its arms, through the Demon Blade and into the ground.

And kept flowing until the creature toppled, jerking and shrinking, and crashed to the earth like a small rockslide. It collapsed in on itself like the remnants of a house fire, then it lay still and dark. Lifeless.

Shassel . . .

Frost realized fully what had happened, and in that instant, as her name filled his mind, something he knew was the shadow of her spirit whispered past him, warm and strong, and freed, and at that same moment he became aware that it was already too late for anything but grief. Grief, and perhaps, a very small joy . . .

CHAPTER SIXTEEN

Winning, yet losing at the same time, left Frost feeling utterly dissatisfied, and nearly drained. The burnt-black carcass of the beast lay crumbling and silent. A hazy smoke that smelled of sulphur, wood and flesh drifted from its gigantic remains. All that it was, all that had been a part of it—Tasche, Shassel, perhaps others as well—was gone.

Sharryl and Rosivok stood beside Frost, waiting patiently and keeping the surviving soldiers away while Frost got to his feet and stood there, teetering, collecting his thoughts. Shassel's death was too big a thing to think about right now, out here in a Grenarii forest. He had always known this day would come, but he had only just found her again, had only begun to make up for the mistakes he had made and the years they had cost him, the life.

"We are riding on to the old castle," Kolhol said, from as near as the Subartans would allow him to get. Frost looked up and saw that the king was already on horseback, as were most of his surviving soldiers. Even now they were assembling behind him.

"You will find no one there, I think," Frost said. "No one alive."

"Then we have burials to tend to."

Frost took a breath, and nodded. "Your son . . ." he began.

"Was still my son, no matter the rest, and I made him a promise, once. I will not leave his remains to be picked at. You owe your aunt that much as well."

"There are no remains, not of Shassel, I am certain of it. Nothing of her is left in this world, save that which exists in memory."

Kolhol seemed to contemplate this for a moment, wheels turning behind eyes just keen enough. "Suit yourself," he said at last, turning in his saddle and looking over what remained of his troops. "I will leave a few men with you as escort. You will go to my castle and be well taken care of, each of you, until I return. Then we can talk. We have much to talk about."

"Take your men," Frost said. "Leave good horses."

"As you wish," Kolhol huffed, clearly frustrated, though he did not delay in saying it. "Promise me you will return and not leave again for Worlish until I have had my say," he asked, before turning his mount to go.

"We will talk again, Lord Kolhol," Frost said. "Be sure of that."

Kolhol kept turning, though he paused once to glance over his shoulder at Frost as if some thought had caught him by the ear and was tugging at him. Then he turned away again, and his men started up the road with him, heading east. In a moment they were gone from sight, leaving Frost, Rosivok and Sharryl alone beside the colossal smoking, reeking corpse of the vanquished demon beast. Frost closed his eyes and breathed a great sigh, but before he could open them a new voice called from behind him, "Ho, Frost!"

A voice Frost thought he recognized, but he had

trouble focussing on such things—on anything, in fact, just now. He shook himself from his daze as best he could and turned as he heard the man call his name again. He saw Rosivok moving to the right and eyeing a group coming toward them through the trees, and not the road.

As though they had been there, waiting for Kolhol and his soldiers to leave, Frost thought. *Waiting to scavenge the beast or those who may have fallen while fighting it, perhaps. Waiting for their chance.*

They kept coming, though now it was clear they held their hands in the open to show they had no weapons drawn. Then Frost recognized the man in the lead, a big man dressed in fine blue and white robes and sporting jewelry that hung around his neck in ridiculous amounts. The men and horses that walked behind him numbered a dozen and looked as if they were on their way to an audience with royalty, rather than trudging about in the wilderness. Each was dressed in brightly colored matching tunics, skirts, and the most ornate armor, with tall helmets topped by red plumes, and heavily engraved breast plates and embroidered surcoats.

The leader waved.

Weakly, Frost waved back. "Cantor."

"Yes, Frost!" the merchant said as he drew up in front of Frost and extended both hands to greet him. Frost accepted the gesture. Cantor's men all drew up short behind him save one, a soldier carrying a fair-sized leather satchel who hurried up to Cantor's side.

"Most impressive," Cantor said. "You know, I have never seen the like. No sorcerer I have ever known could have destroyed such a beast, and so swiftly."

"There was but one," Frost said heavily.

"Who?"

"It no longer matters."

"As you say, no matter. You are remarkable enough."

Frost said nothing else, but Cantor let the silence endure for only a moment. He nodded at some thought of his own and showed Frost a fiendish grin. "I have a gift for you, one I went to great trouble to obtain," he said. "But I will know no sorrow if you choose to throw it away."

Cantor hadn't changed, though Frost had expected that. A riddle was as good a beginning as any, and kinder than some. Frost nodded. "Very well," he said.

With that Cantor gestured. The soldier beside him set the satchel on the ground, undid the leather tie and opened it. Then he grabbed the bag on two sides and shook out its contents. The smell preceded the sight. The bag contained a severed head. Frost blinked as he realized whose it was.

"You know this peddler," Cantor stated.

"Yes, Lurey," Frost answered, tipping his head to one side. He looked up again and signaled the soldier that he'd seen enough. The man used the toe of his boot to kick the head back into the bag before he tied it shut once more. Frost narrowed his gaze. "He was a friend of the family."

Cantor chuckled at this, then shook his head. "Not the friend you thought, I assure you. After all you have been through you are still too trusting a soul, Frost."

But he had learned that, hadn't he? *Trust no one.* Perhaps he could not even trust himself. "I don't trust you," he said.

Cantor grinned. "A good start. Do you remember Taya, the woman who owned the inn where we stayed when we first arrived in Calienn?"

"The one who betrayed me to Andair's soldiers," Frost said. In fact she had come to mind with Cantor's last words.

"Did she?" Cantor said, eyes going wider.

Frost nodded.

"That, I did not know. I know only that she sent

her son as a messenger to me with word of rumors she had overheard at her inn. Talk among soldiers and travelers from Ariman, and one young nobleman too fond of ale, all since you were there. I tell you, that woman is very good at gathering such news, and she is not afraid to use it as she sees fit. I have never known her to betray a friend. Her son said you left without so much as a good-bye. Perhaps there is more to this than I guessed?"

"I knew she was talking to soldiers," Frost said. "I thought she was talking to them about me, telling them about the Demon Blade."

"Ah, yes, I see," Cantor said, rubbing his chin a moment. "You didn't trust her."

"No."

"Good work!" Cantor said with a flair, but then he frowned dramatically. "You were wise to do so, but my guess is you were . . . wrong. I correct myself, Frost, you are not too trusting, you are trusting of the wrong people."

Cantor was grinning again. Frost felt the truth of it lay in his gut hard and heavy.

"Perhaps," Frost said, wondering if he would ever pass that way again, if he would have the chance to speak to Taya again, one day, and ask her face to face. To tell her . . .

He shook the thought out of his head; there wasn't time to dwell on it now, and no gain. "The boy," Frost said. "What did he say?"

"That Andair and Gentaff were getting information from someone close to you. This troubled me. As I have told you, I want this matter of you and the Demon Blade cleared up swiftly and at any cost; it can be a terrible, evil thing, as you and I both know, and I will not stand by and see my world and all that I have built be devastated by it."

Frost sighed heavily. "Go on."

Cantor nodded. "I had the rumor looked into. It

led me to Lurey, your peddler friend. I had him followed after that. His many journeys would amaze anyone, but they would be of special interest to you. Lurey was loyal to his payments and nothing more. I would wager he was Shassel's friend for all these years because she was the only power in the land, other than Andair, and even the king himself could not do many of the things Shassel was capable of. I am told the twins possess a little talent for magery as well. I am sure Lurey had this, too, in mind.

"After you arrived a good many things changed. Indeed, for a man like Lurey, new opportunities arose almost faster than he could profit by them—though he did an admirable job of trying."

"So he betrayed me, Shassel and the twins?" Frost asked.

"To start with. Lurey has been selling information to everyone. To Tasche and Haggel, to Kolhol, to Andair, and even to you. Quite an ambitious fellow really, and successful, unless lives hang in the balance, and many have. Including, with all due credit to me, his own."

Cantor took a bow.

Frost had no words for this, for the pain and consternation that was nearly strangling him. Then one thought rose to his lips: "Shassel is dead because of him."

"If she is dead, that would be my guess. I believe Lurey sold information about her to Tasche and Haggel. They sought her out and captured her only days after meeting with Lurey in secret. Then they brought her to these woods. Something to do with that hideous thing you killed so grandly." He waved one hand at the still smoldering carcass less than fifty paces away. "But by then Lurey was off to points north and west, and back again."

Frost nodded slowly, feeling even more haggard than he had a moment ago, feeling vanquished, just as he had when the demon prince Tyrr had nearly destroyed him. But even then, though the damage had been far worse, he had not felt the pain of it so deeply, a pain beyond the physical, and much more debilitating. He had failed Shassel in every possible way, and for nothing more than . . .

"She was trapped inside that thing, and helped destroy it," he said. "She is dead." He shook his head, eyes closed, then he focussed on Cantor once again. "The Grenarii king, Kolhol, lied to me as well. He must have known more than he said. He is not the trickster Andair is, but he seems intent on his own destruction nonetheless." Frost turned to Cantor again. "Kolhol wanted my help to rid him of this beast, and with luck Tasche as well—perhaps even his own son in the bargain. He knew enough. He rode on to bury his son's body, though he might have had other reasons for feeling uncomfortable around me."

"That he might," Cantor said. "Especially after seeing what you did here. He will have dreams about this day for many nights to come, I think. But with Tasche gone he will want to retain your services as court wizard, once he gets his confidence back. Knowing his reputation, I do not think that will take him very long."

"He should not get his hopes up," Frost replied bitterly. "I promised to see him again, but only to pay what I owe him for all of this."

"Agreed, he should pay, and probably with his life, but probably not soon."

Frost eyed Cantor again. He looked suddenly grim. "Why not?"

"Because another duty awaits you, one far more pressing and dear. My informants are many, and they go many places. Almost as many as Lurey did! I learned as I was coming here that Dorin and Dara are once again the guests of Lord Andair and the sorcerer Gentaff. Andair's soldiers rode in to Wilmar's village after you left and collected the twins again. Tramet and Wilmar with them. They may be dead, all of them, by now, but if Andair had ordered them killed I think he would have left the bodies behind."

"That was Andair's plan all along," Frost said, forcing the words out through tightly clenched teeth while he turned away from Cantor, away from everyone, and stared at the decimated demon creature, both fists knotted. He had wanted to avenge the wrongs of the past, but now he must add all the wrongs of the present to the list. *Far too many.*

I should have hidden them elsewhere myself, he thought, furious at the thickness of his skull. *I should have placed layers of warding spells on them, or stayed with them. I should have found a way to protect Shassel, but . . .*

"This was part of Andair's plan, at least, I am sure of that," Cantor agreed. "Lurey must have told him about Shassel, and he used the information to his own ends. He was always a clever sort, but some of what happened was happenstance, which Andair simply adapted to."

"He knew I would leave the twins to search for Shassel. He only had to find them."

Cantor shrugged. "Agreed. Though he might not have guessed you would learn the truth so quickly, and come to Grenarii. By now he must know that. He wants the Demon Blade, as does Gentaff, but they are as worried that you will help Kolhol as Kolhol is that you will not. Still, they can use their hostages for leverage in either case."

"Of course," Frost said, turning, setting off through the dried and crackling underbrush, stomping his way between dead trees until he reached the ash-gray claws of the beast. Several of its talons were shattered like so much dark crystal, and part of the hand and arm had turned to dust. Frost leaned over the mess, holding his nose, and reached out to grasp the hilt of the Demon Blade. It stayed in place on the first pull. He got closer, half-sitting on the burnt and crumbling carcass, and tried again, until it pulled finally from the earth.

The Blade felt good in his hand as he wielded it, careful not to let it draw from him now—not now, not yet, not here. There would come a time, and soon. He still lacked the knowledge he needed to control the Blade completely, to ensure that it would not kill him or do more damage than he intended, perhaps to those he would protect. He knew it was far too dangerous to use the Blade again, especially in anger. But he knew in his heart and in his soul, as he stood in this forest, his hand tight on the hilt and his ears full of the sound of its smooth metal edge whistling through the air as he swung it once over his head—he knew he must.

Gentaff knew who was to have the Blade, but it was a secret he seemed to want to keep. He also knew full well what he was doing by taking the twins hostage again. *If he will not tell me what he knows, then he will take that knowledge to the grave,* Frost swore in silence. *One he will share with Andair.*

"I hear they have quite a reception planned for you in Weldhem," Cantor said, after Frost had turned once more and made his way back. "Though I know no details."

"No doubt," Frost said. "In any case, I must go. He tricked me years ago and he got away with it. He has tricked me again, but I vow this day that it will not stand." Frost realized he was still swiping at the air in front of him with the Demon Blade, punctuating his words. He made an effort to lower the weapon.

"He has cost me a part of myself and far too much of my life, cost the twins their father and Wilmar and his son nearly everything they had. Now, by whatever measure, he has cost the world a most precious life, and even more lives hang in the balance. For all my travels and years I had thought myself a wiser man, but mistakes have been made on both sides. Andair will not run away this time, and I will not leave."

"The Demon Blade will be the price for the twins' lives, and the others," Cantor said. "But you cannot give it to them."

"I know," Frost replied.

"Then I would tell you one more thing. You can only blame yourself for just so much in life, Frost. No one man is responsible for everything. It is more complicated than that. As you must know."

"I know," Frost said. "But that is not enough." He wrapped the Blade, then put it on his back again and covered it with his cloak.

"We will go as soon as you are ready," Sharryl said, and Frost looked up to find his two Subartans staring at him. Rosivok added a silent nod.

"We'll need to better use our heads this time, I think," Frost told them, trying to add a little bit of smile. It wasn't necessary. They understood.

"When I am through with my tasks in Worlish, I will return to pay Lord Kolhol a visit," Frost said then, speaking so only Cantor could hear. "But what of you?" he asked. "You who has served us all so well?"

"I will wait, and watch, and trust my best interests will be served."

"I could make good use of an army," Frost said.

"I can field a small one," Cantor answered, "but not one large enough to march on Andair at Weldhem. You will need other means, if you have them."

Frost nodded.

"What of fresh horses?" Cantor asked.

"We have these," Rosivok said, nodding toward the mounts Kolhol had left them.

Cantor tipped his head to examine them, then he shook his head, grinned, and slapped Frost twice on the shoulder. "I say no." He gestured to Rosivok to follow him. "My friends," Cantor said, "you will have the swiftest horses in the land. It is the very least I can do."

Frost slowed to let the horses feed and rest only as often as he thought he must. He passed nowhere near the village Shassel had called home for so long, but rode due south into Worlish, then west again, toward Weldhem. He finally admitted to himself that he felt ill, a convergence of factors, fatigue and trepidation among them, frustration and frenzy, and a bit of fever brought on by his poor condition. His mind boiled in the soup created by all of this, and he had no choice but to let it. Fighting how his body felt or the thoughts that swirled in his head would only tire him more, would only stall the inevitable.

Sharryl and Rosivok allowed him his isolation as they all rode out of Grenarii and traveled along the roads of Worlish. On the third day, not far from Weldhem, they came within sight of a small, familiar village at a crossroad, where they turned north and headed toward Wilmar's lands. He had to be sure all of it was true, and he had to know if Wilmar, Tramet and the twins had been taken alive. He was sure someone would know.

Before they had gotten started a pair of young boys approached them and fell in step, running along beside their horses. "We are sent to tell you that someone is waiting for you at the inn," the nearest one said, as he had no doubt been paid to do. "He has important words for you. He said to tell you his name is Jons."

The village had only one inn. Frost found Jons seated at a table in front of it along with his usual four soldiers. One of six tables, though all the others were empty. Frost dismounted. Sharryl and Rosivok did the same, then walked with him, letting the horses wander as they willed. Jons had a cocky smirk on his face. Frost had an overwhelming urge to remove it at the neck.

"You have a message for me?" Frost asked.

"I do, from my king, Lord Andair, as you have guessed. You are to deliver the Demon Blade to him, or your young cousins will die, along with those who have helped you."

Frost held steady. "Who would they be?"

"Surely you know Wilmar and his son, Tramet. At least Andair is sure you do. He has them as well, and he would have me warn you that this time he and Gentaff have gone to great lengths to prepare for your visit. It will not be like before, storm or no storm. Any attempt to turn the situation to your advantage will be met swiftly and will bring a grim result."

Frost had expected every word. He turned to his Subartans and shrugged, matter of fact. "How grim?"

"And in whose mind?" Rosivok asked.

"He cannot answer questions," Sharryl said. "He has no mind."

Frost saw the fire in his Subartans' eyes. They had suffered enough at the hands of their enemies—Frost's enemies—and were more than eager to purchase a share of vengeance. Jons seemed determined to hold himself up as a ready target.

But Frost was not through with him yet.

"Anyone's opinion would do," Jons answered coldly, then, "Have no doubt, it is true. You were lucky the last time, I know that, but luck will not go with you again. As Lord Andair has proven many times already, none of you is bright enough even to learn from your mistakes."

Frost bit his lip, then raised his arm and waved to either side, halting Rosivok and Sharryl as each took a step forward. He tasted blood, then closed his eyes and took a breath before going on. "That, good Jons, is a mistake in itself. But I won't belabor the issue. I would know more important things. Are the captives unharmed?"

"The twins are well," Jons answered freely. "I was there when they and the others were captured and taken away. Wilmar and his son put up a fight. I am afraid they each suffered a beating before they relented. Wilmar was nearly beaten to death, but that is why you all get along so well, isn't it? Fools keeping company with fools."

"Perhaps," Frost said, fists going white as he tightened them.

"What else would you know?" Jons asked, waving at the world around him. "The day? The season?" He grinned again, snide. "The length of the tear in Dara's dress? Or the shape of the mole on her left breast?"

Frost nodded once, and his Subartans leaped forward.

The soldiers at the table were on their feet, swords drawn as Sharryl and Rosivok reached them, but two of them fell in a spray of gore before they could wield their blades. Jons jumped back from the table and pressed his back against the inn's thin daub and wattle wall as he drew his own sword. He began inching his way toward the inn's open door while Rosivok engaged another soldier, deflecting three, then four sharp parries. Sharryl met the fourth soldier from a height advantage as she sprang onto the tabletop. The table wobbled, worrying her balance, but she managed to avoid the thrust when the soldier tried to take advantage, then she swung her subarta across, left to right, and forced the soldier's blade aside just far enough to leave him open. But now a polished, black-handled dagger appeared in his left hand. He tried to slash with it, but in the midst of the effort Sharryl's left leg shot out. Her boot caught the soldier square in the face as the dagger's blade was deflected. The crack of fracturing bone was followed by a groan as the man dropped the dagger and reached to cover his eyes and nose. Sharryl squatted and drove her subarta forward, ending the duel.

Frost moved past Rosivok as his subarta came across to catch the fingers and knuckles of his opponent's sword hand where they wrapped around his weapon's hilt. His sword fell away and the man started to scream as chunks of his digits fell after the weapon. He kept screaming as Rosivok stepped in and drove his subarta through him, then pulled it back.

Frost dodged right, out of the way, as the soldier's body spun and collapsed, then he stepped past.

Jons reached the door just as Frost got to Jons. He swung his blade but Frost stopped short, just out of reach. Frost raised his staff, more than twice the length of Jons' weapon, reached out and touched Jons with the tip. Jons yelped like an animal as he jumped to one side. Frost caught him again, and Jons yelped even louder.

"Leave me unharmed or you will pay a dear price!" Jons shouted, gulping a breath and leaping again to avoid a third jolt from Frost's staff. "I—I am Andair's personal—"

He leaped again. "His personal . . ."

He gasped suddenly, eyes going wide, and looked down. A black-handled dagger protruded from his abdomen, its blade fully embedded.

"No longer," Sharryl said.

Jons let a thin, strained breath slip out. Blood followed it to his lips. He fell to his knees, then he drooped down and lay on his side as the life flowed out of him.

Frost looked at Sharryl.

"It belonged to a friend of his," she said.

"Only fitting," Frost replied, then he raised his eyes to Rosivok as he appeared just behind Sharrly. "Have the innkeeper bring us food and ale, and tell him I will pay him for this mess."

Rosivok went inside, and soon a small feast sat

before them. When they had had their fill, Frost walked to the edge of the village and found a spot where rocks had been taken from the fields nearby and piled for use in building. He sat on the pile and stared up at the stars, thinking of the day to come. He could only imagine what precautions Gentaff had taken, what Andair might be planning to do. He imagined nothing good, but he was not without his own resources. He would not trust, he would not be fooled, and he would not hold anything back. He needed to know all that, needed to believe it. Most of all, he needed to use his wits more than ever before. It was possible that a lifetime spent wandering, learning, atoning, becoming all that he was, had not been in vain. He could not change the past, only the present, and the future.

He spent most of the night bent over the Demon Blade, adapting a spell, a very old and simple one, hoping it would work. . . .

CHAPTER SEVENTEEN

The old gates of the city stood open. As Frost and his Subartans entered they were greeted by rows of soldiers on either side, an impressive show of force obvious to anyone in the city. One man, a very young soldier for the rank he wore on his vestments, came forward to do the talking. He insisted on escorting the visitors up to the castle for an audience with Andair. Immediately.

"And Gentaff?" Frost asked. "Has he fled?"

"I am not told," the soldier replied. "But that is unlikely."

"Very well," Frost said, and they proceeded through the streets where most of the population of Weldhem waited, lining the way to get a glimpse of them. The crowds vanished as the road reached the castle and crossed over the moat. More soldiers waited in the castle's expansive main courtyard. As was to be expected.

Very little of the damage from Frost's earlier visit remained, the charred and bloodied earth had been cleaned, much of the stone and wood repaired. The memories were fresh in Frost's mind, along with the memory of Gentaff himself, of his powerful aura, sharp and sour. He felt that aura again just now. Gentaff was here—in the keep just ahead—but no magical traps were present, at least none that were active or obvious. Frost suspected that might change.

The heavy doors on the raised parapet swung open as the soldiers escorting Frost drew to a sudden halt. A procession emerged onto the high walkway, headed toward the stairs, and began to descend to the courtyard's floor. Gentaff led the way, followed by Andair. After them came a small contingent of soldiers— and among them, bound at the hands and closely held but all quite alive, were Wilmar, Tramet, Dorin and Dara. None of them looked well, especially Wilmar who seemed barely able to walk. Even from a distance his bruises were visible. Frost watched as the soldiers helped him down the stairs.

Andair looked splendid in a scarlet-colored cloak trimmed in silver cloth, and quite in contrast to the dark blue cloak worn by Gentaff. Frost had not laid eyes on Andair for half a lifetime and he almost didn't recognize his old foe. But the resemblance was there beneath the robes of royalty, the same look in the eyes visible even at a distance, a wicked look Frost had not understood once, long ago, but one he was more familiar with these days.

"Lord Andair!" Frost shouted out as the group reached the bottom. "You have seen fit to attend the meeting this time."

Andair acted as if he hadn't heard until he and the others had assembled some fifty paces away, spread out in a line. "And you have come back, just as you were told," the king said, "as your king commands."

Frost made an effort not to bristle at this, to tell himself he had expected nothing less. He needed a clear head, a sharp focus. The clouds of rage would not serve him now. At least not yet.

"Listen to me, Frost, and listen well," Gentaff said, as he stepped out from the others. Without words between them Andair moved forward as well, then he walked to the right, in the direction of the stables on the courtyard's northern wall. A wooden post, waist-high and fat as a man's leg, had been planted in the earth only a few paces from the group. Andair walked past, until the post stood precisely between himself and Gentaff. Then he turned and Frost saw that he held a velvet sack in his hands, one he seemed quite intent about, as he held it up for all to see.

"Andair holds the key to your cooperation," Gentaff went on. "A talisman I made from a bloodstone, a very smooth and perfect one, which I have been saving for years. I have labored over it for days in anticipation of your arrival."

As Gentaff spoke, Andair withdrew the stone from the sack, walked over and placed it on top of the post. Then he stepped away from it, measuring his paces, until he and Gentaff were again precisely ten paces each away from the stone.

"The talisman requires only a single, short phrase to empower it. With that phrase the spell will be released, one prepared especially for you, Frost. It is a physical spell, you know the type. This one cripples a man by making every muscle in his body burn with fatigue, even a sorcerer's muscles. Part illusion, part reality, but altogether effective, and far too complex to defend against quickly enough, even for one such as you."

"We each know the phrase," Lord Andair said with particular glee. "Gentaff has taught me how to use it. If you do not agree to our terms, if you have any tricks in mind, if you try to flee—"

"Or if you try to use the Demon Blade," Gentaff interrupted, glancing back at the twins and the others, who remained surrounded by soldiers.

"—I can activate the spell, just as Gentaff can,"

Andair went on. "It can remain activated long enough to stop you forever, I think. Or Gentaff can. He thinks the spell might kill you. It would be interesting to find out."

"In any event, you cannot hope to stop both of us at the same time, thin as you are," Gentaff added, "and you cannot prevail against the talisman, I promise you."

"However, I am assured that you will live long enough to see my guards take care of everyone else you hold dear in this world," Andair said. "That is the only alternative. You will submit. You have no other choice."

"You have already had a hand in the death of Shassel," Frost said, letting some of the bitterness he felt flow into his voice.

Andair shook his head. "I have heard something of this already. But how can you blame me for another sovereign's actions? Kolhol is my enemy. Grenarii is as hostile a land to me as to you. If misfortune found Shassel there, it says nothing of me."

"You lied to me," Frost said. "A lie that took time to realize and might have taken much longer, time I could have used to save her. That is enough. You have always lied to me, Andair. Now, I have stopped listening."

"Then listen to me," Gentaff said, taking another step forward. He withdrew a short staff no longer than a man's arm from beneath his dark cloak and waved it at Frost like a club. "The talisman is real. The spell is real. The orders given these soldiers to kill their prisoners and then you is real. I have taken no chances this time, Frost. I heard all about the massacre in Ariman, I know you have command of the Demon Blade, and I know what it is capable of. You have no secrets here, and no leverage. Do as I say, nothing less, nothing more. It is your only hope, and theirs."

"It was my hope that you would tell me who the next Keeper of the Blade might be—other than you or Andair, of course," Frost said. "Shassel thought you knew. Perhaps in honor of her memory, and the memory of those who have gone before us, you might now do what you know is right, and tell me after all."

"My memory of her is vague," Gentaff replied.

"And mine bitter," Andair sniffed. "That woman has needed to die for years!"

"*You* have needed to die for years," Frost said as evenly as he could manage, though that proved most difficult.

Gentaff showed a feeble grin at this. "It is good to see old friends getting along so well. But I think all this chatter can wait until some other time. For now we should move things along." He looked over his shoulder at the prisoners, then turned to Frost again. "I will agree to name the Keeper of the Blade, and agree to turn both the twins and Wilmar and Tramet over to you, as soon as you have handed the Demon Blade to me."

Frost stood silent for a long moment, watching the two men, measuring them. The Demon Blade remained where it was, pressed against Frost's back, wrapped in its scabbard.

"Let me tell you what you do not know," Frost said, turning slightly so as to ignore Andair, addressing Gentaff. "Foremost, you do not know how to use the Demon Blade. Even I have not been fully able to understand it; even I cannot precisely control it. What I have managed has taken a great deal of time to learn, and has come at a great cost to many, and myself."

"You will tell us whatever you know," Andair said. "You have no choice. Then I will worry about the rest."

"I have choices," Frost said. "You will ask what you like, and I will answer, but no matter what I tell you it will not be the truth. I feel I owe you that much."

Now it was Andair who boiled, but Gentaff held up his hand to bring pause to the exchange. "All as it should be, I suspect," he said. "I understand completely, but it does not matter. I already knew more about the Demon Blade than most any man alive, perhaps nearly as much as you, Frost. More importantly, I know the results of your work with it, I know the Blade drew the life energy out of every soldier on the battlefield in Ariman. I know that in turn you managed to use that energy to destroy a demon prince. There lies the secret that has been lost for so long. Once the end is known, the means are easily devised for one such as myself. You of all men should agree; you devised a means without even that knowledge to begin with. You say your means are slipshod, that may be true. Mine will not be."

"You don't know what you are doing," Frost chided, "and you will not. You cannot imagine. There is more to the Blade than even you or I can understand, more than even many of those on the last Council knew, I fear. All the legends ever told about the Blade are true, but there are others untold. A darkness unimagined, perhaps unintended. To use the Blade as I have, as you would, is madness."

"As you yourself have said, anything you tell us today will be a lie," Andair said.

"Anything I tell *you*," Frost said. "I speak now to Gentaff, and what I say is truth. Do not brush aside my warnings, else you will find yourself a bigger fool than even Tasche was."

"Was?" Andair asked, though Gentaff was also clearly intrigued.

"A victim of his own ambitions and limitations, as were many others. The Grenarii prince among them. Are you so eager to follow on such a path? To destroy

yourself and others? You will never be able to use
the Blade without bringing disaster. You all know of
Cantor of Calienn, the merchant lord. He knows the
truth of what I speak, the darkness that waits. You
need not take my word for it."

"No!" Gentaff said, showing signs of frustration,
evidence that Frost's arguments were having an effect.
The sorcerer paused as if considering his next words
carefully. "I have given the Blade and its possibilities great thought. The spells needed to activate the
Blade are complex, certainly, but above all they must
be designed to draw energy from all but he who holds
the weapon. That, I think, I have divined; just as you
have. I have more knowledge than you, Frost, even
you would not deny that. I have the means and desire
to make the Blade work, no matter what you think,
and it will be secure in my hands. But there is only
one way we will ever know. The transaction must
proceed."

The entire group left of Gentaff watched and listened with absolute attention, including the twins,
Tramet, and Wilmar, so far as Frost could tell, though
Wilmar's eyes were closed more than open. Frost
focussed on Dorin and Dara and tried to analyze their
expressions. Not bitterness, not now, but he saw other
things there—frustration, fear, anger. They had been
quick to judge him all along, most often as harshly
as possible, and eager to condemn him for the deci-
sions he had made. All rightly so, at least in part.
Frost knew that, but if Dorin and Dara had been too
hard on him, so perhaps, had he; if Shassel's forgiveness was to mean anything, and if he was ever to have
theirs, they must look forward now, not back. All of
them.

Frost turned and surveyed the courtyard. At least
two hundred men had gathered around the perimeter, their backs to the stone walls, obediently waiting and watching events in the center. Whatever

happened, it would take them several moments to reach him, or the others. Not long, but perhaps long enough.

He shouted to the twins, "Tell me, what would you do in my place? You know all that is at stake."

"Frost," Dorin answered, while his sister remained silent. "I have been wondering that very thing. I see no possible solution other than to give them what they want. At least . . . for now."

"Hear the boy, Frost?" Andair said. "Listen to him. If you die defying me, we will have the Blade in any case. The poorer alternative, I think. If you live, there is always hope."

"Yes, try to see the sense in that," Gentaff said jovially.

"But that won't work, because you can never give them the Blade," Dorin added, scowling at Andair. "Never."

"Never!" Dara echoed.

Tramet nodded, apparently unwilling or unable to speak. His father only managed to look up, but his eyes were keen enough, still defiant, even after all he'd been through.

"You are all quite dense," Andair said, shaking his head. "It is no surprise you have fared so badly."

The scowls on the twins' faces said enough.

"A difficult situation," Frost said. "Which will no doubt require a difficult solution."

"The correct decision is not always easy to come by," Dorin said, looking at Frost, eyes hard on him and saying more than words could have.

"So I have learned," Frost said.

"So have we all," Dara added, and Frost found the same depth in her gaze.

He turned again to Gentaff. "Our hosts may be correct, after all. It is hard to argue with their logic, or the reality of this day. Therefore, I yield. I will hand you the Demon Blade, and you will set them free, then set me free with the knowledge of the Keeper. All agreed?"

Andair and Gentaff looked at each other, then both of them said at the same time, "Agreed."

Frost removed his cloak and worked at the harness until he had pulled the Blade's scabbard around, where he began to unwrap it. The twins and Tramet all gasped, and even Wilmar managed to groan in protest. "Don't," Tramet said, speaking at last.

"Don't," Dara echoed.

"Listen to them, Frost," Dorin pleaded. "Don't!"

"I must," Frost said, wearing his most pained expression. "It is the only way. Now, be silent." He pulled the Blade free, then held it up and walked slowly forward, watching as both Gentaff and Andair each held a cautious hand out toward the bloodstone talisman on the post between them. *Taking no chances*, Frost thought. He stopped less than a dozen paces from Gentaff and laid the Blade carefully on the ground. Gentaff waved him off, and he stepped back. Frost waited patiently for what he knew would come next, the pain and anguish, the soul-wrenching brutality that was the sure and certain result of an adept touching the Demon Blade unawares. Gentaff leaned down and spoke quietly over the weapon at his feet, hands held level above it; then he slowly lowered them, but used only his left hand finally to touch it. He grasped the hilt and lifted the Blade up high. Frost noted a brief wince as it crossed the other's features, then nothing but calm as he lowered the Blade and held it vertically in front of him, eyes closed, and began reciting more spells just beneath the reach of surrounding ears.

He knows, Frost thought. But how much more did he know? How much had he guessed correctly or closely enough to serve his purposes this day—or the next.

As if he had read Frost's mind, Gentaff opened his

eyes again, and Frost saw a new and darkening fire burning there.

"This moment has waited decades, but it comes as rightly now as it ever could," the old sorcerer said. "I am not the true Keeper, Frost, I will tell you that, but it will reside in my capable hands and under Lord Andair's protection well enough, and for some time to come. In the meantime you will understand, you of all men, that I cannot allow anything to threaten that. Especially so great a threat as you."

Frost was hearing nothing he hadn't expected. "You have hostages, Andair's army, the Demon Blade, and yet you are afraid of me?" he asked.

"You are a most powerful, potential adversary."

"That has always been true," Frost replied.

"But only so long as you live."

"A problem you would ease, I suppose?"

"I have no choice."

"Nor regrets, I think. How fortunate for you."

"How unfortunate for you, and me," Andair said.

Then Frost saw it, a flicker in Gentaff's eyes, a nervousness in his free hand. Andair continued to steep himself in his gloating, but Gentaff had begun to doubt, as he noticed the depth of Frost's glib mood. Still not enough to stop what was about to happen, Frost guessed, but he needed to be sure. . . .

"I worry little over your threats," Frost said. "I worry most that I will survive to reclaim the Blade, that any in Weldhem might survive, after you have bungled the attempt to use it."

Gentaff glared at Frost, but then he changed that expression willfully and laughed instead—a small, barely audible chuckle like someone who couldn't quite remember the joke. Frost knew the truth, knew that Gentaff was already saying the spells he had so carefully assembled for so long, saying them over and over and adding one to the string each time until he reached the final phrase, when he would add his own binding phrase. The laughter was a show.

Frost could not hear the spells clearly, but with only a bit of unnoticeable enhancement his ears picked up enough to be impressed with how accurate they were, how erudite—not quite like his own but nearly adequate nonetheless.

"You are indeed talented, old mage," Frost said, watching Gentaff's eyes blaze with a mix of exhilaration and triumph as the Blade began to glow, as he felt the surge, and the pull. Gentaff added spells, keeping control, until the Blade grew suddenly brighter than the late day sun.

"You have done everything right, guessed what you needed to guess," Frost added. "Had you only known of the reversal spell I was able to impress upon the Blade last night . . . But how could you?"

Frost glanced at the twins and saw the look of recognition in their eyes and the words hanging just the other side of the moment in their open mouths. To their credit they only watched as Gentaff's jaw went rigid, followed by every muscle in his body.

Then the ancient sorcerer began to scream. The sound rolled from his open mouth and rose higher than Frost might have thought possible, then it fell as Gentaff's body shook in violent spasms. The Blade continued to glow while the sorcerer that held it darkened. Frost knew something of how it felt, though even he had not experienced the depths which the Blade was taking from Gentaff now. The screams went on but grew shrill as the Blade brightened still further, went on even when Gentaff's lungs had long since run out of air. Not an earthly scream any longer. Abruptly the screaming stopped.

Gentaff crumpled to the ground, gasping, his body still trying to let go of the Demon Blade but unable to make the fingers obey. Unable to break the chain of events his spells had set in motion. The Blade had done exactly as he had so expertly commanded—but reflected back in the opposite direction he had intended—back at him.

Gentaff's eyes met Frost's as what remained of him lay on the ground, slowly curling like fresh-cut plants left drying in the sun. The look Frost saw frozen on the dying sorcerer's face was not wisdom or confidence, not gall or anger; it was not even surprise—it was fear. Gentaff knew.

He knew everything. He knew the whole truth of what Frost had said and still more that he had not, and he knew it had been his end.

His sword hand let go. Gentaff lay motionless on the ground, robes draped too loosely about the dried, pallid husk that was all that remained of him. The courtyard was utterly silent.

"What did you do?" Andair blurted out, sounding suddenly hysterical, each word rising one note. His head twitched about, but his eyes did not seem to focus on anything much. "What did you do?" he repeated. "What have you done?"

"I have destroyed the only path I knew to the truth, the only hope I had of ridding myself of the Demon Blade," Frost said, feeling the fatigue of his body and his mind meld together and weigh him down.

"You have also chosen to face the talisman!" Andair howled, his voice cracking with the strain. The soldiers holding the prisoners tightened their ranks as Andair's panic sent him scrambling, but their king seemed to have forgotten them. He reached the post in two awkward bounds and grasped the bloodstone in both hands, then he fell to the ground as he clutched it, obsessed with it, already repeating the chant Gentaff had taught him.

"Sharryl, Rosivok, free the others!" Frost shouted as he lunged after Gentaff's body and seized the Demon Blade.

The Subartans charged the men holding the hostages, moving with a swiftness that caught their two well-chosen first targets fatally unprepared, and surprised most of the rest. Two more soldiers fell an instant later in a clatter of iron and shouting, which caused the others to pull at their prisoners in order to re-form in their own defense.

"Dorin, Dara!" Frost called out next, as he stood with the Blade in hand and turned to them. They already knew, they were already waving hands about and reciting the same phrase in precise unison. Frost felt a twinge of admiration as he watched. Any number of simple spells would have worked, but the one they chose was impressive. An augmentation of the dust kicked up by the ensuing scuffle, it instantly engulfed everyone. Most of the guards began to choke and squint as they waved at dust clouds, and Dorin, Dara and Tramet turned on the guards holding them. The two holding Wilmar let go, joining the battle, but not before one of them put a dagger in him, and left him to collapse on the ground.

Tramet dropped and scurried toward one of the fallen soldier's swords. He came up armed and helped the twins and their two Subartan rescuers. Frost saw Dorin and Dara each collect a sword, but then he knew he could watch their battle no longer. He was about to engage in another of his own.

He looked about, verifying the positions of the guards all around them. Most were staying where they were along the perimeter of the courtyard, no doubt ordered to do so to prevent an escape. Andair could change those orders, but he was still too busy babbling in frustration at the bloodstone in his hand, apparently not getting something about the spell just right. Though he might still get lucky, and he might call in reinforcements at any instant.

Frost had not planned for the talisman, but he had expected plenty of soldiers. He had prepared a

warding spell that would keep Andair's men back for
a few moments at least. He erected the warding now,
using as little of his strength as possible, saving the
rest for what he must do next.

He pressed the Blade's hilt firmly into his left hand,
careful not to fall prey to it, and began reciting the
required spells, weaving them together, adjusting them
yet again in his ongoing attempt to find the means
to use the Blade safely and effectively. He had heard
a part of Gentaff's spells as well, especially the controlling spells, a slight variation he would not have
come by on his own. It felt right as he added this
extra piece into the others, and began the final phrase.

Then the talisman took hold.

The sensation pulled him instantly from his task.
It was much different than that brought on by the
Demon Blade—not a draining of all that was flesh
and bone and spirit—this was pure exhaustion. The
sort that too much physical effort could bring, or too
much magic, though this was as thorough as anything
Frost had experienced. His body felt suddenly, terribly heavy. His arms and legs began to burn as if
he had run for miles full out and lifted barrels for
hours. The big frame and powerful muscles he carried under his extra weight became crippling burdens
to him now, and his lungs ached with the effort of
drawing each breath.

Even in death, Frost saw that Gentaff was a formidable opponent, and he had taught Andair well.

Frost set about trying to interrupt the spell using
an incantation he had tucked away in his memory,
one designed to give enhanced physical endurance
to athletes or soldiers, when necessary. It did little
good. Gentaff's spell was too well constructed, too
complete, and had already taken too firm a hold.
Another wave of fatigue swept him, and Frost fell.

As he tumbled to the earth and stone of the courtyard floor he tried to get an elbow under him, but

managed only a half roll instead that ended with him
lying down, mostly faceup and gasping, nearly para-
lyzed with the relentlessly increasing pain of inspired
exertion.

He tried to focus but found he couldn't concentrate on magic at all. *Part of Gentaff's intent*, he
guessed, giving the dead sorcerer one last nod of
tribute.

His hand still held the Demon Blade. Using both
hands now he managed to haul the weapon up onto
his abdomen until it rested flat across his chest, where
he could at least see it, and he realized it must look
as if he was trying to use it to shield himself from
his enemy. Which was a foolish thought . . .

He looked up to find Andair's face staring down
at him. The panic was mostly gone, replaced by what
might have passed for strained amusement at Frost's
predicament. Frost tried to speak, to serve Andair
with a warning he hoped might at least give the other
pause. But calling out was out of the question. *Perhaps*, he thought, *something less ambitious*.

"I have you, Frost," Andair said, grinning, fully
enjoying the moment as he drew nearer and bent over
slightly. He held the talisman out before him like a
shield, a weapon, and watched closely for any reaction. Frost writhed about, but the movements were
feeble and slow, less than threatening; he opened his
mouth again but managed nothing more than a sickly
wheeze.

Frost rolled his eyes at the sound, and even that
hurt.

Andair leaned over Frost and shook his head dis-
paragingly. "The great sorcerer, laid out on your back
and waiting to die. Powerless. Useless. I am upset
about Gentaff, he was an asset. Now I will have to
find another who can learn the Blade's ways, and that
may take some time." He grinned, though the corners of his mouth twitched with the effort. "But I

have time, and no matter what else, I can always sell it if need be, or trade it for . . . well, I think a kingdom or two, at the very least." The smile disappeared and he narrowed his gaze as he leaned still closer. "I would have needed to rid myself of Gentaff eventually, I think. Despite his knowledge, he was much too difficult at times, too smart for my own good. Not so witless as you, Frost. No, you are an incredible fool, just like Shassel. You both wasted your lives. Such that they were. Though it has worked out well for me."

"No . . ." Frost finally managed to gasp. He could still hear the fight raging nearby, the clash of steel on steel, the shouts of men in battle. He guessed many more of the soldiers around the perimeter of the courtyard were trying to get to him by now, but if they were, his wardings must be keeping them away. At least for the moment. He couldn't feed the warding any more energy, his magic and the strength to power it were beyond him now, taken by the stone. Soon, he guessed, the talisman would take the energy he needed simply to survive. Soon afterward the twins, and Wilmar and Tramet, would die along with Sharryl and Rosivok.

"I know what you are thinking, Frost, but there is nothing you can do, nothing."

"I . . . will . . ."

Andair shook his head. "No, you will not. Not even the magic Blade you hide behind will heed you anymore. It is as useless as you are." Andair straightened up and kicked, a good plant that dug the toe of his boot into Frost's ribs. Then he kicked the same spot again. Frost moaned and closed his heavy eyes, grimacing at the pain in his side and the more unbearable pain being brought by the talisman. Andair held the stone even closer, grinning sharply, mouth twitching again as he saw Frost begin to feel the pain more intensely. Then the king's look turned serious again, and he slowly, cautiously moved the stone even closer, until he touched it to the cloth covering Frost's thigh, just below his hip.

The smell of burning fabric, then roasting flesh rose amidst a dull sizzling sound as Andair watched Frost suffer without protest. He was convinced now that Frost could do nothing, that he was dying. Frost all but believed it himself. Gentaff's magic burned through every fiber of his being, but it was magic after all—the pain, the fatigue—and that was something Frost knew much about. The stone would change him tangibly, it would likely kill him, but that would take time and perhaps more energy than the stone contained; for now it only made him suffer, made him want to die.

He struggled to remind himself who he was and what he was, as his mind whirled in agony and sank, inexorably, toward a creeping darkness that was all too near. Toward relief. He tried to recall the great strength and stamina he had found within himself when he'd battled the demon prince Tyrr. Could that have been the same Frost?

Part of him knew he was still that man, but an equally determined part sought to embrace the fatigue and let it have its way until it let him go completely.

He drew a deep breath as Andair gently put his own sword down, freeing one hand, and reached to take the Demon Blade from Frost. As he did, their eyes met once more.

Frost focussed his mind enough to remember what manner of man lived behind those eyes, to remember the treachery and deceit that had fooled a younger Frost so completely, then fooled him all over again, and again after that. To remember Wilmar's suffering, the twins, *Shassel* . . .

Frost felt a different kind of pain inside him, the pain of frustration, of crushing sorrow and regret. But this was a pain he could use. He could not muster the strength to use his magic to defend himself, but he needed to make Andair pay for all he had done, and keep him from doing it all over again. He needed that more than life itself.

His mind no longer functioned in any proper manner, it swirled in a darkness filled with agony and rage, searching for focus, then focussing on vengeance. Frost used all of it to fuel the will to make his body obey just one last command.

As Andair's fingers touched the Blade and wrapped around it, Frost tightened what he thought must be both his fists, then cried out as he willed the muscles in his arms to pull, and heave. He saw the steel flash as the Demon Blade ascended toward the face of his enemy. Andair's eyes went wide as the edge caught his cheek. Blood ran from the wound as Andair jerked back and brushed the Blade aside. He spotted his own sword on the ground beside his enemy, but as he bent to snatch it up Frost leaned right and heaved again, and felt the satisfying push of resistance as the tip of the sword broke through Andair's flesh, then penetrated deep into his side.

"If it is the Blade you want," Frost whispered, "then you shall have it."

Andair let the bloodstone talisman fall from his fingers as he came almost fully erect again. The Blade's hilt pulled free of Frost's hand. Frost watched the look on the other's face for clues as to what would come next. Andair wrapped both hands around the steel of the Blade, half-buried in his abdomen. Then his mouth fell open and his eyes filled with fright, with disbelief, and then, understanding.

Frost could not be certain Andair had heard his words. He knew he would never get the chance to tell him more. Already Andair's eyes were going dim. Frost heard him wheeze, moist and straining, then he collapsed, the life gone out of him, and Frost was suddenly free.

His pain began to vanish, and his mental fog along with it. He sat up and blinked the dizziness from his head. The twins and Tramet had done well for themselves, all three were still standing, still fighting and serving to complicate the battle enough so that Sharryl and Rosivok could strike more decisive blows. Only four of their guards remained standing, and those had formed a defensive line against the onslaught from the others—a line that was backing slowly toward the wall and the stairs behind them.

But all around, just beyond the edge of the warding Frost had placed about the center of the courtyard, a ring of soldiers five and six deep pressed toward them. And the warding was failing.

Frost watched one man slip through, then another. A flood would follow, and there was no time to build another warding now. He looked down at Andair's corpse and felt a fleeting surge of pleasure at the sight, but he could not allow himself to savor the moment. He and Andair had not finished their business together.

Frost stepped forward, bent over Andair, wrapped both hands around the hilt of the Demon Blade and pulled it loose. As he turned away into the clear he swung the weapon once, flinging most of the blood and gore from it. "Behind me!" Frost yelled to the others as soldiers began to swarm toward him from every side, their shouts joined by others on the parapets above as more soldiers emerged from the open doorways. The twins and Tramet collected Wilmar off the ground while the Subartans protected their flank. Then all of them were running—running toward Frost.

He braced himself, finished the last locution of the Demon Blade spells and raised the weapon up before him. Then he added his binding phrase, and the Blade ignited.

Frost's mind stayed focussed, but his body flinched

reflexively, anticipating the fiery pain that had so often accompanied past attempts, but now he realized that he had gotten the spells more nearly right this time than ever before, that for the moment at least, he was master.

He drew the Blade slowly across and swept the field before him, and an army began to die as the life, substance and essence that comprised them was violently extracted. The Demon Blade's infinite appetite consumed all it touched in a spectrum of blazing, fiery streams that fed into one and rushed to it. But it was the color Frost noticed as he watched these "enemies" dying behind the torrent of crackling fire. The life energies of these men were a mix of blues, oranges, yellows, even bright white. *The goodness in them,* Frost decided, more goodness among some of them at least than had been inside most others he'd slain in the past.

He kept slowly turning, keeping his Subartans and the others behind him, taking all of Andair's army into account until most of the survivors turned and began running for their lives. Frost wavered, thinking of these men, the pained deliberations that must have taken place in their mind between duty and desire—between staying, and going.

Then he felt the pain and ethereal heat of the Blade begin to torture him, or it was something inside him, some part of his soul. He spoke the words and broke off the attack. Then he turned and dropped to his knees. He pointed the Blade and gave one last command. In the space of the beat of a human heart the Demon Blade released the energy it had just consumed. A blinding, raging torrent of blue-white fire crossed the yard and impacted the castle walls, and every stone it touched exploded from within. Frost lowered the Blade and waited, bracing himself as the shock wave reached him and squinting through the dust and debris that blew into him and the others.

He nodded to himself, satisfied, as he saw that the main gates and surrounding structures had been nearly obliterated.

Dozens of soldiers lay scattered on the ground all around. Some were still moving, more would eventually. For others it had been too late. Frost turned around and saw the troubled look on Tramet's face.

He quickly realized the concern; Wilmar lay motionless, barely breathing. Tramet pointed to a spot where blood soaked his tunic on the right side. Frost went to him and knelt beside him. He pulled the tunic up and saw the damage, a sharp wound from the knife blade that cut across several ribs, but it did not appear to go deep. *Wilmar must have moved at just the right time*, Frost thought.

He worried over the wound for a moment, chanting the words of the spell that would help the blood turn sticky and thick, so as to seal the wound. He breathed a great sigh as he felt his efforts finally begin to take hold.

"Thank you," Wilmar said, reaching out to Frost, touching his arm.

"And you, my friend," Frost said. Frost got to his feet, shaking and feeling suddenly very cold. He nearly blacked out, but stayed on his feet somehow until his vision and balance started to return. "And all of you," he added, looking from one to the other. He realized Rosivok's arms were supporting him, were the reason he had not managed to fall again, and gave the big Subartan a special nod.

"How is he?" Tramet asked of Wilmar.

"He will live," Frost said. "The worst is over."

"We owe you our lives, as do so many," Dorin said. He stood side by side with Dara only two paces away, holding Frost in his gaze. The look on his face was like a smile, only deeper, more sincere. Frost felt something tug at his insides, something that made his eyes sting. Both twins moved to embrace him, and Frost did not protest.

CHAPTER EIGHTEEN

Wilmar finally emerged, shrinking from the light of day like a miner ascending from a shaft. Then he began to smile. After all, this was a day of celebration. Four weeks spent in bed or hobbling around in chambers had been more than enough, with only squires and a nurse for company most of the time. Otherwise a slow parade of nobles, gentry, stewards, captains and men-at-arms and, in a recurring dream, the Greater Gods themselves had managed to find him with their most serious concerns.

Tramet and Dara had been to see him every day, the two of them apparently inseparable. Wilmar had welcomed their company, and he had nothing to say against them. In truth, they'd only picked up where they left off. But regular visits from anyone else since the battle and injury that had left him cloistered and helpless were less enjoyable. He was not ready for all of that, but he had made the best show of it that he knew how. Until today. Today was to be different. He was eager enough for fresh air. And whatever came with it.

"Not so piteous a sight as I expected," Frost said, the first one who greeted him. The inner courtyard in the center of the castle's keep was filled with people, nobles and their families, soldiers of rank, merchants and tradesmen, the priests from the Church of the Greater Gods. All here about their own futures no doubt, and that of Worlish, but today, most of all, they were here for the celebration. They gathered about tables set with a bounty of foods and casks of fresh ale. Wilmar couldn't count them all as he looked them over. But some of those present counted for more than the rest.

"Frost," Wilmar said, facing the sorcerer. He was not alone; gathered with him were Sharryl and Rosivok, Dorin and Dara and Wilmar's own son, Tramet. Wilmar held out his hands.

"I hardly notice the limp," Frost said, as he clasped hands.

Wilmar was favoring the wound on his side perhaps more than he needed to, it was no longer so painful and clearly beginning to heal over. "I have not walked so far since—"

"Since Andair died, leaving no heirs," Tramet said, moving to offer his father an arm for support. Wilmar waved him off. He wanted to stand on his own two feet.

"Save the rightful one," Frost said. He bowed ceremoniously. "Once he gets around to it."

Wilmar and the twins mimicked the bow.

"I think Lord Andair secretly wanted this for you all along, don't you?" Dara said, smiling, looking more than pretty enough to make Wilmar jealous of his son's happiness.

"Why is that?" he asked.

Dara turned away slightly, demure. "Why else would he go to such trouble to ensure that no one in his court or even in his army retained any loyalty to him from the instant he fell? They have all flocked to you."

"Frost's patronage has had as much to do with that as anything else," Wilmar pointed out.

"Frost and the Blade," Tramet said. "No one would be foolish enough to come up foul of all that after what they saw in the outer courtyard."

Everyone looked at Frost. He only shrugged.

"Well, I am grateful, Frost," Wilmar said after a moment. "Word of that battle has spread all across Worlish and beyond. They are right. No one would think to oppose me so long as you are here. I even received a messenger from Kolhol of Grenarii. A greeting, along with a promise to observe the sovereignty of Worlish and to support me, should I become king."

"As you shall," Tramet was quick to add.

Wilmar smiled at him. "I have your support at least."

"And my support as well!" another voice called out from across the walkway. Wilmar looked up and saw a large man approaching dressed in a king's robes and sash, his neck adorned with gold chains. Not a king, though, Wilmar knew that much. A merchant lord, and surrounded by servants.

"Cantor of Calienn," one of the servants said, introducing the man as he strode into the others' midst and bowed perfunctorily.

Wilmar nearly staggered upon hearing the name. He knew all that it entailed. He had heard plenty of Cantor, everyone had, but had never met the richest freeman in this part of the known world. He very nearly bowed, but caught himself in time. The two men stood facing one another, eye to eye, while everyone else kept still.

"It is an honor to meet you, and to serve you," Cantor said, easing the moment immeasurably. "I agree with these others completely. Indeed, I am told by many that Worlish is yours for the asking. I can only assume you will ask."

"I may at that," Wilmar said calmly, though he could not help the grin that followed.

"In that case, count on Calienn to support you, and to continue to trade with you. Commerce between our lands need not be interrupted. In fact, I believe it will benefit from your much celebrated honesty. The people of Worlish have waited too long for this moment. I congratulate them all. And you as well," Cantor added, turning to Tramet, "the future prince, if I may say as much."

"Oh, you may," Dara said with that smile again, all while standing as close to Tramet as was humanly possible.

"We all welcome your friendship and endorsement," Tramet said. "It will mean a great deal."

"These are the twins I have heard so much about," Cantor said without preamble, moving along, shaking Dorin's hand first, then leaning in to kiss Dara's. He grinned too fiendishly. "You know, I foresee a day when Dorin here might become a grand duke."

Dara and Tramet both blushed a little. Wilmar found it endearing but he noticed one silent voice. "Nothing to say about it, Dorin?"

"It is all well and good," Dorin replied, though he was curiously melancholy about it, so far as Wilmar could tell.

"Your story is being told all across the land," Cantor said, speaking directly to Frost. "And far beyond, no doubt. Stories that will inspire many to take heed, and others to seek you out."

"I know," Frost said. "Too well. We were just talking about that."

"Then you still have my best wishes in mind, and those of these people you so cherish?"

Frost nodded. Wilmar saw the look in the sorcerer's eye, disquieting, cheerless. He limped nearer. "What is it, Frost?"

"I cannot stay, not now, though I may return."

"You *must* stay," Wilmar protested, fearing this. "You will not leave again. There is no dishonor this time. You have more than made up for the sins of the past, sins forgiven by all but you long before you ever returned. What am I without you, and what of the twins? This is your home, Frost. You are needed here."

Frost listened stone-faced as the others chimed agreement. Only Sharryl and Rosivok were silent on the matter.

"I will not argue, Wilmar, but I have unfinished business," Frost said at last. "I do not intend to be gone so long this time. First I will travel north and visit Kolhol once more. I must speak to him, and be sure he listens." He set his hand solidly on Wilmar's shoulder. "I will tell him you have heard his messenger and agree for now, but that it is only by your grace that you and I do not destroy him, and half his kingdom. Should he change his mood and choose to move against Briarlea, the Demon Blade and an army loyal to you will be his welcome."

Wilmar didn't understand this last. "That won't be true if you leave."

"He will not know where I am, how far I have gone, or when I might return," Frost replied. "Then, there are these two." He turned to Dorin and Dara. "They are both born adepts. Young and inexperienced, but learning fast. When I return I will teach them much more, but for now, Kolhol has no court wizard at all. Having adepts will be to your advantage. Kolhol is a warrior and an opportunist, but he tries not to be the fool. Taken all in all, I think Grenarii will no longer be a threat."

"And then what?" Wilmar asked, waiting until he met Frost's gaze again and holding him there. "What is it that takes you away at all?"

"Cantor speaks a burning truth. Too much unpleasantness will yet find its way here, too many men drawn by visions of the Demon Blade, and the one who controls it. It is a dangerous thing all on its own. More so than I can tell any of you here. More so than Andair or Gentaff were willing to believe—than I would believe myself, for a time. I must go, if for no other reason than to take the Blade away from here."

"You still hope to find the Keeper?" Dara asked, all traces of her earlier mood gone from her young features now, replaced by the weight of this one truth.

"Yes," Frost said. "Gentaff took my best chance of that with him to the grave, but there is someone, I know that much."

"How can you know for certain if you will ever return?" Wilmar asked, and he knew he was speaking for his son and the twins.

"Nothing is ever certain," Frost replied. "But none of us can deny fate. I know the task of rebuilding Worlish is a great one, but you have all that you need." Frost turned to Wilmar and Tramet, then to the twins. "All, and more."

"Frost," Wilmar told the sorcerer, searching for the words. "All Worlish thanks you. As do I, and I wish to . . ."

"There is no need," Frost said. "Your forgiveness and your friendship are enough. I ask only that you be here when I return."

"We will each see that day," Wilmar replied, and they embraced one another. Wilmar felt other arms around him then, Tramet and Dara, then Dorin. His side hurt with the added weight. He didn't say a word as the celebration began.

The sun had already set as Frost, Sharryl and Rosivok left the courtyard, but oil lamps had been lit throughout the castle halls and grounds, casting warm light and soft shadows. Frost had been in just such a place at just such a time, in Ariman, not a year ago. He felt disturbed by the notion, but he could think of nothing he would have done differently, at least not so far, and he took comfort in that. Perhaps with hindsight he would eventually second-guess himself, but not for now . . .

"Dorin has something he must talk to you about," Dara said. Frost turned to find the two of them hurrying to catch up, with Dorin out in front.

"And so do I," Dara added as they came near, both of them glancing nervously at one another.

Frost waited, but they tended not to get any further.

"Yes, speak," he said.

Dorin swallowed as if something were caught in his throat, then he set his jaw and took a breath. "I am going with you," he said.

Frost's eyes widened. "What?"

"I wish to be your third Subartan. I have given this a great deal of thought, and it makes complete sense no matter how you see it. I know I will require much training, and I know the dangers, but I am able and ready for both. I also need to be trained in the arts of magic. You have promised to do as much, but I have no wish to wait untold months, or perhaps years, for you to return. If I go with you, you can begin right away."

He hadn't let Frost get a word in. But already Frost was thinking that perhaps it was just as well. Nothing the boy had said was incorrect. Frost thought of Taya's son, Lan, standing before him much like this, saying much the same things. But Lan had been younger and no mage of any kind; more than that, there had been no blood between them, and Frost had not owed Lan anything. He owed Dorin so very much, almost as much as he owed Shassel. Dorin would learn such things one way or the other, but if he stayed behind he would have to learn them on his own, without the watchful, knowledgeable mentoring of his great uncle and the known world's two most capable Subartans. . . .

Still, it was not as simple as all that. "I couldn't bear to lose you, I have lost too many already," he told Dorin. "And how can I be sure I won't? Besides, I am certain your sister is here to talk us both out of it."

"Nothing is certain," Dara said, using Frost's own words. "And we must think of the future, not the past, at least that is what I am told."

They were in this together. Frost could see the determination in both their eyes. He had seen something like it before, once or twice, looking at his own reflection.

"I can't say I dislike the idea," Frost told Dorin. "Or parts of it. You have a gift and you can be trained to fight, and fight well, I think. But I have no idea where we are going or what we might face, and as you know, I tend to lose my third Subartans. A triangle cannot stand without three equal sides, and each side must agree on what 'equal' means. Therefore I insist that no matter what I think, it is left up to Sharryl and Rosivok. They will decide."

Dorin turned to the Subartans and waited, weathering their scowls at having such judgment thrust upon them.

"He may just do," Sharryl said, tipping her head side to side, considering. "Just."

Rosivok moved toward him and Dorin stayed put. The big Subartan reached out and grabbed the boy's arms, and began testing his muscles with a squeeze here, then a thump there as he released his grip. All the while looking him over like a mule up for purchase. Finally he nodded. "I will see that he does," Rosivok said.

"And you, what do you say?" Frost asked Dara.

"I want him to go, to live his life as he should, and this is something I know in my heart he should do," Dara said. "I am tempted to go with you myself, there is so much to learn, and I am as anxious as my brother. But I am needed here, at Tramet's side. The task of rebuilding Briarlea is a great one, and he has asked my help with it."

"I think my sister is capable of that," Dorin said. "She thinks I am capable of going with you and learning what you can teach. One day, even if you cannot, I will come back, and teach my sister."

Frost had no reply, other than to nod.

"If I could, I would make both of you stay," Dara said softly. "You went away once, Frost, and now I am losing you again, and my brother as well, but I know you must tend to the Blade."

Frost nodded again. His reasons for leaving were not the same this time, but the need was just as great, and the decision was just as difficult. "I have no choice," he said.

"None of us do," Dorin said, and Dara put her arm around him.

"Andair was not the only reason I left," Frost said. "I felt the need to find my own path, to learn the truth about myself. I knew I must find the answers if I was ever to serve anyone else, or myself. I think, perhaps, Dorin feels much the same right now."

Dorin closed his eyes, and Frost thought a tear was about to form. But the boy drew a deep breath, and none did. Instead he opened his eyes again and threw both his arms around his sister, and held her for a very long moment.

"We will not leave for a few days yet," Frost said. "There will be time for all of that."

They parted, and Dorin smiled at his sister as a tear glistened at the corner of her eye, no matter.

"I will come home again, my sister," Dorin said.

"And so shall I," Frost said, feeling a chill, sure that it was true. "So shall I."

ABOUT THE AUTHORS

Mark A. Garland: Mark read a copy of Clarke's *The Sands of Mars* when he was twelve, and proceeded to exhaust the local library's supply of SF, then book stores and magazines like *F&SF* and *Galaxy*. Then he got interested in playing music professionally, auto racing, and eventually a long and torturous management career. But he still found himself compelled to do something creative with his life, so he finally came full circle, back to science fiction and fantasy.

He's spent the last fourteen years reading, going back to school, attending conventions and writing. He has written or collaborated on seven novels and more than fifty short stories, and has recently begun editing a trade newspaper. He lives in Upstate New York with his wife (also an avid reader), their three children, two cats and a dog.

Charles G. McGraw: Dishwasher, car washer, concrete worker, clay pressman, accounting clerk, data processing supervisor, stationery stores and phone guy, writer—it does seems like Chuck has trouble keeping a steady job. He does, however, have the distinction of managing to earn a four-year bachelor's degree in a record twenty-two years, starting at eighteen and finally receiving it at forty. He has co-written and sold four novels.

Chuck has been married for over half of his life, lived all of his life in Central New York and doesn't see either of these changing in the future. He is currently writing a solo novel, is back in school again—this time working on both an M.A. in Writing and an M.S. in Distance Education, running a writer's workshop and hoping to last long enough to retire and teach writing.

Comments are welcome. Write care of Baen Books, or you can E-mail Mark at GarlandMA@aol.com and Chuck at Demonblade@aol.com.